FOOTFREE
AND
FANCYLOOSE

FOOTFREE
AND
FANCYLOOSE

A novel

by Elizabeth Craft and Sarah Fain

LITTLE, BROWN AND COMPANY

New York Boston

Little, Brown and Company

Hachette Book Group USA
237 Park Avenue, New York, NY 10017
Visit our Web site at www.lb-teens.com

First Edition: April 2008

The characters and events portrayed in this book are fictitious. Any similarity to real persons, living or dead, is coincidental and not intended by the author.

ISBN-10: 0-316-05795-9
ISBN-13: 978-0-316-05795-0

10 9 8 7 6 5 4 3 2 1

RRD-C

Printed in the United States of America

The text was set in Granjon, and the display type is JM Libris.

To girlfriends everywhere.
What would any of us do without them?

PROLOGUE

Harper Waddle wondered how she'd survived seventeen years without her own pool. Or at least access to the pool that belonged to Genevieve and Gifford Meyer, the Hollywood power couple who owned the Beverly Hills estate where one of her three best friends, Sophie Bushell, was living in the guesthouse here while pursuing her dream of becoming an Oscar-winning (read: red-carpet-posing) paparazzi-charming actress. Two hours into an afternoon of lying on a deep-cushioned cream-colored chaise, basking in the California sun, Harper hadn't felt so relaxed since her junior year in high school, when she took mistakenly took Tylenol PM in the middle of the afternoon and fell asleep for four hours on the grungy pleather sofa in the student lounge.

"Sweetie, you really need to up your SPF." The singsong voice of Genevieve Meyer buzzed into Harper's consciousness like an annoying fly. "Especially with that pale skin of yours."

Harper opened her eyes and fake-smiled at her hostess. Genevieve was fifty-something, superskinny, with a frozen forehead and frosted platinum blond hair. She looked like she spent every night entombed in a cooler.

"Will do, Mrs. Meyer. Thanks for the advice." Given that

Genevieve was Sophie's (sort of) patron and issuer of invitations to the Meyers' annual black tie New Year's Eve bash, Harper wasn't about to make waves by informing the Queen of Sheen that she'd never had a sunburn in her life.

"You're already showing signs of aging." Genevieve was still talking with great fake concern. "It sneaks up."

What's next? Maybe Genevieve would go on a tirade about her lank dirty-blond hair, or suggest she replace her trademark rectangular black glasses with aquamarine-tinted contacts. At the very least, Harper expected a comment about the freshman fifteen she'd managed to put on since September, despite the fact that instead of going to college, she'd spent the last several months living her parents' basement, attempting to write the next Great American Novel.

But Genevieve's gaze had moved to a twenty-something, tuxedo-clad cater-waiter who was setting up a bar next to the giant stone fountain at the opposite end of the supersized pool. "I told him the *south* side. Why won't anyone *listen?*"

Harper closed her eyes again. Maybe she'd work a Genevieve-like character into her novel — the one she was absolutely, positively going to complete now that she was free from The Lie.

The Lie started last April, when she received a rejection letter from NYU. NYU was the only college to which she'd applied — stupidly, she now realized — because she'd been totally convinced she'd get in. Crushed under the weight of humiliation, she'd led her best friends — Sophie, Kate, and Becca — to believe she'd been accepted. Harper had intended to tell them the truth before everyone went their separate ways in the fall. But when the moment came, she couldn't do it. She'd felt like a colossal loser, a complete idiot. So instead she'd made a passionate speech about following dreams — then dropped the bombshell that she was going to forego college in order to pursue hers.

What happened next couldn't have been predicted. Sophie and Kate had hopped on the so-called Dream Train and decided to nix their freshmen years, too. Becca had gone through with her college plan because skiing on the renowned Middlebury ski team *was* her Dream, but Harper, Kate, and Sophie had assigned her the task of following through on another — much scarier — Dream. That is, falling in love.

The psychic trauma of lying to her friends had killed Harper's creativity. In four months, all she'd managed to write was fifty pages of stilted drivel. It just wasn't good enough. In fact, it was awful. She'd burned the pages in her trash can in a private ceremony on Christmas Eve, then finally confessed everything to her three friends the next morning. Surprisingly (this was the part that always made her teary), they'd forgiven her. Apparently, following one's Dream had merit, even if that following was based on deception.

Now Harper had a clear conscience and was on her way to a mocha-choca latté-ya-ya of a tan. Two days ago, Sophie had called and announced that Becca and Harper were cordially invited to the Meyers' New Year's Eve Blowout. The way she described it, the event would be a cross between the *Vanity Fair* after-Oscars party and a Jay-Z video shoot on some exotic Caribbean island. They'd immediately logged onto Expedia.com and started planning their trip. So what if the plane ticket had cost her three weeks of hard-earned barista tips? And so what if she was supposed to be working on a new and improved college essay for her reapplication to NYU instead of meditating on a poolside chaise? This was her first-ever trip to Los Angeles, and not just any old Los Angeles — it was like she'd gone to sleep and woken up in Tori Spelling's adolescence, or maybe *E! True Hollywood Story: 90210*. And, best of all, she was spending New Year's Eve with two of her three best friends. When she went back to Boulder, she'd be ready to write.

This time, she wouldn't fail. She *couldn't* fail. Because if she did, Harper and her non-freshman fifteen would melt into a plus-sized puddle and die.

"I'll call you at midnight."

From two thousand miles away, the sound of Stuart Pendergrass's voice made Becca Winsberg's insides chaotic. Not just her stomach, which was twisted into happy knots. Not just her heart, which skipped rapidly beneath her pink Polo tee. No, Stuart's voice reached all the way to her *loins*. She'd read enough steamy romance novels to know.

Becca sank onto one of the long stone benches strategically placed throughout the lush gardens rimming the Meyers' extensive estate. As soon as she'd seen Stuart's name on her caller ID screen, she'd ditched Harper by the pool and disappeared down one of the narrow stone paths that wound past blooming bougainvilleas and rosebushes.

"Your midnight or my midnight?" The gushy tremulousness of her voice made her blush.

Becca ran one hand through her less-frizzy-than-usual, shoulder-length auburn-brown waves. She had to relax. Everything was good. There was no reason she couldn't sound gushy and tremulous. Stuart was her *boyfriend,* after all. It was simply that she'd never felt this way before, and it was more than a little frightening. Becca had always believed that there were some people in the world who were *allowed* to be all lovey-dovey and gushy — people who'd been handed a special Happy Pass at birth — and she wasn't one of them. So now she couldn't shake the niggling feeling that her newly minted Happy Pass was a forgery — made in Tijuana and smug-

4

gled over the border — ready to be snatched away by the Love Police at any time.

Even worse was the overwhelming fear that if somehow she managed to fool everyone into thinking she had a right to be so happy, at some point she was going to get hurt anyway. Not toe-stubbing hurt. More the tractor-trailer-to-the-face kind.

Stuart's voice was smiling. "Both," he said, "and I'm going to owe you a kiss when we get back to school."

There was a sexy, masculine gushiness on his end of the phone, too. She didn't have to be afraid. Stuart wasn't like her parents — constantly putting themselves first and letting her down over and over again. Becca could trust him. He cared about her. He wouldn't hurt her.

"I'll make sure you pay up," she sighed.

"I'll call you later."

"Okay."

There was a pause. Becca's heart started pounding faster, as if it were aware of the significance of the pause before her brain was. And then her brain caught up. This wasn't just *any* pause. Oh God, was he . . . ? Was he going to *say* it? Becca inhaled. Was Stuart Pendergrass about to tell her he loved her?

He cleared his throat. "I miss you," he said quietly. "Bye."

She exhaled. "I miss you, too. Bye."

Becca exhaled.

Her hands sank to her lap.

He'd almost said he loved her. She was sure. And given everything they'd been through in the past several months, that awareness alone was a small miracle.

Becca realized she was smiling.

He hadn't said it this time. But he would say it soon. And when he did, she knew just what she was going to say back.

The closet was hot. And stuffy. Sophie Bushell also noted there was a sickly smell, possibly emanating from the open bottle of sweet almond oil — apparently Jackie Kennedy's favorite beauty product — that Becca had sent her from a Vermont country store a few months ago.

Go away, go away, Sophie silently willed, using the visualization technique her therapist-mom taught patients. She'd heard Sam Piper's signature *rat-tat-tat* on the guesthouse door just as she'd slipped into her favorite Isaac Mizrahi for Target red bikini to rejoin Harper and Becca poolside. Her stomach had dropped at the sound, and she'd immediately dashed into the closet (the only space in the little casa without a window) to avoid detection. She knew she'd have to see Sam eventually, but she wasn't ready. Not yet. Not when she knew she was in for a big fat "I told you so."

For several seconds there was silence. Sophie waited. She knew from experience Sam wouldn't give up that easily. He had a habit of knocking on her door until she was shamed into answering it. Finally, she heard tapping at the bedroom window.

"You can't hide forever, Bushell," he called.

Go away, she willed again. And this time it worked. Moments later she heard Sam's footsteps as he clomped noisily away from the guesthouse.

Sophie emerged, relieved that neither Harper nor Becca had been witness to the incident. After four months of pursuing her life's passion of becoming a bona fide Hollywood actress, cowering in a messy overstuffed closet wasn't exactly the image she wanted to project.

Of course, she wouldn't even know this particular closet existed if Harper hadn't made her "I Have a Dream" speech on Kate's roof that night. She wouldn't know a lot of things. Like how to drive on the LA freeways, or how to strategize the best outfit for auditions, or how it felt to spy a paparazzi shot of her supposed boyfriend, Trey Benson, making out with his married costar while she was waiting in line at an Aspen grocery store on Christmas Eve.

I also wouldn't know what it was like to get three lines in an actual movie, Sophie thought, grinning as she remembered the call that had convinced her to return to Los Angeles after professing in Harper's basement that she was never leaving home again.

Staring at herself in the full-length rectangular mirror attached to the closet door, Sophie had no doubt that she *looked* like a soon-to-be famous actress. Her skin was a creamy caramel, she had huge chocolate brown eyes, and her lustrous dark curls had helped her win a national shampoo commercial.

"You've *gotta* be kidding me," she pronounced. It was the first of her three lines, and she'd already practiced it a hundred times. "You gotta be *kidding* me." Ugh. She was eyebrow acting. She *despised* eyebrow acting.

She grabbed a pair of True Religion jeans — bought second-hand at American Rag, because she wasn't earning bona fide Hollywood actress money yet — and slipped them on over her bikini bottoms. Lounging by the pool could wait. Sophie had a performance to perfect.

"Welcome to Ethiopia."

The man behind the chest-high fake-wood counter slid Kate Foster's passport toward her under the glass. She retrieved it, blinking sleepily. A pretty, carefree, blonde smiled up at her from the passport photo. Kate almost didn't recognize herself. Which wasn't entirely a bad thing.

"Thank you."

"Bags are that way," the man pointed with one slender brown hand.

Kate slipped the passport into a secure compartment in her now-worn suede purse and followed the direction of his finger toward Dorothé, one of the French aid-workers she'd met in Paris, who was waiting patiently at the baggage carousels. Dorothé's chin-length brown bob was plastered flat on one side. Kate envied her. Clearly, Dorothé had been able to sleep on the seven-hour flight, while Kate had been too keyed-up to even close her eyes. Kate's mind had been racing five hundred ba-zillion miles a minute for hours, and now she was paying for it. Her exhausted brain had completely shut down, and her body wasn't far behind.

At five AM, the stark-white steal-beamed Bole International Airport was nearly empty, except for the passengers of the 737 Kate and Dorothé had just arrived on from Paris. Blearily, she made her way through a small group of Ethiopian men and women dressed in white flowing wraps that gracefully circled their shoulder and heads, and hauled her scuffed, black North Face backpack off the conveyor belt. Then she followed Dorothé into the warm predawn air of Addis Ababa, Ethiopia's capital.

"This way," Dorothé told her in French-accented English.

Kate followed her tall, willowy companion across the empty airport road and down a cement sidewalk to a black-asphalt parking lot, where several old cars and vans idled in the darkness. Aside from the chatter of the other passengers and the people who'd come to greet them, everything was quiet. A pungent and unfamiliar smell of blossoms hung heavily in the night air.

Two young men in raggedy western clothes approached from the night, smiling and speaking Amharic, Ethiopia's primary language. At Kate's blank look they held their hands out for Kate's and Dorothé's bags and switched to English, saying "Carry, lady, carry."

Dorothé handed over her backpack to one of the young men, then nodded Kate toward the other young man.

"Give him your bag," she said.

"I'm okay. It's not heavy." They were almost to the vans. It seemed silly to hire someone to carry her backpack when she'd been carrying it herself for months.

"They want to earn a few birr," Dorothé explained. "They have no jobs."

Oh. Kate handed the second young man her backpack. He hitched it high on his narrow back.

"Hello, lady," he said, accented heavily, smiling. Kate realized that he was barely a teenager.

Ten steps later, Dorothé stopped at a small white van. She hugged the driver, a tall Ethiopian man with a long nose and prominent cheekbones wearing jeans and a worn blue button-down. Dorothé introduced him to Kate as Ibrahim. Ibrahim loaded their meager luggage in the back of the van while Dorothé handed the young men two birr each.

As the young men nodded their thanks and walked away, Kate did a quick calculation in her head. Eight birr was about a dollar. So two birr . . . about a quarter. And then she was in the van, driving through the wide streets of Addis Ababa toward their hotel. Kate stared out the window. Even in the semi-darkness, she could tell she had entered another world.

Kate thought about the three words that had brought her to Ethiopia. *Take the water.* Harper had taken the line from a favorite poem: "Sometimes a human's clay is not strong enough to take the water." The three words had become something of a mission for Kate, a riddle to solve, a path to finding herself. So here she was, one member of a multi-national team of young men and women who had come to Ethiopia to build wells. She was going to, literally, take the water.

She only hoped she was strong enough.

Please describe a person who has influenced you and why in five hundred words or less.

Adam Finelli has dark hair that curls winsomely around his ears. He wears wire-rimmed glasses that seem to magnify his intense hazel eyes and give him an air of unstudied intelligence. He's committed to his profession, but this doesn't mean he's stuffy or old-fashioned: he dresses in khaki pants and T-shirts, and seems completely comfortable with himself. He begins every week clean-shaven, though by Friday he has an undeniably scruffy beard, as though he's too preoccupied with thinking and reading and talking to worry about unimportant things like grooming. He has palpable passion for what he does.

It's this total commitment that made a huge impression on me. I always knew I wanted to write, but from Adam Finelli I learned WHY. He taught me that writing isn't just about putting together words on a page for one's own amusement. If the words on the page are good enough—honest enough—they can change the world. I'm not claiming to have world-changing abilities yet, but now, thanks to him, I see that anything is possible.

Adam Finelli was my A.P. English teacher. He was also the first man I ever loved, in that way of a woman loving a man. He encouraged me to follow my dreams and offered support when I began a novel, an incredibly ambitious project for someone my age. But once our relationship progressed to the kissing sta

I HARPER WADDLE AM INSANE.

WHO WRITES A COLLEGE ESSAY ABOUT MACKING THEIR TEACHER?

NOTE TO SELF: START OVER. WRITE ABOUT MOM.

ONE

My ass is *huge.*"

"It is not."

"It's huge!"

"Bec, tell Harper her ass is not huge."

At the sound of her name, Becca snapped to attention. Harper and Sophie stood squared off in the middle of Sophie's guesthouse living room. Their conversation had barely registered through the happy fog Becca had been in since Stuart's call.

"Um. . . . Ass. Not huge."

But Harper turned to Sophie, victorious. "She hesitated."

"She's in Stuart-land," Sophie countered.

Harper looked at Becca suspiciously. "Ass or Stuart?"

"Stuart," Becca confessed, bracing herself for the reaction.

Harper rolled her eyes and flopped down next to Becca on the over-pillowed cream-colored couch. "Well, I hope you were at least thinking about *Stuart's* ass."

Becca felt herself blush — the combined curse of her pale skin and inherent tendency toward embarrassment. Anyway, Harper's ass was definitely not huge. Maybe it was slightly larger than it had been four months ago, but failed romances with English teachers and sitting in front of a computer screen twenty-four seven trying to write the Great American Novel will do that to a girl. She couldn't help feeling a little sorry for Harper: everyone else had gone away to other places and had all sorts of adventures, good and bad. Harper had been stuck in her parents' basement, burning her manuscript pages in despair and messing up what sounded like a semi-promising relationship with Mr. Finelli. Faced with blushing Becca and show-off Sophie, Harper had the right to be a little intolerant.

Becca thought about doing something supportive — like give her a hug, or maybe just a friendly squeeze of the leg — but Harper had already bounced back to her feet. She and Sophie, their argument forgotten for now, were huddled together at the window, peering out at all the furious pre-party activity. Becca leaned back on the comfortable sofa and sighed. This guesthouse was unreal. It was the size of at least four Middlebury dorm rooms put together — Becca could probably fit most of her college stuff, including her bed and desk, into Sophie's huge closet — and about 200 percent more chic.

Outside the guesthouse, strings of party lights flickered on around the Meyers' figure eight–shaped pool. A miscellany of blue-uniformed workmen and gardeners broke into a cheer. Work crews had been swarming the massive grounds all day, setting up chairs and tables, stringing lights, and primping and pruning the foliage for what Sophie described as *"the* New Year's Eve party to be at this year."* Becca was sure she was right, though a tiny skeptical part of her wondered how, exactly, Sophie could be so sure. Last New Year's Eve they were all playing let's-juggle-with-pretzels at Kate's house; Los Angeles was still a dream for Sophie. She liked to act all woman-of-the-world, but this was all new to her, really, just as much as it was new to Harper and Becca.

Earlier in the afternoon Becca had felt guilty watching the workers set up tables and heat lamps as she lounged by the pool. But then she realized that when she got back to Middlebury in all her bronzed glory, Stuart Pendergrass would be there to appreciate it. Appreciate *her.* So she had eschewed her usual modest one-piece for the slinkiest little black number Sophie could find in her seemingly bottomless bikini drawer. If Becca was going to be in a real relationship, she didn't want to be there with a pasty-pale stomach.

"Whoa." Sophie checked her watch. "Party starts in ninety minutes. We gotta jam."

Harper sprang back from the window. "I call the shower!" she shrieked, and was through the bathroom door and stripping off her yellow tee before Sophie had taken two steps.

"If your ass will fit!" Sophie yelled as Harper slammed the bathroom door. Grumbling something about finding the perfect outfit, Sophie disappeared into her bedroom. Which left Becca free to go back to Stuart-land. Even now, she could hardly believe it was true. She, Becca Winsberg, had a *boyfriend.* An *amazing* boyfriend. Stuart was smart, funny, strong. His softly tousled brown hair and dark eyes made her weak every time she looked at him. But the most wonderful thing about him was his ability and willingness to understand her and forgive.

Even when Becca had done something unforgivable.

It wasn't as if she'd set out to lose her virginity to her best friend Kate's ex-boyfriend. But over Thanksgiving, when she'd still been afraid to acknowledge where her budding relationship with Stuart was going, she'd unexpectedly seen Jared Burke at a party in New York City. Years of longing and unrequited adoration had caught up with her, and the retrospectively idiotic belief that Jared was the love of her life had caused her to hurt two of the people she cared most about — Stuart and Kate. She'd realized it almost immediately — but still too late.

After some tense moments, Kate had managed to forgive her. But it had taken a grand dramatic gesture, the most gutsy and terrifying thing Becca had ever done, to even get Stuart to talk to her again. At the urging of her Middlebury roommate, Isabelle Sutter, she'd scheduled a last-minute stop-over on her way home and appeared, uninvited, on his parents' doorstep in Kansas City the day before Christmas Eve. She could hardly believe it was only eight days ago that she had delivered her rambling, confessional apology on the front steps of the Pendergrass house. Stuart had been stunned, but he'd listened. Really listened. And understood. Then, finally, forgiven.

Her hand drifted again to the sterling silver charm bracelet around her wrist. Stuart's Christmas present. Her heart shifting up a gear, Becca remembered the first time she'd seen him. How she'd hated him, standing on the Middlebury track field with a group of his football team buddies. Becca had mistakenly believed he was talking trash about her after he'd watched her make a mad dash across the center grass to rejoin her first ski team practice. She'd been so concerned about not pissing off her idol, Coach Jackson Maddix, that she hadn't even been aware that people were watching her leap over hurdles, football equipment, and haphazardly scattered athletic bags. And then she'd seen Stuart laughing, and immediately detested him. Her tendency to dismiss all jocks as rude and offensive — a relic of middle school, when the boys were still *so* immature and Becca was still painfully self-conscious — hadn't helped his cause.

But Stuart had patiently and steadfastly earned her trust. And, eventually, he'd explained that he hadn't been laughing at her at all. He'd been telling his friends that he'd never seen anyone so hot jump hurdles like that. Which was about the sweetest and most amazing thing she'd ever heard, partly because Becca had never considered herself hot. With friends like Sophie and Kate, she'd gotten used to a certain amount of fading into the woodwork.

Not that she and Harper weren't pretty enough — just not heartstopping like Sophie and Kate. Those two had hit the genetic jackpot — a fact she was reminded of when Sophie returned from her bedroom in a slinky red jersey dress and matching sling-back heels. Sophie's creamy light brown skin glowed against the bright red of her dress, making her look every inch the movie star. Which, Becca supposed, was the whole point.

"Too much?" Sophie ran her hands through her wild, dark curls. An utter lack of body fat didn't keep her friend from having curves, Becca noted wryly.

"It's definitely not too much material."

"So I look hot."

Becca nodded. "Angela would freak." Sophie had been on a first-name basis with her New Age-y mother ever since her parents got divorced when she was ten.

Sophie smiled like she'd just won an Academy Award. "Cool. It's a Stella McCartney. Genevieve let me borrow it. She said it clings to her in all the wrong places, but I don't think she has any wrong places anymore. Not since the last surgery, anyway!"

Genevieve Meyers was an old college friend of Angela's — although, according to Sophie, the ageless stick-insect of a bombshell who currently inhabited the mansion on the other side of the pool had been frumpy Genny Perry back then.

Stuart had an aunt named Genny, Becca remembered. Stuart . . . her boyfriend. Her sweetie pie. Her pumpkin. Her *lov*-ah. Her one and only. She couldn't wait to see him again. She couldn't even wait to hear his voice on the other end of her phone at his midnight, which was still, sadly, several hours away. For the first time in her life, she had a boyfriend on New Year's Eve. If only he was going to be here with her instead of at the New Year's Eve bash he and his older brother threw every year at a dive bar in Kansas City for their friends, so they could kiss —

"Yo." Sophie was standing in front of her, hands on her hip bones. There was glaring.

"What?"

"Seriously. Enough already."

"I was just —"

"Oh god, not again." Harper stood in the bathroom doorway, wrapped in a white, fluffy supersized towel that reached past her knees.

Sophie shook her head. "It's like she doesn't even care that John Krasinski's coming to this party. She's all 'Stuart, Stuart, Stuart.'"

Becca blinked. The charmingly understated — and in Becca's opinion, incredibly sexy — actor from the American version of the British TV show *The Office* was the only actor Becca had ever had an active crush on. "Really?"

Sophie sighed. "No. Genevieve says he's out of town. But some of those *Grey's Anatomy* folks are coming. I think they are, anyway. And that thin chick with the old-lady knees — the one who just starred with Tom Cruise. And about a million agents and entertainment lawyers, so watch yourselves. I hear they can get grabby."

"That Tom Cruise chick is not coming," Harper scoffed, flicking her wet hair around like a dog.

"She is, too, shower hog, and she's bringing a plus one."

"Hold the Motorola. Isn't she dating what's-his-name?" Harper groaned and clutched her backside. "I can't be in the same room as *him* with an ass this huge!"

"It's not huge —"

"Becca thinks it's huge."

Becca just shook her head as Harper and Sophie continued their bickery banter. For once in her life, she suddenly realized, she was utterly and completely happy. Her bitterly divorced parents and their respective spouses had managed to maintain civility for the entire four days she'd been in Boulder over Christmas. She had an awesome new dress to wear to the party tonight, purchased on a New York shopping spree with Isabelle. She was in LA for the first time ever with two of her three very best friends — well, four, since she'd started including Isabelle in that highly selective group.

And she had Stuart.

The new year hadn't even started, and already it was the best year of her life.

"You remind me of my granddaughter," the old man confided in Sophie. "She lives on the East Coast, so I don't get to spoil her too often."

Sophie had no idea what a geezer like this was doing at what had to be one of the hippest bashes of the year. Sure, he was dapper, dressed in a crisp linen suit with a silk cravat knotted around his neck, his silvery gray hair neatly combed. But his skin was pale and papery: one prod and he'd probably turn to dust. This was not the kind of older guy Sophie was hoping to hang out with at a fabulous Beverly Hills party. But she'd been brought up to respect her elders, so she smiled politely. "I'm sure your granddaughter adores you."

"She does," he responded, his blue eyes twinkling. "Mainly because I send her a lot of big checks."

As he kept talking — something about the pony he'd bought little Madison when she was seven — Sophie's eyes roamed the party. Even though she knew Trey had planned to stay in Aspen for several more days, she couldn't help fearing that he'd show up tonight to beg her to forgive him. Not that she'd fall for those warm chocolate-brown eyes again. No way. No how. Not even if he offered a starring role in his next movie.

The first floor of the Meyers' giant Spanish-style mansion had been transformed by event planners into an elegant winter wonderland. There were white twinkle lights everywhere, the Persian rugs had been removed in favor of artificial snow, and all of the cater-waiters wore fur caps and boots with their tuxedos. Midnight wasn't for hours, but already lots of beautiful people stood in corners kissing in the New Year. She was on the lookout for famous people so she could point them out to Harper and Becca. They were probably totally excited about all this, however cool they tried to play it. But, thank god, Trey was nowhere to be seen.

The old guy — whose name Sophie had forgotten the moment he'd said it — patted her hand. "Let me take you to lunch. I'll tell you everything you need to know about The Business over Cobb salads at The Ivy."

Sophie considered. It wouldn't kill her to indulge the man. Being a surrogate granddaughter could be a good investment in her karma bank. Besides, she'd been dying to go to The Ivy since she moved to LA in September. It was *the* place to be seen — every second picture in *People* magazine's "Star Tracks" was taken at The Ivy. She'd even heard that some stars would stop there on their way home from rehab, just to let everyone know they were back in circulation. Sophie wrote down her phone number and handed it to him. "Call anytime."

"I will, dear," he responded before moving off, probably in search of a quiet place to take a nap before the clock struck midnight.

Sophie glanced around the room, this time looking for Harper and Becca. They'd been at the party for half an hour, and while she was talking to the old dude she'd already managed to lose them both. She just hoped they weren't doing anything embarrassing, like asking for autographs — although, on second thought, Sophie had to admit they weren't quite as starstruck as she was. It was her *business* to be starstruck, she told herself, trying to look cool. Parties like this were a major networking opportunity for an up-and-coming young actress. It was like one giant audition.

After five minutes of aimless wandering, Sophie finally found Becca stuffing her face with a plate of mini grilled cheeses she'd gotten from the eclectic buffet line.

"I can't believe you know all these people!" Becca exclaimed after swallowing yet another bite-sized sandwich. She looked so pretty in the little black dress she'd bought in New York: the strapless, knee-length Marc Jacobs showcased Becca's toned arms and flat stomach to perfection. With her frizzy auburn hair tamed — Sophie paused to admire her own handiwork — into a sleek-as-humanly-possible chignon, Becca looked kind of like an athletic version of Audrey Hepburn.

Sophie laughed. "I don't know everyone, really."

Suddenly, Becca's eyes went wide. "Is that who I think it is?" She clutched Sophie's arm, nearly causing her to spill Cristal all over her borrowed dress. Sophie ducked out of the way just in time: Genevieve would certainly not appreciate stains on the Stella.

Sophie followed Becca's gaze to a tall, thirty-something, martini-sipping blonde. "Who do you think it is?" Sophie asked, mentally running through the various cast lists of whatever sitcom, drama, or recently released movie came to mind.

"The Downhill Destroyer," Becca answered in a hushed, reverent tone, sliding her plate onto the table. "Picabo Street."

Sophie laughed. In a party overflowing with Hollywood movers and shakers, leave it to Becca to have eyes only for a fellow athlete. "She's won, like, a gazillion gold medals," she continued. "Picabo is *important.*"

"Go talk to her," Sophie urged, giving Becca a gentle push in the right direction. "You guys can swap stories about . . . powder . . . and T-bars."

Becca looked mortified. "I'm not going to *stalk* her." She paused. "But I am gonna call Stuart. He'll die when he hears this."

Sophie grabbed Becca's black velvet clutch handbag before her friend could dig inside for her cell phone. She was glad Becca had found everlasting love, but the girl was getting obsessive. "You can talk to your cuddle-buddy later. Tonight's about us being fabulous," she announced. "If you refuse to chat up Peek-A-Boo, let's go find Harper."

"You're right," Becca conceded. "It's not like I'm one of those girls who can't go five minutes without talking to her boyfriend."

Right. But Sophie didn't say anything. Becca was finally . . . well, happy. She could cut her some slack. For now.

As they wound their way through the crowded party looking for Harper, Sophie semi-discreetly pointed out whomever she recognized to Becca. There was the knobby-kneed chick from the Tom Cruise movie, draped all over her Brazilian supermodel boyfriend. There was the producer who was known for firing his assistants more often than his maid changed his sheets. There were lots of people Sophie had met through the Meyers — mostly attorneys, like Giff Meyer, or other business types who worked on the decidedly non-glamorous side of the industry — but she was hoping for an actual A-lister or hot young director to show Becca.

"There's Harper!" Becca shouted into Sophie's ear, over the increasing din of the party. "She's by the bar, talking to an extremely cute boy."

Sophie pushed her way past a cluster of guys who looked like extras in *Entourage* to see where Becca was pointing. Harper was, in fact, by one of the dozen bars that the caterers had set up for the party. And she was, in fact, talking to an extremely cute boy.

"Are you okay?" Becca asked. "You look a little pale."

"I can't look pale," Sophie reminded her. "I'm biracially unable to look pale."

"Figuratively speaking, you look pale." Becca let out a little snort. "Oh . . . wow. Isn't that . . . ?"

Sam. Harper was talking to Sam. Actually, she was listening to Sam. Listening and grinning like an idiot. Unlike this afternoon, there was no nearby closet for Sophie to hide in.

Sam was the first person she'd met when she arrived in Los Angeles. Sophie had landed at LAX having no idea what to expect, and there he'd been, standing near the baggage claim with a piece of paper that had her name scrawled on it. At the time Sophie hadn't known that he was a fellow struggling actor, or that he was the Meyers' pool boy. She'd just known he was hot. But once she'd gotten past the adorably shaggy blond hair, laser-beam blue eyes, and killer body, Sophie had decided Sam was a jerk. If he wasn't blowing her off, he was talking down to her like she was a wannabe fit only for shampoo commercials rather than a serious actor like him.

But somehow they'd become friends. Or something like friends, anyway. It sounded clichéd, but there was undeniable electricity between them. Sam wasn't intimidated by her looks or her outrageous personality. He challenged her. And she challenged right back. But every time she thought something was going to happen, it didn't. If she was totally honest, this was part of the reason she thought Sam was a jerk: he always had to be the one pulling the strings. And then she'd met Trey . . . and it didn't matter anymore.

Sophie hadn't seen Sam since right before Christmas, when they'd exchanged cryptically meaningful gifts. His was a mix CD of LA-related songs, and she gave him a framed playbill cover from *The Cherry Orchard,* the play in which he'd just appeared. That was before Trey Benson had shown up at the guesthouse two hours before her plane was supposed to leave and convinced her to go to Aspen with him, despite the fact that she hadn't seen or heard from him in weeks.

If only she hadn't left Sam that message. It was a momentary lapse — one she'd tried to forget. But at the time she had just found out that Trey had cheated on her with his married costar, Pasha DiMoni, and she'd been weak. And in that moment of weakness, stuck waiting for six hours at an Aspen bus station, she called Sam and tearfully told him that he was right. Trey Benson *was* an asshole. And so was she for thinking he actually cared.

As soon as the words were out, she'd regretted them. Unfortunately, cell phone technology was not advanced enough to allow her to call back and erase the message. At least, not without Sam's password. And, apparently, Sam was so smug about being right that he didn't even bother to call her back. He was probably waiting to see her in person, so he could make her feel as small and foolish as possible.

Now he was here, tending the bar and talking to Harper. That he would rub her stupidity in her perfectly made-up face was totally unappealing and inevitable.

But, oh well. She might as well get it over with.

"I'm telling you, it was pure, unadulterated shit," Harper pronounced, recklessly waving her glass of Cristal to emphasize the point. "It was so bad I had to burn it."

"You burned your *novel?*" Sam shouted as he poured a glass of Cabernet for a tiny, wrinkly-necked lizard of a woman Harper recognized from a seventies sitcom that reran on Nick at Nite. "You're insane!"

"It was the best thing I ever did," Harper insisted. "Tending to a nearly out-of-control fire in one's plastic trash can is a very cleansing experience."

Harper couldn't believe it, but she was actually enjoying herself. The moment she'd arrived at the party with Sophie and Becca, she'd felt like an imposter — a loser who worked in a coffee shop, lived in a basement, and wrote drivel that nobody else would ever want to read. Her friends were taking huge strides toward making their own dreams come true, while Harper was just chasing her raggedy tail. It didn't matter that Sophie had spent most of an hour on Harper's hair and makeup, or that she'd tried to do some last-minute butt toning with several power lunges around the guest-house. This party was for the rich, the successful, and the beautiful, and Harper was none of the above.

She was, however, observant. Which is how she'd managed to spot Sam Piper tucked away behind one of the less-crowded bars. Despite the tuxedo (minus fur hat and boots, thank goodness) and a shorter haircut, she had recognized him from the cell phone photo of him Sophie e-mailed back in October. According to Sophie, the guy was rude and obnoxious, not to mention irritating. Harper didn't entirely get why Sophie was taking his photo and getting a ride to acting classes with him when he was supposedly the Worst. Jerk. Ever.

Still, when Harper spotted him, she marched right up and introduced herself, fully intending to start a tirade about the importance of treating her friend with the dignity and respect she deserved. Instead, she found herself wondering what Sophie's problem was. Unlike the rest of the people Harper had encountered tonight, Sam seemed . . . *real.*

In the ten minutes she'd been talking to him, Harper had already developed a theory on why Sophie had issues with Sam. Her best friend lived in her own Sophie-centric world. She barely tolerated constructive criticism from Harper, Becca, and Kate, her three best friends, much less from a good-looking guy who wasn't immediately intoxicated by her charms. Not that Harper had any right to judge. She'd turned into a major bitch in the fall when Mr. Finelli tried to dish out some undeniable truths about her writing.

Of course, her former English teacher was a different subject altogether. One Harper didn't care to dwell on at the moment, not if she wanted to get through the night without diving into a pit of self-hating despair. She could never admit it to her friends, but she'd rather be spending New Year's Eve with Adam Finelli than with any number of Beverly Hills glitterati. Not that he would want to spend any time with her at all after the childish, petulant way she'd acted.

"Uh-oh," Sam half-whistled under his breath, popping the cork of yet another bottle of Cristal.

"What?" But the question was rhetorical. Harper saw Sophie heading toward them, Becca in tow, and she did *not* look happy.

"Hi, Sam." Sophie oversmiled and spoke in the formal voice she reserved for people she was pissed off at. "I see you've made Harper's acquaintance." She turned to her left. "Allow me to introduce Becca Winsberg."

"Nice to meet you," Sam greeted her good-naturedly. "I guess you've already figured out that Sophie hates me."

"I — no," Becca stuttered. "I mean, she said you were the pool boy . . . not that there's anything wrong with that. . . ." One of Sophie's false eyelashes was about to fall off, but judging by Sophie's frosty expression, it was not, Harper decided, the time to mention it.

"It's okay." Sam grinned. "I'm just glad she didn't try to keep these friends I've heard so much about away from me."

"She did," Harper informed him. "But I found you anyway."

Sophie shot her a look. "I'm glad everyone's talking about me like I'm not here," she huffed. Then she turned to Sam. "Go ahead. Say it."

"Say . . . what?"

"I told you so."

"I don't know what you're talking about."

They were staring at each other, eyes intense. Harper suddenly felt like an intruder in a very intimate conversation. She glanced at Becca, who'd grown extremely interested in the bottom of her champagne flute.

"We'll just . . . go call Stuart," Harper announced, nudging Becca. "I have a . . . uh . . . joke . . . I've been dying to tell him."

"Great idea!" Becca exclaimed. "Jokes are good. And funny. Ha-ha."

"You're not going anywhere," Sophie countered. "Whatever Sam has to say to me, you guys can hear."

"Sam has no idea what you're talking about." He was pointedly ignoring the crowd of overzealous reality TV stars who'd bellied up to the bar for refills.

Sophie stamped one of her five-inch red Kenneth Cole heels on the fake snow. "Come on. The *message*?"

"What message?" Sam looked as confused as Harper felt.

"I think I have to pee," Becca announced. "Really bad." Sophie glared at her. "Or not. Definitely not. False alarm."

"The message I left on your cell phone when I was waiting for the bus in Aspen," Sophie sternly informed him. "I told you I'd seen a picture of Trey kissing another girl? I said I was an idiot? I said you were right and I was wrong?"

"You went to Aspen?" Sam looked genuinely bemused. "I thought you were going to Boulder for Christmas."

"She went with Trey Benson," Harper clarified. "She thought she was in love. But it turned out she was just another proverbial notch on the belt of a narcissistic teen idol who can't keep his tongue in his mouth." She paused to gulp down the last dregs of her drink. "That sounded a lot better in my head."

"I dropped my cell phone in the pool a week ago," Sam responded, but he was looking at Sophie, not Harper. "It's been busted ever since."

Sophie winced. "Oh." She dropped her head, shuffling some fake snow around with the toe of one shoe.

Becca let out a nervous giggle. "Well! Glad we got that cleared up!"

"We're supposed to be friends." Sam kept his eyes on Sophie. "Friends don't act like total dicks when something shitty happens to one of them."

"You aren't going to say 'I told you so'?" Sophie looked up.

"Given what you obviously think of me, I was wrong," he responded. "We're not friends." He paused, shaking his head as

27

though he was trying to snap out of something. "And since that's the case — I told you so."

There was an awkward silence. Sophie didn't look fierce anymore: her usual confident glow had deserted her. Her beautiful face seemed to droop with sadness. Harper felt really bad for her.

"Aren't we supposed to call Kate soon?" Becca must have noticed as well.

Harper quickly nodded. "And my feet are killing me. I don't think I can last till midnight."

"Let's go." Sophie looked away, obviously unwilling to meet anyone's gaze. "This party's suddenly feeling too crowded."

Five minutes later, the three of them traipsed into the guesthouse. Sophie had made it clear she didn't want to discuss the blowout with Sam, or the fact that she'd left him a tearful cell phone message at her darkest hour. Harper wasn't about to push the point. She was all too familiar with the desire to avoid certain unfortunate conversation topics.

"I need ice cream," Becca announced, kicking off the black strappy Ferragamo sandals she'd borrowed from Sophie. "And Cheetos."

"Just water for me." Harper flopped onto the couch. After witnessing the parade of perfect bodies in the Meyers' house, she had vowed to herself she'd eat nothing but rice cakes until she was fifty.

"I thought the keggers at Middlebury were wild," Becca mused, returning from the kitchen laden with Chunky Monkey, Cheetos, and several other tantalizing processed snack foods. "That party is out of control."

"The square inches of lip per capita was nothing short of astounding," Harper agreed, eyeing a bag of Twizzlers. "How do you stand it?"

Sophie, who was standing in front of a mirror, admiring the deep scooped back of her red dress, looked over at her. "Stand what?"

"The people out here. I mean, they *look* good. But everyone in LA seems so stupid . . . and shallow . . . and . . ."

"I'm sorry we can't all be intellectual powerhouses who write novels in our spare time," she snapped, folding her arms.

Oops.

"I'm sure Harper didn't mean *everyone,*" Becca interjected. "She liked Sam. Right, Harper? You liked Sam?"

"Fuck Sam!" Sophie marched into the middle room and stood glowering down at Harper. "He's self-righteous and condescending — a lot like a certain other person I know."

"Excuse me for having an opinion!" Harper retorted. "I can't help it if there are more fake boobs than brains in this town."

"Hellooo!" Becca called. "We're best friends! And if we're going to continue the Year of Dreams, it is *extremely* important that we lose the judgments."

"Easy for you to say," Sophie commented. "You already achieved your dream. You're in love."

"Which is great," Harper added. "If a tad annoying for those of us who are subjected to the baby voice you use when you're on the phone with Stuart."

"That has *gotta* stop," Sophie agreed, folding her arms again.

"I use a baby voice?" Becca was horrified. "Please tell me I don't use a baby voice."

Harper rolled her eyes. Could the girl be that oblivious? "Every time."

"It's worse than I thought," Becca declared as she opened the bag of Cheetos. "I need an intervention."

"We've got half an hour until the West Coast feed of the ball dropping in Times Square comes on. We'll use that time to break you."

"And we'll call Kate later," Harper suggested.

"So we're agreed?" Becca asked. "The theme of this year is no judgments?"

"Definitely. The Year of No Judgments." Secretly, Harper knew she'd be judging everyone, all the time, in her head. But she could certainly keep those judgments to herself. Or at least try to.

Sophie headed toward the kitchen. "I'll get a bottle of champagne, and we'll toast to it."

A tiny voice inside of Harper was telling her that despite the avoided argument, things with her and her friends were different. They'd all changed, but they weren't necessarily changing together. Sophie seemed more emotionally volatile, as though the insecurities of life as an aspiring actress in Los Angeles were already getting to her. Becca hadn't just moved away to college — she'd moved into a whole new world with new friends and new priorities and even a new (and irritating) romance-related baby voice. Kate was thousands of miles away, probably unrecognizable by now, wearing a beret and drinking something foreign and possibly lethal like absinthe. And Harper herself was secretly disloyal, dreaming of sitting in boring old Boulder gazing into Mr. Finelli's super-intelligent eyes rather than living the high life in LA with her best friends. Is this the way it was going to be from now on — everyone wishing they were with other people somewhere else?

She grabbed the Chunky Monkey and a spoon off the oversized bamboo coffee table. Her non-freshman fifteen pounds could hang around a little longer. Right now, she needed to bond with her girls. And that definitely required ice cream.

Coffee. If Kate could just have one more cup of coffee, perhaps her eyes would stay open and the weight of the blue ballpoint pen in her hand would feel less like an anvil. Trying to take page after page of notes with an anvil between her thumb and forefinger was starting to get more than a little difficult.

But the coffee pot was so far away — all the way on the other side of the massive wood-paneled Addis Ababa Hilton Hotel conference room where Kate and nineteen other young men and women were being officially orientated by Simenen, a short, round-faced Ethiopian man with a strong accent and a pocket protector who ran the Ethiopian branch of Le Project D'Eau (or The Water Project, depending on which side of which ocean one happened to be on). At least, Kate thought wearily, he was conducting the presentation in English. As fluent as her French had become in the last several months, the two hours of sleep she'd managed to grab since she'd landed in Addis Ababa this morning hadn't rejuvenated her brain cells enough to think in a romance language.

Dorothé, on the other hand, seemed perfectly alert. Sitting on Kate's left, she looked far younger than her twenty-six years as she scribbled energetic doodles on a yellow legal pad and sipped casually from a tall bottle of Abyssinian Springs water. Then again, Dorothé had been to Ethiopia several times. She probably didn't even need to be present for the orientation — she already knew all about things like Afrivalvs and hygiene protocol without running water.

A rubberband snapped somewhere in the middle of Kate's brain. Had Simenen just said *"without running water"*? How the hell was she going to take a shower without running water? Or wash her face? She hadn't come to Ethiopia to get pimply. And how had this seemingly obvious fact — that there would be *no running water* in the village where she was going to live — not occurred to her before? What had she gotten herself into? More accurately, what had *Harper* gotten her into? This was, ultimately, Harper's responsibility after all. If she hadn't lied about not getting into NYU, and then proceeded (albeit accidentally) to talk Sophie into bailing on UC Boulder to pursue her dream of being their generation's Halle Berry, Kate never would have . . . well, she would never have realized that she'd been blindly following the path her parents had laid out for her without giving any thought to what she actually wanted from her life. She would have gone to Harvard with her now ex-boyfriend Jared, gotten straight A's, graduated with honors, and never figured out that there was something . . . well, something more.

She didn't know exactly what that something more was yet, but she knew it was out there. It was that elusive *more* — a dream she had yet to discover — that had caused her to abandon Harvard, infuriate her parents, and say goodbye to her sister and three best friends, and travel to the other side of the world by herself. Not that it would have been a *bad* thing to fulfill the dreams her parents had for her. She probably would have excelled at Harvard, then at Yale Law, and not minded working ninety-hour weeks at some high-profile law firm. And maybe that was what she wanted.

But maybe it wasn't. And Kate had waited long enough to find out. Eighteen years was more than enough time spent living someone else's dreams, even if they were stellar dreams. Now it was her turn. The only problem was she still hadn't figured out exactly what her dream was yet — though she did feel like she was getting closer. The last four months had been the most challenging and magical of her life. She'd discovered, while crisscrossing Europe with minimal luggage and money, that there was more to Kate Foster than what everyone saw on the outside — a blond eighteen-year-old high-achiever. There was even more than the good grades and hard work that had gotten her into Harvard in the first place.

Her friends had helped her learn that by forcing her to make her travels more than just a tourist's fantasy. At the end of her second week in Paris — she hadn't known where else to go, and staying on the same continent as her beyond-angry parents was out of the question — Harper had sent her a list of challenges designed to help her find her dream. Sophie, Becca, and Kate's sister, Habiba, had all contributed. Some of the items on the list were silly, like "stomp grapes," and others were more serious, like "touch the Berlin Wall."

It had been number seven on that list ("talk to the ugly guy") that had led Kate to Magnus. Hopelessly lost, she'd gone into a Parisian bar to call a taxi, but the tall Swede had started talking to her before she ever made it to the phone. She'd been captivated by his friendly openness, and having concluded that Magnus was striking looking, but definitely not ugly, Kate had spent the night blissfully in his arms. But the next morning, afraid of getting waylaid from her goal, she'd written him an apologetic note and disappeared into the Parisian dawn expecting never to see him again.

A terrible, disturbing incident in Athens had changed all that. On a circuitous walk to the Acropolis, three teenaged thugs had hauled her into a dark alley, beaten her, and stolen her day pack. A kindly older Greek couple had scared off the attackers, but the experience had sent Kate into a tailspin. She was grateful it hadn't been worse — she hadn't been raped, thank God — but the wounds had been far deeper than her stitched-up forehead, swollen knee, and bruised elbows and ribs. Suddenly, she had felt vulnerable. Weak. And, worst of all, afraid. Upon her release from the hospital, she'd immediately boarded a train back to Paris. She hadn't known where else to go, and on their one night together Magnus had introduced her to an amazing older woman, a professor named Chantal, who generously offered to let Kate convalesce in her guestroom.

Chantal had cared for her, found her a job at a nearby café, and encouraged her to start facing the world again. Best of all, she had called Magnus. Kate would never forget the moment she'd looked up from the cash register to find him standing in the café doorway. She'd expected him to hate her. Instead he'd picked her up and put her back on her feet again — or, rather, on his motorcycle. He'd taken her away from Paris, away from the superficial security she was clinging to — her travels limited to the short journey between Chantal's cozy guestroom and the café — and helped her find security within herself.

Together, they'd remembered most of Harper's list, which had been nestled in her stolen day pack. He'd done several of the items from the list with her, like stomping grapes at a vineyard in Italy and climbing a mountain in the Swiss Alps. Almost like a personal trainer, Magnus had helped her build up her strength until she was strong enough to continue her journey alone. And then she'd accompanied him back to the southern coast of Sweden, kissed him good-bye, and gone to face her fears head-on in Athens. By then, it was almost Christmas, so she'd returned to Chantal's for the holiday. The plan had been to head east, through Turkey, into the Middle East, and then China.

Until Kate bailed on Harvard, she'd been a big admirer of plans. Her parents' favorite mantra was that it was always best to have a plan and stick to it. But in the last few months, she'd learned that while it was good to have some semblance of a plan, sticking to it wasn't always possible. And it definitely wasn't always best. So when she'd overheard Dorothé and Mira talking in the café about taking water from one Ethiopian village to another . . . well, it was the closest thing to destiny Kate had ever experienced. Suddenly, everything was clear. Number 43 on Harper's list, "take the water," which had been haunting her for months, was not only a means to finding her dream, it was a way to make a mark in the world.

It was also a way to get closer to her sister.

The Fosters had adopted Habiba from Ethiopia four years ago, when Habiba was twelve and Kate fourteen. An only child all her life, Kate had been excited about her parents adopting a baby. Then Habiba had arrived, all gangly legs and bright black eyes, a preteen insta-sister, fascinated by all things American and, Kate eventually realized, quietly longing for her new big sister's affection and approval. For the first time in her life, Kate hadn't been able to deliver. It was too much — Habiba was too much. She was too different from the tiny infant she'd been anticipating. One of the many downsides of her parents' affinity for planning was that when plans changed, Kate had a hard time adjusting. She'd done her best, but it had taken leaving home for her to realize how much she truly loved her little sister. And how much Habiba wanted and needed for them to really be sisters, not just teenaged girls who happened to share a bathroom.

Which was how Kate had ended up thousands of miles from home at this conference table in Addis Ababa, yearning for coffee after two solid hours of lecturing that would have done any Harvard professor proud. The session had started with a brief introduction to Ethiopian history — both impressive and, when it got to more recent history, pretty depressing — and then moved on to the founding of The Water Project. The project was initiated seven years earlier by a group of international businesspeople who knew that providing water access to rural African communities not only improved health; it meant local girls and women could go to school or learn new skills, rather than spend up to eight hours a day carrying unhealthy water from rivers and springs several miles from their villages. There was also the political benefit of keeping villages and families from having to fight for the water they needed just to survive.

There was no question that Kate was glad to be here. Glad to have the opportunity to do something meaningful. And excited about everything she was going to experience, everything she was going to learn — not just about her sister's birthplace but about herself. But no running water? *Really?*

Kate sighed. She could handle it. If she'd learned anything in the past four months it was that she *could* adjust. Still, if she was going to get through the next two hours of orientation, she was going to have to have more coffee.

She'd just started to push her chair back, when —

"Kate Foster?"

She turned toward the conference room door, where a maroon-uniformed concierge was looking around the room.

"Yes?" She tried to ignore the fact that all eyes were suddenly on her.

"A telephone call from Los Angeles for you." The concierge gestured toward the lobby.

Kate smiled as she checked her watch. It was midnight in Los Angeles. She'd almost forgotten it was New Year's Eve.

"Sorry," she mumbled. They could look all they wanted. Harper, Becca, and Sophie were waiting.

She pushed back her chair and followed the concierge to the two-story high, 1970s-era, vaguely Asian-looking lobby, where he directed her to a phone nestled in a private nook behind the long brown marble front desk.

"Katie-pie!"

"Do you miss us?"

"How the hell are you?"

Her best friends' voices clamored from the other end of the line. They sounded drunk. Or on a sugar high. Or both.

"Of course I miss you!"

The connection was static-y, but considering the distance, pretty damn good.

"How's my homeland?" Sophie had gone through an Afro-centric phase sophomore year. For exactly three weeks in January, she'd worn only kinte cloth and sandals. Fortunately, the played-for-drama outward manifestation had inspired her to actually learn something about her distant heritage.

"Honey, Africa is *everyone's* homeland — everything isn't always about you," Harper deadpanned.

Kate thought she caught a tinge of real tension in the contours of the joke. But now that they had asked, she didn't know what to tell

36

them. So many things were so . . . well, *bleak* here. Not the land-scape, at least not in Addis Ababa, which was lushly green in Janu-ary, with purple jacaranda trees blooming even in the grimmest areas. Not that Kate had really seen all that much, yet—mainly just the view from the back of the hotel, which had startled her when she glanced out a window, waiting for the elevator on the sixth floor. It had been even more shocking because the view from her balcony on the front of the hotel was like any American resort. Red clay tennis courts, several aquamarine pools with water from natural under-ground hot springs, a poolside restaurant with thatch-umbrella'ed tables, and flower beds everywhere.

But behind the hotel, a shanty town stretched to the horizon. Tin-roofed shacks with corrugated metal fences as far as Kate could see. Children in worn t-shirts and shorts played in a dirt lot on the other side of the tall, gray stone Hilton wall. The air smelled like smoke. Dorothé had explained that very few people in the shanty-town would have gas or electricity. All the cooking was done over wood fires or over small, wood-burning ovens.

How was she supposed to tell her friends, smack dab in the center of LA glamour and excess, about that? So she changed the subject.

"C'mon, give me the skinny," Kate prodded. "Tell me about you guys."

"Becca's in luuuuv," Sophie crooned.

"Stop it." But Becca sounded happy. "Sophie's living in a mansion. The pool at this house has its own waterfall. Can you believe it?"

"No." Kate didn't know what to say. She was in a country where millions of women and kids had to walk miles every day to get a bucket of water. When she heard about a private waterfall in a Bev-erly Hills mansion, she didn't know whether to feel impressed or ashamed.

"Sophie's getting a boob job," Harper intoned.

"Don't start — ohmigod, it's him!" The background noise on the LA end of the phone increased significantly.

"What?" Clearly something big was going on in La-La-Land.

"That guy who was in that movie about the plane crash in the desert. He just walked by Sophie's guesthouse —"

"What movie?" Kate hadn't exactly been keeping up on entertainment news.

"Holy celebrity, he's talking to Scarlett Johanssen," Harper gasped.

"Whose boobs are real, by the way." Clearly something was up between Harper and Sophie.

"Whoever it is, she looks f — ing g fant — tic." A patch of static didn't keep Kate from getting the general idea.

"There's no way you're at the same party as Scarlett Johansson." Kate laughed. This was too weird. She wasn't just thousands of miles away from her friends: she was in a completely different universe.

"Hey." A male voice spoke sharply behind her.

Kate turned to find a pair of almost yellow hazel eyes glaring at her. The eyes belonged to . . . she couldn't remember his name. Something like . . . oh, yeah, *Darby*. They'd been briefly introduced at the beginning of the orientation session, so she knew the tanned, dark blond/light brown–haired American was one member of her five-person team. Together with Dorothé, one other French guy, and another American girl, they would be assigned to a village in northern Ethiopia, near a town called . . . hell, Kate definitely couldn't remember that. She really needed some sleep.

Why was Darby looking at her like that? With . . . was it contempt?

"What?" She held one hand over the mouthpiece.

"Not that your conversation doesn't sound *really* important," he said in a low voice, "but orientation isn't optional. And your rich

38

friends probably don't mind, but that conversation costs about three bucks a minute."

Then he turned and strode back down the hall to the conference room.

Kate felt a wave of heat rush up her neck, all the way to her hairline.

"Kate. . . . Are you there?" Becca's voice intruded on her humiliation.

"Yeah," Kate said, "I'm here." And she was going to be there for at *least* five more minutes. Or three. Maybe two. "Tell me about your hunky quarterback."

As Becca filled her in on the latest Stuart news, Kate stared down the long hall at the conference room doorway.

What an asshole. Indeed, she decided, despite the definite appeal of those hazel eyes, the fact that his name happened to be one meager letter removed from Mr. Darcy's in *Pride and Prejudice* didn't improve Darby one bit.

Dear Kate,

Thought you might need this...

Hello...selam (The e sounds like the e in "her" or the u in "burst." Kind of.)

Mr...Ato

Mrs...Weizero

Miss...Weizerit

How are you?...Dena nesh? (if you're talking to a woman) or Dena neh? (if you're talking to a man)

I'm fine...Dena neny (the ny's kind of like in "canyon")

Thank you...Amese guhnando

Please...Ebakuh (m) or ebakesh (f)

Sorry...Aznallo

OK...Ishi (or maybe more like eshi—you'll pick it up when you hear it)

What's your name?...Semeh man no? (m); Semesh man no? (f)

My name is Kate...Semeh Kate no.

Can you help me please?...Ebakeh er dany? (m); Ebakesh erjiny? (f)

I'm from America...Ke Amerika neny.

Excuse me...Yikerta

Where's the nearest airport?...Yemikerbo airoplan yet no?

That last one's in case you want to come home. I've attached a few more pages of helpful words, and a short Amharic grammar lesson. Good for reading on the plane. Hope it helps you get though the first few days—We miss you.

XO, Habiba

❋ ❋ ❋ ❋ ❋ ❋ ❋ ❋ ❋ ❋ ❋ ❋ ❋ ❋ ❋ ❋ ❋ ❋ ❋

TWO

Without opening her eyes, Becca knew that he was watching her. She smiled.

"What?" Stuart whispered.

He *was* watching.

"You're looking at me."

"You're beautiful when you sleep."

Becca opened her eyes. She looked up across Stuart's bare chest to his smiling deep brown eyes. "When I sleep, huh?"

The morning sun was just beginning to make its way through his dorm room window, bathing him in yellow light.

"And every other moment of the day." He brushed a hand gently through her long auburn hair and down her back, hindered only by the strap of the way-sexier-than-she-was-used-to black lace bra Sophie had insisted she purchase at a lingerie boutique on Melrose.

"Good recovery." Becca sank deeper into Stuart, letting her head return to the perfect spot against his chest.

It was almost unimaginable that she could be here, nestled against him, one hand against his chest, the other casually resting on his narrow waist, as if she were old hat at cuddling in bed with nearly naked men. She brushed her leg against his, reassuring herself that there were still boxers between them. And, of course, her black French-cut lace panties. She was probably in love, but she wasn't a floozy.

"I had a dream about you," he breathed against her ear.

"How did you sleep long enough to dream?" They'd been up most of the night, talking and . . . other things.

She felt Stuart's chest rise and fall beneath her cheek.

"You make me really happy," he whispered. His voice sounded almost nervous.

Suddenly, Becca couldn't breathe. She forced a deep breath into her lungs, willing her heart to stop its profound throbbing. It was several breaths before she found courage and her voice. "Me, too."

For several long moments, they were silent as she listened to the sound of his breath and smelled the warm, soothing, cedarish scent of his skin.

Not for the first time in the last several hours, Becca found herself thanking the universe for having the foresight to send Stuart's roommate, Lee, abroad to Australia for the semester, leaving Stuart with a very spacious and, more to the point, private single room. Unfortunately, Lee had left most of his belongings, including several Metallica posters and psychedelic tapestries. Stuart's side of the room, on the other hand, was more sedate. His dark oak desk was a disaster area, with papers and books piled haphazardly around his laptop, but the walls were bare except for a large Gustav Klimt print from The Tate in New York. His standard-issue twin bed, covered with a thick navy-blue down comforter, sported blackwatch-plaid flannel sheets. Given that the temperature outside was probably somewhere in the negatives, she had developed a quick affection for flannel.

Becca could hardly believe, now, that she'd been so nervous about seeing him again. The nerves had started on the flight from LA to Boston and intensified when she hopped onto the smaller plane connecting to the tiny Middlebury State Airport. And they'd only gotten worse as she picked up her luggage, took the shuttle to campus, and — as she'd promised — made her way straight to Stuart's room. She'd tried talking the insecurities away, keeping up a steady mental stream of "he likes you, it's okay, he really likes you, everything will be fine" as she walked first down the brick pathway toward his gray, stone, almost medieval-looking dorm, then up the gloomy staircase, and finally down the carpeted hall that led to his door. She'd stared at the faux-brass number 9 until someone started coming down the hall toward her and she realized she'd look like a freak if she just kept standing there staring.

Once she knocked, it took barely a second for Stuart to open the door. The moment she'd looked into his eyes, the nerves melted away. He'd taken her in his arms, and she hadn't left them since. Except for a couple times to pee.

Stuart's fingers slowly entwined in the hair at the nape of her neck, sending shivers down Becca's back.

"Tell me your favorite memory," he said quietly.

What was it about his voice that made her get all shivery?

"Other than right now?"

"From when you were a kid."

That was a tough one. Most of Becca's memories from childhood were centered around screaming parents — raised voices that drove her to her room as she tried not to listen to the escalating accusations that eventually drove one or the other of them out the door. In that way, the inevitable divorce had been a relief. It was seven years since she'd moved into the tiny gabled room in her stepfather's house — seven years of dealing with a stepbrother and stepsister she could never find common ground with, as well as her mother's bottomless bitterness about her father and his younger new wife, with whom, her mother informed Becca, he had been having a two-year affair.

Martin, Becca's stepfather, had proven himself to be an okay guy. He was an accountant who'd met Becca's mother when she was trying to sort out her chaotic post-divorce finances, and he was pretty average in most ways — height, build, hair loss. What Becca appreciated most about him was his general tendency toward silence, and the fact that he never engaged in her mother's attempts to pick fights. The mere fact that his presence, on the whole, calmed her mother's daily storms to rarer, seasonal squalls had created in Becca a certain level of affection for him.

Her stepsiblings, on the other hand, were another matter entirely. Their mother, Martin's first wife, had left when the kids were small, moving up to Oregon to live in some sort of strange religious farming collective. Martin had tried his best to do the job of two parents, but his long working hours meant he ended up both ignoring and indulging his children. Becca felt sort of sorry for Carter, her twelve-year-old stepbrother, who acted out both at home and at school in a vain attempt to gain some attention and favor from his father. But with sixteen-year-old Mia, it was harder to find sympathy. Becca had tried to be friends with her, but Mia was undeniably a brat. And a bulimic. From the moment Becca had set foot in their house, Mia had gone about making her life miserable. Easily threatened, Mia had seen Becca as a rival for her father's affections — though she clearly wasn't. Martin was no more interested in Becca than he was the latest slew of reality TV shows — he'd check in now and then, but never really got involved with the story line.

No, all of Becca's best memories were with her friends. Harper, Kate, and Sophie had seen past the shy, protective barrier she'd erected with great care and deliberateness. They let her be herself — not the most talkative of the bunch, but funny and, at times, insightful. They'd seen her as brave, and that made her feel brave. Becca, with her friends, had an escape, a refuge. And, for the first time, unqualified acceptance and love. She certainly didn't get that from her father and stepmother, who seemed to view her as little more than an occasional garden accessory, donned when it suited their carefully controlled and maintained greenhouse of a life.

"You there?" Stuart kissed the top of her head.

"I'm just trying to figure out my favorite one," Becca covered. She'd told Stuart a little about her family, but this was definitely not a moment she wanted to spoil. "Maybe when we all went camping the first time sophomore year. Sophie refused to go without an Aero-Bed, Harper got poison ivy peeing in the bushes, and Kate brought her laptop to work on an English Lit paper."

"Sounds like a blast." He grinned.

"It *was*." Becca nudged him in the ribs. "I know it sounds weird, but I've never laughed so much in my life. It was just . . . *fun*. You'd love my friends."

"Speaking of friends," Stuart said, squeezing her hand, "we could go meet Isabelle for lunch."

Shit. Isabelle. Becca had forgotten all about her. She'd meant to call from Stuart's room last night and let her know she was back. But as soon as she'd seen Stuart's smiling face, as soon as he'd taken her in his arms . . .

Oh well. Isabelle would understand. Still, she should call her and ask how her vacation was.

But then Stuart was kissing her neck, and Becca decided that her roommate — and everything else in the world — could wait until later.

"Mr. Finelli. He's the one."

"Mr. Finelli is *not* the one," Harper countered, handing Habiba Foster the Rainy Day Books Café smoothie she'd dubbed the Green-Eyed Monster during the first weeks of her non-college career as a barista-writer. "I say that for reasons I don't care to go into."

47

Harper had enough on her mind without being forced to think about Mr. Finelli. She had a novel to write, her NYU essay was a literary travesty, and she was supposed to be starting a new diet and exercise regime — consisting of dozens of carrot sticks, hundreds of sit-ups, and lots of running up and down the basement stairs — today. All of which, of course, was in addition to the marathon sixteen-hour shift she'd agreed to in a moment of insanity.

A shift that would not involve brewing coffee side by side with Judd Wright, her old school friend — make that ex-friend — who'd managed to make sure they were never working at the same time since he'd basically told Harper he never wanted to speak to her again. She'd gone into one of her trademark rages, biting Judd's head off when he was trying to give her well-meaning advice and accusing him of being a jealous, unsupportive loser. The trip to Los Angeles had been a nice respite from all the drama back home — well, aside from the ridiculous, almost knock-down-drag-out with Sophie about whether LA was fake — but now that she was back in Boulder, Harper's score on the angst scale was off the charts. *Anyone* could see that.

But once Habiba had an idea, she didn't let go. It was one of the things about Kate's fourteen-year-old sister that Harper found most annoying. Especially because she was usually right. "He's not the one because you guys kissed?"

Harper almost choked on her nonfat decaf latte. After four months on the job she'd finally acquired a taste for coffee. "How did you *know* that?"

Kate would be killed. Slowly. With much pain and begging. Harper couldn't believe one of her best friends had revealed the intimate details of her personal life. Even if the person she'd revealed them to was one hundred percent trustworthy.

"I didn't. Not until you just told me." Habiba shook her head and drummed the counter with her fingertips. "I can't believe you fell for that."

48

Neither could Harper. Okay. *She* would be killed. At the hands of herself. Slowly. With much pain and begging. The very *thought* of Mr. Finelli, aka Adam, made her feel like she was going to spew nonfat decaf latte all over the morning pastries.

Harper had been in love with Mr. Finelli since the first day of A.P. English class her senior year, when he'd read Yeats poems aloud for the whole period. He was an inspirational teacher, totally encouraging her dreams about writing. And he was also totally hot. Young, hot, brainy, literary — he was the man of her dreams. She'd assumed that love would remain forever unrequited until a few months ago, when something so surreal had happened that Harper still wondered if she'd been abducted by aliens one night while she was sleeping and taken to a parallel universe. Mr. Finelli had liked her. Like, *liked* her, liked her. He'd actually said that. With words. "You're funny and brilliant and adorable," he told her — not that Harper had obsessively replayed this scene in her mind hundreds of times or anything.

He'd kissed her, at which point Harper had bravely declared she couldn't see him again until she'd completed the first fifty pages of her novel. At the time, she'd been absurdly proud of herself for putting her Dream before her desire. Of course, that was before she'd finished the pages and given them to Mr. Finelli to critique. Before he'd offered some gentle constructive suggestions and she'd responded by accusing him of being jealous of her obvious talent. Before she'd stormed like a jackass out of his apartment.

"Can we pretend I didn't just tell you I kissed Mr. Finelli?" Harper asked. "I'm really not in the mood for insights."

If only the Rainy Day Café were busy right now, she would have an excuse to stop talking to Habiba, but this was the mid-morning slump: there was nobody waiting in line. Where were the annoying customers-with-complicated-orders when she needed them?

"The point is you have to get a new college recommendation," Habiba continued, moving swiftly past the whole kissing thing.

"And Mr. Finelli is the one to ask. You were one of his best students, he loves your writing, and he knows how much getting into NYU means to you."

Harper slid open the glass that protected the pastries from random sneezes and grabbed the chocolate chip muffin she'd sworn she wasn't going to eat this morning. "Suffice it to say, I have acted in a way that makes what you're suggesting impossible."

"Being afraid isn't an excuse," Habiba informed Harper, her dark eyes serious. "NYU is too important to let fear stand in your way."

With that, she picked up her Hello Kitty backpack and headed for the door. As Harper watched her go, she realized that Beebs was starting to remind her of someone — Kate. As happy as she was that those two had started the sisterly bonding process, there were definite disadvantages. Now that Kate and Beebs were communicating on a regular basis, Harper felt like Kate was watching her from afar through the eyes of her Ethiopian sister. And Year of No Judgments or not, Kate always had an opinion. On everything.

Harper pulled off the top of her muffin, inhaling its sweet scent as she took a bite. This whole idea of starving herself was insane. When a person's life was as screwed up as hers, sugar fuel was not only a comfort, it was a necessity. Now that her tormentor was gone, she was glad there weren't any customers. If just one tourist asked for extra foam today, someone was getting an espresso machine to the head.

"We're out of onion bagels," Harper informed a disturbingly preppy headband-wearing CU student ten hours and seventy-eight customers later. *Because I ate them all,* she added silently. *Along with most of the cream cheese.*

"You guys really need to stock better," Miss Headband told Harper, in that whiny, born-to-be-a-bitch voice of every preppy girl who came into the café. "I'm going to Starbucks."

"Bye, then." Harper smiled benignly, hardly mourning the loss of a potential customer. Students never left good tips.

Besides, the end of her shift was in sight, and she'd already decided that today was a bust as far as college applications, writing, diet, and exercise were concerned. She planned to go home, flop on her mattress, and read back issues of *The New Yorker* until her eyes bled. The only matters that stood between her and whatever insights into contemporary society that Malcolm Gladwell had to offer were refilling the Splendas and mopping the perennially coffee-ground-covered tiled floor behind the counter. She knelt down to grab handfuls of the little yellow Splenda packets from a huge cardboard box that the staff kept under the cash register.

"Are you still open?"

Harper's stomach sank. She knew that voice. She wasn't prepared for this right now. There was a speech to remember, or a disguise to assume, or a knife to plunge into her chest.

"Uh . . . no!" She closed her eyes, hoping the voice would magically disappear back from whence it came from. *This is not happening. This is not happening. This is not happening.*

"Harper? Is that you?"

Damn! She started to stand up, forgetting that her head was currently stuck deep into the space under the register.

BAM! A sharp, shooting pain traveled the length of her body as her head made contact with the bottom of the oak counter top.

"Owww . . ." Dizzy. She felt dizzy. And faint. Or maybe those were the same thing. Either way, passing out was a definite possibility. And not a bad one, all things considered.

"Are you okay?" The voice was closer now. A lot closer.

Harper tried to stand up as gracefully as possible, but her belt loop snagged on a corner of the cardboard box and she nearly banged her head again trying to get disentangled. Mr. Finelli, aka Adam, was staring down at her, his aquamarine eyes showing concern behind his sleek wire-rimmed glasses. She managed the weakest of smiles. "Oh! Hi, Mr. Finelli. I didn't realize that was you."

"Right."

He was as beautiful as he had been a few weeks ago, the night she'd ruined her life *forever* by being a total and complete ass in his presence. His short, dark hair was endearingly messy, and he was wearing faded jeans and a heather-green sweatshirt that made his eyes look even more intense than usual. Just seeing him made her hurt all over — a pain that was different from and deeper than the throbbing in her head.

"I'm sorry — I hit my head." As if that weren't obvious. As if he cared.

"Yes, I see that."

He was still standing there. He hadn't turned and fled. That had to mean something. Right? *Tell him you're sorry. Tell him you've loved him since he read the Yeats poem "When You Are Old" aloud. Tell him you need a new recommendation letter for your NYU college application.*

The list could go on forever. There were a million things she wanted to tell him. That he'd been right about the fifty pages of crap she'd given him. That she'd finally figured out what her novel was about. *Really* about. That she'd thought about him the entire three and a half days she was in LA, though she pretended — even to herself — that she didn't.

The problem was, she didn't know where to start. Sometimes a person just didn't have the words to say what she was feeling.

So she just stood there. And said nothing. Moments passed. The phrase "awkward silence" sprang to mind. Finally . . .

"I . . . I . . ." It was all she could manage. It was pathetic.

Mr. Finelli shifted uncomfortably and half-smiled. "I guess it would probably be best if I went to Starbucks."

Harper nodded. Of course he would. He'd go to Starbucks, where he'd stand in line behind Miss Headband, and they'd bond over high-calorie coffee drinks and whatever novel she was reading for her sorority book club — probably something about the triumph of the human spirit. Eventually he'd overlook her whiny voice and addiction to pastel colors, and they'd get married and fly to Ireland for their honeymoon, where he'd recite Yeats and she would only care about bumping into Bono and The Edge and whatever those other two guys from U2 were called. And Harper would be a writer-barista forever, doomed to spend her nights mopping up stray coffee grounds and banging her head over and over on the underside of the counter. Alone. She had to say something.

"Rumor has it Starbucks has great onion bagels." She tried to smile — and failed.

He smiled back, maybe a little wistfully this time. "You know what, Harper? I don't get you."

Neither do I, she answered silently as he walked slowly toward the door. Once he was gone, she put her fingers gingerly to her head. There was already a lump. But compared to the size of the one in her heart, it was nothing.

"Which bed do you want?"

Standing in the doorway of the round mud and straw hut that was to be her home for the next several months, Kate stared at Dorothé.

Bed?

From what she could see, there were no beds at all. But if Dorothé meant to ask which *goat-skin cot* she preferred . . . well, it was hard to say. There was the one next to the low, round clay cookstove. Or there was the one just to the right of the indoor chicken enclosure. Neither seemed appealing. So she pointed hopefully at the cot under the one crooked glass-free window.

"I think Jessica got that one already," Dorothé sighed.

Yes, that was twenty-year-old Jessica's backpack, settled snuggly under the sagging goat hide. So *that* was why the third young woman on their five-person team had ditched the village elders' elaborate welcome ceremony. Kate had been in the middle of having her feet washed by the most adorable little girl she'd ever seen when Jessica had slipped off one of the low, wooden stools they'd been directed — through a series of hand signals and broken English — to sit on, and snuck through the crowd of gathered villagers in the direction of the compound that their driver, Isaac, had pointed out as theirs. If Kate hadn't been so annoyed, she'd have been impressed — though she never would have missed the welcome ceremony. Every man, woman, and child in Mekebe village — at least two hundred people — had assembled for their arrival and escorted them to a large dirt-floored ceremonial hut with what could only be described as great fanfare. Or, possibly, hoopla.

Women had ululated and danced. Men drummed. Children, utterly lacking shyness, had taken all five of them by the hand, grinning and clamoring in Amharic.

"We're considered honored guests," Darby had explained to the group at large. It was a fairly innocuous statement, but Kate had found it irritating nonetheless.

In the ceremonial hut, where the air smelled strongly of frankincense, they'd been instructed to leave their backpacks with a smiling elderly woman, and then been led forward through a crowd of Ethiopian men and women, many draped in graceful wraps called *natalas* wound loosely around their shoulders. Many of the natalas were white, others were bright reds, purples, and greens — all had a beautiful woven border at both ends. Kate made a mental note to get one for Habiba.

When they reached the main part of the hut, they'd been presented to Tafesse, the village elder. Tafesse's natala was a faded red. He tossed one yellow-trimmed end stiffly over his arm as he labored to his feet from a carved wooden armchair. Isaac first introduced Darby and Jean-Pierre, which gave Kate time to study Tafesse. His wrinkled cheeks and stooping back made him appear at least eighty, though she'd already discovered that it was nearly impossible to accurately guess anyone's age. There were so many things that aged people prematurely here — disease, malnutrition, hard manual labor under a punishing sun. But there was no question Tafesse had been around a long time.

When it was her turn to greet him, Kate — as she'd been instructed — held her right hand under her left elbow to shake his hard, boney hand. He held her much-softer hand tightly for a moment, a sincere smile in his aged, black eyes.

"Wel-come," he said slowly in a rich, rumbling voice.

"Amese gendando." Kate smiled. Thank you.

Still holding her hand, Tafesse turned to a group of elders assembled behind him and said several quick words in Amharic. They nodded in response, smiling at Kate.

"He says you're very pretty."

Darby, standing just behind her, shared the compliment with clear displeasure. Kate suddenly felt self-conscious.

She ignored Darby, nodded a thank-you to Tafesse, and stepped aside as Isaac presented Dorothé and Jessica. When the introductions were complete, Isaac led them across the grass-strewn dirt floor to several waiting stools, all three-legged and hewn from thick, dark wood. Children stepped forward with brightly colored plastic buckets of precious water to wash their feet. Given the orientation process that Kate had just been through, she knew that the girls and women in this village had to walk more than three miles to the nearest water source — a river that was barely a trickle in the dry season. So this was a privilege indeed.

A rail thin little girl with dark brown skin and a smile as wide as the Blue Nile removed Kate's tennis shoes and socks, beaming up at her.

"Welcome, you." The little girl smiled shyly. Kate, recognizing the deep purple dress the girl was wearing as a school uniform, decided she was probably about ten. The short-sleeved dress hung loosely over the girl's bony shoulders and was coated in a thin layer of the dust that seemed to rise of its own volition into the air.

"My name is Kate," she recited in Amharic, grateful once again for the primer Habiba had sent her.

The little girl's smile grew impossibly wider as she drew a wet cloth over the tops of Kate's feet. *Faranji* hardly ever spoke Amharic, and the gesture was appreciated by more than just the little girl. Several people around Kate nodded approvingly and repeated her name. Kate grinned, pleased to have not completely bungled the accent. The girl gently placed the wet cloth in the water bucket at her feet, and reached for a dry one. Her face was long and slender, and her forehead high and wide. But it was her eyes that captivated Kate. They were round and bright and completely alert — as if she were watching, waiting for something incredibly exciting to happen, surely just moments away.

The girl glanced up bashfully as she finished drying Kate's feet and pointed at herself. "Angatu."

Then she nodded quickly and disappeared back into the crowd. *Angatu,* Kate had repeated to herself several times. Angatu, Angatu, Angatu. Not that repetition would make the name stick. Getting used to Ethiopian names was going to take some time.

Once all four pairs of feet were washed — Jessica had already disappeared — coffee was served. Well, not really coffee. At least, not like any coffee Kate had ever tasted. This coffee was roasted on a low fire right in front of them. They watched as a young woman in a white natala tended the pale green coffee beans until they were browned, and then ground them with a pestle in a small wooden bowl. Once the beans were ground, she poured them into a clay pot and kept a sharp eye as the coffee brewed over the small fire. Finally, she poured the hot, deep brown liquid into small, white porcelain cups. All the while, a group of men and women from the village danced, rolling their heads and shoulders to the beat of several drums, their knees raising rhythmically between intricate footwork. With her first sip of the traditional Ethiopian coffee, Kate had known immediately that she'd never tasted anything so staggeringly yummy. There must have been sugar waiting in the cups, because the thick, dark coffee met her taste buds with a sweet richness that she couldn't wait to describe to Harper.

The taste was still on her tongue now as she stood in the doorway of her new hut home, trying to decide between two less-than-fabulous cot options. Considering her lack of affinity for chickens . . .

"I'll take that one." She pointed at the cot by the cookstove.

Dorothé grinned. "Think I got the better end of that deal. Did I mention we cook mainly with dungcakes?" Somehow, a French-accent made even the word "dungcakes" sound lovely.

"Lucky for me — I love the smell of dung in the morning."

Kate had realized about an hour into the bone-jarring, two-hour drive from the Bahar Dar Airport over bumpy dirt roads that she had to make a choice. She could either turn her sense of humor dial up to extra-high, or she could spend the next few months sobbing. So humor it was.

At least for the moment.

All in all, their compound was quite nice. A six-foot fence con-structed from mostly straight eucalyptus branches wreathed the two *tukuls* (round, thatch-roofed mud huts) and a large dirt and rock yard. Kate, Dorothé, and Jessica would be sharing one *tukul* while Darby and Jean-Pierre, the last member of the team, shared the other. Six or seven chickens and a large, impressively feathered turkey roamed freely. Someone had taken the time to plant several plants (probably *enset,* Kate decided) along the inside perimeter of the fence. In one corner, a purple-flowered jacaranda tree shadowed a three-sided storage shed made of mud and straw. Inside the shed, several enormous white industrial plastic bags bulged with teff, a common Ethiopian grain, as well as barley and wheat. The grains were a gift from the village. Since their arrival coincided with the end of a successful harvest season, all the farmers in the area — and pretty much everyone was a farmer — had contributed.

"Home sweet hovel!" Jessica stood in the doorway, her hands on her slightly over-round hips. She wore khaki shorts and a fitted emerald-green polo shirt. Her short red hair was tousled adorably. Her eyes, the same bright color as her shirt, sparkled with mischief. Everything about her screamed *cute.*

Kate hated cute the way Harper hated perky.

From the moment they met, Jessica had rubbed her the wrong way. She seemed to have an almost paternalistic attitude toward Ethiopia and Ethiopians. Every time she opened her mouth it was to say something condescending or rude — unless one of the guys was around. Particularly Darby. In front of him, Jessica was extra-cute and constantly proclaimed her deep love for the continent of Africa as a whole.

The night before, at Darby's suggestion, the five team members had met in the Hilton Hotel bar for some get-to-know-each-other time. For the most part, the evening had been great. They'd had round after round of *tej,* Ethiopian honey wine, and shared their reasons for signing up with Water Partners. Dorothé, in her usual acerbic, French-accented way, explained her commitment in global geopolitical terms. Jean-Pierre quietly explained the subject of his recently completed graduate work, which had something to do with the horrific repercussions of the European colonization of Africa. Only when work was completed did he realize that book research couldn't compare to actual experience. When it was his turn, Darby said that he'd gotten overwhelmed by the tenor of eliteness at Princeton and needed to spend a semester reconnecting to "the real world."

"Now Kate," Dorothé had urged, lifting her third glass of *tej.* "Tell them about the Year of Dreams."

Kate had gotten through Harper's announcement, and telling her parents she was taking a year off when Darby interrupted, "So, you're here basically because of peer pressure and to piss off your parents."

Kate froze. She couldn't imagine a more warped description of why she was here. He hadn't even given her a chance to get to Habiba, or the List, or destiny. But Darby had already turned to Jessica.

"What about you, Jess? What's your story?"

"I guess it's like yours," Jessica gushed. "Everything at UCSB just seemed so fake. You know, the whole Greek thing, and everyone just took their privileged lives for granted. I couldn't take it anymore."

Darby'd nodded like he totally got it. Kate wanted to vomit — and the urge only grew stronger moments later when Darby left the table to talk to another team leader and Jessica leaned in conspiratorially.

"That was total bullshit," she whispered. "I got rejected from the study abroad program in Monte Carlo, and everything else was all filled up. How much does *that* suck?"

Now Jessica was plopping down on her by-the-window cot, and talking about Darby like they were long-lost soulmates.

"Did you know his parents were in the Peace Corps? He totally grew up in Africa, like all over," she prattled on. "Ethiopia, South Africa, and a bunch of other countries I can't remember. This is, like, his home."

Kate glanced at Dorothé, who seemed as mortified as she was at the thought of spending months in a mud hut with this chick. Grabbing a packet of travel toilet paper out of her backpack, Kate headed for the door.

"Where's the . . . ?" she asked Dorothé, pointedly not looking at Jessica.

Dorothé pointed toward a small shantylike outhouse on the perimeter of the fence. The roof was made from corrugated iron and looked like it was about to slide off into the dust.

"Pit latrine," she declared. "Best one in the village."

Great. Pit latrine.

As Kate headed toward her new flushless toilet, she thought about the letter she'd been trying to write Magnus since she'd arrived in Ethiopia. There were so many things to say that she'd had a hard time figuring out where to begin. The trip so far could mostly be summed up in images: the scores of women she'd seen trudging down Entoto Mountain outside Addis Ababa bearing twice their weight in eucalyptus branches on their shoulders to sell for pennies at the market; the small children herding oxen along the side of the dirt roads; the orphans begging as they drove through the streets of Bahar Dar, their gaunt faces covered in dirt, their eyes as hungry as their empty stomachs.

Kate forced back impending tears. Sense of humor, she reminded herself. Not that any of this was funny. Maybe that was part of why she couldn't figure out what to write to Magnus. She'd always been honest with him — even when she didn't want to be. But she couldn't be honest with herself about how existence here seemed so perilous, so fragile . . . she just couldn't think about it. Not yet. Maybe over time it would get easier. In the meantime, maybe she could just tell Magnus about Angatu, with her bright eyes and sweet smile.

Yes, she would write him about that.

"Rolling!"

"Sound!"

"Speed!"

"Action!" The director's deep voice rang out from somewhere behind the camera. His name was Eli Berg, and he had a voice that carried two city blocks.

Sophie's heart hammered in her chest. This was it. Her moment. *Do it,* she screamed to herself. And then —

"You've got to be *kidding* me!" she exclaimed, staring at the bountiful brown curls that adorned the head of Devon Riggs, the star of the movie. Sophie had never heard of him, but the casting director had informed her that this movie was going to make him the next Vince Vaughn. Devon wasn't as tall or funny or charismatic as Vince Vaughn — in fact, he was on the short side and his eyes were kind of googly. But he was cute enough, Sophie thought, and the last offbeat comedy he appeared in was, allegedly, the sleeper hit of the Sundance Film Festival.

Stud was about a bald guy, played by Devon, who has no luck with girls until he wakes up one morning having mysteriously grown a full head of hair. Sophie was playing Morning, his zany neighbor who's always bumping into him in the hallway. In this scene she was supposed to register understandable shock at the sight of formerly bald-as-an-egg Devon in all his hair glory.

"Cut!" Eli screamed. His hair was even crazier than Devon's wig, and his bushy eyebrows grew in one insect-like line across his forehead. "Let's reset."

Sophie's heart slowed down. It was seven fifteen AM, and she'd just completed the first take of her first line in her first movie (she'd decided not to count the line Trey had given her in *Bringing Down Jones* for obvious reasons). Phew. She retreated to her canvas chair — it didn't have her name on it, but who cared? She had *a speaking role in a movie* — and Devon slouched into the seat next to her.

"Great reaction," he told her. "But next time make it bigger. This is comedy."

61

"Bigger. Got it." The guy could have told her to do a cartwheel delivering the line and she would have followed the order without question. Two hundred people at Sundance couldn't be wrong!

This was the most major opportunity of Sophie's life. Millions of people would see the movie all across America. She could imagine the reviews. *With only three lines, Sophie Bushell steals* Stud. *Sophie Bushell makes* Stud *magic.* Stud *births new star in Sophie Bushell.*

Her phone would be ringing off the hook with offers. Maybe she'd get to do a movie with Angelina or, better yet, Meryl. Everyone who was anyone had done a movie with Meryl. Or she could star in her own TV show. Maybe a sassy, must-see series for the CW about four friends who ditch college to pursue their dreams.

By that time Trey Benson would be a has-been. He'd knock at the door of her airy, super-modern bachelorette pad — with understated Asian décor and an infinity pool — nestled in the Hollywood Hills, begging for a job. Of course, Sophie wouldn't be there to answer the enormous front door herself. She'd be on location in Paris. Her assistant, Kimberlee or Ashlee, would report the incident when she called Sophie with a list of couture designers clamoring to dress her for the Oscars.

She'd be nice to Sam, though. She couldn't help but want him to succeed, even if he was a dick most of the time. Even if they weren't currently speaking. After all, he'd been her first friend in LA. Her only *real* friend.

Sophie was just glad Devon, at thirty, was too old — and too short — to be her type. The last thing she needed was her big break exploding in her face over an on-set romance. And anyway, she was done with actors.

"Too bad this piece of shit is going straight to DVD," Devon remarked as he used the reflection of the LCD screen on his cell phone to adjust one of his brown curls. "The script sucks, but I think it'll be good for a few laughs."

"What?" She must have misheard. It was the nerves.

"We don't have a shot at getting released in the U.S. This baby's going to be on the shelves of video stores." He paused. "In Germany."

Germany? How did Germany get involved? Sophie seemed to be watching from far away as her shiny bubble of hope burst into smithereens.

"Didn't your agent tell you?" Devon asked, still adjusting his Bo-Peep curl. "We lost the studio backing we needed to make the picture viable." He grinned bitterly. "So much for my break-out role, huh? Better luck next time."

"But the casting director said —"

"Casting director?" Devon snorted. "They'll say anything to get you to agree to a role. That's why you've got to make sure your agent stays on top of things."

"My agent's been on vacation," Sophie lied quickly. "I guess that's why I didn't get the news."

No way was she going to admit to Devon Riggs that she didn't *have* an agent. She did supposedly have a lawyer. Gifford Meyers had agreed to be her attorney — and take five percent of whatever she made for life — over a handshake at lunch. So far, he hadn't done much but call two friends to get her into a few auditions and give her standard day player contract a cursory glance before she signed it.

"Man, this wig is making my head melt." Devon was clearly done with the conversation. "The shit I do for my art is unbelievable."

"People, this isn't *Gone with the Wind!*" yelled Eli, saving Sophie from having to respond. "Let's get moving. I want to be shooting in the bedroom by lunch."

Five minutes later, the cameras had reset and they were finally ready to shoot another take. Devon stepped out of his fake apartment door, where Sophie/Morning was waiting with a bulging bag of trash she was supposed to be carrying to the Dumpster. She took one look at the thick, curly brown wig. And thought about her big break turning out to be a tiny fission.

"YOU'VE GOTTA BE KIDDING!" she shouted, dropping the bag of trash. It was a bigger delivery, just like Devon had requested, but this time she wasn't acting at all.

Thirteen hours later, Sophie pulled the silver BMW borrowed from the Meyers into the terracotta mansion's expansive circle drive. She was exhausted, everything ached, and she was hungry. But she also felt exhilarated. Sure, she'd moped for a few hours after Devon delivered the news that *Stud* was going straight to DVD in Germany. But eventually the thrill of being on location, acting in an actual movie — even if it never made it to the big screen — overrode her disappointment. Germany was a sizeable country. And millions of people rented DVDs. Including Germans.

Besides, if she was good enough to get this part, she was good enough to get another one. Plus she still had an awesome place to live, the three best friends in the whole world (even if they did live thousands of miles away), and a job as a hostess at Mojito that was hectic but fun as long as her manger, Celeste, was in a decent mood. Life was *not* all bad.

While she waited for her *next* big break, Sophie had decided she'd start learning German. There was no harm in being prepared for stardom in Central Europe. She grabbed the brand-new English-German dictionary she'd bought at Barnes & Noble on the way home and headed up the burnished tile path that lead to her little *casita* hidden deep within the manicured gardens.

For a moment, Sophie was scared. The front door was open. And all the lights were on. She'd heard about a rise in home invasions in Los Angeles during the past few months. Why had she never followed Harper's advice and gotten a can of mace to carry around in her purse? Just as she was about to turn and sprint to the main house, where she could dial 911 in safety, Sophie heard a voice.

"We'll make this wall all mirrors. It will be divine." The voice unmistakably, undeniably, belonged to Genevieve Meyer. It sounded like she was . . . decorating.

Sophie tentatively entered the guesthouse to find Genevieve and a very tall, very tan young man in a black t-shirt and pants standing in the middle of the living room. *Her* living room. Genevieve, dressed in a lavender terry-cloth running suit that probably retailed at somewhere around six hundred dollars, was waving her hands excitedly.

"And we'll put a leather sofa in here," she gushed. "This place really needs some good leather." Genevieve paused long enough to notice Sophie standing in the doorway, English-German dictionary in hand. "There you are!"

"Hi, Mrs. Meyer." No matter how many times her host told her to call her by her first name, Sophie couldn't bring herself to do it. She glanced at Tan Man, whom she assumed was a decorator. She knew Genevieve was generous. But redecorating her guesthouse? It was too much. "You really don't have to —"

"Sophie, I want you to meet Marco," Genevieve interrupted. "He's my nutritionist and personal trainer. A total genius."

"Nice to meet you," she responded.

Marco smiled, flashing a set of professionally whitened teeth. He looked like he'd walked straight out of an infomercial — perfect teeth, perfect hair, clothes that hugged every inch of his muscular frame. Sophie was confused. Was this a hint? Did Genevieve think she needed to drop a few pounds? Okay, so maybe she'd eaten more than her fair share of chocolate over the holidays. Sophie thought the extra couple pounds actually made her butt look *better*.

"Now that you're doing so well, I thought it might be time." Genevieve smiled brightly. Her lipstick was a perfect match for her lavender running suit, but it made her look like she'd been sucking on a grape Popsicle.

"Uh . . . time for what?"

"To get your own place. You're a young woman, you need your own space. Giff and I are cramping your style."

No, you're not! Sophie screamed in her head. *This is my own space. I love it here!* But Genevieve was oblivious to her inner monologue.

"I already left your mother a message all about it. Marco's going to move in here once I've done the place to his liking. His last apartment had such bad energy, the poor darling. And if I want to keep my figure I need him near me *all* the time."

But Sophie barely heard the last part of what her benefactress — correction, ex-benefactress — said. Her semi-perfect world had just crumbled around her, and there was nothing she could do about it.

Genevieve laid one French-manicured hand on her shoulder. "Of course, all of this is only if it's okay with you, sweetie. You know you're welcome to stay here as long as you like."

Sophie was desperate to tell Genevieve that, no, it wasn't okay with her. She didn't want to go anywhere. But the only thing truly linking her to the Meyers was a decades-old friendship between Genevieve and her mom, Angela. She could hardly demand to stay.

"Sure," she agreed, forcing herself to smile. "I'll be out by the end of the week."

And just like that, Sophie Bushell, formerly of Beverly Hills, was homeless.

RESIDENTIAL RENTALS

Downtown/Metropolitan
Including Hollywood

MID WILSH – MIRACLE MILE
LG Bach w/lots of charm
Util paid
$650

Charm = mold in the kitchen

HLYWOD HLS
Rm to rent. $400.
Charm room with frpl and ceil fan
Vu of Hlywd sign
No Scientologist haters, pls.

Twenty thousand extra to "be cleared"

HLYWOD
1 bd, 1 ba, new kit, no pets
$1600 pls. utl.

WLA STUDIO
$800+
Hi Ceil, Cntrl A/C
Blks to shops

Gone

WLA
Help! I need SF to share rm in 2 +2
Twin bed prov. Snoring OK
$350

Not THAT desperate

FAIRFAX
1 + 1 Remdld kit and ba
Urban delight, $700
Act fst, too gd to miss

Last tenant overdosed

NORTHRIDGE
$575 Guest Rm.
Util. inc.
Female Pref.
Non-Smkr

Northridge = no social life

THREE

M addix hates me again."

Becca plopped down on the cold snow beside Isabelle and fingered the wristband of the winter-white Spyder ski jacket that her father had given her for Christmas.

"Maddix doesn't hate you," Isabelle reassured her. "You just blew one run."

In her gray cashmere turtleneck sweater and fitted black ski pants, Isabelle looked like a model in a ski magazine. Her curly, shoulder-length brown hair was pulled into a poof-ball at the top of her head. A black ear-warmer and matching wool gloves completed the look.

In the distance, far below them, the pretty New England town of Middlebury was sprinkled with fresh snow. With its white-steepled church and twisting river, it looked Christmas-card perfect. Usually Becca loved this view, but she couldn't enjoy it today. It was the first real training session of the new semester and she *had* totally blown her first run. She certainly hadn't meant to. She'd tried to focus when the buzzer sounded. But even Coach Maddix — her skiing god, the entire reason she'd wanted to come to Middlebury in the first place — standing right beside her couldn't push *him* out of her head.

"I was thinking about Stuart," Becca confessed.

"No!" Isabelle assumed a look of mock shock.

"He's going to say it." Becca's heart pounded just thinking about it. Isabelle's sarcasm barely registered. "I can tell. He's going to say it really soon."

Isabelle sighed. "You know, you could say it first."

"No way. He has to say it."

"Love isn't sexist. There's no *rule.*"

"Of course there is. The he-says-it-first rule. Anyway, I could never."

"Okay . . ."

Becca caught a tone in Isabelle's voice. Had she been talking about this too much? No, definitely not. She'd barely *seen* Isabelle in the week they'd been back. She'd spent every night in Stuart's room, and with their new class schedules she and Isabelle hadn't even managed to have lunch together. They'd met up in their room a couple of times, but ski practice was the only chance they'd had to really see each other. Which meant she could only have talked about Stuart three times. And that was definitely not too much.

Isabelle was probably just stressed about the first ski meet against Amherst, one of their big rivals, which was coming up this weekend. Yeah, that's probably all it was. She hadn't been skiing her best, either.

"What about the sex?" Isabelle stood up, brushing snow off her butt.

Becca stood up, too. Mainly because she didn't want their conversation to be overheard by the entire ski team, although she knew she had to get back to top of the mountain and try to do better if she didn't want Maddix to ream her in front of everyone — like he did way too often last semester.

"We haven't . . ."

Isabelle looked at her like she was nuts.

"I know. It's just . . . I want to wait."

"So basically what you're saying is, you're not going to say it, he has to say it, and until he does, you're not going to sleep with him?"

Becca blinked. What was Isabelle's problem? It wasn't like that. Well, it *was* like that, but was that so wrong? Maybe she was too hung up in romantic notions, maybe she was just freaked out at the thought of having sex again — her first and last experience hadn't exactly made her anxious to get back on that particular horse — but whatever it was, it was how she felt, and it wasn't wrong. Was it?

Her doubts stuck with her all the way back to the top of the Snow Bowl, the mountaintop ski area that was home to the Panthers, Middlebury's ski team. But as she jumped off the lift and headed into the starting box to face Maddix, she shook them away. Focus. Just focus, she told herself.

Coach Maddix looked at her coldly as she stepped up. Every ounce of energy in his six-foot-four frame was directed right at her as she clomped toward him on her skis. His chilly blue eyes took in all the details of her stance, from the distribution of her weight to the bend of her knees. If there was fault, he would find it.

"You gonna go shit side up on this one, too?"

"No, sir."

Becca tightened her grip on her poles and stared down the mountain. The glare of the sun showed the danger spots — all the places she'd hit on her first run that she was going to avoid this time. If she'd been paying attention, Becca would have seen them before. *Don't make that mistake again.* She adjusted her goggles, retightened the grip on her poles, and got into position. This mountain was hers.

Becca nodded.

"Go!" Maddix shouted.

She went. Stuart was forgotten. Isabelle didn't exist. Her friends, family, classes — none of it mattered. All that mattered was the mountain, and her skis. Nothing in the world was better than this when all the pieces came together — the skis were like synapses, sending messages back and forth between Becca's body and the snow. She swooshed from gate to gate, blue and red flags barely a blur as her knees rose and fell, her poles stuck and lifted, her hips leaned fractionally this way or that. The air, barely above freezing, burned her cheeks as she picked up speed. Never once did she fear falling. Tumbles happened, but not today. Today, she was a machine. She was on fire. She was . . .

Yes! Becca crossed the red chalk finish line at the bottom of the run and immediately headed for Carey, the assistant coach, who had a cell phone to his ear.

"Time?" she panted.

"You took off six seconds," he announced, hanging up the phone. "Maddix says 'very salty.'"

Coach Maddix rated performance on a salt scale that no one precisely understood, except to know that having salt was a good thing, and not having it was . . . well, say goodbye to the team.

Becca grinned with relief. Very salty, indeed. That would show him. One bad run didn't mean she'd lost it. And with the time she'd just delivered, she would definitely be one of the lead skiers at the competition this weekend, even though after an ankle injury last semester Maddix had moved her to giant slalom, a tough event she'd never skied in competitively before. But that was cool. No problem. She could handle it. It was just about keeping her head in the game. Staying focused. Not letting Stuart impede too much on her — Stuart.

He'd said the funniest thing last night. They'd been in the middle of a very tight game of *Grand Theft Auto: Vice City Stories,* and she'd just sideswiped his red mustang with her police cruiser. "I got that on video, pig," he'd yelled. "You're going down!"

Then he'd taken her down in a barrage of kisses. Then the kisses had gotten slower, longer, deeper. Becca felt her nipples tighten just thinking about it, and her breath grow shallow. Whenever she finally did have sex with Stuart, she had no doubt that it was going to be good. Damn good. Probably great.

Isabelle was almost down the mountain now, black goggles shielding her eyes.

"C'mon, Iz!" Becca shouted, as her roommate zipped across the finish.

"Two seconds over," Carey called, shaking his head.

Isabelle wasn't exactly in grand form today. Fortunately, she mostly skied because she liked it. She didn't really care about the whole competition aspect. Still, maybe something was up with Abe. He was a friend of Isabelle's from high school, and she'd always had a killer crush on him. Isabelle had been ecstatic when they'd finally hooked up over Thanksgiving, but when Abe had returned to Harvard, and she'd come back to Middlebury, they'd only talked a few times. Then things had heated up again over Christmas. Now that they were back at their respective schools, maybe the relationship had cooled?

"Nice run." Becca grinned as Isabelle snapped out of her skis.

Isabelle shook her head. "I sucked."

Becca snapped out of her skis as well and they walked toward the long, blue van that would take them back to campus. A few more people had to complete their runs, then Maddix would give them one of his loud, ferocious lectures about being "salty" enough to take down Amherst this weekend, and they would head back. No reason to stand around waiting in the cold when they could wait in the heated van.

"How's Abe?"

Isabelle was quiet for a second, her face a hard-to-read mask. "Fine. Good."

"Are you going to see him sometime soon?"

"Yeah. Maybe in a few weeks."

73

"Did I tell you what Stuart —" Becca began. But Isabelle turned back for the ski lift.

"I think I'm going to get in another run," she said over her shoulder. "Try to get my time down a little."

Becca nodded. Something was definitely off with her friend. She was not her usual chatty self today. As soon as Isabelle was back down the mountain, she'd ask her about it.

Several skiers were in the van already. Two of her lunch buddies — Luke, a stocky sophomore from Baltimore, and Taymar, another freshman, who was from Detroit — greeted Becca with congratulations on her final run.

"You're gonna kick some Amherst ass this weekend." Luke slid closer to Taymar, making a space for Becca in the back row of the van — and also, she noticed, giving him more leg-on-leg contact with the self-proclaimed "goddess of color." Luke's crush on Taymar was getting more obvious every week.

"They won't know what hit 'em," Taymar agreed with a flick of her long dark braids.

"Thanks." Becca grinned.

"What're you wearing to the dance?" Taymar, along with Isabelle, was one of the few real fashionistas on campus.

Becca paled. God, what *was* she wearing?

Taymar laughed. "You can raid my closet. What're you, a six?"

She nodded. Raiding Taymar's closest would be better than an hour at Neiman's — not that there was Neiman Marcus in Middlebury, Vermont.

"Come over before, I'll hook you up. Stuart won't know what hit him."

"Guy already walks around in a love-daze," Luke added wryly. "Go easy on him."

Becca blushed. A love daze? *Really?*

She barely even noticed when the rest of the team climbed into the van. And when they got back to the main campus, Isabelle had hopped out and was on her way across the Common to their dorm room in Batell before Becca had even reached the sliding van door.

Well, whatever was wrong, she'd definitely ask Isabelle about it the next time she saw her. But right now, Stuart was waiting. They had plans to hit the cafeteria by his dorm, then spend the night reading Schopenhauer.

And for someone walking around in a "love-daze," what could be more romantic than that?

"French doors, exposed brick walls, hardwood floors . . ." Sophie's eyes roamed the apartment as she lied to her mom via cell phone. "It's gorgeous, Angie."

And it was. If one's definition of gorgeous included mold-covered walls, roaches, and carpet that had been around since the Truman administration. The ad had described the studio as "charming." Shithole would have been more appropriate. This was the sixth apartment Sophie had dragged Celeste to today, and each was worse — and in a worse neighborhood — than the last. She was growing more nostalgic for her heydays in distant Beverly Hills by the minute.

"Oh honey, it sounds lovely." Her mother paused. "When I got Genny's message I was so worried."

"I can take care of myself." *Of course, I may be living on skid row,* she added silently.

Angela sniffled on the other end of the line. "I'm so proud of you."

Okay, now she'd done it. Sophie felt a lump form in her throat. "Thanks. Me, too."

"This is a real process of self-actualization for you," her mother continued in her therapist-speak. "Be sure to call Dad and tell him the good news."

Sophie's parents had been divorced for almost as long as she could remember, but they were much more civilized about it than Becca's dysfunctional parents: they'd done the whole "staying friends" thing for her sake. Which was great, except that their ongoing communication always made it harder for her to get stuff by either of them. She could never play one off against the other, or tell them different stories if she wanted to stay out late at a party or go somewhere her mother considered age-inappropriate. Sometimes Sophie wished they were less civilized — she could have had a lot more freedom.

By the time Sophie hung up, she'd added crown molding, a spacious terrace, and a bird's-eye view of the Hollywood sign to the imaginary details of her imaginary apartment. Maybe she felt a tiny bit guilty about her lie. But Angie always said visualization was the key to success. If she pictured the ideal apartment long enough, maybe she would find it.

Celeste, her dyed-blue hair a perfectly tousled mess, emerged from the puke-colored bathroom with a strange look on her face. "I think something's living in the toilet," she announced. "It sort of . . . bit me."

Sophie was less shocked that there was a critter in the toilet than by the news that Celeste had actually *used* it. Apparently, years of living in Los Angeles had inured her to the grosser things in life.

"There's a place for rent just down the street on Sunset." Celeste held up the classified section of the *L.A. Times* and read aloud in her most peppy-sounding voice. "Only five hundred dollars a month! Ad says it's cozy and quaint!"

"In other words, it's a hundred square feet and has outdoor plumbing," Sophie groused. "I might as well move into a refrigerator box."

76

Celeste put a comforting arm around her coworker's shoulders. "I know it seems bad. But remember, everything happens for a reason."

Maybe Celeste was right that everything happened for a reason. But that didn't mean it happened for a *good* reason. Sophie's check from her straight-to-DVD debut was due any day now. At which point she could possibly afford a place that didn't have *ick* as its defining quality.

Technically speaking, Sophie had told Genevieve she'd be out of the guesthouse by tomorrow morning. But as far as she was concerned, Marco and his professionally whitened teeth could wait.

The closed toilet seat was hard and unforgiving, not unlike a church pew. It was also, in Harper's opinion, sacred. Because here, on this cracked, dingy, off-off-white toilet seat, she was writing her novel. *Really* writing it.

Every day. Like clockwork.

Despite a numb butt and an aching back, Harper's fingers flew over the keyboard. She'd started the ritual last week as a result of abject terror. Terror because now that she knew exactly what she wanted to write, something would come along and get in the way. Doubts. Fantasies about Mr. Finelli. Mental apologies to Judd for being such a huge bitch before Christmas when he was just trying to be an honest friend. Whatever. She was determined to let nothing penetrate her concentration, her will, her *commitment,* to writing this damned thing.

So every day, either before or after her shift at Rainy Day Books Café, she slipped into her favorite once-were-black sweats (The Gap, circa 2002) and locked herself in the bathroom with her laptop. Only then did she turn on the computer and pull up the Word document that contained what she hoped would someday be the Next

Great American Novel. For as long as the battery lasted, Harper wrote. And when the power gauge showed she was down to five percent, she saved her work and shut off her Vaio for another day.

In the safe space of her small cell, straddling the toilet, Harper was able to block out the rest of the world. She was also able to stop herself from playing Spider solitaire, which was perhaps her greatest achievement of all. When she thought of the hours she had wasted moving one card on top of another on that little green screen, she wanted to shoot herself.

And there was another key element to her new process. Maybe it was a bit superstitious. All right, a lot superstitious. But she was convinced that if she allowed herself to think about the book outside of her sacred bathroom time, she'd ruin it. So Harper spent every waking moment she *wasn't* writing *not* obsessing about what she'd written or what she planned to write. So far, it was working.

Honey, are you okay? she typed quickly, the words flowing. Then she stopped. Where had that sentence come from?

Her answer came from a knock at the bathroom door. "Honey? Are you okay?" It was her mother, and she sounded slightly concerned. As if she'd been knocking at the door for a while, inquiring repeatedly as to her daughter's well-being. Oops.

"I'm fine!" Harper called back. "Writing!" *Translation: Go away.*

There was a pause on Mrs. Waddle's side of the door. "You're writing in the bathroom?"

"Long story." *One I'll tell you later. Like, after I've finished my book.*

"Do you think that's healthy?"

Harper sighed and heaved herself off the toilet, carefully balancing the black laptop in her hands. She might as well show her mom she hadn't gone completely insane. She opened the door and poked her head out.

"I'm kinda in the middle of an important scene. Can we talk later?"

Mrs. Waddle indicated her marinara-covered apron. "I'm kinda in the middle of something, too. Lasagna for sixty." Her mother catered parties all around Boulder part-time and considered her hours in the kitchen as holy as Harper considered hers in the bathroom. "But I wanted to pass along a message from your English teacher."

Harper almost dropped her computer. "My — what? Who?"

"Mr. Finelli," she clarified, apparently unaware that her oldest daughter was suffering from what surely felt like a heart attack. "He called while I was saucing my noodles."

"Oh. Okay." Harper started to shut the door, desperate for the conversation to end. She needed to process this information immediately, and she needed to process it alone. Her heart was thudding its way out of her clothes at the very mention of Mr. Finelli's name. So much for her creative focus.

Her mom reached out to stop the door from closing. "Don't you want to know what he said?"

No. "Uh . . . sure."

Mrs. Waddle grinned, her blue eyes lighting up. She wiped her hands on the apron, apparently unaware that the sleeves of her yellow sweater were smeared with sauce, too. "He finished your new recommendation for NYU. He sent it to them and all the other schools on your list this morning."

"But how did he — I mean . . . great. Thanks, Mom." This time when Harper shut the door, her mother didn't stop her.

Harper set her computer carefully on the sink and leaned against the wall, the cold white tiles offering relief to her now-clammy forehead. Had Mr. Finelli decided on his own to write her a new recommendation? Was it some sort of gesture that he wanted to give her another chance? Hope flickered.

Then died.

He had told her mother that he'd sent the recommendation to *all* the schools on her list. There was no way he knew what that list was, since last time around she'd only applied to one school. And no one else even knew where she was applying. Well, no one except . . .

Harper was going to strangle that Habiba for going behind her back. Right after she offered her free Green-Eyed Monsters for life.

I'm a paper pusher, Kate thought, wearily gritting her teeth. Three thousand miles from home and she was standing on the fringes of the action, holding a clipboard. All around her, men, women, and children were hustling and bustling — carrying and chopping eucalyptus branches, hauling wheelbarrows full of dirt, cooking *injera,* organizing tools. And what was she doing? Pushing paper. And why? Because Darby Miller was a jackass.

At least the morning had started well. She'd woken up excited, barely even aware of the cot-induced aching in her back. She'd swallowed her anti-malaria pill with a swig of the iodine-treated river water she was beginning to get used to, and then thrown on her shoes. Dorothé, who always seemed to hear the village roosters well before she or Jessica did, had already been up and dressed. Their regular breakfast of scrambled eggs, *injera,* and *berbere* was cooked and waiting. Even Jessica was ready when Darby and Jean-Pierre knocked on the door.

This was well-digging day. Or rather, it was starting-to-dig-a-well day. Rome wasn't built in a day, and apparently wells weren't either. There were crews to train, ground to be cleared, machinery to be set up, animals to be moved, kids to be wrangled . . . everyone was in the thick of it, except Kate. And why? Because of Darby. Apparently, he didn't think she was capable of using any muscle besides her brain, and he didn't seem to think much of that muscle either.

"Think you can handle this?" he'd asked that morning, holding out the clipboard and a blue Bic pen.

"I'll muddle through," she'd answered coldly. She was familiar with the mechanics of working a pen, for God's sake. And the single sheet of paper on the clipboard — a schedule of who should be doing what, where, and for how long — wasn't exactly neurosurgery. Especially since everyone who lived in or around the village was extremely motivated. The village council were the ones who'd gotten the whole project going — contacting Water Partners, donating as many supplies as they could, raising money for maintenance once the well was built, and hiring a local man as the well's custodian. This was a village-wide project, and everyone wanted to be involved in some way. Even the children were excited to be there.

So Kate had spent most of the morning walking around the site — a parched former grazing field just outside the western boundary of the town — checking up on other people's progress. Not exactly a challenge. Jean-Pierre and his industrious team were ahead of schedule assembling the components of the well. Dorothé and her crew, armed with shovels and hoes, were right on track with the clearing and grading of the land. Darby had assumed the responsibility of training Tesfaye, the young man the villagers had chosen as their well custodian. And then there was Jessica. Darby had given her the task of helping the children keep the cows and oxen away from the site until a fence could be built. Considering every kid over the age of four was an expert animal herder, that was pretty much a no-brainer.

In fact, Kate thought, maybe Darby had actually given Jessica the easiest job. Maybe she shouldn't be so totally offended at being Clipboard Girl. It was, after all, important to stay on schedule — and he trusted her with keeping everyone else on pace. He hadn't known when he'd given her the job that morning that everyone was going to be so competent. Maybe he thought he'd need her as a troubleshooter, his right hand gal. Maybe what she was doing was important after all.

Kate decided to give Darby the benefit of the doubt. As annoying and offensive as she sometimes found him, there were good things about him, too. He was smart. He was cute, not that that mattered. He was an excellent organizer. He spoke Amharic almost fluently. He had great respect for the men and women in the village. And he liked kids. Every evening since they'd arrived he'd organized impromptu soccer games in their compound. Boys and girls from tots to teenagers had spent hours laughing, running, and kicking a ratty old soccer ball around their dirt yard until dinnertime. It had given Kate a chance to bond with Angatu.

Her nightly discussions with the bright-eyed little girl had improved her Amharic greatly. She was now capable of carrying on a simple conversation, and usually understood at least the gist of what was being said around her.

So she understood when a gaunt young woman approached, asking politely for help in Amharic. A baby was wrapped snuggly against her back with a thick woven canary-yellow cloth, and a red clay jug balanced on her head. The baby's legs, poking out of the cloth, were thin — but, Kate noticed, barely smaller than his mother's bone-thin arms.

"Yes," Kate answered in Amharic. "Can I help you?"

The woman took the jug from her head and spoke several quick sentences. Kate understood enough to know she was from another village, and she was asking for water.

"Oh no," Kate replied, noticing for the first time the woman's bare feet. How far had she walked to get here? "There is no water yet. The well is not finished."

A look of sorrow crossed the hollowed planes of the woman's face. Kate's heart was pierced. She held out her hand toward a shady spot under some nearby eucalyptus trees.

"Come, sit with me." She smiled. "I'm Kate."

"Rebekkah." The woman nodded as they sat down on the dirt beneath the tree.

Rebekkah untied the cloth around her back, and swung her baby to her chest. Her village was several miles to the east of Mekebe, she explained, and had no well. The river had run dry, so she'd walked all this way with her baby boy. He was ill, and needed water, but . . .

She grew quiet. Kate's eyes dropped to the sleeping baby in Rebekkah's arms. Yes, his arms were thin, but his belly was round. Too round.

Kate gritted her teeth against tears. *No.* This was unacceptable. It was unacceptable for her to be sitting under this tree with this woman and her sick child who only needed water. It was unacceptable for her to have to tell this woman that there was no water to give. It was unacceptable that there wasn't even a clinic for Rebekkah to take her son to for treatment. It was not acceptable that the river had run dry. None of this was acceptable.

"Wait here," she instructed, running for her compound.

In barely five minutes, Kate was back with two large bottles of the fresh spring water that they'd brought in the van from Bahar Dar. Rebekkah's eyes grew wide.

"Amese genando," she breathed quietly. *"Amese genando."* Thank you.

"Take these," Kate gestured. "The well will be working in a few weeks. Come back then."

Rebekkah thanked her several more times as she returned her baby to her back. Then she reached out and took Kate's hand. She held it for a long moment, her deep brown eyes expressing her gratitude more clearly than any words, and turned toward the road leading away from the village.

Kate swallowed several times to get rid of the lump in her throat. She grabbed the clipboard and hurtled toward the *tukul,* where Darby was working with Tesfaye. Kate had come to Ethiopia to take the water, and goddammit she was going to take it. Wherever it was needed.

"I need you." The words were out before she was even all the way through the door.

Darby stood up. In the small mud hut, its only furnishings a rickety wooden chair on either side of the cooking stove, he seemed an incredibly imposing presence. "What is it? Did someone get hurt?"

"We need to build another well."

"What are you talking about?"

"I just met a woman from Teje, it's a village about five miles east of here. They need a well."

"Lots of villages need wells," Darby said in his most patronizing tone. "It's more complicated than that."

Whatever Kate had expected, she hadn't expected this. The lack of concern, the obvious annoyance on his face.

"Don't you care?" she snapped, pushing back loose strands of hair from her flushed face. "This woman has a sick baby —"

"I'm surprised *you* care," Darby snapped back. "Far as I know, there are no famous people in that village. Isn't that what you're interested in?"

Kate stared at him, stunned. She was coming to him with a real need, and he was throwing the Scarlett-Johansson-lookalike conversation in her face — a conversation he shouldn't even have overheard, about something that didn't even interest her. She'd just been having fun, joking around with her friends. What was he going to do, make her pay for it for the rest of her life? Or, the rest of her time in Ethiopia, which was all that mattered, because she would never, ever see him again under any circumstances after that anyway?

"Forget it," she finally managed to say, shaking her head in disgust.

Kate didn't remember walking back to the well site. Or the round of checkmarks she made on her clipboard over the next hour. All she could think about was Darby. Would his opinion of her change if he knew she had gotten into Harvard? If he knew, really, why she'd come to this place so far from her home, and yet so close to her sister's heart?

Maybe if he knew it would make a difference. But . . . really, it didn't matter. For one thing, she didn't even know if Harvard was going to let her in again for the next school year. And for another, she was never going to tell Darby, anyway. He was free think whatever he wanted about her.

He was free to think whatever he wanted about Jessica, too. And about Coke versus Pepsi, and the Red Sox, and global warming.

Nothing Darby Miller thought about anything mattered to her at all.

Not one, eensy-weensy, teeny-tiny, little iota of a bit.

Sophie *really* wished she hadn't worn the two-sizes-too-small Cole-Haan black patent-leather pumps she bought on sale at Loehmann's last month to go apartment hunting. Her feet were covered in blisters, and her calves felt like they'd been set on fire. Then there was the blinding headache that had started sometime between viewing the kitchen-less bachelor on Vine Street and the roach-infested one bedroom on Hollywood Boulevard. *Hot bath,* she envisioned as she opened the door to the guesthouse. *Must have hot bath. And Advil.*

"Hey, lover, where are all your boxes?" Mr. Man-Tan, Marco, grinned at her from behind a giant zebra skin–covered throw pillow he was holding against his chest.

Shit. Sophie had been too focused on her physical pain and psychic stress: she'd failed to register that Marco's classic Mustang convertible parked in the driveway meant he was actually here. In *her* guesthouse.

"Boxes?" Sophie hadn't planned for her move beyond today's disastrous hunt for a semi-livable apartment.

"Don't worry, girl. You can use mine when I'm done unpacking." Marco gestured toward the kitchen which was filled to the point of bursting with cardboard boxes, each carefully labeled in black marker with everything from "power drinks" to "mood music."

Technically she was supposed to move out by tomorrow. Sophie hadn't realized that *technically* meant Marco would show up with all of his worldly possessions tonight.

For several moments, she stood in stunned silence. It was only when she smelled a telltale whiff of Gucci *eau de parfum* that Sophie realized she and Marco weren't alone.

"Sophie, darling, what's wrong?" Genevieve, dressed in Marni jeans and a skin-tight black t-shirt, had emerged from the bedroom. Marco was wearing a similar body-hugging outfit — he could be Genevieve's evil twin, Sophie decided, if her ex-benefactress weren't so small, blond, and old enough to be his mother. Genevieve was staring at Sophie with a look of slight concern. "You look like you stepped on the scale and discovered you've gained twenty pounds."

"Nothing — I just —" *Don't have a place to live,* she finished silently. "I know I'm supposed to move by tomorrow . . ."

"If you need more time, just say the word," Genevieve informed her breezily with a girlish flip of her fluorescent hair. Her hair looked a shade lighter every time Sophie saw her. "You and Marco can work out the details." She turned back toward the bedroom. "I'll be figuring out what to do about new curtains."

Sophie was awash in relief. She wasn't going to be homeless. At least, not tonight. Genevieve was shallow, materialistic, and often kind of ridiculous, but she was not the type of woman to throw her old college friend's daughter out onto the tree-lined streets of Beverly Hills.

"Genevieve's such a sweetie," Marco commented as he and his throw pillow swaggered toward Sophie. "So generous."

"Mmm . . ." She was too busy wondering how long before they'd be gone and she could get in the bathtub to pay much attention to Marco.

"I want you out." He was standing right next to her now, and he'd dropped the lilt in his voice in favor of a low, threatening growl. He clutched the pillow as though it were a battering ram, and for a moment Sophie wondered if he was planning on suffocating her with it. The tone of his voice was decidedly scary.

"What?" she demanded. She wasn't going down without a fight.

"I want you out tonight. I don't care where you go, just get out." Marco was staring her down, his eyes deadly serious.

Who the hell did this guy think he was? She was tempted to punch him in his Day-Glo white teeth.

"Sorry, Marco," she responded, once she decided that she hadn't misheard him. "No can do. But you can leave your stuff until I find a place." Firm but polite. Always the best policy.

He stepped even closer. She could smell the wheatgrass on his breath. "You don't understand. You're leaving. Tonight."

Sophie's nostrils flared, metaphorically speaking. "You can't just —"

"You're an aspiring actress, and I'm the personal trainer to every agent and casting director in this town," Marco informed her, tossing the pillow aside. "If you're not out of here within the hour, I'll blackball you. If you think I don't have that power, just ask Eloise Drummond."

"Who's Eloise Drummond?"

He gave an evil smile. "Exactly."

Genevieve reappeared from the bedroom, waving a piece of leopard-print fabric. "This material is perfect for drapes!" she announced, holding it up to Marco's body like she was outfitting him for some cheesy remake of *Tarzan*.

Sophie took a deep breath. She was scared of being homeless. But she was more scared of Marco ruining her career.

"Good news!" She tried to sound cheerful. "I just got a call. My new apartment came through. I'm leaving tonight."

"You're going to be so happy there." Genevieve beamed. "And I won't hear of you taking a cab. I'll call the car service to pick you up and take you anywhere you want to go."

It was at that moment that Sophie realized the silver BMW Series-3 she'd driven for the last four months had been part of a package deal. Guesthouse and car. Car and guesthouse. The two went together. Which meant Sophie was officially without wheels in a city where nobody — *nobody* — walked anywhere.

Less than an hour later, Sophie watched as the bored-looking, forty-something driver threw the last of her hastily packed duffel bags into the trunk of his black Cadillac. She climbed into the back of the big car and closed her eyes, taking in the leathery smell of luxury for what might be the last time.

"Where to?" the driver asked, not even turning his head to look at her.

Sophie paused, wracking her brain. The Farmer's Daughter Hotel, famous for hosting naïve Midwestern girls on their way to nowheresville? Muscle Beach, where men on steroids mingled with voluptuous teen runaways? The airport, where she could buy a one-way ticket on the next flight home? "Take me to the corner of Melrose and Vine."

The drive from Beverly Hills to Hollywood took less time than she had imagined. The neighborhoods were twenty-five minutes and a lifetime apart. Sophie gave the driver an extra five dollars for hauling her bags up the two flights of narrow wooden stairs that led to her destination. She waited until he was gone, then she steeled herself and knocked on the door. A moment later, it opened.

"Hi, Sam," Sophie said brightly. "Can I move in?"

English 234 – Modern African-American Literature
Professor Anita Smith
Class Hours: M,W,F 11am-12:15pm
Office Hours: Th 3-5 / Humanities Bldg. Room 204A

Becca
Pendergrass

*Stuart
and
Becca*

Grade: 1/4 class participation
1/4 final exam
1/2 papers

I ♡ Stuart Pendergrass

PLEASE NOTE: Papers purchased off the Internet will receive an "F." Papers with sections cribbed from Cliff's Notes or, even worse, from someone else's scholarly work will receive an "F." Offending student will be referred for disciplinary action. I, personally, will do my best to see that anyone who knowingly rips off anyone else's work is expelled. Got me? Good.

Enjoy your reading.

✳ Stuart & Becca ✳

SYLLABUS: *I ♥ Stuart*

Week 1: *Their Eyes Were Watching God* (Zora Neale Hurston)

Week 2: *Invisible Man* (Ralph Ellison)

Week 3: Paper #1 (Topic TBD)

Becca Pendergrass

Week 4: *The Color Purple* (Alice Walker)

Becca
♡
Stuart

Week 5: *Native Son* (Richard Wright)

✳ Mrs. Stuart Pendergrass ✳

FOUR

Fun in a bun?" Harper stared at the straightest bangs she had ever seen as she proffered a tray of mini hamburgers to a girl whose name tag read "Maggie" in bright blue bubble letters. With her severe hairstyle and preppy button-down shirt, Maggie didn't look like the kind of girl who knew much about having fun, in a bun or anywhere else.

Harper felt a headache starting behind her right eye. It was either a sign that the apocalypse was imminent or a sign that staying up for eighteen hours yesterday had been a bad idea. She was currently hoping for Option A. Her mother's offer of extra cash for helping her cater a party at one of the administration buildings on the UC Boulder campus had seemed harmless enough at the time. Then again, Harper had been half asleep. And her mother had failed to mention the party was for freshmen who'd made the Dean's List first semester. Passing appetizers to her academically thriving peers was not Harper's idea of a good time. Even if she was making twenty dollars an hour.

"Oh, they're adorable!" Bubble-letter Maggie cooed. *So much for my insights into character,* thought Harper, trying to maintain her fake service-person smile while Maggie's fingers swooped in on the tray. "And what a clever name! I'm a debate champion, so I'm, like, totally into words."

It was then that Harper realized Bubble-letter Maggie must be Maggie Hendricks, the girl Sophie had been assigned to room with her freshman year at CU. Sophie's one meeting with Maggie over coffee at Starbucks had been part of what drove her to ditch school and move to LA. Harper suddenly felt like she was in some weird sci-fi movie, where she could see how her life would have played out in a parallel universe. A universe in which Sophie called her in her dorm room in New York every other day to complain about Maggie and her obsession with pro and con arguments. A universe in which Harper was a guest at a college function rather than the hired help.

But I'm glad things turned out the way they did, she reminded herself. None of these carefree students were writing their first novel. Harper was.

"I'll be by with the Cheesies in a second," she promised Maggie Hendricks, referring to the tiny grilled cheeses her mother had made this morning. When she got back from Los Angeles, Harper made the mistake of listing all the novel miniature appetizers served at the Meyers' New Year's Eve party. Mrs. Waddle, who liked to think of her offerings as cutting-edge, had immediately designed a new catering menu, complete with a "catchy" name for each item. Harper was dreading dessert, when she had to pass out mini pieces of double-chocolate cake her mom had dubbed "Bite Me's."

I'm writing a novel. I'm writing a novel. I'm writing a novel. Harper repeated the mantra over and over as she threaded her way through the crowd. The room was large and elegant, with high ceilings, heavy drapes hanging at the tall windows, and oil paintings of various donors or founders — old rich guys, basically — on every wall. It beat the coffee-grounds-and-laptop ambience of the Rainy Day Café any day. But by the time she made it back to the kitchen, where her mom was stuffing itty bitty French fries (aka "Silly Spuds") into itty bitty paper containers, Harper had managed to convince herself she actually felt sorry for all these dorm-living, beer-drinking losers. They were all too busy going to class and surviving Rush Week and making out at keggers to even think about writing the next Great American Novel.

"I'm a hit!" her mom crowed. "I can't get this stuff out there fast enough." She handed Harper a tray of the Silly Spuds, grinning madly. "Your friend with the curly black hair ate four Cheesies before he let me leave his side."

"My friend?" Harper's stomach clenched. "You mean — ?"

"The one who always comes in through the basement window instead of the front door. I told him you were here."

Harper cracked the kitchen door open an inch and peered out at the crowded party. Her eyes traveled past several lip-glossed sorority-types, a few hard-core geeks probably talking about their engineering homework, and three black-clad Goths of undetermined gender pretending to be above it all while scarfing as much free food as possible. Then she saw him.

Judd Wright, the curly black-haired eschewer of front doors who'd filled in as Harper's closest friend while her closest best friends were at the ends of the earth pursuing their dreams. Damn. She couldn't believe she'd missed seeing him earlier. The aroma of wee burgers must have put her in some kind of stupor. Instead of one of his trademark distressed — and distressing — Phish T-shirts, he was wearing a navy blue polo that looked like it had been ironed. And there wasn't a stray coffee ground in sight.

They hadn't talked once since that ill-fated night at Dan's Big Lot, when she'd terrorized her way through several subspecies of Christmas trees. Hot shame washed over Harper as she remembered her irrational behavior. The word bitchy didn't begin to do it justice. Before he dropped her off at home, Judd had informed her that she'd become insufferable and he no longer wanted to live in "Harper's World."

93

She knew she had to apologize. And she'd intended to. Ever since Harper had realized he was one hundred percent right. In the days leading up to Christmas, the stress of lying to her friends, combined with learning that Mr. Finelli hadn't thought the first fifty pages of her first attempt at a novel reached masterpiece status, had turned her into a person who didn't deserve the company of fellow humans.

She'd had her apology speech written for weeks. It had been perfected down to the word, and it was a doozy. Unfortunately, she was a pro at avoiding unpleasant conversations. Especially ones that required her to be humble. She'd therefore dealt with the Judd situation by skulking around Rainy Day Books Café, hoping she wouldn't run into him.

"Harper, what did you do?" her mother asked, putting aside the Silly Spuds and giving Harper a long, knowing look.

"Me? Nothing." She tried and failed to smile innocently.

Mrs. Waddle shook her head. "Whatever it is, just apologize. You'll feel better. Trust me." With that, she gently shoved Harper and her tray of itty bitty French fries out into the party.

For a moment, she considered her options. 1. Throw her tray of mini fries into the air, creating a distraction that would allow her to flee. 2. Go back into the kitchen and hide until the last freshmen had headed off to a keg party. 3. Get on her knees and grovel, begging Judd for his forgiveness.

Her mother was wrong. However this turned out, she would *not* feel better. Nonetheless, Harper took a deep breath and steeled herself. She was nothing if not a glutton for punishment. Besides, being humiliated in front of a roomful of well-adjusted eighteen-year-olds would be good fodder for her writing. Especially given her outfit — the ill-fitting black skirt and polyester white button-down shirt she always wore when she worked for her mom.

She marched up to Judd and planted herself between him and Maggie Hendricks, who'd drifted to his side and was apparently in the middle of a monologue on the topic at her latest debate tournament. "Silly Spud?" she offered, holding up her silver tray. "They're all the rage on the Coast."

Judd's eyes flitted toward her. Then *through* her. "I never thought about the flat tax that way," he said to Maggie, as if Harper weren't there. As if she were *air*.

Maggie brightened. "I know! Isn't it fascinating to think about the global ramifications?"

Harper turned to her. "Excuse me. I'm sure everything you're saying is incredibly relevant to the world we live in, but I need a moment with Judd."

Maggie's mouth dropped and she took a step back. "Oh — sure."

"Judd, I'm a misanthropic twit," Harper began, fixing her gaze on his nose — looking him in the eyes was too hard. "I am a worthless, spineless human being who doesn't deserve to have you as a friend. There are maggots, and there's me. I'm lower than a maggot on the food chain, and that's saying something. I acted like a complete and total bitch, and you were right to tell me —"

"Harper! Stop." Judd interrupted.

"I haven't gotten to the part where I compare myself to the flies that hover around dog shit on a hot summer afternoon —" She liked that part a lot. Very evocative.

"Why can't you just say you're sorry you were a jackass like a normal person?"

Harper gave him a wan smile. "Because that would be boring?"

He shook his head. "You're unique, y'know that?"

A ray of hope. She used her free hand to shove her glasses higher on her nose and gave him her best puppy dog look. "Does that mean you forgive me?"

He raised an eyebrow. "It's either that or spend the rest of the year checking the schedule at the café every five minutes to make sure I don't have to be in your presence."

She suddenly felt as if the weight of the entire Dean's List — no, make that the entire CU freshman class — had been lifted from her shoulders. Judd forgave her. They were going to be friends again. She wouldn't have to spend every Friday night watching bad movies on TNT by herself. If the situation had been reversed, she wasn't sure she would have let it go so easily. In fact, she was pretty sure she wouldn't have.

Maggie cleared her throat. Harper had completely forgotten she was there, which was no easy feat, considering the girl was wearing pink corduroy pants embroidered with tiny green whales. "*I'd* like to hear the rest of your speech," she announced. "I love speeches."

"Sorry, I already forgot it." Harper shrugged and looked back at Judd. He'd earned the right to hear what he wanted to hear from her. Nothing more, nothing less. "I'm sorry I was a jackass," she offered simply. "Please accept my apology."

"Like it never happened," Judd assured her.

They grinned at each other, their friendship flooding back into the space between them. For the millionth time in her life, her mother had been right. Harper felt better.

"Pass the bread, please, Jake."

"Here you go, Sandra."

"Thank you, Jake."

Becca stifled a grin. Her parents were being so . . . *polite*. It was weird. And awesome. She glanced at Stuart, who was sitting beside her, eyeing her mom and dad warily. She'd warned him this dinner could go very badly, very quickly, and he seemed to expect the calm, seemingly tamed animals that were Sandra Howard and Jake Winsberg-Weldon to go suddenly crazy and start tearing each others' throats out. Which wasn't entirely out of the question.

The last time they'd had a "family dinner" like this, Becca's mom, dad, and stepmother had tossed rapid-fire insults at each other like automatic ball-release machines — one after the other, with barely the space to swing back. And in the rare, brief pauses, they'd managed to fit in snide asides and derisive glares. Finally, Becca had lost it completely. Her shy, quiet nature had vanished in a tornado of fury. She'd released in one long verbal barrage everything she'd been holding back for years. Yelling at her mom for blaming her for the divorce, her dad for being a cheat, her stepdad for being spineless, and her stepmom for being a self-centered bitch. Then she'd stomped out and gone back to campus to get excessively, stumblingly, pass-outingly, reputation-dashingly drunk.

But this night was entirely different. For one thing, Stuart was here with her instead of Isabelle. For another, her stepdad Martin had stayed home in Boulder to keep an eye on Mia and Carter, the evil stepsiblings. Only her mom, her dad, and his wife, Melissa, had traveled to Vermont to see her race. And, as they had over Christmas break, they really seemed to have taken Becca's loud, but no less honest, tirade to heart. With the possible exception of her stepmom Melissa, who had spent the evening with her lips pursed tightly together, they were making a genuine attempt to put their difficult past behind them and get along for the sake of their daughter. They were trying to be grown-ups. Becca admired the effort. She even found it slightly amusing. And touching.

"Did your coach say anything after the race?" her father wanted to know, pressing a hunk of bread into a small dish of olive oil and absentmindedly dripping dots of oil on the red tablecloth. Thanks to perfectionist Melissa, he looked dashing in a black suit and white button-down shirt. Her mom had dressed up, too, in a dark green flowy dress. Becca was pretty sure that the cleavage the dress revealed was at least partially responsible for Melissa's pursed lips.

"He nodded at me." Becca grimaced, feeling almost underdressed in her black pants and red cowl-necked sweater. This restaurant, with its Tuscan frescoes and candlelit tables, was one of the nicest in Middlebury. "That's big for him. He doesn't exactly do compliments."

"I saw him when your time came up on the board." Stuart put his arm around her. "He was psyched."

Her mother stroked the pendant dangling from her neck, possibly to draw even more attention to her cleavage. "He probably didn't expect you to do so well. You're a freshman, it's a new event for you. . . ."

"I didn't want you guys to come all the way here to watch me lose," Becca admitted.

"Even if you'd lost, it would have been worth the trip." Becca's mom smiled.

"Completely," her dad agreed.

Even Melissa managed a meager grin. Becca felt her heart beat a little faster. And not just because Stuart looked so edible in his black sweater and khakis. Or because he was beaming at her in that way of his. Or even because her mom was looking approvingly back and forth between them. No, this heart thumping was all about finally feeling, for the first time in her life, like she was part of a normal family. Or, at least, as close to normal as she was going to get.

"Excuse me." Melissa scooted her chair back and headed swiftly to the back of the restaurant toward the restrooms. Becca's mom watched her go, then leaned toward her dad.

"You know what this restaurant reminds me of?"

Her father looked blank for a moment, then laughed. "That place in Denver. What was it called?"

"Something Italian . . . Castellis?"

"Castellianos!"

Becca watched, amazed, as her mother reached out and put a hand over his, which was resting on the tablecloth. She was even more amazed when her father didn't pull away. She couldn't remember ever seeing her parents actually *touch*.

Becca's mother looked at her. "Our first date was there."

Their first date? Somehow she had never imagined that part of her parents' relationship. But of course, they would have had a beginning like any other couple — a first date, a first kiss, meeting each others' parents, the first time they had sex and said they loved each other.

"And then we'd have dinner there on the seventeenth of every month," her father added. "Our anniversary."

What was happening? Her parents were *reminiscing*. Like they didn't want to gnaw each others' hearts out for a pre-dinner snack. Under the table, Becca reached for Stuart's hand. It was less a romantic gesture than an effort to keep herself grounded. She needed to feel something stable, secure, sane . . . and Stuart was definitely the sanest person at this table. She exhaled as he gave her hand a little squeeze and rubbed his thumb gently along the side of her hand.

"And every time, your mom would have the penne a la vodka."

"And your father never had the same thing twice."

There was a long pause. Her parents' eyes were locked. They were grinning at each other. It was the strangest thing Becca had ever seen.

"Those were good times." Her mother turned to look at Becca. "We didn't always hate each other, sweetie. I bet you thought we did."

"Yeah," Becca admitted, confused. "I guess so."

"No." Her dad shook his head. "We loved each other once."

"Once." Her mother smiled sadly. "But we screwed that up, didn't we?"

"We were young and stupid." Becca's father looked at her and Stuart. "Don't be stupid," he advised solemnly. "Trust each other."

Becca suddenly felt as if she and Stuart were under a spotlight. She hoped he wasn't as uncomfortable as she was.

"We'll do our best," Stuart replied with a respectful nod.

Melissa returned to the table and the mood was broken. Becca's dad slid his hand away. Her mom's mouth grew thin, and she took a long sip from her glass of Pinot Grigio.

"What'd I miss?" Melissa asked, casting a significant glance at her husband.

"Nothing exciting." Her parents were avoiding each other's eyes. Everything was back to normal — or, rather, the new and improved version of normal.

But for Becca, the last two minutes had somehow changed everything. Her parents had *loved* each other. When they'd looked at each other, she could see the faded remnants of it on their faces. She'd never seen it before, and she would probably never see it again. But she *had* seen it.

She turned to Stuart, and he winked at her.

"No pressure," he whispered with a smile. Becca almost laughed. How was it that he knew exactly what to say?

The waiter brought their dinners, and as Becca scooped up a forkful of veggie lasagna, she had a sudden, terrifying thought. The feelings that she had for Stuart were just like the feelings her parents had once had for each other. They'd once believed they would be together forever — not that she thought that about Stuart. Yet. It was far too early and she was far too young for that. But what did it all mean? Would she and Stuart fall out of love? How long would their relationship last? Would they do horrible things to each other, make each other feel hurt, and angry, and bitter?

It was inevitable, wasn't it?

"Trust each other," her father had said. But it wasn't as easy as that. Becca had seen and experienced enough to know that trust was as elusive as smoke. She realized her fear of trusting Stuart was part of the reason she hadn't had sex with him yet. It was why she wanted him to say he loved her first. Because she thought if those things

100

were in place she would be able to trust him with her body, and with her heart.

But even if she did trust him . . . did it really matter? Her parents had trusted each other once, and it had brought them nothing but misery. As much as she wanted to believe that nothing would ever happen to make her feel anything less than complete and utter love for Stuart . . . now she knew that her mom and dad had once felt the same way.

And — the thought made Becca's stomach lurch — her father's love had faded first. Even if her feelings for Stuart never changed, even if she loved him until the day she died . . . there was no guarantee his feelings for her would last.

All Becca had to do was look across the table at Melissa to know that her father was proof enough of that.

"Does this outfit work?" Sophie strutted in front of Sam, blocking his view of the game of *Halo* he'd been playing since three o'clock that afternoon. He was propped up with cushions on the sagging red couch, just a few feet away from the TV.

Sam craned his neck to see around her. "Great."

"You didn't even look." She stepped sideways so that he had no choice but to observe her conservative soft green tweed skirt and matching jacket.

When she'd shown up at his doorstep a few weeks ago, Sophie had half-expected Sam to kick her and her considerable amount of luggage to the curb. While he hadn't exactly been welcoming, he *had* allowed her to stay in the spare bedroom that technically belonged to Sam's roommate, the elusive J.D.

Luckily for her, J.D. was an assistant to an A-list celebrity (identity confidential) and spent ninety percent of his nights at one of his boss's numerous palatial homes. He and Sam had agreed to allow Sophie to stay on the condition that she paid two hundred dollars a month and slept on an Aerobed in the living room whenever J.D. was home. The two-bedroom Hollywood apartment wasn't the lap of luxury that the guesthouse had been: all the furniture was of the kit-set pine IKEA variety, the sofa looked like it had been used as a trampoline, and they used plastic cups instead of glassware. The only decorative touches were an old *Rebel Without a Cause* movie poster above the television and a string of red hot-pepper Christmas lights strung around the kitchen. But the apartment was just messy and generic rather than dirty, and Sophie liked the *Melrose Place*–style pool in the courtyard.

Neither she nor Sam had mentioned their blowout the night of the Meyers' New Year's Eve party, and Sophie hoped it would stay that way. She had a nagging feeling that she'd been the one in the wrong, and apologies weren't her style.

"Are those *panty*hose?" Sam asked, finally tearing his eyes away from the alien swarm he was obliterating with grenades on the high-definition screen. "No one in LA wears pantyhose."

"They happen to be appropriate for the occasion," Sophie sniffed. Lunch at the Ivy with Mr. Geezer had morphed into dinner at the famous Polo Lounge in the Beverly Hills Hotel, but she was finally making good on her promise to have a meal with the grandfatherly type she'd met at the New Year's Eve bash.

"If you don't want my opinion, don't ask." Sam reached out and shoved Sophie out of the way of the TV screen so he could go back to his game.

Some girls might have chosen that moment to return to the bathroom to touch up their lip gloss. Sophie chose to yet again block his view. "The Polo Lounge isn't Sky Bar or Lotus," she informed him. "They have standards."

Sam swept a loose strand of shaggy blond hair out of his eyes and shrugged. He was dressed in baggy cargo shorts and a CLUB SANDWICHES NOT SEALS t-shirt. "Whatever. Who's this dude again?"

"Peter Alterman. And he's not a dude. He's, like, seventy. I'm doing a good deed." *And getting an awesome free dinner,* she added silently.

Sam furrowed his brows. "Why does Peter Alterman want to take you to dinner?"

"Because he misses his granddaughter." Huh. Sam had obviously heard of the man. She was dying to ask why, but she didn't want to look like an idiot for not being in the know.

"Maybe the pantyhose are a good idea, after all." He paused as if he was weighing his next words carefully. "Anyway, you look really pretty."

Sophie sighed deeply and left Sam to his game. Boys were so frustrating. Especially this boy. What was up with the comment about pantyhose being a good thing, after all? And saying she looked pretty? Was it a real compliment or was he being sarcastic? She couldn't even tell if he was relieved that her "date" was a man of doddering age. *I shouldn't care,* she reminded herself. *I don't care.* Living with Sam was complicated enough without throwing romantic tension into the mix.

Forty-five minutes and two buses later, Sophie presented herself to the hostess at the Polo Lounge, one of LA's most famous restaurants. She'd never been to the Beverly Hills Hotel — the Mission-style stuccoed "Pink Palace," surrounded by tall palm trees and lush gardens — and she'd certainly never stepped inside the fabled Polo Lounge. This was the place where stars like Humphrey Bogart, Marlene Dietrich and Marilyn Monroe — not to mention Frank Sinatra and the Rat Pack — used to hang out at the bar. The Beatles swam in the pool! Elton John threw birthday parties here! And now she, Sophie Bushell, was going to have dinner in one of its classic green booths. One day, she hoped, her name would be part of the Polo Lounge's star-studded history as well.

At the desk, Sophie gave her name to the hostess, scanning the opulent dining room for her elderly dinner date. Apart from the booths, everything else — tablecloths, vases, drapes, and all the flowers — was a soft peach-pink. It was all so elegant, so old Hollywood.

The young white-blond woman, scantily clad in a paisley halter dress with nary a scrap of nylon in sight, smiled at her. "Mr. Alterman isn't feeling well. He asked that you meet him in his suite."

"He lives here?" Was he so lonely he needed the constant companionship of bell boys?

"Just until the remodel of his house in the Colony is done," she answered. Sophie stifled the urge to whistle. Even she'd heard of the Colony, an exclusive neighborhood in Malibu where homes regularly sold for well over ten million dollars. "Go to the lobby and the concierge will show you upstairs."

The Art Nouveau hotel lobby, with its giant sparkling chandelier, was overwhelming. It made the Meyers' place look like a modest bungalow. A polite concierge escorted Sophie up to the third floor in the elevator and gestured in the direction of Mr. Alterman's suite. Sophie was tempted to find the fire stairs and bolt. She'd signed up for an elegant evening at an expensive restaurant, not a night of spooning chicken soup into Grandpa's mouth. But a heavy door down the hall was already opening. Mr. Alterman appeared in a black silk smoking jacket — the kind she'd seen only in old British movies or an *E! True Hollywood Story* about Hugh Hefner — and braided burgundy-colored slippers.

"Sophie, my dear! You made it!"

Karma bank, she reminded herself as she smiled and walked toward the suite. She noted that he still looked papery in that sweet-old-gentleman way, but not exactly *sick*. What was left of his silver gray hair was so perfectly slicked back he might have just come from a salon, and his pale gray eyes were bright. "Hi, Mr. Alterman. Thanks for having me."

"Of course, my dear, of course. I'm always thrilled to converse with the young people." He stepped aside to let her pass.

The cream-colored living room of the hotel suite was huge and lavishly appointed with antique chests and ornate gilded mirrors. She glimpsed an enormous bathroom off to the side and paneled doors leading to two bedrooms. Mr. Alterman pointed toward a table laden with silver-topped dishes. A bottle of Cristal chilled in a silver ice bucket, and Sophie was positive she smelled chocolate-covered strawberries. Clearly, chicken soup was not on the menu.

"I didn't know what you like, so I took the liberty of ordering everything on the menu. So sorry we had to meet up here in my dreary room."

"No problem." Sophie sank into a plush beige velvet chair in front of the marble-topped table and prepared to dig in. She was still waiting for the check she was owed from her three lines in the movie, which meant she was so broke that her diet these days consisted mostly of Ramen noodles and the occasional designer hot wings or hand-cut frites begged from the chef during her shifts at Mojito. "Just be ready for me to pop a button on my skirt by the time I eat all this," she half joked.

She spread a white linen napkin over her lap, feeling more relaxed than she had since Genevieve dropped the moving bombshell. A pleasant evening with doting Mr. Alterman was exactly what she needed to get back on track. And if he was a big deal, as this suite and Sam's peculiar reaction to his name seemed to indicate, maybe he really could help with her career. God knows she needed help. Since she moved out of the guesthouse, Gifford Meyers — her only Hollywood connection now that Trey was out of the picture — seemed to have forgotten she existed.

"Before we begin . . . I have a request."

Sophie looked up from the incredibly tender-looking beef dish she was about to devour. "Sure. Anything." She'd give up her first-born child for this spread.

"I had a feeling about you the night we met." He smiled. "I'm glad to know I was right."

Mr. Alterman tugged at the black silk sash holding his smoking jacket closed. It fell to the floor, quickly followed by the matching silk lounging pajamas he wore underneath. And there he stood. Completely naked.

In her state of shock, Sophie made two observations. One, his hair was silver-gray *all* over. Two, despite his advanced years, Mr. Geezer either had no problem with erectile dysfunction or he was a great advertisement for the wonders of Viagra.

Before she ran out, Sophie grabbed the bottle of Cristal and a handful of chocolate-covered strawberries. She'd definitely earned them.

Standing at the door of her empty mud-and-straw hut, Kate studied the crevices on the joints of her fingers. Every shallow wrinkle was filled with a fine coating of reddish brown Ethiopian dirt. The dirt was in her teeth, eyes, nose, each miniscule pore on her face. And it felt *great*. Finally, after a week of clipboard duty, today she'd gotten down and dirty with a wheelbarrow and a hoe. Woo hoo! She loved manual labor! Or maybe she just loved doing something a particular someone didn't think she *could* do. Whatever, it had been a great day. And she had Jessica to thank for it — because if Jessica wasn't completely incompetent and lazy, she never would have had the chance to show her stuff.

With the fence around the well site finally complete, Darby had given Jessica the new duty of overseeing the construction of a drainage field. The first day, things had gone relatively smoothly. But every time Kate came around with her clipboard, Jessica's team had fallen farther and farther behind schedule. The excuses were plentiful. The men didn't want to work. The women had wandered away. The tools weren't strong enough.

Kate was new to Ethiopia, but there were a few things she was pretty sure of. The men didn't shy away from work. The women weren't wanderers (unless they were going to get water, and that hardly counted as "wandering"). And the tools were pretty damn good. They'd been used for hundreds of years to plow what was largely a volcanic landscape, so flimsy they weren't.

Finally, when the grading was several days behind schedule and all of Kate's ideas and encouragement had fallen on Jessica's deaf ears, Kate had gone to Darby. She hadn't asked him — she'd *told* him that she was taking over the grading team and passing the clipboard off to Jessica. He'd listened, given her a curt "fine," and that was that.

Jessica couldn't have been happier. She'd flounced off with the clipboard and Kate hadn't seen her since. Kate was pretty sure that the second the six village men and women figured out that Kate — or anyone other than Jessica — was going to be working with them from now on, their smiles would have lit the dark side of the moon. Over the next several hours, she'd heard all about how Jessica's constant chattering had annoyed everyone, to such an extent that the women *had* disappeared every now and then. So had the men — once or twice they'd even intentionally broken a tool to have an excuse to leave and effect repairs. Then there was the added annoyance that came from Jessica's certainty that she, and only she, knew the right way to do things. Which, Kate concluded from the state of the site, was exactly the *wrong* way.

Fortunately the team was well motivated once Jessica was gone and extremely skilled. It was just a matter of clearing wheelbarrow after wheelbarrow of volcanic rock, grading the soil underneath, and then returning a layer of the smaller rocks to mark the borders of the drainage field.

By the end of the day, Kate's muscles felt as mushy and wobbly as Jell-O. So the note that was left on her bed was a welcome surprise. "We're going out for dinner!" it read in Dorothé's European-slanted writing. "Meet us there at 7."

"There" was Mekebe's only restaurant, known simply as "Abebech's place." It was little more than a small cinder-block square in the center of town with an outdoor patio surrounded by corrugated metal fencing. There were several mismatched chairs and tables, and festive colorful sheets draped overhead obscured the crumbling ceiling. The food was inexpensive, extremely tasty, and cooked fresh every day by the proprietor. It wouldn't have ranked even a quarter of a Michelin star, but there was no way Kate could show up in her present state. Her gray t-shirt was soaked through with sweat, and dirt had rendered her blue jeans a mottled brown. She was pretty sure she smelled like she'd been rolling in dung all week.

She changed her clothes and spent several minutes at the wash basin in the yard before finally making her way to Abebech's place. Dorothé was already seated with Jessica, Darby, and Jean-Pierre at a large round table in the back corner of the enclosed patio.

"You missed the first round!" Dorothé waved at her over a line of empty beer bottles. The only available seat, Kate noted with displeasure, was beside Darby. She sat in it anyway.

"We've all given our reports," Jean-Pierre grinned. "How's the drainage field coming?"

"It's still behind schedule," Kate replied evenly, with a glance at Jessica. "But it's getting there. We got most of the land cleared today."

"You must have a magic touch or something." Jessica was looking as wide-eyed and innocent as ever. "I just couldn't get that team in gear."

"Not magic at all." Kate looked at Dorothé. "Have you mentioned anything about the well for Teje?"

"Not yet," Dorothé responded. "I thought you should be here."

Kate had told her all about Rebekkah and the conversation with Darby that had followed. Dorothé had agreed that they should at least approach the villagers in Teje about a well. Clearly there was a need and they were already in the area.

But before Kate could make her case, a little girl approached and set a bottle with the familiar bright yellow label of the local St. George beer on the table in front of her. The pale liquid had the strange smell of cooked corn, but after a long day of working outside, any beer was better than none at all.

"Thank you." Kate smiled, surprised to see Angatu. Shouldn't she be at home getting ready for bed? "Is Abebech your grandma?" she asked in Amharic.

Angatu shook her head, sending her coarse shoulder-length braids into a spin. "I have no grandmother. I work for her. She lets me stay in the back room."

"Oh." Kate couldn't think of anything else to say. Angatu gave her a small smile and walked back toward the kitchen.

"I don't understand," Kate said in English, gazing around the table. "She lives in the back room? By *herself*?"

"She's an orphan," Darby announced in his usual know-it-all tone. "Her parents died, and after some unpleasantness, Abebech took her in."

"Unpleasantness?" Jean-Pierre wouldn't accept the abbreviated explanation either.

"She and her sister worked for a local farmer after their mom and dad died, but he wanted to marry the older sister —"

"How old was she?"

"I think the sister was about twelve. This was several years ago. Angatu was only about four —"

"He wanted to marry a *twelve-year-old*?" Kate gave Darby a horrified look, even though it meant twisting in her seat to face him. She didn't like sitting this close to him and, judging from Darby's body language, he didn't like sitting next to her either. "And don't give me the 'it's a different culture' speech."

109

"Well, it is." He nodded. "Anyway, the sister ran away, and Abebech took in Angatu."

"What will she do?" Kate wondered, breaking a moment of silence, not even realizing she was speaking out loud.

"What will who do? You're not making any sense." Jessica took a long sip of her beer.

"Angatu. I mean, Abebech isn't exactly young. What if something happened to her —"

Darby shook his head.

"What?" Kate couldn't help but snap.

He shrugged. She glared at him. What was wrong with this person? Didn't he care about *anything*? Why was he even here?

"I'm not hungry." She stood up. "I'm going for a walk."

Moments later Kate was on the dirt road leading back to the compound. Her tired legs moved by rote, and kept moving as she approached her gate. She couldn't go in yet. She had to keep moving, so she walked.

Of course she had known that there were people in the world less fortunate than she was. She'd seen them on TV a thousand times and read about them in newspaper articles. She'd seen them on the streets of Boulder and all around Europe. Homeless people, sick people, people with hardly any money or family or support struggling to make ends meet. Still she found herself stunned to her center, deeper than her heart, beyond the reaches of her brain. Maybe because she had never known anyone personally with such unfair disadvantages, none of it had ever seemed real. But Rebekkah and her sick baby were real. Angatu was real. These were real human beings with voices Kate had actually heard, smiles that had been offered to her with generosity and openness. The injustice overwhelmed her and it came down to mere geography. Kate was born in Colorado. Angatu was born in Mekebe.

That made all the difference.

Being born in Colorado meant having a house with running water and food to eat at every meal with snacks in between. It meant medical care, education, recreation. That her parents most likely weren't going to die from AIDS and she wasn't going to get malaria. That she could have animals as pets, without having to tend to them for hours a day and not go to school and then eat them for dinner. That when she was little she could play with her friends after school instead of fetching water for her mother.

It meant . . . everything.

Why was she chosen to have been born on one hemisphere versus the other? Why had she been so . . . lucky? Was luck even the word?

The children here were loved and happy, but everything was so *hard*. Kate had never thought of her life as easy. She'd known, of course, that it was. It just wasn't something she'd ever had to think about. At least, until Habiba had arrived. And then she'd started to see it. But she'd never really known what Habiba's life had been like before she became a Foster. And it begged the inevitable question. What if?

What if her mom and dad hadn't adopted Habiba? Would she have been married off at twelve, or would she have been like Angatu, going to school half days so she could work for her room and board? It was unbearable. Kate felt the weight of it pressing out from her chest as her tired arms shook.

"God." She looked up at the millions of stars that lit the night sky. She'd never been religious, but in that moment she couldn't think of anyone else to ask. "How am I supposed to take this?"

"You just do." The voice was quiet, matter of fact.

Kate whirled around. Darby, holding a torch, was barely ten steps behind her.

"Do you have the answer to *everything*?"

He looked at her for a moment, then lifted his shoulders. "Hey — you want to be hyena food, that's your business."

"What are you talking about?"

Kate looked around her. She'd been so lost in thought she'd walked right past the last village compound on the road, and straight into the countryside. Her stomach tightened as she heard a howling in the distance. Shit! She really *could* have been hyena food.

"Don't be ridiculous," she replied, trying to sound nonchalant. "I was about to turn around anyway."

Which she did. And for the entire walk back to the compound, they spoke not one single word. Darby walked silently behind her, the torch held high in the darkness. At the compound gate, Kate reluctantly turned to him. As much as she hated to admit it, she really should thank him for coming after her. There was a chance, however slim, that he might actually have saved her life or at least saved her from some kind of very unpleasant bodily harm. Even if he was the biggest know-everything asshole on the planet, there was no reason for her to sink to his level. At a minimum, she could be polite.

As she started to open her mouth, she looked straight at Darby, and his eyes . . . they actually *glowed* in the firelight from the torch. Maybe he hadn't saved her from bodily harm after all. Because something very unpleasant indeed was happening in her belly. Something like oversized butterflies gone berserk. What was wrong with her? She *hated* this guy!

"What?" Darby gave her an impatient look.

Kate sucked in her breath. Right. She *did* hate this guy.

"Nothing." She shook her head and stomped away.

As she crawled into her goat-skin cot and pulled the flimsy mosquito netting around her, Kate recognized that she knew next to nothing about this world or her place in it. The only thing she knew for sure was that if Darby Miller ever had to save her from hyenas again, she'd rather just get eaten.

Dear Magnus,

Hejsan! Puss pa dej. I feel like it's been a zillion years? like if I ran into you in the street in Mekebe, you wouldn't even remember me.

DAMN—I don't know what to write to you. What if I don't ever see you again?

You mean so much to me that I can't bear to admit that's a possibility.

Okay, I'm throwing this away. There's too much to tell you anyway—most of it about how much I hate Darby. He's the opposite of you. He's rude, smug and intolerant. Meeting you changed my life in the best possible way, even if I didn't know or appreciate it at first. And now I'm forced to spend time with the kind of jerk who's-well, probably like the guys I would have met this year at Harvard. Another thing I don't want to think about right now.

Sorry this is all so vague. I'll write you when I know what I want to say. I know I miss you. I guess could just write that. Okay, I'm going to start over. On a postcard.

FIVE

Becca stared at the disgusting compilation of mismatched foods on the crumb-covered table in front of her. A slice of whole wheat bread, covered with peanut butter, clam chowder, sugar, pepper, Cap'n Crunch, and topped off with a colorful spray of raw green pepper slices. Just looking at it made her feel queasy.

"I'm in for five." She reached for the wad of bills in her North Face backpack. "But you can't throw up."

"No way I'm puking." Mason shook his head. "My stomach is a steel trap."

Stuart, standing behind Becca, put his hands over her eyes. "You're not going to want to see this," he laughed.

She leaned against him and grabbed his fingers. "I am woman. I am strong."

For the last few weeks, Becca had found herself eating lunch with Stuart and his friends almost every day. With their class schedule, it was just easier to go to the dining hall by his dorm than to walk all the way back to her side of campus. And — surprise of surprises — she was enjoying it. Not all football players were the moronic jerks she had always assumed they were. With the exception of today's adolescent bet, they were actually pretty smart. Becca had never really had the opportunity to see guys hanging out in their natural environment. Guy friends, she'd noticed, were different than girl friends. They gave each other shit constantly, for one thing, and they didn't tend to delve into overly emotional subjects. Not that they didn't get deep — they talked about war and politics and the AIDS epidemic, but from a more intellectual perspective than an emotional one. They definitely didn't talk about their feelings — at least not in a group, and not in front of girls.

When she and Stuart were alone, on the other hand, he had no problem talking about his feelings. He still hadn't said he loved her, but he was constantly telling her how smart she was, how funny, how beautiful. No one had ever seen her the way he saw her, and she was addicted. Becca wasn't sure anymore if she could survive a day without her Stuart high.

Of his friends, she particularly liked Mason. Like Stuart, Mason was a sophomore and played some kind of offense on the football team. Tall, broad-shouldered and blond, his outrageous sense of humor was disarming and at first had left Becca feeling slightly ill at ease — like the afternoon she and Stuart were making out in his room and Mason, stationed in the dorm room above with a crowd of Stuart's football buddies, used a fishing line to dangle random pieces of male and female underwear outside their window. But she'd quickly realized that Mason didn't have a mean bone in his body. He just liked being the center of attention, and he especially liked making people laugh.

Although in this instance making people laugh and making people nauseated were verging on one and the same.

"Here goes." He picked up the overladen slice of bread. The group around the table started to whoop. Besides Becca and Stuart, there were four other football players, and one other girlfriend, a petite brunette named Delia who was dating Pete, the big defensive tackle. Stuart laughed and joined his friends pounding the table with their fists. Becca grinned. This was so . . . *college*. There was something oddly liberating about being in a group of people doing something so utterly stupid. When had she decided she had to be so perfect and demure all the time? Wasn't it time she just let go? Without the help of an alcoholic beverage?

"May-son!" She joined in the thunderous chant.

Energized by the surrounding attention, Mason shoved the entire foul pile into his mouth in two huge bites. His face turned bright red. He gagged . . . but he didn't puke.

"Thank you very much!" He scooped up the stack of crumpled bills on the table.

Becca looked at Stuart. "Worth every penny."

"That was unbelievably disgusting." Stuart grinned, then added, straight-faced, "What do you see in these people?"

"The things I expose you to," Becca shook her head in mock despair. "I'm so sorry."

Stuart grabbed her tray, and slid it on top of his. "Let's get out of here. Study Group starts in ten."

Damn. "I'll meet you there." Becca gave him a quick peck. "I forgot my notebook. I'll just run back and get it."

After a brisk five-minute walk across campus, she opened the door to her dorm room to find Isabelle, dressed in pajama pants and a big gray Middlebury sweatshirt, slumped on the floor in the middle of their room. She was bawling, her face puffy, her eyes red and swollen. Even her cheeks had joined the act, turning a bright, blotchy pink.

"What are you doing here?" Isabelle accused, between sobs. *Whoa.* Where had that come from? Sure, they hadn't seen each other much lately, but that didn't mean they were strangers all of a sudden.

"What happened?" Becca knelt on the floor beside her roommate and rubbed her back. "Sweetie, what is it?"

"Abe b-b-b-broke up with me!" Isabelle wailed. A thin line of snot dripped down her lips, but she didn't even notice. Becca reached for a box of tissues and pressed one into Isabelle's hand.

"He's crazy. You're amazing —"

"Stop it!" And there was the hostility again.

"Are you mad at me?"

Isabelle's poofy eyes grew wide. "How could I be mad at you?" she spat. "I never even see you anymore!"

Becca leaned back, startled. "I'm . . . I'm sorry," she stammered. "I mean, I know I've been hanging out with Stuart a lot —"

"Forget it," Isabelle interrupted, staring down at the tissue she was still clutching. "It doesn't matter." She heaved in a huge breath, eyes overflowing, and then she was sobbing again. Becca, feeling guilty and unfairly accused all at the same time, started rubbing her back again.

"So . . . when did this happen?" she began, trying to think of something to say.

"Last . . . week!" Isabelle heaved.

Becca took her hand off her roommate's back. Last week? Abe had broken up with her a whole week ago and she didn't know about it? How could that be? She'd definitely *seen* Isabelle in the last week. At least a few times probably. They'd had lunch on Saturday and crossed paths in their room once or twice. She'd seemed down, but when Becca asked how she was doing, Isabelle said she was fine.

"Why didn't you tell me?"

"How am I supposed to tell you?" Isabelle scoffed. "You're . . . *happy* all the time . . . always babbling about Stuart and how great *Stuart* is and how *Stuart* makes you laugh and . . ." She ripped another tissue from the box and blew her nose.

Wow. That hurt. And it hurt mostly because Isabelle was right. She *was* happy all the time. And she *did* talk about Stuart a lot. But how could she have known it was hurtful since she didn't know that Isabelle was so unhappy?

118

"I'm sorry. I'm really sorry. Do you want to talk about it?"

Isabelle shook her head, and wiped her nose with the sleeve of her sweatshirt. "You wouldn't understand."

"Of course I would. I've been hurt before."

"The Jared thing." Isabelle managed a small smile.

"Exactly. So spill it."

She sighed and looked at Becca sadly. "He said he met someone." Her face crinkled, and she began sobbing again.

"Oh, sweetie . . ." Becca stroked her hair.

"She's a junior at Harvard. Like his R.A. or something. He said she's funny. *I'm* funny!"

"Of course you're funny! You're *so* funny."

"I'm funnier than she is!"

"You're definitely funnier!"

"And I'm prettier. He even said I was prettier! I asked!"

"Well, there you go."

Isabelle's face grew serious. "But that means he likes her for her personality. She has a better personality than me."

"If Abe thinks that, then he doesn't have very good taste in personalities."

"The worst thing he said . . . I can't even say it."

"Tell me."

Becca's eyes landed on the Bose alarm clock behind Isabelle's head. It was already after two, which meant she was late for her Study Group. Well, she was just going to have to be late.

"You have somewhere else to be." Isabelle's was flat.

"No . . . well, yes. Study Group for a Psych exam tomorrow. But it's fine."

Isabelle's eyes were hostile again. "Just go."

"I don't have to go —"

"Of *course* you do," Isabelle snapped. "*Stuart's* waiting."

"Isabelle —"

"You know what? You can't just ignore me for a month, and then come in here and act like you're my friend —"

"I *am* your friend —"

"No, you're *his* girlfriend. And that's about it, these days. Just leave me alone. Okay?" Isabelle abruptly stood up and marched over to her closet.

Becca sat for a moment, stunned, and then clambered to her feet. "I'll . . . I'll come back later, and we can talk. . . ."

"Don't bother." Isabelle turned her back on Becca and pulled a new blue sweater from the closet. "I'll be fine without you."

Becca didn't realize she'd forgotten her notebook again until she was halfway down the hall. But there was no way she was going back. She'd had enough accusations for one day. Her first impulse was to call Sophie and Harper immediately and debrief. Though she realized they probably wouldn't have much sympathy. Considering she hadn't exactly been returning their phone calls lately, they were probably even more pissed at her than Isabelle, in fact. Which was even more reason that she should call.

And she would. Right after Study Group. Only, even as she made the promise to herself, she knew it was going to be a hard one to keep. Not because she didn't love her friends. She absolutely did. But when she was with Stuart . . . she just didn't think about them that much.

Or, if she was being honest with herself . . . at all.

Note to self. Buy Mace. Sophie was still out of breath as she slid her key into the stiff metal deadbolt lock Sam had put on his apartment door. She'd sprinted the three blocks from the bus stop to his building, shouting crazily the entire way to ward off potential attackers. Beverly Hills, this neighborhood was not.

The apartment was dark and quiet as she entered. She'd seen Sam's gray Honda Civic parked out front, so she knew he was home.

Apparently he got to go to bed before two AM, like a normal person. Sophie had been on night shifts at Mojito for weeks, determined to have her days free for auditions. Which meant that she usually had to leave the apartment at seven in the morning to make it via bus to some godforsaken spot in the Valley for a nine o'clock cattle call audition. If she was lucky, there were more cattle calls in the afternoon. She'd make it to Mojito by five, where she'd change into the hostess outfit crammed into her black Gap tote and fake-smile her way through the dinner shift. By the time she got to Sam's after her nightly sprint, she was so tired she was numb.

Sophie tiptoed through the living room, navigating her way around the furniture as she headed to "her" room. Halfway there, the silence was interrupted by a loud snore. She jumped, startled by the sound. Sam didn't snore. Was it possible she was so exhausted she'd fallen asleep while walking? No. There it was again, louder this time.

Shit. J.D. was home. Damn this guy she'd never even met for wanting to stay in his own bedroom. Oh well. At this point she could doze off leaning against the refrigerator. She changed courses and headed toward the bathroom. The layer of fuzz on her teeth indicated a strong need for brushing, but she'd already recklessly decided to forego her skin care regime for one night. Let the zits come, even if it meant she wouldn't look her best for the *Ugly Betty* bit-part audition next week. Tonight sleep was more important than a great complexion. As Sophie neared the bathroom, she noticed one of the guys had left the light on for her. *That's nice,* she thought sleepily, opening the door.

"Oh!"

"Oh!"

She was suddenly very awake. A tall, stick-thin, beautiful girl with long blond hair that reminded her of Kate's cowered at the tiny sink, the fear on her face making Sophie think of the shower scene from *Psycho.* "I didn't —"

"Neither did I —" Sophie stammered, averting her gaze from the girl's almost nonexistent matching red lace bra and panties. "Sorry, I'll just —"

The girl seemed to relax now that she realized Sophie wasn't Norman Bates, and her terror was replaced with a wide, full-lipped smile. "You must be Sam's roommate. I'll be out in a second."

"Right. Sure. No problem." *You must be Sam's roommate.* The implication of the comment was clear. The girl was with Sam, not J.D. As Sophie quickly turned to leave, her foot bumped against something on the floor, sending it skidding across the cracked tile.

"Oops. That's mine." The girl giggled softly. "I was so startled when you came in, I dropped it."

It wasn't until the girl had the object in her hand that Sophie realized what it was. A diaphragm. She'd seen them in her gynecologist's office in Boulder alongside charts about the dangers of STDs.

"Yeah, well, they're slippery little buggers," Sophie responded casually on her way out of the bathroom, feeling the need to seem well-versed in the ins and outs of diaphragms.

She couldn't get the image of the round birth control device out of her mind as she rummaged through the hall closet in search of the AeroBed. Obviously this girl was about to have sex with Sam. One didn't insert one's diaphragm in preparation for a game of Scrabble. Unless . . . maybe *she* wanted to have sex with *him,* but *he* didn't want to have sex with *her.* It was possible. Sam didn't necessarily *know* she'd gone into the bathroom to armor herself against his sperm. He could have thought she was peeing or reapplying her lip gloss. Of course, she *had* been wearing her underwear. . . .

Stop! Sophie ordered herself. None of this was relevant to her life whatsoever. Sam could do whatever he wanted with whomever he wanted anytime he wanted. It had nothing to do with her. What was relevant, however, was the fact that the Aerobed had disappeared from the closet. Great. Just great.

As she collapsed on the too-squishy sofa, shifting so that her butt wasn't hitting the loose spring in the middle cushion, Sophie couldn't help but notice that other faint sounds had joined J.D.'s rhythmic snoring. They were undoubtedly sounds of the moaning variety, and they left little question as to whether or not the girl in the bathroom was putting her diaphragm to good use.

Sophie stared at the ceiling. Sam was a regular guy with regular urges. But did he have to fulfill them *here*? Couldn't he have gone to her place?

"Yes! Yes!" The girl's cries were muffled but loud enough to echo through the small apartment and probably out the open window into the courtyard.

Sophie turned over and punched one of the collapsing cushions as hard as she could. All she could think of right now was a line from an old Bette Davis movie: "Fasten your seat belts — it's going to be a bumpy night."

Kate was trying to keep up. But Darby and Mulugeta, the village elder from Teje, were talking too fast for her imperfect Amharic. She glanced at Dorothé, who gave a tiny, confused, headshake. She had no clue what was going on either. Jean-Pierre and Jessica had stayed behind to monitor the progress of the original well in Mekebe — not that Jessica, anyway, would have been much help. She hadn't bothered to learn more than three words of Amharic. And they were probably *me, myself,* and *I.*

So Kate waited. There was nothing else she could do. Darby was in charge — a point he'd made clear upon their arrival in the village that morning. They'd barely stepped out of the borrowed 70s–era

Land Rover when he informed her that he would be doing all the talking. She had tried to protest, but Darby'd cut her off.

"One word from you," he'd said, pointing straight at her nose, "and we're out of here. Got it?"

"Am I that threatening to you?" she'd replied icily.

"I don't want you screwing anything up." His response was just as cool.

"Who do you think I am? Britney Spears? I do tend to be fairly competent in most things I attempt to do —"

"Just don't talk. Okay? You railroaded me into coming here, now I'm here, so let me handle it. Or we could just go back and forget the whole thing."

Kate gritted her teeth. The only thing she wanted more than smacking Darby upside the head with a tree branch was getting a well built in Teje. That was far more important than playing power games. "I won't say a word." She nodded.

Of course, Kate now realized, that wouldn't have been a problem anyway. Mulugeta spoke a slightly different dialect than she was familiar with, and he was making no attempt to slow down his speech so she, or anyone else, could understand it. Seated on a wooden armchair outside the front door of his *tukul,* Mulugeta's graying temples contrasted with his smooth brown skin. His cheeks were round, and his chin narrow. His mouth was small, while his lips puckered unpleasantly, even when he spoke.

He certainly seemed wealthy enough to support a well, Kate decided, looking around the compound. There were several pigs, as well as the usual chickens, oxen, goats, and cows. There was even a house, built of mud and straw, with a real glass window in the front. Women and children moved busily, tending to animals, grinding *teff,* and cooking an Ethiopian stew called *wot.*

It all would have made her feel extremely optimistic — except for the one word she kept hearing Mulugeta repeat. *Money.* It seemed to be at the beginning of every sentence. If only she could have understood what came after it. Reading Darby's face told her it wasn't good. He seemed to be growing increasingly frustrated, and he was *never* frustrated. With anyone but her at least. In every other situation, he was always calm and smiling and tackling things with open-minded flexibility. But Mulugeta was getting to him and Kate was dying to know why.

She found out soon enough. Darby stood up, shook hands with Mulugeta, and headed for the compound gate.

"Let's go," he announced.

Kate looked at Dorothé. Did he seriously think he wasn't going to have to tell them what was going on?

"What happened?"

"Not yet."

"Why not —"

Suddenly, he smiled at her warmly and put an arm around her shoulder. Kate looked at him like he was crazy. Darby pulled her close. "Shut the hell up," he ordered sweetly, "until we're out of sight. Can you do that?"

Kate didn't know what the hell was going on. But she decided to play along anyway. If it would help getting the well built, she was fine with having Darby's arm around her shoulders for a minute. The only problem was that a certain amount of queasiness came along with Darby's arm. She disliked this guy so much that his touch actually made her feel nauseated. Because the feeling in her stomach certainly couldn't have been anything else.

As soon as they were out of the gate, she pulled away.

"So?"

"All the land around here is his. And he won't let us dig on it."

"Why not?" Dorothé looked as frustrated as Kate.

"He wants to be paid."

"What?" The Water Project did not pay for land, Kate knew.

Since every well they built benefited an entire village, the land was donated, sometimes by individuals, sometimes by the village itself. Either way there was no money in the budget for land.

Darby shrugged. "The guy says he's a descendant of Haile Selassie. He's got delusions of grandeur."

Haile Selassie, the former leader/emperor/dictator of Ethiopia, had all but destroyed the ecology of the countryside and ruined the rural farmer with his policies, but nonetheless he was revered. Any descendant of his was not someone to be trifled with. Still . . . maybe there was a way to make Mulugeta see that a well would benefit him personally. If he could be convinced that he would seem even *more* powerful by allowing them to build a well on his land . . .

Across the street, Kate spotted Rebekkah in the yard of a small compound.

"Rebekkah!" She smiled and waved. Rebekkah looked up at her and lifted a thin hand.

"I'll be right back." She gave Dorothé's arm a squeeze, then ran across the dirt road. Rebekkah met her at the gate.

"Hello!" Kate greeted her in Amharic. "How's your baby? Is he better?"

Rebekkah stood motionless for a moment, then looked down at the ground.

A knot formed slowly in Kate's stomach, then made its way up through her chest to her throat. She wanted to reach out to Rebekkah, but she felt unable to move.

"My son is dead." Rebekkah's voice was hoarse.

"I'm sorry," Kate whispered.

"There was nothing you could do." Rebekkah gave a weak smile, and then turned away.

Kate stood for a moment, then turned back toward Darby and Dorothé, her throat unbearably tight. There was nothing she could do. The truth in that was hard to deny. And yet she still felt that, in some way, Rebekkah's loss was her fault. Her fault, and Darby's, and everyone's. People were *dying. Children* were dying. Because they didn't have clean *water*? Wells were relatively cheap and the labor was fairly basic. It was truly, Kate knew, just a question of will.

"Fuck him," Kate said stonily, rejoining Darby and Dorothé. "We're doing this."

"Don't be stupid —" Darby started to disagree.

"You want to know what's stupid?" She swallowed hard, trying to get rid of the knot constricting her throat. "Dead kids. Dead kids are stupid. If we don't build a well —"

"Kids are still going to die."

"How can you *say* that?" Kate was horrified.

Darby lifted his hands, then dropped them to his sides. "I'm just telling you the truth. There's no quick fix. We do what we can, one thing at a time. In the long run, we make a difference. But in the meantime, kids die. Women die, too. So do men."

Kate stared. How could he just . . . *say* it like that? Like it didn't matter? Like it wasn't wrong and horrible and inexcusable in every conceivable way?

Dorothé reached out and squeezed her forearm gently. "We'll keep trying."

"Don't get your hopes up." Darby pulled the Land Rover keys from his pocket. He unlocked the passenger door and held it open for Dorothé. Once she was inside and the door was closed, he turned to Kate.

"Listen, some people aren't cut out for this. It gets to them. They feel it too much."

They feel it *too much*? As far as she was concerned, there was no such thing.

"Right," she breathed, "it seems to me, some people don't feel anything at all."

"I'm realistic —"

"That's a cop-out —"

"Just listen to me. I'm trying to say, if this is too much for you, don't feel like you have to stay."

There wasn't any hostility in his voice, but that almost made it worse. Apparently he not only thought she was stupid, but also overly emotional and incapable of living up to her commitments.

Kate opened the Rover door and climbed into the backseat.

"A pack of hyenas couldn't drive me away." She looked straight ahead, her eyes deadly.

Darby nodded once then closed the door.

As they drove back to Mekebe and the night descended around them, Kate thought about her commitments. To her family, to her friends, to Magnus. She could do better. Write more letters, find a way to get to Bahar Dar, and maybe even call or e-mail. Because no matter what Darby said, she wasn't going home. After nearly two months in Ethiopia, her view of the world had been turned upside down and sideways and inside out. But, somehow, she could feel herself coming back to center. And with all the unknowns, there was one thing of which she was sure. No matter what, she was strong enough.

"1972 Cutlass. Mint condition. Four thousand. Take it or leave it." J.D. stepped away from the big, boxy yellow convertible and peered at Sophie over his tortoiseshell Persol sunglasses.

Sophie and Sam were standing on a windy tree-lined street in Holmby Hills, where J.D. had told them to meet him. He'd been mysterious about the reason for the meeting on the phone with Sam, but had insisted he was offering Sophie a once-in-a-lifetime opportunity. Considering she had her first day off in two weeks, she'd been tempted to roll over and go back to sleep. But the prospect of actually meeting the phantom J.D. — whose bed she was borrowing — had been irresistible. The night she'd heard him snoring, he'd been gone by the time she woke up half an hour late the next morning.

Sophie bit her lip, staring longingly at the car. The movie check had finally come through, but after taxes it was a lot less than she'd hoped for. Four thousand would wipe out her bank account.

"She'll take it," Sam told J.D.

"Great." Despite the fact that it was ninety degrees outside, J.D. appeared totally untouched by the heat in his perfectly ripped-up True Religion jeans and bright orange Izod polo shirt. He was in his early twenties and pretty buff. His black hair was cut short and spiky, and his white teeth reminded her of Marco's, though luckily J.D. didn't have that hideous man tan. "I'll take cash or check."

"Hold on! Don't I get a say?" Sophie huffed. Sweat was trickling down her pink Target tank top, and her denim miniskirt felt like a heavy blanket wrapped around her butt.

Sam rolled his eyes as he stuck his hands in the pockets of his army green cargo shorts. "This is Los Angeles. Not having a car is, like, a sin."

"It's worth way more," J.D. pressed on. "Only reason I'm giving you this good of a deal is because my boss needs room in the hangar for his new baby blue Aston Martin. Pronto."

In the fifteen minutes she'd officially known J.D., he'd informed her that actors were "hunks of meat" and "pussies" ("no offense") and that the real power in Hollywood was in the hands of producers. He planned to be a movie mogul by the age of thirty — the degrading job of assistant to a star was just a necessary step on the ladder.

"His hangar? Like an airplane hangar?"

J.D. shrugged. "The man likes cars."

"Who *is* this guy?" Sophie asked. "John Travolta? Ben Stiller?"

J.D.'s face remained irritatingly blank. "I'm contractually unable to confirm or deny anything relating to my employer."

"Let it go," Sam advised. "I've plied him with gifts, alcohol, and rent breaks, you name it, and he still hasn't told me."

As Sophie turned her attention back to the Cutlass, imagining cruising down the 101 with the top down, Sam's cell phone rang. She already recognized the ring tone. Sam stepped away to gush over the phone to Ellie Volkhauser, the beautiful blonde with the runaway diaphragm, leaving Sophie alone with J.D.

"If you don't say yes, you'll regret it for the rest of your life. I know these things." J.D. leaned against the vintage car like he was presenting it in a used car lot. "Think how confident you'll be driving onto the studio lots for auditions in this baby."

"Auditions are jokes," Sophie sighed. "Without an agent, I have no chance."

She'd realized in the last few weeks that Gifford Meyer, her supposed lawyer with his millions of connections, was an out-of-sight, out-of-mind kind of guy. Her three lines in a straight-to-German-DVD movie didn't get casting directors jumping out of their chairs to meet her, either.

J.D. took off his sunglasses and assessed Sophie from head to toe. She was reminded of the way Mr. Geezer — standing buck naked in his hotel suite — had looked at her. That was an incident she'd go to her grave *not* telling Sam about. Sophie stared back, daring J.D. to hit on her.

"I know a guy at CTI. Just got off a desk and was promoted to agent a few weeks ago. I'll text him, tell him he'd be crazy not to take you on."

CTI, also known as Creative Talent International, was one of the Big Three agencies in Hollywood. Having an agent there could mean the difference between hostessing for life and getting an Academy Award. Her experience with Mr. Geezer, however, had made Sophie too smart to fall for the line.

"FYI, I've sworn off men," she informed J.D. haughtily. Which was true. Between Trey, Mr. Geezer, and whatever *hadn't* happened with Sam, she was done with guys. All they did was distract her from her career and make her eat In-N-Out burgers and gallons of Pinkberry sprinkled with chocolate chips. "I will not go out with you for any reason." She smiled coldly and crossed her arms across her chest. "So if you think tempting me with some bogus connection is going to get you in my pants, you're sadly mistaken."

J.D. raised one meticulously groomed eyebrow. "FYI, I'm gay."

Sophie suddenly felt stupid. "You're — what?" Really stupid.

"I like men. I have no interest in your pants." He shrugged. "This town runs on favors. Offering you the car is one. Offering to text my agent friend is another. Feel free to get on your knees and thank me anytime."

Sophie wasn't going to mess this up further. She dropped to her knees, ignoring the blazing hot asphalt that was probably burning off the top layer of her epidermis.

"I'll take the car. And the agent."

"I never . . . used my bra as a sling when I sprained my elbow," Harper announced. She raised her glass of Diet Coke and took a huge swig.

"I never . . . hid from Brad Jorgowski in the girls' locker room," Judd stated, lifting his Red Bull.

"Ugh. That guy was such a bully." Harper drank as well. Judd wasn't the only one who'd sought refuge from B.J. (as Harper had referred to him behind his back since tenth grade) in the girls' locker room.

"One more thing we have in common," Judd laughed. "A shared history of fear."

They were sitting by the fireplace at the Hardrive Café, one of CU's most popular student hangouts, with two of Judd's college friends. The hipster coffeehouse had bunches of computers with Internet access, as well as a pool table for those who could tear themselves away from reading blogs or updating their profiles on Facebook.

After the disastrous UC Boulder Fiji Island Party last fall, Harper had vowed she'd never socialize on campus again. But Judd had insisted she'd love Poppy and George. Harper was so grateful that Judd had forgiven her for being a bitch-from-hell, she would've hung out with him at a dentist's office in Lincoln, Nebraska.

The four of them were currently playing "I Never," which consisted of going around the table, revealing embarrassing truths about oneself by saying, "I never did such and such." If anyone had done that thing, he or she had to drink. They'd substituted the alcohol usually used in the game with each person's nonalcoholic beverage of choice. Which was a good thing. Harper could imagine herself getting drunk and self-pityingly declaring, "I never got into college." The shame. The shame.

"I never passed out at the sight of blood," George exclaimed. He didn't drink, but Poppy, sitting next to him, did.

"You promised you'd never tell a soul about that!" she shouted after she set her white ceramic mug back down on the table. "No fair."

"Brutal world, isn't it?" George grinned. He had straggly strawberry-blond hair, freckles, and wide green eyes that seemed to be constantly smiling. "Don't blame me that this game is all about honesty."

Poppy shook her head, clearly exasperated. With long, straight dyed-black hair and light-blue oval eyes, she had the kind of severe good looks that Harper usually found off-putting. But in the hour she'd known her, Harper had already realized that Judd had been right to introduce them. They both loved epic novels, bad TV dating shows, and practically any kind of junk food. Poppy had even asked her to read some of the poems she planned to submit to the *Freestone,* a local literary journal.

According to Judd, Poppy and George had been best friends since the first day of freshman orientation, when they'd bonded over their shared disdain for anything with the word "orientation" in it. They kind of reminded Harper of her and Judd, except Poppy and George seemed a lot closer. And Harper doubted Poppy had ever ranted her way through a Christmas tree lot. She didn't seem like the ranting type.

Part of Harper felt guilty that she wasn't at home right at this minute, locked in the bathroom, typing away on her laptop. But an author needed to interact with the world occasionally in order to have anything to say about it. Plus this was her first social outing since she'd gotten back from LA.

"You want honesty?" Poppy challenged. She gave George's arm a playful flick. "I'll give you honesty."

George held up his Poland Spring bottled water, ready to drink. Clearly he expected her to reveal some humiliating moment from his past. "Go ahead. I've got nothing to hide."

Poppy paused dramatically. "I never kissed George." She took a sip of her chai latte, blushing prettily.

George set down his water. "Well I can't drink to that. I've never kissed *myself.*"

Harper had had the clear understanding that Poppy and George *weren't* a couple, which explained the shocked look on Judd's face as he stared at his friends. "You guys? When? Where? How? What did I miss?"

"Relax, man." George leaned back in his chair. "It's no big thing."

"We're *friends,*" Poppy emphasized. "Not a couple."

They smiled at each other, obviously sharing some kind of private joke. Harper quietly sipped her diet Coke. The writer in her was interested in watching the dynamic of these two relative strangers. Maybe there was something she could use in her book.

"So . . . what? You guys got drunk at a party, kissed, then realized you'd be better off as friends?" Judd asked, clearly confused.

"Not exactly." George raised his water, obviously ready to move on to another topic. "I never cheated on my SATs." He drank and so did Judd. Harper gave Judd a knowing look.

"I copied *one* question off Gina Percy's test," he insisted, putting his hand over his heart. "And I still feel guilty about it."

As the game continued, George suggested they add a bet. First person to get up for a bathroom break had to buy drinks for everyone the rest of the night. Considering the enormous amount of liquid they were consuming, it was quite a challenge. Harper felt like her bladder was going to burst by the time Poppy finally conceded defeat and ran from the table. Harper, thankful she wasn't going to have to spend all of yesterday's tips on the group's beverages, quickly followed.

Once they'd both finished in their stalls, the girls stood side by side in front of the bathroom mirror. Poppy, looking svelte in black skinny jeans, a peacock-blue scarf belting her long gray sweater, freshened her clear lip gloss. Harper readjusted her impossibly messy ponytail and felt a pang. It was the kind of moment she'd shared with Becca, Sophie, and Kate a million times, and she suddenly missed them the way an ex-addict missed his vice of choice. She focused on her stubby ponytail, trying to ignore the gnawing ache inside of her.

"Are you okay?" Poppy asked, glancing over in the mirror, lip gloss still in hand. "You look, like, extremely sad."

"It's just you kind of remind me of my best friends." She managed a smile. "That's a good thing."

Poppy nodded, getting it. "My best buds are all back on the East Coast. They take the train into Boston to see each other all the time. If it weren't for George, I'd be a basketcase."

Harper nodded, too. She couldn't imagine having a guy — any guy — as her best friend. There'd be so much she didn't feel comfortable talking about. Tampons . . . armpit hair . . . Mr. Finelli. But if it worked for Poppy, yay for her.

"It's cool that you guys are so open with each other," Harper began. "Especially given . . . you know . . . whatever happened."

Poppy rubbed her lips together, perfectly smearing her shiny gloss. "It's still happening."

"But you said —"

"We said we weren't a couple. And we aren't. We didn't say we weren't fooling around." She idly wound a strand of her long black hair around one finger as she spoke. "George and I are 'friends with benefits.'"

"What does that mean?" Harper asked, giving her ponytail a final, definitive, tug.

"It means during the day we hang out like regular friends. But at night . . . we get the benefits."

Harper was both appalled and impressed. The arrangement sounded so . . . sophisticated. And messy.

"What if one of you, y'know . . . ," Harper trailed off. This was way too personal a conversation to be having with someone she barely knew.

". . . Decides he or she wants to actually date someone?" Poppy dug in her soft brown leather shoulder bag, totally unconcerned about spilling all. "Hasn't happened yet. But when it does, we'll just go back to being friends without benefits. No harm, no foul, right?" She pulled out a roll of Altoids and held them up in triumph.

"I guess." Harper envisioned Mr. Finelli. There was no way she could be friends with him, and not because he was her former teacher. It was the memory of his soft-yet-firm-yet-melting lips that got in the way. And the fact that she'd made a total idiot out of herself in front of him numerous times.

"You and Judd should give it a go," Poppy commented, zipping her bag shut and smacking her pristine lips. "Trust me, it'll help with those lonely nights."

"Judd? And me? I don't —" Harper suppressed a nervous giggle. The thought of making out with Judd was beyond absurd. His wardrobe of Phish t-shirts alone barred any possibility of that ever happening.

"Don't freak." Poppy patted her on the shoulder. "It was just a suggestion."

But as they rejoined the guys at the table, Harper couldn't help but find herself wishing she were back in her basement apartment, locked in the bathroom. She avoided looking Judd in the eyes, and each time Poppy glanced her way, she felt herself blush.

At least she'd learned something tonight about writing a novel — that fictional characters were a lot less complicated than real-life people.

ELLIOT
Turning on the tears might work
with A.C., but not me. Find
someone else's shoulder to use.

Trina cries harder, but manages to get the words out.

TRINA
That's not what I'm doing.

ELLIOT
You've been lying so long I think
you're actually starting to
believe yourself.
(then)
That's not only scary, it's
pathetic.

OFF Trina, still crying, watching Elliot exit.

INT. PAIGE'S HOUSE - PAIGE'S BEDROOM - DAY

Paige does homework on her bed. A.C. paces.

A.C.
I don't get it. I'm decent
looking, at least to the extent
that I have no visible scars.
People laugh at my jokes. I'm a
gentleman -

PAIGE
Trina's in love with Elliot. Face
it and move on.

A.C. opens one of Paige's dresser drawers, rummages.

A.C.
Admit defeat? Never.

A.C. pulls out a LACY BRA, holds it up.

A.C. (cont'd)
Why didn't you ever wear this
while we were going out?

PAIGE
Because when we were going out, I
was eight.

SIX

Sophie drove through Creative Talent International's vast underground parking structure and carefully pulled into spot 345 as the white-uniformed attendant had instructed. Still unfamiliar with the dimensions of the Cutlass (it was twice as big as the silver BMW she'd borrowed from the Meyers), she narrowly missed banging into a massive concrete pole as she inched her mobile forward. She didn't breathe until she'd managed to put the car into park and leaned back against the black vinyl seat, sighing with relief. She was about to meet her potential agent, Matthew Feldman, and starting off what she hoped would be a long and fruitful relationship with an accident in the parking lot would definitely get them off on the wrong foot.

The seven-mile drive from Hollywood to Century City had taken half an hour, longer than she'd expected. Sophie had kept the top of the convertible up to prevent hair blowage. But since the air conditioner didn't work nearly as well as J.D. had promised, a layer of sweat covered every part of her body not directly in front of the vent. Digging under the front passenger seat, she pulled out the roll of paper towels she kept for emergencies.

Sophie glanced in the rearview mirror to make sure the parking attendant, Lord of the Underground, was nowhere to be seen. Feeling like she was breaking some kind of agency law, she quickly tore off a square sheet of paper and reached into her blouse. She patted away the drops of perspiration that were rolling from her armpits down her sides, praying she hadn't soaked through the gold silk of her Donna Karan blouse. It was a gift from Angela two Christmases ago, and Sophie had sworn she'd only ever wear it on the most special of special occasions. Then she reached into the backseat and pulled out the five-inch-heeled, super-skinny Manolo Blahnik boots she'd borrowed from Celeste. They were her boss's most prized possession, and if Sophie broke a heel or scuffed the beautiful soft-as-butter black leather even the tiniest bit, she could wave goodbye to a cool nine hundred dollars.

Ten minutes later, her hair and makeup flawless, boots in place, she stepped off the elevator and into the hub of CTI. Everywhere she looked, she saw steel and glass, along with an awe-inspiring view of LA's vastness, from the Hollywood Hills to the towering skyscrapers of downtown. Beneath her, cars looked like an army of ants, slowly crawling through the city. The agency's offices were modern to the point of ridiculousness, but the combination of the view and the decor generated its desired effect.

Sophie was scared shitless.

She took a moment to imagine that she was already a client at the infamous agency, popping by on her way from a *Vogue* cover photo shoot to thank her agent for the gorgeous bouquet he'd sent for last night's smashingly successful premiere. *Everyone knows me and loves me. I belong.* The visualization technique usually worked. But after thirty seconds of picturing herself as CTI's golden child, her knees were still shaking.

"Can I help you?" The headset-wearing young woman at the front desk eyed Sophie coldly. Her black hair was cut in a sharp asymmetrical bob like Victoria Beckham's, and in her pearl satin halter top she looked as thin and glamorous as a model. She looked Sophie up and down with undisguised distaste. "Or are you delivering something?"

"Sophie Bushell. Here to see Matthew Feldman." Sophie hoped her voice wasn't shaking as much as her knees. This was a lame start: if she allowed herself to be intimidated by the receptionist, how would she cope with a power-suited agent whose handshake was probably strong enough to break fingers? She stared through the wall of glass that separated the reception desk from the agents, wondering which of the offices belonged to the man she'd come to see.

The woman hit one of the thousand buttons on her phone, muttered something into her headset, and turned back to Sophie. "Through those doors, left at the conference room, right at the water cooler. Keep going past the copy room until you hit the Lichtenstein. Veer right, then a sharp right, and you're there."

What? "Uh . . . thanks."

Sophie strode through the enormous double-glass doors, ignoring the feeling of impending doom that came with the receptionist's intricate directions. She'd just look at names on office doors until she found the one that said Matthew Feldman. How hard could that be?

It turned out to be virtually impossible. Sophie wound her way through hallway after hallway, each one identical. She was pretty sure she'd passed the same water cooler four times. None of the doors had names on them, and every time she stopped to ask an assistant-type where to find Matthew Feldman, he or she made a point of talking into his or her headset, sending the clear message that Sophie, even in her nine-hundred-dollar Manolo Blahnik boots, was beneath speaking to. She was starting to feel like a character in one of those Franz Kafka books that Harper had always talked about junior year — all soul-destroying mazelike corridors and evil faceless bureaucracies conspiring to drive the hero insane.

And then she saw it. An oversized piece of pop art that had to be the Roy Lichtenstein piece the snooty receptionist had referred to. Thank god for the coffee table art books her dad had piled around his eco-friendly house. Sophie veered right, then took a sharp left. She found herself in front of a door, the first she'd seen that wasn't made of glass. She paused, willing away a severe case of the shakes. *He's expecting me. I'm supposed to be here.*

She took a deep breath and pushed open the door. About half a dozen men in dark suits sat around a huge conference table, an untouched spread of bagels, lox, and fresh fruit in front of them. O-kay. She wanted to simply back out of the room, but the men had all turned to her and were staring expectantly.

"I'm, ah, looking for Matthew Feldman?" She smiled, her voice disloyally trembling. "He's an agent here."

"Feldman finally got taken off Overton's desk? Miracles do happen." The remark had come from a twenty-something guy with slicked-back hair who was sitting on a metal stool at the back of the room, a computer in his lap.

"Sorry. I guess I'm in the wrong —" Sophie broke off as she noticed one of the men staring at her from his massive wing-backed chair at the far end of the table. He was impeccably dressed, and his silver-gray hair was swept just so off his forehead. He reminded her of . . .

Ohgodohgodohgod. I know what his penis looks like.

"This is a partner meeting." None other than Mr. Geezer, a.k.a. Peter Alterman himself, delivered the news. "That means we're all partners. Try the bullpen where the junior agents set up shop until we decide to fire them."

She gave a slight nod and quickly backed out of the room, shutting the door firmly behind her. Back in the relative safety of the glass corridor, she could drop the fake smile and freak out. Why didn't Sam warn her that Peter Alterman was a big-time partner at CTI? Her career was probably dead in the water. She'd rejected his sexual advances, not to mention stolen his food and drink, so it was extremely unlikely he'd allow one of his junior agents to take her on. She had to face facts: even if she managed to track down the elusive Matthew Feldman today, security was probably waiting to escort her from the building. Mustering as much dignity as was possible under the humiliating circumstances, she race-walked toward the exit. Or what she thought was the exit.

Winding her way out of the maze of CTI proved to be much harder than winding her way in had been. Every corner, every desk, every door looked the same. Maybe she should give up. Curl herself into a fetal position on the cold marble floor and wait to die. It couldn't take *that* long.

"Sophie Bushell?" An extraordinarily short twenty-something guy with curly brown hair that seemed to be matted to his head was approaching from the other end of the hallway. Everything about him was brown, in fact: his shirt with the rolled-up sleeves, his pants, his bronze tie. He was like a mini-version of Regis Philbin.

"Maybe." After the scene in the conference room with Mr. Geezer, she wasn't sure it was a good idea to admit to anything, including her name.

"I'm Matthew Feldman. J.D. sent over your headshot." He shot her a wide grin. "You have that terrified look. Common to the CTI uninitiated."

Could it be possible? Was Matthew Feldman actually . . . nice? If so, she was doubly sure that this agent-actress relationship shouldn't be. Once Mr. Geezer found out Sophie was on Matthew Feldman's roster, he'd be ushered out the door.

"This isn't a good idea," she blurted out. "How do I get out of here?"

He gently took her elbow and started guiding her through the labyrinth. "I figured you got lost. Happens all the time. That receptionist is such a bitch. Failed actress. Doesn't want anyone else to have her shot, so she tries to ice out every prospective client."

Matthew Feldman spoke in rapid-fire sentences, punctuating each word as if he'd just discovered it in his vocabulary. Instead of showing her to the exit, he took her deeper into the belly of the beast, where they stopped inside an enormous room filled with cubicles. He stopped at one and indicated that she should sit on the ergonomically correct chair in front of the tiny desk.

"I don't have my own office yet. Spring. Believe me. It's happening."

"Listen, you're really nice to talk to me and all . . . but if you want that office, help me get to the door."

"Wow. The self-confidence is killing me. You're a hoot."

"I'm serious."

Sophie spilled the whole story — meeting Peter Alterman at the New Year's Eve party, having no idea who he was. Going to his suite thinking she was doing a good deed for a lonely grandfather, then stealing the champagne and strawberries when he stripped down to nothing in front of her. When she finished, she expected Matthew Feldman to look at her in horror and point to the door. Instead, his intent gaze turned into a huge smile.

"If this agency turned down every aspiring actress who Alterman hit on, we wouldn't have any clients. Relax."

"Really?" Sophie saw a tiny ray of light at the end of the long, cold glass-and-steel tunnel.

He reached over her head and pulled a script from the middle of a teetering stack on his metallic gray desk. Its cover was CTI's signature green, and the agency's logo was emblazoned across it. "Pilot. Mid-season replacement. They're recasting the role of Paige. Read it. Love it. Know it."

"Um . . . why?" She stared at the script in her hands like it was an artifact from some faraway land.

"You're auditioning for it. I'll call tomorrow with the details."

Stars. She was seeing stars. Not of the J. Lo variety, but the ones that were little black dots in front of her eyes. Passing out was not far behind.

"Does this mean. . . . Are you saying you'll represent me?"

He shrugged. Sophie noticed that despite the best efforts of his tailor, the legs of his suit pants were pooling slightly around his ankles. "Let me explain something. I'm a junior agent. Which means I'm shit. Literally. Which means I'm desperate. So are you, from what I gather."

"I have fifty-two dollars in my checking account," she admitted with a rueful smile. There was something about Matthew Feldman that required honesty.

"So we're a perfect match." He stuck out his hand for her to shake. "Let's get rich and famous together."

Even as Sophie gave his hand a firm shake, she felt as if she were having an out-of-body experience. But she was smiling. Smiling so big her cheeks hurt. Matthew Feldman was shit in the world of agents. She was shit in the world of actresses.

Like he'd said, they were a perfect match.

Harper understood that her best friends were all busy individuals leading their own productive lives. They had wells to dig, auditions to attend, boyfriends to make out with. But couldn't just *one* of them answer the damn phone? On the other end of the line, Becca's phone went straight to voice mail.

"Hey, it's Becca. Leave a message." *Beep.*

"Hi, Bec, it's Harper. You may remember me. Dishwater blond hair, glasses, butt bigger than Seattle? We used to talk until you stopped returning my calls? I have news. So friggin' call me!"

Harper hung up her cell and dropped it on the lumpy full-sized mattress she used as a bed. Twenty minutes ago, she'd been elated. That night, after a few hundred hours locked in the bathroom with her laptop, she'd completed the first five chapters of her novel. And they were *good* chapters. Funny, engaging, heartfelt. . . . After all the writer's block, the false starts, the gut-wrenching self-hating anguish of the last few months, she'd finally found her voice. The one Mr. Finelli had been so adamant she had, hidden somewhere beneath the layers of contrived bullshit.

But what good was elation when there was no one to share it with? She was officially what her dad would refer to as a "sad sack." *Still, I'm a productive sad sack.* She waited for the thought to make her feel better. It didn't.

She'd been feeling so good when her laptop battery ran out of power at the end of Chapter Five that she'd actually changed out of her filthy writing sweats and into her best jeans (some way over-priced pair made by Paper Denim, purchased at the urging of Sophie in LA) and a form-fitting brown cashmere sweater Santa had brought for Christmas. What a waste. As Harper picked up her faded pink sweats, ready to change back into sloppy writer mode, she heard rapping at the small sliver of glass near the basement ceiling that functioned as her one window.

She looked up to find Judd's face, half-obscured by an orange ski hat, pressed against the dirty glass. Once he caught her eye, he moved away from the window to hold up a large pizza box and a six-pack of Miller Lite.

"What are you doing here?" she asked once she'd let him into the basement. "You showing up messes with the pity party I was about to throw for myself."

He handed her the six-pack. "You're done with your first five chapters, right? We've gotta celebrate."

She stared at the beer in her hand, stunned. She and Judd were back to sharing shifts at the Rainy Day Café now that he no longer hated her. She'd told him a few days ago about her goal to complete the chapters by tonight, but given that he'd been wrestling a garlic bagel from the toaster at the time, she hadn't realized he'd been listening.

"Harper? Are you going to stare at that beer or drink it?" He set the delicious-smelling pizza down on the fake wood coffee table she'd bought at the Salvation Army.

The lump in her throat made it hard to answer. "Thanks, Judd. Really. Thanks."

He shrugged off her gratitude. "Hey, I'm just here for the pizza."

"Thanks for letting me come with you."

"No problem."

"It's a nice day for a drive."

"Mmm."

For the last hour, Kate had been trying to make casual, polite conversation with Darby. It was a challenge on several fronts. For one thing, the dirt road to Bahar Dar was a series of pits and bumps that barely allowed for a regular breath, much less regular dialogue. For another, the malfunctioning passenger-side seat belt was so tight around her throat she was pretty sure she'd actually stopped breathing once or twice. And last, but by no means least, Darby seemed determinedly incommunicado.

Personally, she couldn't have cared less. They could have spent *ten* hours alone in the overheated, ancient, borrowed Land Rover without exchanging a word, and she would have been just fine with it. It wasn't like she was dying to get to know him better. Quite the opposite. But there was a bigger picture. A larger goal. And that goal had driven her from her cot this morning, and propelled her into the so-called yard at a ridiculously early hour to ask him if she could join him on his supply run to town. He'd stood there, implacable in his well-worn button-fly Levi's and faded orange t-shirt, listening as Kate had explained how she wanted to e-mail her friends and family from the Bahar Dar Internet café. He'd looked at her suspiciously, but she wasn't lying. She had been out of touch for far too long — particularly with Magnus.

Most of all, though — and this was where his Spidey senses were semi-accurate — she was hoping to use these two hours of alone time to get him to change his mind about building a well in Teje. So she'd pulled on her tightest jeans and cleanest black tank top, determined to be attractive, charming, and friendly.

"Jessica says you've been in Africa most of your life," she tried again, gazing out the window though there was nothing much to look at but open dusty fields and a broken-down fence. She didn't want Darby to feel too cornered.

"Mmm-hmm."

"What countries have you lived in?"

"Ethiopia, South Africa, Mali, the Sudan . . . a few others."

"That must have been incredible."

"Mmm."

Was it so hard for him to have a normal conversation? To answer in complete sentences or actually open his lips? He seemed to be able to do it with everyone else, just not with her. Kate had been misjudged before — because she was tall and blond, and people claimed she was pretty, her intelligence usually wasn't the first thing people noticed. But she'd never been misjudged for so *long*. Hadn't she proven herself yet? Shown him that she wasn't some ditz who came to Ethiopia on a lark?

Clearly, she hadn't. But she wasn't going to let that stop her.

"Listen. About the well in Teje —"

"There isn't a well in Teje. And there isn't going to be."

"Why not?" Kate couldn't believe how infuriating he was. "The community wants one, Dorothé and I have talked to several people who could spearhead an organizing effort —"

"It doesn't matter, because we don't have access to the land."

"I understand that." She tried to stay patient. "But we shouldn't just give up. I mean, how much could Mulugeta want for an acre? In American money, it's just not that much. We could get donations —"

"As usual," Darby drawled, his biceps flexing as he swerved around a particularly immense hole, "you're only seeing the microcosm."

The *microcosm*? Was he serious?

"What I see are human beings who have a very specific need," she enunciated slowly. Her voice grew deadly quiet. "And we have the ability to fulfill that need. And you, for some unimaginable reason, don't even want to try."

Darby apparently had had enough. He jerked the car over to the side of the road, slammed it into park with such vigor that Kate actually jumped, and turned to her, eyes blazing.

"Okay, let's say we buy the land from Mulugeta. What then?"

"Then," she stated the obvious with an uncontrollable twinge of sarcasm, "we build a well!"

"And what about the next village? And the one after that? If we pay for that land, the people in power in every village are going to start demanding payment. And all the money that we have for training, for personnel, for equipment . . . that's all going to go to land. And we won't be able to build as many wells, not even *half* as many. Is that what you're saying you want? To start paying money to the only people who really don't need it so we can build fewer wells for the people who do?"

Kate didn't know what to say. She stared at him, furious with his cold, heartless logic and trying not to notice that the pulsing muscle in his cheek was actually kind of sexy. *God, stop thinking he's sexy!* Really, one minute she was complaining that Darby thought she was a ditz and the next minute she was acting like one. Sexy or not, he was not right. Or at least, not entirely. He was, however, definitely cynical. And cynicism, she was fairly certain, wasn't the most effective approach to finding creative solutions to difficult problems.

She took a deep breath, leaned back against her seat, and looked out the window. The dusty, tree-dotted landscape stretched into more dust and more trees, harsh and unchanging for miles. And then in the distance rose a string of hazy mountains.

She had climbed a mountain before. With Magnus — a guy who actually appreciated her, believed in her. Darby had no clue what she was capable of. But *she* knew. She, Kate Foster, was capable of anything. And that knowledge was the only thing that mattered.

Because whatever Darby Miller might have thought, this fight was far from over.

"I should drink more often," Judd proclaimed, cracking open another Miller Lite. "It's very relaxing."

Harper nodded. Over the past several hours, she and Judd had consumed the six-pack he brought, plus a couple more she'd pilfered from her dad's stash in the garage. Neither of them was drunk, but the combination of the alcohol and greasy extra-cheesy pizza had made them both lazy and comfortable.

"It's weird to feel like my dream is coming true," she murmured, apropos of nothing. The thought had been rolling around in her mind all night. "Like I can do anything I want to if I really set my mind to it."

Judd was lounging next to her on the mattress, the empty pizza box between them. He was wearing his I NEED A HUG t-shirt and his oldest pair of jeans. He'd taken off his shoes, and his socks were mismatched and ratty. "So not getting into NYU wasn't such a bad thing after all?" he asked, propping himself up on his elbow.

"Not if I finish my book. And I *will* finish." She knew that now, the way she knew she'd have to wear glasses the rest of her life or that her sister Amy would always be thinner than she was. "Do you have a dream?" she asked. "Something that seems totally unattainable but maybe *is* attainable?"

He thought for a moment. His curly black hair was even messier than usual, and his t-shirt was stained with pizza sauce. "I'm too embarrassed to say."

"Pretend we're playing 'I Never,'" she responded. "Total honesty required."

"Iwannalosemyvirginity." He said it fast, but despite the fact that she'd had several beers, she managed to translate.

Harper had been expecting him to say he wanted to climb Mount Everest or open his own coffee shop or become a member of the next incarnation of Phish. Then again, Judd was an eighteen-year-old guy. According to every study she'd ever read in women's magazines, the thing that guys thought about most often was sex. Still, she wasn't sure how to respond. Something like "good luck with that" didn't seem sufficient.

"I'm a virgin, too. If it makes you feel any better." She hadn't *planned* to say that. It just sort of came out. He swiveled his head to look at her.

"You and Mr. Finelli never . . . ?" He left the question hanging there, his eyes boring into her. Harper felt her face getting red.

"No!" she yelped. "God no! We never even . . ." She didn't know how to finish the sentence. Never made it to second base? Never made out for more than a minute? For some reason, the conversation she'd had with Poppy in the bathroom at Hardrive Café came floating back. Harper pushed it aside. *Maybe I really am drunk.*

"Not that it's any of my business," Judd added quickly. "You don't have to tell me anything about it."

"Good." She'd known, deep down, that Judd was aware on some level of what was going on between her and her former English teacher last fall. But now she'd as much as admitted it, and that was as far as she intended to go on the subject. Judd was a friend, but he was also male. Unlike Poppy, Harper felt that meant there were still certain topics that were off-limits. Like her fantasies about Mr. Finelli.

"Amelia Dorf."

"Huh?" Harper wondered if she'd dozed off and missed part of the conversation.

Judd averted his eyes, staring somewhere over her shoulder. "That's who I'd like to lose it with. Ideally. She doesn't know I exist."

"You don't know that. I mean, I didn't know Mr. Finelli noticed me beyond my incisive English essays until he kissed me." Okay, so maybe the topic wasn't *entirely* off-limits. It actually felt good to talk to Judd about this stuff. For a guy, he was surprisingly easy to open up to.

For a few minutes, neither of them said anything. They just lay there, sipping their beers and contemplating their respective love lives. The silence wasn't awkward. It was just silence. Harper had forgotten how good it felt to be quiet with someone.

"I like Poppy and George," she said finally. "I'm glad you dragged me out of my cave to meet them."

"Yeah, they're cool." Judd sat up, readjusting the pillow behind his back. "George told me something pretty wild while you and Poppy were in the bathroom."

"Did it involve the words 'with benefits'?" She couldn't resist stealing the thunder from his bombshell.

"She *told* you?"

"Yep. She also said you and I should try it." Had she said that? Out loud? What was *wrong* with her?

Judd looked shocked and slightly pale. "Well, that's just . . ."

"Insane," she finished. "We're not even —"

"Totally." He toyed with the edges of the pizza box, tearing the cardboard into tiny strips.

Okay. Now this *is awkward silence,* she thought. She was keeping her mouth shut for the rest of the night. The rest of her *life.*

"Unless it's not," Judd replied quietly. "Insane, that is."

Harper felt the tiny hairs on the back of her neck stand up. It was a feeling not unlike she'd experienced when she'd watched *Silence of the Lambs* alone one night at four AM. Except . . . this wasn't entirely unpleasant. It was actually kind of thrilling. In a weird, surreal sort of way. *Say something. Respond.*

"Mmm . . ." It was all she could manage.

"We're both unattached. . . . We get along. . . ." He paused. "And I happen to think you're extremely pretty."

Harper knew she was blushing again. The heat from her face could probably melt the snow on the ground outside. As much as she knew she should hit Judd with a pillow and tell him to shut the hell up, she couldn't.

The truth was, she'd been thinking about the "friends with benefits" thing for the last four days, ever since Poppy made her revelation. She'd found herself staring at Judd at odd moments, like when he was mopping the floor at the café or grinding coffee beans. It wasn't that she was *attracted* to him exactly. She just wasn't *unattracted.*

"I'll shut up now," Judd declared. "And I should probably go. It's late —"

"Don't go," Harper heard herself saying. "Maybe it's not . . . insane."

"Really?" It was a whisper, but she heard him loud and clear. "You'd consider it?"

She hadn't realized they were moving closer to each other. But somehow they'd each maneuvered their bodies so that their faces rested against their pillows, just inches apart. "We'd need rules," she stated firmly. "There would have to be boundaries."

Judd nodded, his head moving against the pillow. "No 'benefits' behavior in public," he suggested.

"And no sex." Harper didn't want him to have illusions about his virginity dream. "You can still hold out for Amelia Dorf."

"Either one can end it anytime we want," he added.

"Right. No harm. No foul."

There it was. The statement of their intentions and the rules that applied. Her heart was hammering painfully in her chest and she was having trouble breathing. It was one of those moments when she knew something fundamental was about to change forever and she wasn't sure if the change was a good thing or a bad thing.

"I guess we should kiss," he began slowly. "Make it official."

Harper nodded, but neither of them moved. Physically their bodies were almost touching. Mentally they were still a million miles apart. How did two people go from what they were to what they were about to become? Even if they were still just friends, it was a huge psychic barrier. Judd got up his nerve first. He closed his eyes and jutted his face in her general direction.

They bumped heads, and Harper's glasses slid sideways on her face, but eventually their lips found each other. They were both so self-conscious that it was almost painful at first. Then she felt herself relaxing, slowly, tentatively. Judd's lips were warm and soft and reassuring. She felt something stir inside of her.

"Can I touch your hair?" he whispered when they broke apart several minutes later.

"Yes, it's allowed," she whispered back.

Suddenly, they were kissing again and it wasn't tentative this time. She felt his hands tangle in her hair as she reached out to run her fingers through his. It was rough against her skin and smelled like apples. *I'm making out with Judd Wright.* She felt stunned at the notion.

But she let herself go. Let herself enjoy the sensations that were coursing through her body, stronger and stronger as their kisses deepened, as more parts of their bodies found their way to each other. Harper didn't think about Mr. Finelli. She didn't think about her friends, so far away from her that sometimes it felt as if they were gone forever. She didn't think about whether or not this whole thing was a huge mistake. She didn't think at all.

The next time she was aware of anything beyond the touch of Judd's lips, it was three o'clock in the morning. They both stared shocked at the digital clock on the overturned milk crate next to her bed. Two and half hours had passed, but it felt like a minute.

"I should go," Judd said, although his voice lacked conviction. "I have a history test in seven hours."

"I've got to be at the café in three," she responded as evenly as possible, as though this evening wasn't a big deal in any way. "And it's delivery day."

"Sucks to be you." Judd grinned as he stood up. Delivery day was the worst because it involved standing in the freezing cold, unloading huge amounts of everything from coffee to hand soap from a truck. "Maybe you'll get lucky and there'll be a snow storm between now and then."

Just like that, the kissing was over and they were back to being friends. Friends with benefits. But friends, nonetheless. *It's going to be okay. It's going to work.* She walked him to the window where they both stood for a moment, unsure how to leave each other. A hug? A kiss? A wave?

In they end they shook hands. It seemed right, as if they were sealing a deal. In a way they were. "Thanks for a great night," Judd muttered, not looking her in the eyes, before he slipped through the window and out into the night.

Harper watched him jog through the snow to his decrepit teal-colored Saturn. Not one of her friends had ever called back to hear her news. Strangely enough, it didn't bother her anymore.

Kate stared at the circa 2000 model computer screen and wished she could go back in time. Not to 2000. She barely *remembered* 2000. Just to a few months ago, when she always knew exactly what to say to Magnus. When just looking at him made her feel like everything that confused or scared her was simply the next thing she was going to learn to laugh about.

Why was it so hard to compose a stupid e-mail to him? She leaned her elbows on the grimy counter. How the three computers in this tiny cinder-block room that flattered itself with the title "Internet café" managed to work amid the dirt and grime was a mystery. But somehow they did, at least long enough for Kate to read and reply to e-mails from Harper, Sophie, Habiba, and her parents. Becca, not surprisingly, had sent only one blissed-out e-mail about Stuart about three weeks ago. According to Harper and Sophie, she had basically dropped off the planet. No one was surprised, but there were definitely ill-couched hurt feelings. Habiba had sent Kate even more Amharic phrases — many of which, she was happy to discover, she already knew. And her parents had sent updates on the whole readmittance-to-Harvard thing. Apparently it wasn't all that difficult — she just had to sign some papers and the 'rents had to send in more cash. She still wasn't sure Harvard was what she wanted, but she definitely wanted to keep the option open.

Then there was Sophie. Kate felt loath to admit it, but her e-mails all seemed so . . . superficial. It made a certain amount of sense, given that she was living in LA with celebrities and other fake-boobed people, pursuing a dream that was . . . well, Kate was trying not to judge. Sophie had a real talent, a gift. She could make a difference in the world with that gift if she used it the right way. Kate just hoped she wouldn't get caught up in the surface-y part of the LA dream. The part where the only thing that mattered was the outside of a person instead of the inside. Because Sophie's dish had always been a wee shallow, and this year was all about going deep. She was a smart girl, though, and Kate felt confident she would figure that out on her own.

And Magnus. He'd sent her six e-mails, each more charming and sweeter than the last. She'd started fifteen different responses, knowing her time was running short and Darby would be returning from his errands any minute. Magnus wrote from Stockholm that he missed her. She missed him, too, even though she hadn't had a lot of time to think about him lately. Maybe she should just start with that.

"I miss you," she typed, feeling like Carrie Bradshaw e-mailing the adorable Aidan after seeing him at the opening of Steve's bar. Only a lot grungier.

"Hey, you ready?" Darby beckoned from the door. Behind him, the streets were bustling with women and children walking home to prepare dinner, men herding goats, donkeys carrying loads of teff and other grains. Kate wanted to tell Darby she was *not* ready. She wanted to reach out to Magnus and confess all of her confusing emotions and fears so he could make her feel better. He always made her feel better.

But trying to get everything down would literally take hours. Even if Darby didn't already hate her, he wouldn't wait that long.

She sighed and pushed "send." "I miss you" was enough for now. She closed out her account and slid her chair back, cringing as the metal legs squealed against the cement floor.

"Let's go." She didn't bother to smile.

Once they were back in the Land Rover and out on the open road, she tried the conversation thing again.

"My boyfriend will be really happy to hear from me. He's Swedish." She wasn't sure why she wanted Darby to know she had a boyfriend. "I met him in Paris. And then we did a bunch of traveling on his motorcycle. South of France, Italy, Switzerland . . ." She trailed off. What was wrong with her? She wasn't a babbler. She was an intelligent conversationalist!

Darby didn't even seem to hear her. Then, as if the truck knew that the sun had just set and they were in the absolute middle of literally nowhere, it made a loud clanging sound and stopped.

"Shit," he muttered. He steered them over to the side of the road and hopped out into the darkness.

"What happened?" Kate started to open her door.

"Stay there!" His tone brooked no argument. "Lock the doors!"

Lock the doors? Was he *trying* to scare her? But she did what he asked, watching Darby pop the hood. And then waited for what seemed like forever for him to come back. When his face finally reappeared at the driver's door, she leaned over and it snapped open.

"What is it?" she asked as he climbed in. "And why did I have to lock the doors?"

Darby nodded toward the back of the truck. "Don't want the supplies to get stolen. The back's full of water, vaccines, new tools. . . ."

Right. Of course he wasn't concerned for her personal safety.

"Plus," he continued, looking warily out the window, "there are still rebels around here. They call themselves militia, but it's hard to tell the difference."

Oh. Rebels. Fan-*tas*-tic.

"So . . . can you fix it?"

Darby shook his head.

"Are we going to walk?"

"Too far. And the hyenas."

"So . . . somebody's going to come by, right? Somebody who's not a rebel-slash-militia person?" Kate knew, even as she asked the question, that it was highly unlikely. They'd only seen two other trucks on this road the entire day. Most transport was done by donkey cart, and all the donkeys had been safely tucked away in their yards by now.

Darby shut off the headlights and Kate was instantly immersed in deep, dark, black. Darker than if she had closed her eyes. There was *no* light. Anywhere. Even the moon and stars were extinguished by a heavy layer of thick clouds. The whole earth had suddenly turned into a vast black void.

Her breath caught in her throat.

"Don't worry." Darby's voice was quiet. "Your eyes will adjust."

It was the first kind of nice thing he'd ever said to her and it turned out to be true. After several minutes, during which she sat silently trying to control the panic in her breathing, she could make out the shadow of the mountains in the distance. She could even sort of see Darby. At least, the outline of him. And the outline of something else, in his hands. . . .

"Is that a . . . *gun*?"

"Shotgun. Keep it under the seat. Don't worry, I'm sure we won't need it."

"You've been a jerk to me for two months." Her voice rose a pitch. "So when you tell me not to worry two times in less than an hour . . . I. Am. Going. To. Worry. Okay? And you have a *gun*."

"Okay. Sorry. Worry away."

"I will."

"Feel free."

Kate let him get the last word. If this kept up, she was starting to think she might grab the gun and club him in the teeth with it, or dump him out of the car and let the rebel/militia have their way with him. This whole stalled truck thing was probably his fault anyway. He'd probably forgotten to fill the gas tank, or the radiator, or whatever other truck parts needed filling.

After about a million years of tense quiet, the silence was broken. "Tell me about this boyfriend."

"Why?" Kate was as close as she ever came to pouting.

"We're going to be here all night. Might as well."

What the hell. So she told him about Magnus. How funny he was, and caring, and how he had come to her when she needed him most. She told him about how Magnus had gone back to university in Stockholm to finish his degree in philosophy. And she told him finally about the year of dreams, and how Magnus totally got it and supported her.

When she was done, there was a long silence. Then finally Darby nodded slowly. "He sounds like a pussy to me."

Kate clenched her fists. She really was going to kill him. And she wouldn't need a gun. Her bare hands would do just fine. "Excuse me?" she breathed quickly.

"Anyone can ride around on a motorcycle and climb mountains. What's he actually *doing*?"

"You," she began, "are the most pompous, self-satisfied, egotistical, superior, smug —"

"I get it." Darby cut her off. He sounded almost . . . *chastised*. "Enough with the adjectives."

Kate turned in her seat to face him, but didn't say anything. She just stared at him through the black. For a very long time. She could see from his profile that he wasn't looking at her. *Wouldn't* look at her. And that made her feel as if she had won.

Somewhere, not so far away, a pack of hyenas began to cackle. Her heart stopped.

"It's okay," Darby said quietly. Kate found herself staring at the outline of the gun on his lap. She hated herself for it, but that gun made her feel safe. More specifically, that gun in *his* hands made her feel safe. Because if anything did happen, she knew, somehow, that he wouldn't hesitate to use it. Even if he didn't like her and thought her boyfriend was a pussy.

She couldn't resist one final jab. "By the way, Princeton Boy," she began, sounding a little smug herself, "I was supposed to be at *Harvard* right now."

Although it was too dark to see Darby's face, Kate was pretty damn sure she'd finally managed to surprise him.

Fractures (broken bones): First Aid

What To Do If You Find Yourself Waiting Nervously at a Hospital:

❑ **Sit in an uncomfortable orange plastic chair.** Settle in. Buy a coffee from the machine. Read a six-month-old magazine with a torn cover. You'll be there for some time.

❑ **Bond with your other family members.** They may drive you crazy normally, but this is not a normal situation. If you find yourself crying and holding hands, do not be alarmed.

❑ **Try and restrain feelings of resentment and/or animosity towards members of the medical profession.** They're doing their best. Really. Actual hospitals aren't like the ones on TV: everything takes hours, and nobody—especially your doctor—will be young and good-looking.

SEVEN

I will kick ass. Say it."

"I will kick ass."

"Louder. I will kick ass!" Matthew Feldman was yelling into his end of the phone, forcing Sophie to move her cell a few inches away from her ear.

She glanced around the studio parking lot. It seemed empty enough. "I WILL KICK ASS!"

Walking toward Far Flung Productions, where she was going to read for the part of Paige Dalloway in *Heartland,* Sophie was determined to ace this audition. The mid-season replacement pilot was about a group of beautiful-but-angst-ridden teens in the Midwest who "find each other while discovering themselves." Matthew Feldman had sent over the scenes she'd be using for the audition two days ago, and Sophie had spent hours rehearsing each line in front of the tiny toothpaste-flecked mirror in Sam's bathroom.

"I WILL KICK ASS!" Her agent's loud voice got a decibel or two louder.

"I WILL KICK ASS!" Sophie stopped herself just as she was about to pump her fist triumphantly into the air. A security guard was headed in her general direction.

"Good. That's what I like to hear," Matthew Feldman panted. She could imagine him pacing around his tiny barren cubicle, straining the cord attached to his headset. "Call me the *second* you get out of the audition."

"I will."

"Swear."

"I swear." So this is how it felt to have an agent. Somebody who cared about her. About her career. Almost as much as she did. The idea thrilled her.

"I've got a lot riding on you, Bushell. Don't fuck it up." He paused. "But no pressure, okay?" Then again, there was something to be said for going it alone.

She tossed her RazR back into her black Gap tote and took a deep breath. Worrying about Matthew Feldman's disappointment if she didn't blow away the producers would only induce panic. She'd simply put him out of her mind, pretend that this was any other audition on any other day. She'd nail her lines and let her work speak for itself. Well, her work and the new True Religion prefaded jeans and clingy yellow halter top she'd bought for the occasion.

Sophie opened the door of the tiny pale green bungalow that housed Far Flung Productions and entered the air-conditioned office. Usually in this situation, there would be other actresses sitting in chairs or pacing, each murmuring the same lines she had been practicing for however long she'd had her sides. But today the office was empty. Stopping at the reception desk, she signed in, printing her name in bold dark letters. She grinned when she saw the space where it said "Agent's name" beside her own. How many dozens of times had she left that space blank, glaring evidence that she was nobody in this town?

I will kick ass, she kept repeating to herself like a mantra as she wrote "Matthew Feldman — CTI" in the small box. And she knew she would. This was her time, her moment. She'd paid her dues and she was finally going to be rewarded for it. The knowledge made her tingle from head to toe.

"Sophie! Hi!"

The voice was familiar. A waitress from Mojito? A girl from her acting class? She turned to find Ellie Volkhauser, aka the Diaphragm Dropper, beaming at her from behind a giant pair of white Chanel sunglasses. Her beauty was so overwhelming it was oppressive.

"Ellie . . . hey! What're you doing here?" Dealing with Sam's ditzy new girlfriend was not on the agenda.

"Auditioning for *Heartland*." She came closer and lowered her voice. Her shiny long blond hair brushed Sophie's shoulder as she spoke. "Supposedly they axed the girl who was supposed to play Paige Dalloway because she refused to get a boob job. I just heard about it last night. Lucky, right?"

They're only seeing a couple of people. You're on a very short list. They loved the shampoo commercial. Sophie's fists clenched. Ellie was auditioning for *Heartland*. And she'd just heard the role was available *last night*?

Matthew Feldman had explicitly told her that almost no one knew *Heartland* was looking for a new actress. They were recasting under the radar because they hadn't informed the original actress she was fired yet. Apparently there was some concern the girl might try to commit suicide — or worse, file a lawsuit. The only reason Matthew Feldman knew was because the creator of the show had been one of his old fraternity brothers at the University of Michigan. But Sophie had no doubt how Ellie had weaseled her way in here today.

As far as she knew, Sam was the only person outside of herself and Matthew Feldman who knew about today's audition. Sophie had told him after her meeting with the rookie agent, and he'd seemed happy for her. It had been one of those moments when she remembered why they were tenuous friends to begin with.

A short, stocky woman wearing a flowing multicolored peasant dress emerged from one of the closed doors behind the reception desk. "Oh, good. You're both here. Ellie, let's start with you."

"Wish me luck!" Ellie whispered. As if she really thought Sophie *would*. As if she hadn't marched into Far Flung Productions to steal the part that *belonged* to Sophie.

As soon as the Diaphragm Dropper and the casting director disappeared, Sophie yanked her cell from her tote. Her fingers trembled as she dialed furiously.

Sam answered on the second ring. "Hey, Bushell, how was the aud —"

"Guess who's here?" she interrupted. "Your *girlfriend.*"

"Ellie? She is?" He sounded genuinely surprised. Then again, he was an actor. A struggling actor, but an actor nonetheless.

"It seems a little bird informed her of the super secret fact that *Heartland* is looking for a new Paige Dalloway. I wonder who that could have been."

"You think I said some —"

"This is *my* part, Sam. *Mine.*" Sophie's breath was shallow and her palms were sweating. She hadn't felt so close to losing control since she was standing in line at the Aspen grocery store on Christmas Eve and saw the tabloid photo of Trey kissing Pasha DiMoni.

"If the part's yours, you shouldn't be afraid of a little competition," he retorted. "Cuz that'd be lame."

"I'm not scared of competition!" she shouted into the phone. But it wasn't true, and they both knew it.

"Before you make a total ass out of yourself like you did New Year's Eve, let me let you in on a little fact. I didn't tell Ellie about your *Heartland* audition. She did *not* hear it from me. Got it?"

"Oh." Despite all evidence to the contrary, she believed him.

"So instead of getting yourself all worked up over another actress, I suggest you go in there and show the producers what *you* can do."

Sam paused and his anger filled the silence. "And next time you want to accuse me of some nefarious scheme, here's another suggestion. Don't."

The line went dead. She could picture him slamming his phone shut, possibly even throwing it into a pool if he happened to be near one. The worst part was that he was right. She *shouldn't* care who was up for the part against her. Even if it was diaphragm-wielding Ellie.

Ten minutes later, Ellie emerged from her audition. Sophie could hear the producers laughing heartily as she walked out, a shit-eating grin spread across her impossibly gorgeous face.

"Everyone's totally nice," Ellie informed her. "You'll have a blast."

The casting director appeared in the door. "Sophie Bushell?"

She followed the flowy-dress woman into a large, nearly empty room where several producers lounged on sofas with notebooks and bottled water, trying to shut out both the conversation with Sam and Ellie's infuriatingly sweet smile.

The casting director gave her a nod. "Whenever you're ready."

Sophie nodded back. This was her chance. She had to go for it. *Before you make a total ass out of yourself . . . I didn't tell Ellie about Heartland. . . .*

"I don't get it. I'm decent looking, at least to the extent that I have no visible scars," the casting director began, reading the role of the character named A.C. "People laugh at my jokes. I'm a gentleman —"

Everyone's totally nice. You'll have a blast. There was silence. Silence that Sophie realized she was supposed to fill with Paige's Dalloway's dialogue. "Trina's in love with Elliot. Move it and face on." She paused, and cringed. "I mean, face it and move on."

And with that first flubbed line, she knew she was going to blow this audition. Matthew Feldman's voice chimed in alongside Sam's and Ellie's. *I've got a lot riding on you, Bushell. Don't fuck it up. But no pressure, okay?*

She was tempted to run screaming from the room, but stood her ground and eyebrow-acted her way through the rest of the scenes. Not because pride necessitated that she gut it out no matter how torturous it was for everyone there — rather, she knew that as soon as she left, she'd have to call her agent.

And she wanted to put that off as long as possible.

"You know this is going to lead to disaster, right?" Harper didn't want to hear it. Especially when Sophie, who'd called from her oversized used convertible while driving down the multi-lane madness of the LA freeway, sounded like she was in a wind tunnel.

Harper held her Motorola cell with one hand and expertly poured Guatemalan coffee beans into the grinder with the other. "If I knew it was going to lead to disaster, I wouldn't be doing it."

She glanced across the Rainy Day Books Café, where Judd was wiping down a coffee spill on a table. Sophie had called last night, despondent over a pilot audition that she'd bungled with too much "eyebrow acting," whatever that was. To get Sophie's mind off her stalled Oscar-bound career, Harper had launched into the whole story of how she and Judd came to be "friends with benefits" a few nights earlier. The good news was that Sophie had forgotten about the pilot for at least an hour as she grilled Harper on every detail, down to the texture of Judd's tongue. The bad news was that she was now calling every fifteen minutes with a new thought on the subject.

"Someone's going to get hurt," she declared dramatically. "It's inevitable."

"What happened to the Year of No Judgments?" Harper asked, tossing the empty bag of coffee beans into the already overflowing trash.

"That's not a judgment. It's a fact."

She sighed, almost regretting having told Sophie the whole thing. Maybe private lives were better off left . . . private. "Either of us can get out at any time. No harm, no foul."

"Whatever. You should see this girl, Ellie. She's, like, *inhuman,*" Sophie was clearly ready to get back to her favorite subject — herself. Which right now was just fine with Harper. "She looks genetically engineered."

Beep. "Hold on, Sophie. I have to get the other line." It was probably Amy asking her to bring her home an espresso. Again. She clicked over, ready to remind her sister that last time she brought coffee home, she scalded herself between her thighs.

"Harper, it's Mom." Her mother sounded weird. Like . . . bad weird. "Dad had an accident. We're at the hospital —"

Hospital. Accident. Dad.

"We don't know anything yet —"

"I'll be right there," Harper interrupted, her voice sounded tinny and far away. *Dad. Hospital. Accident.*

She snapped her phone shut and grabbed the scuffed red backpack she carried everywhere, ignoring a mother with a stroller who'd stepped up to the counter and was patiently waiting to order. *Mocha latte with soy milk,* Harper thought automatically, seeing the woman's kind, familiar face. *Accident. Dad. Hospital.* Her legs felt like lead as she raced toward the café door, fumbling in her backpack for her keys as she went.

"Harp, what the hell —," Judd called as she passed.

"I can't —" She just shook her head and continued out the door, knowing Judd would be understanding and supportive if she told him. But saying the words would bring tears and she didn't have time for tears. *Dad. Dad. Dad.*

Fifteen minutes later, she ran into the lobby of the hospital and spotted Amy first. Her usually perky sixteen-year-old sister was slumped in one of the orange vinyl waiting room chairs, head in her hands. Mrs. Waddle sat next to her, ramrod straight, looking ready to spring to her feet at a moment's notice. And she did spring up, the moment she saw her elder daughter.

"Sweetie, hi." Her mother took Harper in her arms, still smelling sweetly of the six apple pies she'd been baking for some couple's fiftieth-anniversary party.

"Dad?"

"He's in surgery. He was inspecting the work a few of his guys had done on the roof of a new house and fell. That's all we know."

Mr. Waddle was a general contractor. He walked on roofs every day. Harper never thought twice about it, never worried. So stupid! How could she not have seen the danger he faced?

"Is he going to be —"

"She doesn't *know*," Amy snapped. "Jesus!" She shook her head. "Sorry."

Harper nodded and went to sit beside her sister. They usually circled one another's orbit on the periphery. Sometimes sitting at the kitchen table together, eating bowls of Shredded Wheat or arguing over who got to borrow their mom's Honda Odyssey — but they'd never been into sisterly bonding. Now Amy reached for Harper's hand, and she took it. Their mother sat on Amy's other side and Amy took her hand, too.

As they hung onto one another, sitting in silence, Harper tried to force thoughts of her father out of her mind. If she made herself blank, tabula rasa, nothing bad could happen. But she couldn't stop the images from flitting across her brain. Him sticking his head in her room to announce that her mom would "quote 'kill'" her if she wasn't downstairs in five minutes. Her dad teaching her how to drive, pushing imaginary pedals on the passenger side of his Ford Super Duty when she didn't brake fast enough.

Guilt flooded in as she remembered how just a few months ago she'd totally believed he was having an affair with a redheaded woman named Margo. Harper had confronted the woman at her house the morning after Thanksgiving, only to discover that her safe, stable dad wasn't cheating, but rather was helping a colleague with a house she and her fiancé were building.

He's going to die. My father is going to die. She swallowed the bile that rose in her throat. This was her fault. She wasn't sure *why* it was her fault, she just knew that it was.

The hours dragged on. Most of the time Harper sat with her eyes closed, blaming herself for whatever had happened. At odd moments, totally random thoughts entered her mind, like how she'd hung up on Sophie earlier with no explanation, or how she hoped Judd remembered that they were supposed to inventory the storage room before they closed tonight.

When an older scrub-wearing doctor finally approached them three hours later, Harper felt the breath being sucked out of her body. Amy's nails dug deep into her skin, and she was grateful for the pain.

"He's going to be fine," her mom reassured them quietly. "I feel it." She stood to greet the man who had their whole lives in his hands.

The doctor smiled, but Harper couldn't tell if it was a good-news smile or a sorry-your-world-just-crumbled-around-you smile. This infuriated her: she wanted to shake that noncommittal look off his face. Didn't he realize how long they'd been waiting to hear something? "Mrs. Waddle, I'm Dr. Emory. Your husband had a pretty nasty fall." Harper felt an incredulous giggle escape her mouth. Amy squeezed harder.

"But he's all right." Her mother wasn't asking a question, she was stating a fact.

Dr. Emory nodded. "His right leg was fractured in three places, and he broke his right arm and his collarbone. He's not going to be able to work for quite a while, but he'll be fine." He paused and smiled again at her — a real smile this time. "Your husband has a hard head. He's got a bit of a concussion but nothing beyond that."

He's not going to die. The relief was so powerful that Harper thought she might faint.

Mrs. Waddle hadn't cried the entire three hours plus since Harper arrived. None of them had. Now she broke down, her shoulders heaving as tears ran down her face. She reached for Amy and Harper blindly, holding out her arms for them, and they hugged her, burying their faces against her hair. Harper felt her mom's love for her dad wrenching through her. *Dad. Accident. Hospital.* He was going to be fine. The doctor said so. Harper fought back her own tears. She didn't want her father to see her eyes swollen and red.

When they were finally allowed in to see him, he was still groggy from anesthesia and painkillers. It seemed like half his body was covered in plaster, but his face looked almost like it usually did, his blue eyes smiling, his graying hair swept haphazardly across his forehead.

"My girls," he murmured, reaching out with his left hand, the one that wasn't covered in bandages. They gathered around, each touching whichever parts of his body seemed the least injured.

Amy and her mother started babbling simultaneously, but Harper stayed quiet. There just weren't any words. Several minutes passed before her dad gazed in her direction and grinned.

"Too busy figuring out how this is fodder for your book to talk to the old man, huh?"

They stared at each other for a moment and Harper looked down, realizing that a tear — her own — had fallen on her father's plaster cast. But she managed a smile. Despite the stark hospital room, the casts, the IV taped to his hand, he was still *him.*

Everything was going to be all right.

"Do you want some . . . uh . . ." Stuart held up a bottle of red wine. "I have some — I thought . . . y'know, since it's Valentine's Day . . ."

Becca suppressed a smile. Standing in the dead center of his dorm room, Stuart fumbled nervously with a corkscrew.

"Actually, I think I'm good," she replied quietly, smoothing the skirt of her black Marc Jacobs dress. "But if you want some, go ahead." She took a deep breath, aware of how her C-plus breasts heaved upward in the strapless top. Stuart was aware of it, too. In a quick move, he set the wine bottle on his dresser with a *thunk*. "Oh. No. I'm good."

Then he just stood there, arms hanging awkwardly at his sides, looking half stunned at her, unsure — as if she hadn't sat exactly like this on the edge of his bed a hundred times in the last three months. As if they hadn't even kissed.

It was almost more than Becca could take. She wanted to throw her arms around him and hug him. For once, *he* was more nervous than she was. And that meant she'd been reading all the signs correctly — the roses he'd had delivered to her dorm room this morning, the fancy Valentine's Day dinner at La Bistro Blanc in town, his perfectly starched blue button-down, and his uncharacteristically nervous throat clearing in the car on the way back to campus. This was the night. He was going to say it. And then they were going to have sex. Or make love or whatever you were supposed to call it. Becca was sure there was a difference, but she wasn't sure if she could pin it down just yet. That would probably take some more experience than she actually had, although she imagined being with Stuart would be a thousand times more like making love than it had been with Jared. That had definitely been just sex — and an awkward, uncomfortable loss of virginity. No love there.

Becca patted the bed next to her and smiled. "C'mere."

But Stuart didn't move. "Bec . . . ," he began. Okay, now she was getting nervous. He looked pale.

"There's just something . . . I have to tell you."

Oh God, he *didn't* love her. Not only was he not in love with her, he was in love with someone else! Someone perfect and funny and beautiful and not completely screwed up. Fuck. Becca wished she'd accepted the glass of wine.

"What?" She was barely breathing.

Stuart seemed to read her face. In two steps, he was beside her on the edge of the bed and gripped her hand. "No, it's good." He smiled, although she thought he still looked slightly queasy. "I've just never . . . I've never said this before."

Becca started to shake. So much for not being nervous, she thought, drawing a ragged breath. Now that she thought about it, maybe she'd been nervous all along — so nervous she'd passed right through the normal symptoms into the bizarre calm with which she'd been possessed all day.

She stared at Stuart. She loved his face — the slight uneven tilt of his upper lip when he smiled, the crinkles around his almond-shaped brown eyes when he read, the tiny freckle on the left side of his nose. She loved his hands — the football player calluses on his palm, the fine dark hairs on his fingers, and the pulsing vein at the base of his wrist.

"I love you," she whispered, unable to look at him.

Stuart lifted her face with a finger under her chin. He was smiling. Becca wondered vaguely if it was possible for a guy to look radiant.

"I thought you wanted me to say it first."

Had she been that obvious? "I did. It just . . . I . . ." She didn't know how to explain. All her rules suddenly seemed stupid. She loved him. She wanted him to know and now he did. Oh God, this would be a really bad time to throw up.

Stuart kissed her lightly, and every nerve that Becca hadn't been feeling all day broke free now with a vengeance. She barely even told her *friends* she loved them. Much less a guy. Much less *this* guy, whom she actually did love.

"I've never known anyone like you. I love you, Becca."

Hearing the words out loud, even when she'd known they were coming, suddenly made everything real. What was happening with Stuart . . . it wasn't just dating or hanging out. They were a *couple*. They *loved* each other.

"You're the only person I know who smiles and cries at the same time." He grinned. "Have I told you I love that about you?"

Becca couldn't speak, so she kissed him, and though they'd kissed more times than she could count, she felt something different as he kissed her back. This kiss was slower, deeper, more satisfying. It was the difference between really good grocery store chocolate cake and the triple chocolate fudge brownie cake she splurged on once a year at the best restaurant in Boulder. It was everything.

He loved her.

The knowledge was unexpectedly emboldening. Without breaking the kiss, she reached behind her back and unzipped the top of her dress, pulled away, and stood up. The slim-fitting Marc Jacobs slipped to the ground with a faint rustle, and Becca fought the urge to cover herself up. She'd been in her underwear with Stuart before, but only in bed, not standing up. Not where he could really see her. And not in this particular lacy black bra-and-panty set bought with Sophie's guidance.

Stuart stared at a spot on her clavicle. He didn't seem to be breathing.

Becca stepped out from the pile of her dress, and walked toward him. His arms wrapped around her, and he stood to kiss her. First her mouth, then her neck. She reached for the buttons on his perfectly pressed shirt, undoing them slowly, hardly able to believe that her fingers were still able to function. She was going to do this. She was going to have sex . . . make love . . . with Stuart. Once she did, everything would be different. There would be no more doubts, no more fears. He would be hers, and she would be his.

"Becca," he whispered, pulling back. He ran his hands up her bare back. "Are you sure about this?" Becca could have sworn she heard his breath catch as he inhaled. She nodded. She was sure.

Twenty minutes later, with Stuart on top of her — *inside* her — she was less sure. He'd been completely gentle and caring. Careful, even. And everything leading up to the actual *inside her* part had been great. But now that he was there, she just felt so . . . uncoordinated. Or something. How was she supposed to move; what was she supposed to do? Why oh why hadn't she accepted the wine? Why had she wanted to be completely sober and aware of everything? Maybe a little less awareness would have been better. Not that anything was wrong. Just . . . what was she supposed to be *doing*? It all felt so . . . kind of mechanical. Not painful like the first time, at least, so that was an improvement. And of course she loved him. So that was different. And better. This actually *meant* something. They were connected, literally. That was important. But, still, she was sure there was more that she should be doing. She didn't want to be the girl who just lay there. But what were the options?

Dammit, why hadn't Sophie called her back today? Or Harper? Not that either of them were experts, yet some advice would've been helpful. Were they mad because she hadn't exactly been good at returning calls lately? She really could have used some serious girl talk, and talking to still brokenhearted Isabelle — on Valentine's Day no less, when Isabelle was planning to spend the evening at the library — had seemed too cruel. Finally she'd called her mom out of sheer desperation. Not to talk about sex of course; just to talk. For once they'd had an actual, real conversation. Her mother had asked about Stuart — even asked if she was in love with him. Becca hadn't wanted to tell her mother before she told Stuart, so she'd hedged and her mom had been oddly supportive about the whole thing. "When it's love, you know," she'd proclaimed. "Love overwhelms you."

Well, Becca was definitely overwhelmed. And not just with love. At the moment she was mostly overwhelmed with where she was supposed to put her limbs. When had arms and legs become such awkward extremities? Not sure what else to do, she ran her hands down Stuart's back, and wrapped one leg around his naked hips. That was something. Women on T.V. who theoretically knew what they were doing did that. Should she moan? Movie sex always had lots of moaning. But she'd never moaned before and it might sound funny. It might distract Stuart. She didn't want to distract him. She wanted him to . . . well . . . be done. Then he would hold her and that was always good.

And then something happened and she *did* moan. Softly. She couldn't help it. Something felt *good*. *This* was what it was all about. This good feeling, this tingling and tension in her stomach. Lower than her stomach. She breathed against Stuart's neck and moved her hips against him.

Okay, maybe she could get the hang of this. Only now *Stuart* was moaning. Or grunting, some sound she couldn't quite identify that didn't really sound like him. He said her name three times over, and then his back arched. Becca looked up at his face. His eyes were closed and there was sweat on his brow. His hair was mussed from her fingers, his mouth open and tense. He was moving faster and she wanted him to keep moving — just that fast, just right there. But she couldn't actually *say* it. Having sex was one thing. *Talking* while having sex was quite another thing entirely.

And then Stuart sagged on top of her. He released a ragged breath against her neck and stopped moving.

Okay then. So that was that.

She was embarrassed and weirdly proud all at the same time.

"Are you . . . okay?" he asked. His eyes were blurred, his face mere inches from her own. He kissed her lips gently.

Becca nodded. She was okay. But she'd wanted to be *good,* she thought, as he rolled away from her. She'd wanted to be more than good — wild, uninhibited, crazy. The best sex he'd ever had or would ever have. So much for that.

Stuart reached under the sheets and she heard a rubbery, snapping sound. The condom. He wrapped it in tissue and reached over her to drop it in the white plastic trash can next to his bed. That was real. Very, very real. Then he wrapped his arms around Becca, cradling her as he lay back down on the bed.

"I love you," he said for the second time, his fingers sweeping through her hair.

He loved her. And she loved him. This was it, official. Sexed, sealed, and delivered. She ran her hand over Stuart's chest, listening as his breath slowed and deepened — and then she looked up at him sleeping. Lying naked in bed with Stuart didn't settle anything, she realized, quite the opposite. Maybe it ended the beginning of their relationship . . . but it was just the beginning of the rest.

She missed Harper, Kate, and Sophie desperately. More than missed them. She *needed* them, needed to hear their voices, needed them to remind her that she could do this. That she was worth it.

Although loving Stuart was the biggest and most important thing she'd ever done, she wasn't sure she could do it alone.

"I'll do the talking."

Dorothé, standing with Kate at the door of Abebech's ramshackle little restaurant, nodded. "Better you than me."

Together they stared at the back table where Mulugeta was sitting. Dressed in his finest natala, he sat like an emperor awaiting his noon meal. Two young women draped in colorful natalas — Kate assumed they were his wives? — stood behind him. She could never get used to this idea of Ethiopian men having multiple wives, as though women here were like cars back home — the more money you had, the more you could afford to own.

In his left hand, he held a long, thick *dula,* the wooden staff that Ethiopian men carried to herd animals or to rest on during long church ceremonies — although she doubted Mulugeta had ever herded a cow, and if he went to church, he certainly didn't seem to understand its precepts.

"Did you check on Darby?" Kate's voice was low. She smiled at Mulugeta, who nodded regally.

"He's having lunch at the site." Dorothé briskly adjusted the white natala draped around her plump shoulders. "He'll be there the rest of the afternoon."

Okay, good. The last thing Kate needed was him barging in to screw things up. Unwilling to let Darby have the final word on building a well in Teje, two days ago she had sent Mulugeta a note inviting him to a luncheon in his honor at Abebech's restaurant. With Dorothé's help, she'd planned every detail, from the date (the Afrivalv was being installed today, which would hopefully keep Darby from even noticing their absence) to what she and Dorothé were wearing (tradition Ethiopian natalas and long white skirts), to where they would sit (in the private table on the small back patio), to what Abebech would serve (goat meat, fish balls, lentil wot, injera, and beer).

"Let's do this," Kate stage-whispered. "Remember — it's all about the flattery."

Kate plastered on her most obsequious smile and led Dorothé to Mulugeta's table. She shook his hand deferentially and took the seat to his left. Dorothé, before sitting in the chair to Mulugeta's right, expertly poured fresh roasted coffee into Mulugeta's waiting ceramic cup.

Five minutes of pure flattery was about all that Kate could stand. Once she'd exhausted every subject she could think of on which to expound about Mulugeta's superiority — the beauty of his wives, the health of his cows, the impressive size of his compound, the sparkling clean green Land Rover he'd arrived in — she finally got to her point.

"Of course, being as wise as you are, you know how greatly a well would benefit your community."

Mulugeta's eyes shuttered. He'd clearly known the subject was coming, but he wasn't going to make it easy for them.

"And it would be of great help to you as well," Dorothé nodded, leaning forward in her chair. "You could wash your Land Rover whenever you want."

Kate tried not to smile.

"I understand you are a descendant of the great Haile Selassie," she baited, trying to look starstruck. "Is that really true?"

"He was my great uncle," Mulugeta declared proudly, assessing the goat meat that Angatu had just set down on the table. Kate smiled at the little girl, who winked back before she returned to the kitchen to fill up her arms with the rest of the meal. Abebech and Angatu were both in on the plan and Abebech had even spread a ceremonial layer of fresh green grass on the floor beneath the table.

"He was a great, great man." Kate was trying as hard as possible to keep the judgment from her voice. Haile Selassie had indeed been great, but not very good. His repressive policies were responsible for the near destruction of the rural farmer, and had done immense damage to the Ethiopian landscape as well, which, in turn, had led his already drought- and famine-prone country even deeper into tragedy. "And think of the example you could set for other men like you. Men who don't have your superior intelligence and aristocratic heritage." Angatu had spent a solid hour tutoring her on the

Amharic translation of words like "aristocratic" and "heritage" the previous night.

Kate could tell that Mulugeta was starting to thaw. He twirled a succulent bite of goat around in his thin-lipped mouth, and ripped off a hunk of injera with his left hand.

"For a girl, you make some excellent arguments," he said pensively.

Kate glanced at Dorothé and held her breath. This was it. He was going to agree. She could feel it.

"You are right, of course, that we should have a well," he continued. "I have thought so for some time."

Yes! Kate tried to stay calm.

"There are several steps to take before we can start digging," she replied calmly. "We'd like to meet with the people in your village to tell them what must be done. Do we have your permission to set up a meeting?"

Kate held her breath. Mulugeta dipped a hunk of injera into the lentil wot, a thick, spicy red stew. He put it in his mouth and chewed slowly, swallowed, and took a long drink of beer.

"You have my permission."

"Thank you," Kate breathed. "You won't be sorry —"

"But as I told your young man," he finished. "There is still the matter of payment for the land."

Kate's heart sank. More than sank — it plummeted. And then froze in the chilly depths of disappointment-tinged anger. She wanted to pick up the bowl of lentil wot and hurl it at his mean, arrogant face. He *knew* that his village needed a well but he didn't care, unless he was getting paid. No matter who suffered.

Dorothé gripped her hand under the table. The young French woman shook her head grimly. Take it easy, her eyes instructed. Kate wrapped a shaking hand around her St. George beer, forcing herself to concentrate on the bottle-sweat that seeped through her calloused fingers.

"I'm sorry, but as you know, we don't pay for land. I hope you'll change your mind. Excuse me."

She stood up and unceremoniously started for the door. Mulugeta could go fuck himself. She wasn't going to keep sitting at a table with a man who was, for all intents and purposes, a murderer. She was done with flattery. But she wasn't done. There had to be another way and she would find it if she had to . . . what? What the hell was she going to do?

Abebeck passed the kitchen door and caught Kate's eye with a quick wave of her dish towel. "You come see me tomorrow," she whispered, a sparkle in her small dark eyes. "Come late. I will help you." And then she closed the door.

Kate glanced back and saw that Dorothé had also risen and was following her out. At the table, Mulugeta's eyes were blazing. Apparently, he wasn't used to being walked out on — especially not by two *girls*. Well, he was just going to have to get used to being mad. He was already mean and greedy, so what difference did it make being pissed off as well?

Halfway back to her hut, Kate had the presence of mind to wonder about Abebech's words. How could she help?

Tomorrow night, she was going to find out.

From: rebeccawinsberg@middlebury.edu
To: waddlewords@aol.com, katherinef@ucb.edu, HerDivaNess@aol.com
Subject: News!

My dearest chicas—

So I have news. You've probably been expecting it—or maybe not since
we haven't been talking so much lately—but IT happened. On Valentine's
Day, which I know is extra cheesy, but it was really romantic and
mostly good (not at all like the last time with a certain name I will
not write here).

The weirdest part is that he actually loves me. He said it. And I
love him. I said it too. So… dream accomplished! Can you believe?

Deep breath. Trying to stave off panic. Miss you guys so, so much.

XO, Bec

EIGHT

Do you think I should get a tattoo?" Harper murmured sleepily. "Maybe a skull and bones . . . or a rose. . . ."

She and Judd were lying on one of the twin beds in his extremely narrow dorm room, talking and making out. Sometimes the talking was more prevalent. Sometimes the making out was. They were supposed to be working a shift together at the café, but it was closed due to a major snowstorm that had shut down the entire Pearl Street Mall. She'd spent the morning working on her book, but once the battery of her laptop had run out, Judd had convinced her to use her old Uggs, the ones she'd once spilled ink all over, to trek the quarter mile to the CU campus.

According to the rules of their arrangement they weren't supposed to engage in "benefits" until it was dark outside, but they both had agreed the rules didn't apply to snow days. If Harper were being honest, she'd have to admit that she'd been dying for an excuse to get out of the house.

Her dad had been home from the hospital for a few days, and seeing him so helpless . . . it was intense. He was trying to stay in a jovial mood, but she could tell that he was in constant pain. And Amy had told her she'd heard their parents whispering about money. Months out of work was going to put a strain on the Waddles' permanently stretched budget, a fact that made her feel slightly queasy every time she thought about it. Spending a few hours kissing Judd and *not* thinking about her father's numerous injuries was a welcome respite from reality.

"I think you should get one . . ." He lifted up her gray RipCurl sweatshirt and kissed the spot just above her right hip bone. ". . . right here."

Harper closed her eyes, savoring the feel of his soft, full lips. It was weird what a familiar sensation that was becoming. A few weeks ago, the idea of kissing Judd would have made her either burst into hysterical laughter or gag. Now it seemed perfectly normal.

Almost too normal. Not in the complicated, leading-to-disaster way that Sophie had warned her about, but more in the it's-really-hard-to-stop-even-though-we-have-a-no-sex-policy way. The more she and Judd explored one another, the more she found herself losing herself in the moment. The hot, sweating, panting moment. She had to admit: sometimes she even found herself fantasizing about doing It with him. There were worse things than losing one's virginity to one's sort-of best friend, right?

He was just so . . . comfortable. In retrospect, she'd been painfully self-conscious during her brief encounters with Mr. Finelli. Kissing him had been thrilling, but she'd been too busy thinking about the fact that she was kissing *him* — her former teacher, whom she'd worshipped forever — to relax and enjoy it. With Judd, she never had that problem.

"But it shouldn't be a rose or a skull and bones. You should get an espresso machine."

Harper pulled the pillow out from under her head and smacked Judd in the face. "Perish the thought! Once I'm done with my novel

I never want to *see* another espresso machine or anything else having to do with this year, much less have a permanent reminder tattooed on my hip."

He glanced up at her. "So you're definitely out of here next year, huh?"

"God, I hope so." She rolled her eyes. "Another no-school semester in Boulder and I'll either bore myself or everyone around me to death. Or both."

"It's not *that* bad," Judd responded quietly. He flopped over onto his stomach, wedging her closer against the wall on the tiny, hard-as-floorboards bed. "I mean, there are a *few* good things about being here."

Harper instantly felt bad. Just because *she* considered living in Boulder a crime against her humanity didn't mean it sucked for the world at large. The world at large consisting, in this case, of Judd. But she was a *writer* and it was her duty to herself to experience something besides quaint small-town living. New York would be amazing — better than amazing — but at this point she'd settle for anywhere outside the Colorado area.

"I didn't mean that the way it sounded." She wriggled further down on the bed so they were forehead to forehead. "You like Boulder. It suits you."

"Because I'm so boring?"

Okay, she obviously needed to work on her delivery. From presentation to content, she was a mess. Debate diva Maggie Hendricks, Sophie's would-be roommate, would *not* approve. Harper was about to try to further dig herself out of the verbal hole when there was a light knock on Judd's dorm room door. He instantly shot off the bed, tugging his green J. Crew v-neck sweater (one of the few items of clothing he owned that she approved of) into place.

"Come in!" he yelled, heading toward the door.

187

An extremely petite girl with stylishly cut short dark hair and black cat-eye glasses poked her head in. "Oh, sorry. Didn't know you had company."

Harper was already sitting straight up on the bed and leafing through a dog-eared course catalog, the picture of innocence. She smiled at the elf girl and waited for Judd to get rid of the distraction.

Instead, he opened the door wider. "That's okay. It's just Harper."

"Hey," she greeted the girl. *Just Harper?* Was that some sort of retaliation for insinuating that he was boring?

"Everyone on my floor went out for a snowball fight, but I'm more in hot chocolate mode."

"Judd can give you some," Harper offered, nodding toward the supplies cluttering the top of the mini-fridge. "He brings it home free from the café where we work."

"Or I could make you some," Judd suggested cheerfully. He rattled the doorknob as though he was nervous. "I'm pretty proficient with the microwave."

There was a moment of awkward silence. The girl looked back and forth between Harper and Judd like she was trying to figure out if she was interrupting something. *Yes, you are,* Harper silently informed her. She wanted to clear up this Judd-as-boring thing and get back to making out.

Then again, *he* didn't seem in a hurry to get rid of the girl and almost seemed like he wanted her to *stay.* Harper had a sudden nasty suspicion that three was a crowd, and she was number three.

"What's your name?" she asked since Judd obviously was too much of a guy to do the polite thing and introduce everyone.

"I'm Amelia." She smiled warmly, still half in and half out of the doorway. "Nice to meet you."

Amelia. As in . . . the girl Judd dreamed of losing his virginity to. Amelia Dorf. Harper glanced over at him and caught him looking at her. *He knows. He knows I know.*

Okay. No problem. Judd's major crush had just interrupted a serious makeout session. According to the bylaws, her next action was clear. She should gather up her woolen bobble hat, double-lined North Face parka, ragged mittens, and ink-stained Uggs and get the hell out. Push aside friends-with-benefits activity to clear the way for the path of True Love.

"Amelia's in my Intro to Religion class," Judd was saying in a forced-banter kind of way. "She's got some pretty firm opinions on Mormonism."

"Mmm . . . don't we all."

Get up, Harper ordered herself. *Leave!* She had no issue with this. None. Their whole deal was based on a firm grasp on the no harm, no foul concept. Which dictated that she not give a shit that he wanted her out of his room to make delicious hot chocolate for virginity-losing-worthy Amelia.

So why did she have a hollow pit in her stomach?

"I just remembered I have to get home," she announced, tugging her parka off the back of Judd's chair. "To, uh, give my dad a sponge bath." She turned to Amelia. "Not in a creepy way. He fell and broke a bunch of bones and my mom's having to work extra to make up for the loss in income. . . ."

She was babbling. "I'm so sorry —" Amelia looked, not surprisingly, like she'd gotten more than she bargained for on her quest for cocoa à deux.

"It's okay. He's gonna be fine. Hard head." She'd managed to get some semblance of a hold of the majority of her belongings and was heading for the still-open door.

"Harper, you don't have to go." But Judd was already reaching over to the mini-fridge for the canister of Nestlé powdered hot chocolate with mini marshmallows.

"I'll see you tomorrow," she said to the door, not wanting to catch his gaze, and brushing past Amelia as she hurried out.

She raced down the dorm hallway, with its endless identical closed doors, leaving a trail of hole-ridden mittens in her wake. She couldn't help but wonder if Sophie had been right after all. The pit in her stomach felt suspiciously like the real Green-Eyed Monster. Then she thought of her dad, lying in bed, and decided it wasn't jealousy at all. It was guilt. She should have been home with him instead of whiling away selfish hours with her so-called friend-with-benefits.

As far as being a daughter went, she had a lot to make up for. As far as things with Judd went, everything was status quo. No harm, no foul.

"Wait up."

Kate stopped at the compound gate and gritted her teeth. It was the last voice she'd wanted to hear and the absolute last footsteps she'd expected to be drumming the dirt behind her. She could have sworn Darby had gone to bed an hour ago. He was one of those early riser types — the second it got dark, and the village kids went home, his head hit the pillow. It was his *thing*. Why change now?

"What?" She knew she sounded annoyed, but she honestly didn't care.

"Where are you going? It's late."

She deliberated, knowing she couldn't tell him where she was *really* going, but she'd never been a very good liar. So she told a partial truth. "I told Angatu I'd tuck her in."

Kate had been going to Abebech's restaurant as many nights as she could over the last few weeks. Since the older woman had resolutely decided that she was *not* in fact going to help her with Mulugeta, she'd had plenty of time to spend with Angatu. In between bouts of trying to convince Abebech to tell her whatever secrets she obviously knew about the Teje elder, Kate had learned to make injera, roast fresh coffee beans, and clean the wood-burning oven. She'd also

190

learned several Ethiopian children's games and songs, which she'd started singing every night to Angatu when she went to bed.

There was a bittersweetness to every moment she spent with the ten-year-old — it reminded her of memories she should have had with Habiba. Habiba hadn't been that much older than Angatu when she became Kate's sister four years ago. But Kate had never sung her a bedtime song or braided her hair. She'd never listened — *really* listened — to her talk about her past. There were whole years that she'd lost, that she couldn't make up for. All she could do was hope to do better in the future. Toward that end, she'd started writing Habiba almost daily, telling her in great detail about everything from the progress of the well to the vagaries of the rainy season in Ethiopia.

Darby was now looking at her suspiciously.

"What?" she demanded, deciding to brazen it out and stare him straight in the eyes. Darby laid a protective hand on the compound gate, as though he was going to stop her leaving.

"I just . . . wanted to remind you we start on the well in Kelem tomorrow."

They'd finally put the finishing touches on the well in Mekebe a few days ago, an occasion marked with a celebration even larger than the one that had heralded their arrival in the village. Every time Kate passed the schoolhouse on the main road, there were more and more children — including Angatu — attending lessons. Now Darby, Jean-Pierre, and Jessica would be spearheading the well in Kelem, a village several miles away, while she and Dorothé continued working with the villagers in Mekebe on an expanded latrine system.

Kate had volunteered for latrine duty and prodded Dorothé to do the same so they could stay under Darby's radar as they tried to find new approaches to the Mulugeta problem. Jessica, of course, had been more than happy to get up early for the hour drive to Kelem if it meant she didn't have to be anywhere near "shithouses," as she charmingly called them. Plus she was always angling for ways to spend more time with Darby. If Kate hadn't found it so pathetic, she'd have almost felt sorry for her. Darby had made it clear on more than one occasion that he wasn't interested in the aggressively adorable redhead — although he was always nice about his brush-offs, which almost made Kate like him. Almost.

"Yeah," she finally replied, noticing that Darby's lean, muscled arms even looked tan in the dark. "Dorothé and I are all set. We're meeting the village team at seven. So . . ."

"Okay." Darby looked at her for a second, then shrugged and walked away.

It took the entire walk to the restaurant for Kate to stop replaying his annoying "okay" in her head. What was he trying to say? Did he think she and Dorothé weren't up to latrine duty? If so, that was sexist. And stupid. Especially since Dorothé was already *waaaay* experienced in the latrine-digging department. Had he wanted to give her a lecture on not slacking off now that he wasn't going to be around every second of the day? As if she would! Did he want to tell her she was amazing and beautiful and smart and —

Whoa. Kate stopped in the middle of the road and gave herself a mental shake. Clearly, the lack of rich, comforting, familiar American food was getting to her. If she'd had mac and cheese at any time in the last three months, she would never have had such a thought. And she most definitely would not have such a thought ever again, not when there were real life-and-death matters to attend to.

It was those life-and-death matters she repeated to Abebech for the twelfth time once Angatu was tucked into her floor pallet and covered in coarse, wool blankets.

"You know something about him," Kate urged Abebech. "Something I can use. Please, you said you would help me." She tossed several empty brown beer bottles into the large metal trash can, wondering when recycling would make it to rural Ethiopia. Probably around the time she got Abebech to spill the goods on Mulugeta. But with a heavy sigh, the elderly woman dropped her thin, brittle frame into a white plastic chair just inside the kitchen door. Her gray hair was cropped close to her head, and her dark eyes were tired.

"You do not give up," she observed in weary Amharic.

Kate smiled, thinking that Abebech probably knew a lot about not giving up. She'd been left on her own when her husband died almost two decades ago, a widow in a society that wasn't friendly to women alone. And yet she'd managed to start this restaurant and make a place for herself in the community. The struggle of it was evident in her stooped back and craggy cheeks, and Kate had noticed that the second the last customer was out of the restaurant at night, her brisk, efficient movements slowed to a pace that better suited her old bones.

"I will help you," Abebech said in her quiet, measured voice, "but you must help me."

"Of course," Kate said.

"The girl." Abebech's eyes locked on Kate's. "When I am gone . . ."

She couldn't finish the sentence and didn't have to. Kate had already spent a great deal of time thinking about Angatu. She was alone in the world, as Habiba had been, with only Abebech to keep her from becoming one of the homeless waifs Kate had seen on the streets of Addis Ababa. Even in Mekebe, there were several children on their own, orphaned by AIDS or poverty, or some combination of both. They worked as farmhands for little or no wages and lived on their own in rented rooms in the compounds of relatives — if they were lucky — or their employers, who charged them for the privilege.

"She has a sister, Masarat." Kate's throat was tight. "I'm already trying to find her."

For the last several weeks, she'd been asking around the village for word of Angatu's sister, and had discovered that the girl — or young woman, as she would have now been eighteen — had probably gone to Addis Ababa to look for work. Kate only hoped Masarat wasn't one of the women she'd seen carrying firewood down Entoto Mountain. Or worse.

"I'll find Masarat. And if I can't . . . I'll find a way to take care of Angatu." She took Abebech's hand, not knowing exactly how she would keep the promise, but Kate didn't make promises lightly. She knew she couldn't go home and live with herself if she hadn't found a way to keep Angatu safe. More than safe — she wanted her to have the opportunities that every young girl should have. An education, a career someday that she loved, a husband — in that order — and children if she wanted.

Thinking about Angatu's future was perilous ground. Her feelings for Angatu and her feelings for Habiba blurred together and filled Kate with such sorrow and such hope that her emotions threatened to overwhelm her, so she turned them off entirely and made it a practical matter. She would find Masarat. She would reunite Angatu with her sister and help them build a life together. Beyond that, she couldn't yet think.

"Please. Tell me about Mulugeta." Kate pulled a dirty white plastic chair from a nearby table, and sat down. She put her hand over Abebech's.

The old women nodded slowly. "He cannot know I told you."

"Agreed."

A look of scorn came over Abebech's face as she spat out Mulugeta's name. "That man is no descendant of Haile Selassie. His uncle was a servant in the palace."

Kate's eyebrows rose. This was *good*. Mulugeta's status was built on a foundation of big ol' lies. She didn't know exactly how she could use this information, but there had to be a way.

"The uncle," Abebech continued, "when Haile Selassie was overthrown by the Derg, he stole from the palace to buy all that land in

194

Teje. From what I know — and I know it from my husband's brother, who *was* in Haile Selassie's inner circle — he sold several gold vases from the Emperor's living quarters. Mulugeta knows this. But who can accuse him? There are so few left who lived through that time. . . ."

Abebech's voice trailed off. "If you shame him — the people will not stand for his greed. So. Now you know."

Yes, now Kate knew. Mulugeta had a secret. The hard part was figuring out what to do about it.

The guys who lived in 3F were having a party again. Sophie could hear Coldplay blasting as she climbed the two steep flights of wooden stairs that led to Sam's apartment. Usually this fact would have pissed her off. Her long hours had turned her into the kind of person who anonymously called the police to register a noise complaint when other people were trying to have fun.

But tonight she didn't care. It was midnight and for once she wasn't totally zapped of all energy. Maybe she'd even change into her favorite red A&F halter dress and wander down to 3F and join the party herself. She smiled as she remembered the source of her sudden second wind. Matthew Feldman had called her cell during the dinner rush at Mojito to inform her that the part of Paige on *Heartland* still hadn't been cast and that he was planning to take out his former college buddy tomorrow night for an expensive steak dinner at Morton's, during which he'd convince said buddy to let Sophie have another audition. This time, she would *own* Paige Dalloway.

She rounded the corner and headed toward the apartment. The door was open and two twenty-something model-types were standing outside of it, smoking cigarettes as they leaned over the railing that overlooked the courtyard. Sophie realized the Coldplay wasn't coming from 3F. It was coming from 3B. Sam's apartment.

Passing the models, she walked in to find the small two-bedroom overflowing with fabulous-looking people in fabulous-looking clothes. Beer bottles and shot glasses covered every available surface, and the air smelled sweet and pungent. Sam stood in the tiny kitchen squeezing limes into a pitcher. He was wearing his goofiest Hawaiian shirt, which meant he was in a good mood.

Sophie knew she wasn't an official roommate, but a little *warning* would have been nice. There were certain private items in "her" bedroom she would have hidden had she known the apartment was going to be overrun with drunken strangers. More importantly, she would have reapplied her makeup before leaving the restaurant. *Be nice,* she commanded herself as she walked toward him, realizing she couldn't justify yelling at the guy for inviting people over to his own place, even if he could have been more considerate about it.

"Hey, Sophie! Margarita?" Ellie had popped out from seemingly nowhere. *She was probably on the ground, kissing Sam's feet,* Sophie thought uncharitably, noting the leave-nothing-to-the-imagination pale pink slip dress her diaphragm-loving buddy was wearing. "We're celebrating!"

"Sure. Why not?" She was still embarrassed about her reaction to seeing Ellie at the *Heartland* audition. After a long conversation with Harper, Sophie had decided that along with swearing off men, she'd also swear off immature outbursts for the foreseeable future. Her dramatic call to Sam seemed even sillier now that neither of them had even gotten the part.

"What're we celebrating?" she asked as Sam poured a fresh margarita into a clear plastic cup half full of ice.

He hesitated. "Ellie got that part," he finally said. "She's going to be Paige Dalloway on *Heartland*."

"What?" The smile was frozen on her face.

"I got it!" Ellie squealed. She grabbed Sophie and pulled her into a tight embrace. "You must have been my good-luck charm."

It wasn't possible that Ellie had landed the role of Paige. Matthew Feldman had promised that she was going to get to audition again. And she couldn't audition again if someone else had been cast.

"I just found out two hours ago!" Ellie continued, gesturing wildly with her drink. "I'm supposed to be at work Monday. Can you *believe* it?"

"No, I can't." Sophie caught Sam staring at her. "I mean, of course I can. Congratulations."

"They held off telling me until the other actress finally got word she was fired. Luckily, she's in rehab so nobody thinks she'll make much of a stink." Ellie shook her butt from side to side with glee.

Matthew Feldman, she reminded herself, was a junior agent. Information was currency in this town, and as low man on the totem pole, he obviously didn't merit much currency. His information was out of date. She never had a chance.

"Wow . . . that is lucky," she responded woodenly, feeling the immediate need to get out of the kitchen and into "her" bedroom. If she was not alone in .03 seconds, she was going to spontaneously combust. "I'm gonna, um, change into something festive. I'll be right back." *Or I'll crawl out the window and hide in the laundry room until the Princess Perfect party is over.*

"You'll get the next job!" Ellie called as Sophie headed toward the bedroom. Apparently, she'd just remembered that *maybe* the competition wouldn't be quite as excited as she was about her plum gig.

Thank God that Sam had posted a KEEP OUT sign on the door to J.D.'s bedroom. Once she was inside, Sophie yanked off her hostess wear and collapsed onto the bed in her Victoria's Secret leopard-print bra and thong. Every last bit of hope she'd mustered since getting kicked out of the Meyers' guesthouse and finding out her supposed big movie break had disintegrated onto the shelf of a German video store had been wrapped up in the role of Paige. Maybe if she lay here long enough, staring at the dusty ceiling fan, she could convince herself that she didn't care that Ellie got her part. Maybe she could find a silver lining. Then again, she also might start to cry, and bawling in her room while fifty people were whooping it up five feet away was simply too pathetic.

Finally, she groaned and rolled off the bed. If she could make it through getting dressed she could make it through the rest of the night. She was slipping into her red halter dress when the door opened behind her.

"Sorry!" Sam's voice seeped through the material that was currently over her head.

In a flash, she tugged the dress into place. "No problem. I was just changing. Obviously."

For a second he just stood there. Someone had put an eighties dance mix on the CD player in the living room. Sophie could hear Cyndi Lauper's nasal voice and feel the vibration from everyone dancing under her feet.

"Was my half-naked ass so traumatizing that you can't speak?" She picked up her MAC blush brush and swiped it across her cheeks.

"Matthew Feldman's in the living room. I guess he got the news and wanted to tell you himself."

"Poor guy. He's the only person who wanted me to get that part more than I did." She was impressed with the breeziness with which she made the statement. Who said she couldn't act?

"The party wasn't planned. It just sort of happened. Just so you know."

"Hey, it's your place."

"I'm sorry, Bushell. Really."

The gentleness in Sam's voice was almost too much to bear. She'd rather hear one of his snide, sarcastic remarks than be subject to his kindness. "No biggie. Really."

"I didn't tell Ellie about the part." He walked toward her. "You know I'd never do anything to hurt you, right?" The sincerity was at odds with the ironically over-loud Hawaiian shirt. She was excruciatingly close to crying.

"Hey, if I can't get a role on the strength of my own talent, it wasn't mine to begin with." She shrugged instead of bursting into tears. If only she'd managed to act this convincingly at the audition.

Sam smiled at her. "You sound very mature."

"It's a new thing I'm trying out."

Sam took another step closer, then put his arms around her. Her first instinct was to pull away, but the comfort of his arms felt too good.

"Promise not to tell anyone I want to kill myself?" she whispered, her cheek pressed against his shoulder.

"Promise." He squeezed her tighter.

Sophie closed her eyes and inhaled the scent of the lavender shampoo he'd borrowed from her this morning. In a minute, she'd go console Matthew Feldman. But for a few more moments, she was going to let Sam be a friend. As it turned out, he was pretty damn good at it.

"You should really answer your phone."

"I'll answer it . . . when you're *dead*!"

Staying low, Becca crept around a corner, pulled out her AK-47, and shot Stuart in the face.

"Gotcha!" she cackled. Damn, she looked good in thigh-high boots and a skimpy tank top. *Grand Theft Auto* freaking rocked, she decided, maneuvering her AK higher over her sexy prostitute hips. Who knew being completely amoral could be so entertaining? Especially on a Saturday afternoon, when the freezing rain blanketing much of New England had resulted in the cancelation of this weekend's ski meet with the University of Vermont. The icy weather outside made the thought of cozying up in Stuart's dorm room and playing video games on his computer while gorging on greasy pepperoni pizza even more appealing than usual. And it was usually pretty damn appealing, particularly since it was the middle of the afternoon, and Becca wouldn't have to worry about whether or not they were going to have sex. It turned out they were night sex people. At least she was. In the dark with no lights suited her just fine.

All in all the sex was definitely improving. But it still sort of freaked her out. Being bare-ass naked in front of another human being — even one she loved — wasn't her natural state of being. She'd had more than a few moments of freaking out about the new intimacy of her relationship as well. Was she supposed to act different with Stuart now that they were sleeping together? There was no question her feelings for him had changed. Or, not really changed — just gotten *more*. Scarier. The fear sometimes made her awkward, unsure of what to say or how to act.

Fortunately, she'd managed to get a hold of Harper, who'd recently entered into some kind of friends-with-benefits relationship with Judd Wright, a geeky-cute guy who went to high school with them. Harper gave her an excellent piece of advice. "Just think of him as a friend," she told her. "A really, really good friend. You don't have to act any different than you always have. Only you have sex. Not that Judd and I do that — but you get the point."

In a weird way, Harper's advice had helped. Whenever she started to feel panicked by her emotions, Becca just reminded herself that Stuart was a really, really good friend. Her best friend in some ways. Unlike Harper, Sophie, and Kate — and even Isabelle — he saw her every day. And none of her girlfriends had ever seen her naked. They hadn't even seen her *breasts,* at least not out of a bra.

Thinking of Stuart as simply a really good friend — with some pretty intense benefits — took some of the pressure off. Sitting in his room now, she felt no pressure at all. The afternoon would have been perfect, in fact, if Stuart's phone would stop ringing. It had been going nonstop for the last half hour. In the last fifteen minutes, Becca's cell phone had joined the clamor as well. Neither of them was willing to pause the game, however, so the dual phones kept right on ringing. Maybe it had something to do with both of them being athletes. The whole competition thing. Just like football and skiing, *Grand Theft Auto* was all about The Win.

Just as she was about to get stomped in the face by one of Stuart's thugs, there was a loud, angry knock at the door.

"Yeah, who is it?" Stuart called, momentarily distracted. Becca seized the opportunity to make her hooker run like hell.

"Open the damn door, will you?" Isabelle voice yelled from the other side of the door. She sounded pissed. Uh-oh.

Becca sighed. "I think we have to pause it."

Stuart pressed a button, then gave Becca a kiss on the cheek. "You're kicking my ass. Just one of those little things that make you cooler than every other girl on the planet."

Becca smiled and kissed him back. The kiss had just started to pick up some heat when the pounding started again.

"Okay, stop making out!" Isabelle shouted.

"Coming!" Becca scrambled to her feet, blushing. How did she know they were kissing? "What is it?" she said, opening the door.

Isabelle stood in the hallway, her hands firmly planted on her hips. "I tried calling," she explained, obviously tense. "You have to come back to our room."

"What's wrong?" Isabelle was scaring her. "Did something happen?"

"Yeah, something called 'your stepsister.' She's here."

The words landed on Becca's eardrums and bounced off like rubber balls hitting lead. That simply wasn't possible.

"She can't be." She shook her head. Mia was sixteen years old and lived in Boulder. Period. She was *not* in Middlebury, Vermont.

Isabelle glared at her. "You're not back in our room in five minutes, I'm bringing her over here." Then she stomped back down the hall.

Becca looked at Stuart, who looked almost as shocked as she was.

"I guess . . . I have to go," she muttered, pulling on her boots and looking around the room for the long gray scarf she'd flung on the floor hours ago.

And as she walked in a daze back to her dorm room, she knew as surely as she knew Coach Maddix's Olympic gold medal–winning time that her lazy Saturday afternoon was about to get much more complicated.

Becca did not love Mia.

Truth be told, she didn't even *like* her. She never had. Not since she was ten and Mia was eight and Martin had introduced them at the front gate of the Denver zoo. Becca's mom had arranged the outing as a getting-to-know-you event for the children, since — although Becca hadn't known it at the time — she and Martin had just gotten engaged after months of under-the-radar dating.

Mia's first words to her, standing under the KIDS UNDER TEN GET IN FREE! sign were "Hey, fatty." Becca, who hardly considered herself a 'fatty,' had looked at her stunned and then, unsure what else to do, smiled politely. Her soon-to-be stepbrother Carter, then only six, had laughed. Martin hadn't even noticed. In those ten seconds, the terms of their relationship had been set forevermore. Mia said mean things and Becca ignored them. Mia got away with everything while Becca held her tongue.

Still, for just a fraction of a second, when she opened the door to her dorm room and saw Mia's tear-swollen face and magenta nose, Becca almost felt sorry for her. Isabelle was handing Mia what looked — from the overflowing trash can — like her millionth tissue.

"I'm sorry for being so pissy," Isabelle began. "I just . . . I didn't know what to do, and you wouldn't answer the phone. . . ."

"No, I'm sorry," Becca corrected.

Mia looked up at her venomously. "You should be. This is all your fault!"

Becca was used to Mia's vitriol, but with this accusation she seemed to have reached an entirely new level of animosity. She had no idea what Mia was talking about.

"How did you get here?" It was all she could think of to say.

"I took a fucking train!" Mia's straight brown hair hung down her back in a greasy mess, and she looked startlingly thin.

"From Boulder?"

"Where else would I be coming from? China?"

"So . . . your dad doesn't know you're here." Becca took a deep breath and tried to ignore the hatred radiating her way. "Have you eaten?"

"Of course," Mia snapped. She blew her nose hard into one of the tissues Isabelle had given her.

"Without throwing up?"

Mia rolled her eyes. That's a no, Becca thought. Great.

Isabelle took her chance to escape. "I'll just . . . run down to the cafeteria and pick something up," she announced, backing toward the door.

"Thank you." Becca gave her an apologetic look, and Isabelle made a this-is-so-weird face as she slipped into the hallway.

Becca sat on Isabelle's bed, not sure she wanted to be within striking distance of her stepsister's seething rage. "So what's going on? What's my fault?"

Mia's eyes grew immediately suspicious. "Your mother didn't tell you?"

Now she was even more confused. "Tell me what?"

"About your fucking parents!"

"What about them?"

"Hello? They're getting *back together.*"

Becca laughed. Out loud. Mia might as well have said her mom was an alien from the planet Zorthon who'd started a shih tzu breeding kennel in Martin's attic. It would have been *more* believable than . . . seriously, it was insane.

And then Becca's laughter faded. *Love overwhelms you,* her mother had told her, not in her usual bitter, angry way. She'd sounded . . . now that Becca thought about it . . . almost girlish. Like she was . . . in love?

No. It couldn't be. Her mother hated her father. Her father felt nothing whatsoever for her mom. And they were both married. To people who weren't each other. Maybe neither of them was all that happily married, but married they were.

Then again, they *had* had that weird moment over dinner. Becca's pulse started pounding somewhere in the vicinity of her temples.

"You don't know what you're talking about." Her voice sounded hoarse and thick.

"You're happy about it, you bitch." Mia sniffled, scrunching up another tissue. "You know you are."

"I . . . I'm not." Becca decided to let the "bitch" comment pass. One of them had to behave in a semi-civilized manner. "Just . . . tell me what happened."

Punctuated by crying jags, she proceeded to tell her that over the last several weeks her mom had been staying out nights. Martin, never one to raise his voice, had actually *yelled* at her. And then, Mia had come home from school to find Becca's mom's clothing gone from the house and her dad wasted on Jägermeister.

"Jägermeister?" Becca frowned. *That* didn't sound right.

"He found it in Carter's room."

That made sense. Where else would a forty-eight-year-old man get Jägermeister but from his fourteen-year-old son?

"But," Becca managed to say, "that doesn't mean she's with my dad." The pounding in her temples had now become a radiating pain from the back of her head to her jaw.

"When she came back to pick up her furniture, your dad was there." Mia's eyes welled with tears again. "He was driving the U-Haul. I wasn't supposed to be at home, but I saw him. You do the math."

"My mom doesn't *live* with you anymore?"

"I'm telling you, she lives with your dad."

"But my dad lives with Melissa," Becca panicked, trying to play catch-up and failing.

"Not. Anymore. What are you, brain dead?" Mia almost seemed to feel sorry for Becca now. In her own masochistic Mia-centric way.

Becca picked at a grease spot on her faded Sevens. They were her favorite jeans and she'd had them for years, molding to her body like a second, exceptionally comfortable skin. They always made her think about shopping in Denver with Sophie, Kate, and Harper. About high school. Now they would always make her think of — this.

She felt an insatiable urge to rip off all of her clothes. The jeans, her white t-shirt, the gray cable-knit sweater that smelled like Stuart. All of it. She wanted to strip down and disinfect everything. She wanted to scream and run away. Run anywhere.

Instead, she looked calmly at Mia. "We have to call your dad. You have to go home."

Six hours later, after calling Martin and putting her stepsister on a flight to Boston, the only thing she could remember before dozing off — in her own bed, across from sleeping Isabelle — was the haunting sound of Martin's voice on the other end of the phone. He'd sounded desolate. Lost.

Becca, on the other hand, felt nothing but empty.

MOJITO

930 HILGARD AVE.
LOS ANGELES, CA 90024

Server: Amber	DOB: 0X/XX
Table 14/1	1:52 PM
Guests: 3	

#40059

Order Type: Dine In
Area: Patio
Day Part: Lunch

Cristal Brut	343.75
Caesar Salad	17.95
Caesar Salad	17.95
Caesar Salad	17.95
Sub Total	397.60
Tax	29.90
Total	427.50
Balance Due	427.50

Have a pleasant day!

Mojito
930 HILGARD AVE.
LOS ANGELES, CA 90024

Server: Amber	DOB: 0X/XX
Table 14/1	1:55 PM

Visa
Card #XXXXXXXXXXXX3715
Magnetic card present: **BENSON, TREY**
Approval: 361329

Amount: 427.50

+ Tip: _100.00_
= Total: _527.50_

X _Trey Benson_
Approval: 36139

Merchant Copy

NINE

"Could you tell my waitress to make my garden salad a half order?" The request had come from a girl the size of an emery board.

Sophie finished filling her glass from the pitcher of icy cucumber water. "That's all you're going to eat for lunch?" She knew she sounded like a nagging mother, but something *had* to be said.

"I just had three almonds," the girl informed her, eyes fixed on her Treo. She was so thin her collar bones jutted like coat hangers through her thin jersey top. "I'm, like, stuffed."

"One green leaf, coming up." Sophie was slightly satisfied to see that the stick figure's lunch companion, a twenty-something guy dressed in the ultra-shabby manner particular to extremely wealthy young people in LA, was checking out her own ample butt. Let the fashion magazines say what they wanted. Men liked a little somethin'-somethin' down there.

She headed back to the hostess stand, where several parties were waiting to be seated. It was the middle of the lunch rush at Mojito, and the terrace was filled with the usual combination of pouting figure-free models, power-suited businessmen, and attractive up-and-coming actors. She made sure to keep her shoulders back and boobs out, just in case anyone who was anyone was there to discover her. As she walked, Sophie made mental notes about where to seat the customers. The older distinguished-looking man who appeared to be with his much younger large-breasted mistress would probably slip her a twenty if she led him to the secluded table at the back of the patio. The bearded, baseball-hat-wearing movie-producer-type would throw a fit if he wasn't seated front and center. The actor —

Fuck.

Sophie couldn't feel her fingers. She'd forbid herself from even *thinking* about Trey Benson since New Year's Eve, when she made a secret resolution to banish him from her mind. She'd done a pretty good job of it, aside from the night with Mr. Geezer, when she'd made herself go over a list of every guy she'd come into contact with in Los Angeles in order to come to the conclusion that she was swearing off men. But here he was, posing casually next to *her* hostess stand.

And he wasn't alone. Two of the glossy, over-buff guys from his entourage were standing nearby, texting on their cells. Even worse, one of the stars of *Laguna Beach* or *The Hills* or whatever the hell it was called now was draped on his arm, looking up into his long-lashed dark eyes like he was some kind of demigod. Gag. Sophie's first thought was that she hated herself for ever having gazed at Trey in the exact same fashion. Her second thought was that she had to hide. Her first words to Trey Benson since that horrible night in Aspen could *not* be, "Hello, let me show you to your table."

Panic rising, she stepped behind a huge potted ficus tree and scanned the floor for an escape route. The patio was unfortunately fenced off to keep out unsavory types. The only way out was right past Trey and his blonder gal-pal hanger-on. Shit. Shit. Shit! She bit her lip as she watched Celeste swoop down on him. The restaurant had a strict "no celebrity waiting" policy, which meant that if Sophie wasn't going to do her job, Celeste would do it for her. Naturally, he looked as hot as ever in a pair of sleek dark-wash jeans and a simple white t-shirt. *Asshole.*

She glanced even more desperately around the crowded patio, trying to come up with some semblance of a plan. A few feet away, three women in dark pant suits who looked like TV executives gossiped over Waldorf salads. The fourth chair at their table was free. In the words of Blanche DuBois — tragic heroine of her favorite Tennessee Williams play, *A Streetcar Named Desire* — she would have to depend on the kindness of strangers. Ditching the water pitcher behind the ficus, Sophie impulsively double-timed it to the table and slid into the empty seat.

"Nobody's going to hire that drugged-out wild child to star in her own show. Too much trouble —" The woman whose narrow wire-rimmed glasses were pushed down past the bridge of her nose stopped talking when she noticed the newly arrived fourth member of her party.

"Hi, all," Sophie greeted the stunned women, her heart racing. "What're we talking about?"

They glanced at one another, trying to figure out if one of them knew her. Finally, the one with most expensive-looking haircut addressed her. "You look familiar. Did you do a guest spot on *Medium*?"

"She was our hostess," said Spectacle Woman dryly.

Sophie gave them her most empathy-inducing grin. "Could we act like we're having a meeting or something? I've got some serious boy trouble at two o'clock."

The three women subtly looked to the right, where Celeste was leading Trey and his followers to a prime table they kept open for any star who happened by for a meal. Each one's eyes widened ever so slightly.

"Trey Benson?" Expensive Haircut stage-whispered.

She nodded. "Big time."

The third woman, who was wearing the same emerald-cut engagement ring she'd seen Jennifer Garner sporting, leaned in. "I always went for actors before I met my fiancé. He's a lawyer. Mean as hell, but at least he's loyal."

"What'd he do?"

Sophie was grateful they were letting her sit at the table, but not so grateful she was going to spice up their lunch with her humiliating tale. "It's too awful to talk about." She shook her head in despair.

Spectacles handed over the untouched glass of Chardonnay she'd ordered with lunch. "Drink this. You'll feel better."

Sophie sipped the wine, studiously avoiding eye contact with Trey or the rest of his group of acolytes. She was vaguely aware that had the situation been less dire, this would be a perfect opportunity to pitch herself as the next star of the CW. But chitchat, even about her career, wasn't on her agenda at the moment. The women had been given their bill, so they'd be leaving soon, and she'd go with them. Once she was safe from Trey, she'd take refuge in the kitchen until he was gone.

Expensive Haircut gasped. "He's heading this way! Look natural!"

Sophie tilted her head back and laughed as if the TV executive had said something incredibly witty. She looked anything but natural, but it was the best she could do. "You are *so* hi-larious!"

Out of the corner of her eye, she saw Trey *et al* walking toward them. Apparently, he wasn't satisfied with the usual celebrity spot and needed his own special table. She desperately wanted to look away as he came fully into her line of vision, but her eyeballs weren't taking commands from her brain.

In moments, their eyes would meet. Sophie could imagine the fake apology speech he'd issue, begging for her forgiveness, promising to call, blah, blah, blah. She almost *wanted* the confrontation. It would feel good to give him her patented "you don't exist in my world" stare before she turned back to her high-powered new best friends and toasted them with her goblet of borrowed wine. She could practically *feel* the female executives holding their collective breath as Trey came nearer and nearer.

Then it happened. He saw her. And she saw him. Their eyes

locked. Sophie waited for him to say something. No way was *she* going to talk first. But his gaze moved past her without the faintest glimmer of recognition. The reality hit hard. Not only was Trey *not* going to beg for forgiveness, he wasn't even going to acknowledge she existed. The weight of the humiliation was so staggering her vision went blurry. She blinked, trying to bring everything back into focus.

"Ouch." Expensive Haircut reached over and patted her arm.

"Don't let it get to you, honey," Emerald-cut Diamond consoled. "They're all walking I-machines."

Sophie slumped in the hard metal chair. That day in Aspen, she hadn't thought Trey Benson could hurt her any worse than he already had. She'd been wrong.

Becca was a big fan of romantic comedies. Good, bad, and moderately bearable — she'd seen them all. Most of them more than once. From the classic Hepburn and Tracy films (*Without Love* and *Woman of the Year* were her all-time favorites), to the newest releases starring people much prettier than they should be having much worse lives than they should be. Until, at least, they were rescued by love. She watched them when she was happy. When she was sad, she *gorged* on them, gobbling them up like a drowning man gobbled a last air-gasp before sinking inexorably to the cold, numb depths.

So of course it made sense that Harper's first question to her — once Becca crawled out from under her yellow down comforter, propped Isabelle's borrowed portable DVD player on her desk, hiked up her blue Middlebury sweatpants, and sluggishly picked up the phone — was, "So what's the binge of choice?"

"The Holiday," Becca replied glumly. The Kate Winslet-Cameron Diaz-Jude Law flick fit solidly in the "moderately bearable" category. "I've watched it four times."

"Yikes," Harper squealed. "That *is* bad. Is it Stuart?"

213

Becca crawled back into bed, taking the phone with her. She shoved the sleeves of her Fairview High sweatshirt to her elbows, gathered her trusty down comforter up to her chest, and propped the phone on the pillow beside her ear.

That was enough exercise for the day. She'd skipped her Econ class that morning and her prospects for making it to Psych weren't too hot. Ski practice was out of the question.

"It's my parents. Mia says they're back together."

"Your parents hate each other," Harper said definitively.

"Mia swears it's true. She *came here* to tell me about it."

"Mia's in Vermont?"

"I sent her home." Tears filled her eyes.

"Okay," Harper replied decisively, her voice all business. "Tell me what she said."

"My mom moved out of Martin's house. Mia saw my dad helping her move furniture."

The silence on the other end of the line stretched for several seconds. "Weeellll," Harper responded finally, "give me the whole story." Becca did, from Mia showing up in her room, through her tearful accusations, and finally to putting her stepsister on a plane at Middlebury State Airport.

"Mia's not exactly reliable. I mean, running away and showing up at your dorm room is an obvious cry for attention from Daddy."

"I know," Becca sighed. "And she's never liked me, but . . . she took a *train*. There's got to be something to it. That's why I thought, maybe . . ."

"What?"

"Well, you spied on your dad last semester, and I thought . . ."

"That was insanity," Harper reminded her warily. "All that stuff about my dad having an affair was just me being completely insecure and freaky, remember?"

"I know. But, I have to know if this is real."

214

"You could call your mom," Harper stated the obvious.

"Martin said she moved out. I don't even have her phone number." It was so weird. How could her mom have moved without even telling her? It made the possibility that her parents really were together seem more likely. They wouldn't have wanted to tell Becca anything until it was somewhat settled, and it sounded like everything had gone down fast and furious.

"Did Martin say anything else? Anything about your dad?"

"I didn't ask." How could she have asked Martin about that? It wasn't like they were close. And he'd seemed so insanely upset.

"All you would have to do" — Becca tried to pitch the idea in the most effortless-sounding way possible — "is hang out outside my dad's apartment for a few hours. See if my mom's there. Or follow her home from work and see where she goes."

"What does Stuart say about all of this?"

Now it was Becca's turn to pause. He hadn't said a whole lot. She hadn't given him the chance to. Ever since she'd put Mia on the plane two days ago, she'd been hiding out in her room. Not because she didn't want to see him, she just didn't want to see anyone. She felt too . . . something she couldn't quite put her finger on. Maybe she just didn't want him to see her so thrown by something or maybe she just wasn't ready to share this kind of stuff with him. It was too . . . awful. Too ugly.

She also felt stupid for letting herself believe that maybe, finally, her family wasn't going be a complete disaster anymore. In her Stuart-stupor, she'd allowed herself to forget that she lived in a family of centipedes — everyone had thousands of squiggly little psychic feet, and every foot had a fucked-up shoe with very flimsy laces, dangling dangerously, just waiting to drop. Complaisance was the enemy, and letting her guard down was not allowed. But she had. So of course the falling shoe was now of the military-boot variety — steel-toed, heavy, and very painful upon contact.

"He's been really great," she hedged, staring up at the ceiling.

"Bec," Harper began carefully, "you know this isn't your fault, right?"

"Yeah, of course," Becca replied too quickly.

"Becca Winsberg . . ." There was an almost parental warning in Harper's voice that sent Becca over the edge. She took a deep breath and, despite her best efforts at self-control, started sobbing.

"Of *course* it's my fault. If it's true, it's totally my fault! I made them act like they didn't hate each other!"

"Sweetie," Harper comforted her, "your parents are screwed up. That's not your fault. Nothing they do is your fault. You gave them a chance to act like grown-ups and instead they acted like idiots. If it's true."

"Please, Harp." Becca hated herself for being so desperate. So pathetic. "You have to find out for me. I can't figure out what to do or how to feel until I know. And I can't ask them. I can't call my dad's house. What am I supposed to say? 'Hey, is Melissa there? Why not? Because you're trying to ruin my fucking life again??!!'"

She pulled herself back from the brink of hysteria. "Sorry."

"Okay." Harper exhaled. "I'll do it. Meanwhile, does Isabelle have any Xanax?"

Becca laughed, wiping her tear-streaked face with her corner of her comforter. "Thanks, Harp."

"It's good material for my future novels. Really, I should be thanking *you*."

By the time Becca got off the phone, she felt good enough to swap out *The Holiday* for *Guess Who's Coming to Dinner*. It wasn't *Woman of the Year,* but at least it was Hepburn and Tracy. That meant she was feeling better. And better, at least for the moment, was all she could ask for.

Back home in Boulder, Kate had hated IM'ing. Could anything be more boring than exchanging one-liners with people you would call on the phone if you actually had anything important to say? Not to mention the inconvenience issue. If she was online, she had a purpose for being there — checking e-mail, researching for a paper, getting updates from MSNBC.com on the latest world news. IMs were just irritating interruptions.

Her ex-boyfriend Jared had been the worst culprit. "W'sup?" would suddenly appear with an annoying high-pitched *bleep*. "Nothing," she'd usually type back, then add pointedly: "Working." The intended brush-off never stopped him. One time he'd actually wanted to have *IM sex*! Breaking up with Jared was definitely the best thing she'd ever done. Or him breaking up with her. "Taking a break," he'd called it at the airport. Whatever. If it was a break, it was a permanent one, and she was glad of it.

At this moment, however, her feelings about instant messaging were completely transformed. Leave it to Habiba to figure out a way to maneuver through the web of the Web so that she and Kate could have what proved to be the next best thing to a conversation. She'd sent Kate instructions in her last letter, as well as a suggested date and time for them to "meet." Since it was eleven hours earlier in Boulder than in Ethiopia, it was after midnight Habiba's time — about an hour later than they'd planned to begin their trans-oceanic chat. Kate had intended to be prompt, but her ride to Bahar Dar was with a village elder who didn't quite appreciate her need for punctuality, and whose ancient German sedan couldn't go more than twenty miles an hour anyway.

She'd arrived at the Internet café late, then had to quickly follow Habiba's step-by-step instructions — which had included downloading software, then winding her way through a variety of free Web sites. Finally, she'd sent her first message ("**You there, H?**"), and gotten a big yellow smiley face with an "**I'm here!**" in return.

They were talking! And this conversation was anything but inconsequential. Habiba was dying to hear about Angatu. Kate had written so much about the younger girl in her letters that Habiba said she felt like she knew her. Habiba had even sent a letter to the director of her former orphanage in Addis Ababa, asking the woman for help in tracking down Masarat. It was a long shot, but it was all she could think to do, she'd explained, and she wanted to do *something*.

"I think it's really great, what you're doing," the screen read. "Angatu's lucky to have met you!"

Kate smiled, imagining her little sister sitting in her bedroom at home with her ankles crossed, at the antique sewing table she'd converted into a desk for her laptop. Her always-tidy room would be completely dark at this hour, except for the green-shaded reading lamp on the corner of her oak desk. She'd be barefoot, wearing her pajamas — probably pink sweats and a gray Harvard t-shirt. Kate felt a pang of yearning to be with her little sister again.

"I miss you a lot," Kate typed. "I can't wait to get home so we can hang out."

The screen bleeped.

"You'll be going off to Harvard! I'll hardly see you!"

Kate knew that was true. What she would give to have gone back in time four years to fix the mistakes she'd made. Which was probably the main reason it was so important to her to reunite Angatu and *her* sister.

"I was thinking of trying to get mom and dad to let me come visit you."

Kate blinked at the words. It was last thing she'd expected Habiba to say. "You'd want to come back?" She pressed "send." Their parents had asked her several times if she wanted to visit Ethiopia, and Habiba had always said no. What had changed?

There was a long pause before a response appeared. "There's a lot of stuff I miss. I guess." Kate read the words aloud quietly. "Maybe I'm just not scared anymore. I think I felt like if I went back maybe

218

I wouldn't get to come home again. It doesn't really make sense — it's not like mom and dad were gonna ditch me or something!"

Kate's heart hurt. "Of course they wouldn't!" Then she added, "You don't feel that way anymore, do you?"

"Nope" came the swift reply. "This is home. This is where my family is. Hey — did you have Joe Macintosh as your PSAT tutor?"

Kate laughed out loud at the change of subject. For all her emotional maturity, Habiba was definitely fourteen.

"Yes. How bad is his breath?????"

A seriously unhappy-looking little yellow emoticon popped up along with "I keep asking him if he wants gum."

"Don't ever let him drive you home. His car smells worse!"

"Good to know. Thx!"

Kate had one other thing to discuss with her younger sister. She'd finally come up with a plan to expose Mulugeta that wouldn't compromise Abebech. No one would know where the information had come from. Mulugeta might suspect, but without proof he wouldn't be able to do anything about it. Once the villagers knew he wasn't who he said he was — he was just a rich man using his power to step on the throats of those less fortunate — they wouldn't listen to him anymore. As Abebech had explained, shame was a powerful social tool in any society, but in Ethiopia — a deeply religious country — it would be even more powerful. Kate wasn't above getting down and dirty if it meant saving just one life. The look on Rebekkah's face when she'd revealed that her baby had died was all the motivation she needed.

"If I send you something, could you translate it into Amharic for me?"

"Sure. What is it?"

As Kate started to fill Habiba in on the details, she realized she was grinning to herself. Taking on Mulugeta was . . . kind of *fun*. And doing it with her baby sister was even better. Plus it felt good not being intimidated. She was finding a creative solution to a difficult problem — exactly what Darby *couldn't* do. She only hoped it worked, because if it didn't, she could be landing herself, Abebech, and Dorothé, not to mention Darby, Jean-Pierre, and Jessica, in a world of trouble. But she wouldn't think about that, not when she was having such a good time hatching a plot with Habiba. Wasn't that what sisters were supposed to do?

Even sisters who grew up half a world apart.

"I can't believe I'm doing this." Judd stared at Harper through an enormous pair of silver mirrored sunglasses he'd pilfered from the Rainy Day Books Café lost-and-found box.

"Trail mix?" she offered, shaking a plastic bag of mixed nuts and granola. "Nuts have the good fat."

Lately, she'd been putting more effort into losing her non-freshman fifteen, which included substituting potato chips and the Rainy Day blueberry muffins with healthier snacks. So far she'd lost two pounds.

He picked out two almonds and chomped down. "You're avoiding the subject at hand."

They'd been sitting in Judd's teal-colored Saturn for the last forty-five minutes, watching as a trail of divorcée-types entered and exited the seventies-era apartment building where, rumor had it, Becca's mother had taken up residence. In her father's apartment. Harper had been trying to ignore the obvious déjà-vu nature of the situation. A few months earlier, she'd dragged Judd into her paranoid fear that her dad was having an affair with the woman she'd dubbed Red-Headed Tramp, forcing him to stalk Mr. Waddle with her. His car still had the dent in the front-right fender that came from the ensuing short-lived car chase.

"This time, our stakeout has nothing to do with my insanity," she insisted. "I'm doing a duty."

Even though Becca had been a less-than-attentive friend since achieving her Dream of falling in love, Harper couldn't turn her back on her in a time of crisis. True, she could have tried to gather evidence of the supposed affair going on between Becca's parents on her own. But she had an ulterior motive when she asked Judd to provide his services, hoping some solid alone time might yield information about Amelia. He hadn't said much about their cocoa date, and Harper hadn't felt like she could pry. But for some stupid reason she'd found herself waking up in the middle of the night, wondering if anything had happened between them. Not to mention . . . they hadn't taken advantage of their "benefits" since the blizzard that day.

A long moment passed. Judd took off his sunglasses. Harper ate more trail mix. She couldn't decide if they were sharing a companionable silence or if neither knew what to say to the other.

"So . . . how's Amelia?" She leaned forward as a middle-aged woman who resembled Becca's mom strolled out of the apartment building carrying a tennis racket. False alarm. Last Harper had heard, Becca's mom hadn't had a boob job.

Judd studied the photos Becca had e-mailed her so he'd know whom he was looking for. "Good, I guess."

Another nonanswer. Screw that. "Any progress on the virginity front?" As a friend with benefits, it was her *right* to know what was happening in his love life.

He put his hands over his face and groaned. "I *really* don't want to talk about this."

"Why?" She forced herself to close the bag of trail mix and stuff it in the glove compartment. Healthy or not, the stuff was packed with calories.

"It's just . . . weird." Outside, it was getting dark. Cocooned in the car, her face in shadows, Harper felt freer than usual to say what was on her mind.

"Because we make out?"

"I don't know . . . yeah." He turned to her. "Nothing happened, okay?"

"Okay. Whatever. I was just curious." She patted his jeans-covered knee. "Better luck next time."

Harper tried not to identify the little leap of her heart as joy. Or maybe it was joy. Not because she was relieved Judd and Amelia didn't hook up — she didn't care about that. If the little leap *was* joy, its source came from her satisfaction at her evolving communication skills with the opposite sex. If Mr. Finelli ever talked to her again, maybe she wouldn't be such a stuttering idiot.

"If I say something will you promise not to get mad?" Judd asked, brushing an almond crumb off of his black Rainy Day Café sweatshirt.

"I promise I won't hit you." It was the best she could do. Getting mad was an involuntarily reaction.

"When you were so convinced your dad was cheating on your mom, it was really all about your writer's block. True?"

She had no idea how the question related to Amelia. "True," she admitted. Humiliating, but true.

"I think this preoccupation with catching Becca's mom and dad together . . . It might be about you not wanting to deal with what's going on at home with your dad." So it *didn't* relate to Amelia. Fine. He leaned as far away from her as the compact car would allow. Apparently her word that she wouldn't hit him wasn't assurance enough.

"That's crazy." She opened the glove compartment and took out the bag of trail mix again. A few more bites couldn't do *too* much damage to her thighs. "I'm telling you, Becca *asked* me to do this."

"I'm starting to think you and all your friends suffer from a case of severe disassociation."

"I hope she's wrong. She's *probably* wrong. But I promised I'd sit here until midnight. And that's exactly what I'm going to do."

"And explain why it's a *bad* thing if her parents have rekindled their romance? Most kids with divorced parents fantasize all the time about their mom and dad getting back together." Judd took the bag of trail mix and helped himself to several more almonds.

"It's complicated." Talking about her own stuff with Judd was one thing. She was allowed to say whatever she wanted to about herself. But she wasn't about to spill the details of her especially sensitive friend's inner life with *anyone*. That was sacred.

Judd nodded, apparently ready to drop the subject. "So you're not upset about your dad?"

An increasingly familiar knot formed in her stomach. It was the one she got every time she pictured her father lying in bed, trying to pretend that nothing hurt. "He's totally going to be okay. It's, like, so not a big deal."

"Well, if you ever want to talk about stuff at home, I'm here." He smiled and ran his fingers through his even messier than usual black curly hair.

"So noted." They were looking at each other, and it felt like they were going to kiss, but in a way that was different from the other times they'd kissed.

Before Harper could overanalyze that particular thought, a navy blue Volvo station wagon pulled into the complex parking lot. She clutched Judd's arm.

"Becca's dad has that car."

He did a quick check of the photo printout then followed Harper's line of vision. It was completely dark now, but the lights in the parking lot illuminated the Volvo. Mr. Winsberg got out and shut the car door. Then the passenger side opened and Becca's mom appeared.

"It's them!" Harper's pulse quickened. The whole time they'd been camped out in front of the building, she'd been assuming nothing would actually happen.

Becca's mom's auburn hair was hanging loose around her shoulders and she was wearing high heels. She was laughing at something Mr. Winsberg said as she sashayed around the car and took his arm. Well, that sort of physical contact didn't necessarily mean anything; even Becca said her parents had gotten along better than usual at Parents' Weekend. Maybe they were getting together in a friendly manner to discuss what assholes they'd been to their daughter all these years and figure out a good way to make amends.

Except then they kissed. Not a chaste peck on the cheek but rather an end-of-a-romantic-comedy-when-all-four-dozen-misunderstandings-are-resolved movie kiss. Tongues were definitely being used. Unless they'd jumped on the "friends with benefits" bandwagon, the Winsbergs were getting back together.

"Holy shit!" Judd peered through the window, the bag of trail mix forgotten in his lap.

Harper reached into the backseat and fumbled in the pocket of her parka for her Motorola cell. She snapped it open and pressed on the camera feature. In a matter of seconds, she focused and clicked the picture, though apparently she didn't need to hurry. Becca's parents showed no sign of unlocking lips anytime soon. She turned away, having seen enough.

"They're really going at it," Judd commented, as though this were Monday Night Football. "Wow."

Harper stared at the lit screen of her phone. She was tempted to delete the picture and report to Becca that she hadn't seen anything. Her friend was finally happy! Why unnecessarily complicate that with something as dicey as a possible family reunion?

Judd sighed and leaned back in his seat. "They're heading inside the building. Looks like they have every intention of continuing inside."

"Eew. Those are Becca's *parents* you're talking about."

He grabbed two of the belt loops on her brown Levi's corduroys and pulled her toward him. "Kind of got me in a mood."

Harper felt her cheeks grow hot. "Here?"

"Why not?" He leaned in. "Nobody's watching."

She knew she should call Becca and tell her about the evidence she'd gotten personally. She *did* have to tell. If Becca found out Harper had kept this from her, there'd be hell to pay. Then again, it was a lot later in Middlebury. Becca might be asleep or in a heavy makeout session with Stuart. No point in interrupting. Judd's lips looked quite inviting and the poor guy deserved some reward for keeping her company, not to mention solace for striking out with Amelia.

Once Becca saw the photo, the two of them would have a nice long chat with about it. For tonight, her friend duty was officially complete.

So she hauled herself and her non-freshman thirteen into Judd's lap. Tongues would definitely be used.

MASARAT

What I know:
- Age: 18
- 5'3"
- 100 lbs.
- Scar on her left arm
- Left Bahar Dar for
  Addis Ababa four years ago.

What I don't know:
- What she looks like now
- Where she lives
- What she does
- Who she knows
- If she's married with children by now
- If she wants anything to do with Angatu
- If she's still alive

TEN

Kate would never again take for granted the wonders of a washing machine. She scrubbed a dirty white tank top in a plastic tub of soapy water, remembering that she'd actually had some pretty nice underwear when she got to Ethiopia. Now — thanks to the harsh scrubbing-with-a-rock technique — they were largely in tatters. Her poor bras were tinted gray and ratty, and her t-shirts malformed and dingy. Only her jeans and khakis had survived at all intact — they actually seemed to look *better* with wear.

Her hands were another matter as she could never manage to get through a load (was laundry still called a "load" when it was being washed in a red plastic bucket?) without scraping her knuckles on the rock. Then there was the hanging process. With five people in the compound, the clothesline in the yard was always full. And she was hardly going to hang her bras and panties in the front yard for all the world — or at least the village kids who played soccer there every night — to see. It was the one thing she and Jessica agreed on: undergarments deserved a special drying spot. So they'd hung up their own line inside the hut, near the cookstove — which was good because their undergarments dried faster; and bad because they frequently smelled vaguely of dung.

Kate dropped a formerly white, formerly lacy bra into the bucket and added some fresh water and a dollop of soap flakes. *Ah, now* this *is the way to spend a Saturday night.* She rhythmically ran the rock up and down against the silky fabric.

"You've got that hand motion down pat." Darby seemed to realize what he'd said as soon as the words were out of his mouth — and then he saw what she was washing and stopped, several feet away. "I mean . . . uh . . . with the rock."

Kate suspected he was blushing, but with the tan it was hard to tell. She was oddly unembarrassed. Who cared if he saw her underwear? She sloshed the bra around in the water then held it up, letting it drip over the bucket as she inspected it for dirt.

"Did you want something?" she asked, rubbing a sprinkle of soap into an imaginary spot in the B-cup. It may not have been the sexiest bra he'd ever seen, but given how long they'd been in Africa, it was definitely the sexiest bra he'd seen in a while. Maybe it was her turn to be mean to *him* for a change. She knew she looked good — the white natala wrapped around her waist like a short skirt showed off her tan, and her pink t-shirt was just snug enough to stretch across her rounded breasts.

"Yeah. . . ." Darby was looking everywhere but at the dripping brassiere. Kate felt a perverse pleasure in his discomfort. "I just wanted to say it's good you're letting go of getting a well built in Teje. It's not going to happen, and you seem okay with it. That's good. So . . . that's all."

She slowly rinsed the bra in the basin, swishing it back and forth; then she picked it up and shaped the jagged lace gently. Right. He *would* think she'd given up on the Teje well. That was what she wanted him to think. If he got any inkling of her plan, he would try to stop her.

"It was stupid of me to push it." She pretended to be conciliatory. Darby stared at her for a moment, seemingly looking for words.

"I've been hard on you. I know that. It's part of my job. But I may have jumped to certain conclusions early on. . . . If I did, I was wrong."

Oh. Kate's chest was constricting uncomfortably. He looked so . . . *sincere*. And . . . hot in that faded orange t-shirt he wore all the time. His light-brown hair, which hadn't been cut since they got to Ethiopia, was shaggy and windblown, his lower lip was sun-creased, and his eyelashes had faded to a pale blond.

"You have a knack for this." He shoved his hands in his jeans pockets. "You're great with languages, you're not intimidated by anything, you work hard, you've made a place for yourself in the village. . . ."

The more he talked — about her initiative, organizational skills, blah, blah, blah — the more Kate found herself wishing desperately that he would shut up. For one thing, with every word he spoke a fluttering in her stomach grew worse. And that was bad. *Darby* wasn't supposed to say nice things to her. They didn't like each other — he didn't like her, and she didn't like him. That had been their dynamic from the very first day, and Kate didn't want to change that. Certainly not *now*. Because if Darby *didn't* dislike her, and if she didn't dislike Darby . . . well, not telling him about her plans for Mulugeta didn't seem as excusable. She couldn't tell him about that, knowing without a shadow of a doubt he would do everything in his power to stop her — she wasn't going to let that happen.

Then there was Magnus. She hadn't gotten a letter from him in a while and she hadn't sent one in even longer. But still — Magnus was important to her, and she loved him. Or something. She cared about him enough that it wasn't right for her to start having feelings for anyone else, that was for sure.

The fact that Darby didn't seem to totally hate *her* didn't mean she couldn't still hate *him*. Maybe that was best. Was she just supposed to forget about how shitty he'd been to her because all of a sudden he decided he *didn't* think she was a complete waste of space?

That hardly seemed fair. No, she would go on hating him. It was the right thing to do.

Darby seemed to be looking at her expectantly. What had she missed?

He frowned. "So . . . do you want to?"

What? Had he asked her out on a date? Did he actually like her?

"I don't think so," she replied cautiously. "But tell me more."

"Well, you'd have to go through about six months of training, probably in South Africa, and then you'd be qualified to be a team leader —"

"A *team leader*!"

"Rrriight . . . that's what I just said."

"I know! I just . . . you think I'd be a good team leader?" Kate wasn't sure if she was flattered by this suggestion or disappointed that he wasn't asking her out.

Darby shrugged. "Sure. Were you *here* when I was talking to you just now?"

"Sorry, you surprised me."

"Unless you're going to be at Harvard next year." He seemed to be invested, somehow, in her answer.

"I don't know yet." Kate shook her head. "I mean, probably, I guess."

"I'll be back at Princeton," he said. His eyes held hers, and for several seconds neither of them said anything. Then Kate remembered: she didn't like him. She *couldn't* like him. For several reasons. One of which was that he was unlikable — despite all current evidence to the contrary.

Still, she couldn't seem to form any actual words.

"Your bra's dripping," Dorothé observed aloud, coming around the corner. Her eyes drifted back and forth between the two of them.

Kate crumpled the bra into a ball as Darby spun toward the front yard. "Think about it," he said quickly over his shoulder. Then he was gone.

Dorothé raised an eyebrow in her amused, French way.

"Don't be stupid," Kate snapped. "It's *Darby*."

"*Oui, exactement.*" Dorothé grinned, not at all put out by the snapping. She held up a piece of paper. "I heard from my friend in Addis. It's not good news. She knows two girls around that age called Masarat, but neither has a sister. She said she'll keep an eye out, though."

"Thanks." Kate couldn't help but feel disappointed.

"Now, tell me what I interrupted." Dorothé grinned. She looked *très chic* in a long African-print skirt, a tight white t-shirt, and beige sandals.

"Nothing. Seriously. He was just suggesting I train to be a team leader."

"That's quite high praise from him."

"Mmm-hmm." Kate dipped her hands back into the wash basin. Now seemed like a good time to return her attention to her laundry.

"Americans," Dorothé laughed quietly. "You received the package from your sister?"

"Not yet," she replied, feeling a nagging worry in her gut. "I think it'll be a couple weeks."

As her comrade went back to the hut to prepare dinner, Kate thought about Habiba's package. As soon as it arrived, she would use the contents to expose Mulugeta. Even if no one else knew she was responsible — and if all went as planned, no one *would* — Darby would know.

Then he really would hate her. For good. If she had cared about him at all, the thought would have been very upsetting.

So it was a good thing she didn't.

Sophie's eyes snapped open. It was the middle of the night and she'd been dreaming that Trey Benson had tracked her down in line at the Ralph's grocery store on Third Street. In the middle of the frozen food section, he'd gotten on his knees and plead for her mercy. She'd stood there, holding a Lean Cuisine spaghetti-and-meatballs, shocked. Before she could tell him what an undeniable asshole he was, Trey started to cry. Big-time crying with sobs and hyperventilating and everything. A crowd gathered, a member of the paparazzi snapped a close-up photo, but the tears just kept flowing. . . . It was a good dream.

As she stared now at the digital clock beside her bed, she realized the crying hadn't just been a dream. It was 3:15 AM and *someone* was bawling for real. Someone outside J.D.'s bedroom door. She tried to ignore the anguished sounds for a few minutes and go back to sleep, but it wasn't letting up. Finally she threw off her covers and slid out of bed, pulling on a pair of red Juicy sweats with the oversized CU t-shirt she'd worn to bed.

Sophie tiptoed across the room and opened the door a crack. Peeking out, she saw Diaphragm Ellie hunched on the sofa in one of her signature see-through nighties. The girl's face was buried in her hands, and she was wailing like a wounded rhino. *This is not my responsibility,* she told herself. Most likely, Sam and Ellie had had some kind of fight. She'd probably turned into a total stuck-up bitch since she got the part in *Heartland.* He'd called her on it, and she'd told him he was a nobody loser in the heat of the moment. Then he'd dumped her ass and thrown her out of his bedroom. Now Ellie was crying her eyes out — as loudly as possible — in the hopes that Sam would emerge from his room, say he was sorry for whatever, and beg her to come back to bed for make-up sex.

But Sophie knew two things Ellie obviously did not. One, Sam was extremely stubborn. Two, he was an extremely heavy sleeper. If he'd zonked out before Ellie started her crying jag, he'd never know about it until he woke up in the morning and saw her red, puffy eyes. Sophie sighed. She might as well go out there and offer a shoulder. Unless she got Ellie to stop sobbing, she could kiss the rest of her night's sleep goodbye.

"Uh . . . hey," she greeted her. "Are you okay?" Sophie noted the girl was in dire need of a tissue. There was snot everywhere. It was seriously gross.

"I — I'm sorry . . . did I w-wake you up?"

Uh . . . yeah. "No . . . I, um, had to pee. Too much Diet Coke before bed."

Ellie just nodded and went back to crying. "You and Sam had a fight?" she prompted. The sooner she started her comforting routine, the sooner she could go back to dreaming about Trey Benson's ultimate humiliation.

She shook her head, unable to speak. Jesus, this was seriously over-the-top. The girl either needed antidepressants or she was a better actress than Sophie had assumed. She hadn't seen tears like this since the funeral of Storm Chase, a character in her once-favorite soap *Cloud Bursts*.

"I can't just stand here and watch you bawl." Sophie decided a dose of fake tough love was in order. "Tell me what's wrong."

Ellie managed to catch her breath for two seconds. "I can't . . . it's too embarrassing."

"You dropped your diaphragm again?" *Great.* "And Sam saw?"

She was rewarded with the tiniest smile. Then the tears started springing out again. Sophie sat down beside the new Paige Dalloway and grudgingly put an arm around her bony shoulders. "I promise you'll feel better if you let it out."

She knew it was the kind of thing her mom said to reluctant patients. Even in therapy, people often didn't want to voice out loud whatever was bothering them. According to Angela, they were usually too ashamed. Until she moved to LA and met Trey, Sophie had never truly understood shame. Now she got it all too well.

Ellie glanced over at her. "Promise not to tell anyone?"

"Sure." Sophie's curiosity was actually piqued. This should be

235

juicy. Naked pictures on the Internet? A soft-core porn video in her past? Ellie used to be Elliot? What?

"They wrote a new scene for the pilot of *Heartland*. Paige tells her mom she hates her and it's, like, totally emotional. It shoots tomorrow and I *know* I'm going to totally bomb it."

"That's what all this is? Nerves?" Sophie had heard of people barfing before a major scene, but this sounded pretty ridiculous.

"One of the other actors in the cast, Frazier Jung, heard me rehearsing in the makeup trailer today. When no one was listening he told me I sucked and he said they were going to fire me like they did the other girl." She paused, her face beginning to crumple again. "And he's right. I *do* suck. I've never even had acting lessons. I was modeling and all this just sort of . . . happened."

Sophie tried to ignore the happy feeling that was a result of someone telling Ellie she might get fired, and she also tried to ignore the burning resentment she felt at the idea that she'd been beaten out by a girl who'd never even done a scene study. She was, after all, trying to be more mature these days.

"Frazier sounds like a shit. He's probably mad because he was doing it with the other actress or something and she dumped him before they fired her. Ignore him." Sophie patted her on back as she averted her gaze from the stream of snot coming out of Ellie's nose.

"Sophie, I'm *terrible*." She wiped her nose. "I mean, I love my mom. I can't imagine hating her or anyone else. It's like, there's just nothing to dig from, y'know?" She sighed deeply. "My life's been too blessed."

Sophie really wanted to hit her. "Do the speech right now. I'm sure it's not as bad as you think."

"Now? I can't." She still sounded miserable, but the tears had stopped. What bothered Sophie the most was that even with puffy eyes and mucus all over her face, Ellie was gorgeous.

"Do it," she ordered. "Or I'm telling Sam."

Ellie took one look at her and seemed to register that this wasn't an empty threat. She cleared her throat and began. "Mom, you don't care about anything except hating my dad. You're bitter and dried up and a menace. I want to love you, but you make it impossible —"

"Stop! You're right. You suck." It was true. The Diaphragm Dropper delivered her lines like a bored robot. She'd seen better acting from dogs. *Significantly* better. And there was *a lot* of eyebrow action going on.

"I know!" Ellie inhaled deeply, ready to start a fresh round of crying.

"But I'll make you better." Sophie hadn't meant to make the offer, it had just come out. "By tomorrow morning, you'll be Hilary Swank."

"Really?" Her eyes were filled with such gratitude that she almost liked her. "I'll be your best friend forever."

Sophie nodded, sincerely hoping that last part wouldn't come to pass. First, she'd break her of the eyebrow acting, and then she'd help Ellie find a way into the scene, explaining it to her in a way that would help her understand Paige's character and what she was going through. Once she could put herself in Paige's shoes, the words would come out naturally. And Sophie knew exactly where to start. With the scene's core emotion. In this case, that emotion was hate. Something she knew just a little bit about.

"Let me tell you a story about Trey Benson . . . ," Sophie began. If she couldn't go back to crushing Trey in her dream, she might as well use his evil toward something good. Or, at least, mature.

When Becca was a little kid, her parents had owned a cabin on a lake outside Boulder. She remembered virtually nothing about it — not the roaring fire she'd seen in pictures, or the three-pound bass her father claimed she'd caught with her kiddie pole. She didn't even remember being with her parents as a couple. The only thing — literally the *only* thing — she remembered was the dead baby bat.

She had never seen a bat before, so when her mother screamed — *screeched* would be more accurate — four-year-old Becca had come running. She couldn't identify the little black creature resting on the cedar shingle in her mother's hand — although she figured the nail spiked through its chest probably wasn't a good thing. Apparently, her mom had been hammering a cedar shingle into the side of the cabin when she'd heard a squeak. Pulling the shingle back, she discovered she'd nailed right through the little bat's heart.

The bat was tiny — maybe three inches long, with a black mouse head and paper-thin wings that beat weakly a couple of times, with a barely audible *thwap, thwap* against the shingle. And then it died.

That was all Becca remembered.

Tonight Becca felt like that bat. She'd just been minding her own business, hiding out in her own private darkness, when her parents had come along and stuck a spike in her chest. But instead of lying down and dying — which was what she felt like doing — she had these annoying people in her life called "friends." And they insisted on forcing her out into the open regardless of the fact that she felt like that poor little bat.

She'd been fine through the biggest ski meet of the year and she'd actually been fine for the past few days while she went to her classes, made out with Stuart, had lunch with Isabelle and their ski team friends, nodded as everyone made plans for that weekend's Winter Carnival, and skied her guts out at practice.

However, since she'd talked to Harper, every moment of "fine" was an act. Her parents *were* back together. Harper had seen her mom go into her dad's apartment and she'd even seen them *kiss*. Thanks to modern technology, *Becca* had seen them kiss. Melissa definitely didn't live with her dad anymore.

Harper, Isabelle, and Stuart all had encouraged her to call her parents, and she knew she should, but every time Becca started to reach for the phone her fingers refused to dial the numbers. It wasn't that she was angry. Or maybe she was. She couldn't tell what she was feeling exactly, except that it didn't feel good.

The only place she felt almost normal was on the slopes. There, she was so on her game that she was almost reckless. Coach Maddix had been impressed with her time in today's meet and congratulated her on the win — but his praise had been tempered with a hard hand wrapped around her elbow. "Next time you win, do it safely," he'd said grimly. "I want you around next season." Becca had nodded mutely.

She'd been ready to climb into bed after the meet, but Winter Carnival was the biggest weekend of the year at Middlebury, and neither Isabelle nor Stuart were going to let her miss it. So she'd tossed on her stand-by black Anthropologie skirt and silver off-the-shoulder sweater, and put on a smile when Stuart showed up at her door to take her and Isabelle to the party.

Stuart had been great, she had to admit, leaning against him in the crowded party. He'd given her space without ever letting her forget he was there for her. He'd been completely nonjudgmental about her parents, all the while assuring her that whatever they did was in no way her fault.

"Do you want to dance?" he suggested, leaning down to be heard.

Isabelle had long since disappeared, and it seemed as if all two thousand Middlebury students had piled into the student center. A band played a steady stream of 90s hits, and somehow everyone seemed to have smuggled in some kind of alcohol to the school-sponsored event.

Becca didn't want to dance, but figured she should. If she'd actually been fine, she would have danced, so she'd dance. In a minute.

"I'm going to run to the bathroom," she yelled up at him. "Be right back."

The line for the bathroom was eternal. By the time she made it into the tiny bathroom, peed, and wound her way back through the crowd to where she'd left Stuart, she was in even less of a partying mood. To make matters worse, he'd disappeared. Where was he? Becca craned her head in every direction. Had he gone to the bathroom?

Then she saw him. On the dance floor. Dancing with a thin, wispy-looking blonde. Becca had seen her before — Middlebury wasn't exactly a huge school. She didn't know the girl's name, which meant she was probably older. Maybe she was in Stuart's year. Watching her boyfriend dance with the blonde gave Becca a sick something — certainly not a feeling, because she wasn't having any of those aside from "fine" — in her stomach. The girl put her hand on Stuart's shoulder as they danced, moving into him as she said something into his ear. Stuart laughed and took the blonde's hand. *He took her hand.* In Becca's mind, it happened in slow motion — Stuart laughing, then reaching out, taking wispy blonde's hand in his, leaning toward her. . . .

The paper-thin wings of her heart beat weakly. *Thwap . . . thwap.* And then stopped.

The next thing she knew she was in her room, crying so uncontrollably she couldn't stand. She crumpled to a heap on the floor, arms wrapped around her stomach, back heaving.

They *were* all the same. They said they loved you and then they fell in love with someone else. Her father had done it. It had only been a matter of time until Stuart did it, too. She'd known it all along — she'd just been fooling herself in those rare moments when she believed Stuart was different. Maybe he wasn't in love with the other girl yet, but that hardly mattered. There was no point in pretending anymore.

Becca had tried to believe. She really had.

She just couldn't.

"Water. It's essential."

"Water. Why wait?"

"Fight for your rights. Free water now."

Harper shook her head. "Sounds like the water is being held unfairly in prison or something," she told Habiba as she ladled rich mushroom soup into the twelve matching brown mugs Mrs. Foster had lined up on their marble countertop.

They were in the Fosters' kitchen, where Harper was prepping soup and helping Habiba brainstorm catchy slogans for the fliers she was making for Kate's latest well project in Ethiopia. Mr. and Mrs. Foster had hired the Waddle team to cater a dinner party, saying they were both too stressed to cook themselves. But Harper couldn't help but wonder if the party was really just an excuse to throw her mother some business. The fact that her dad was out of work for the foreseeable future wasn't exactly a secret around town. She was torn between feeling grateful and resenting being a charity case. None of which she planned to tell her mother or anyone else.

Beebs sighed as she studied the flier she'd written in Amharic. "I know Kate really wants to impress Darby with these. I just want to come through for her, you know?"

Harper couldn't imagine her own sister worrying about "coming through" for her. Amy flitted through life oblivious to other people's angst. Like lately. She'd pop in and out of her parents' room, filling in their dad on the details of her day, but she never offered to make him dinner or help out around the house. Did Amy even care that Harper should be locked in her bathroom working on her book right now instead of helping out their mother? No, she did not. She was too busy keeping up her cheerleading duties and maintaining her 24/7 grooming schedule.

"This Darby guy is a clown," Harper grumbled. "Where does he get off telling Kate what she can and can't do?"

Beebs touched the brass beads of her choker necklace, which meant she was thinking. "Darby's definitely challenging," she declared finally. "Challenging can be good."

"Living without running water and electricity is challenging enough. She doesn't need some know-it-all breathing down her neck."

"I'm pretty sure she likes him."

"You think everyone likes everyone." Which was true. Of course she was usually right.

"We'll see." Habiba helped transfer the mugs to one of the five hundred antique silver platters the Fosters had lying around their house before she headed up to her room to redo the flier for Harper's inspection. Beebs was clearly better than Kate had ever been at getting out of participating in their parents' intellectual dinner parties in which everyone argued for hours in impenetrable academia-speak.

As Harper carried the tray of steaming hot soup out to the now-seated guests, she passed her mom, who was coming in with the empty appetizer platters. "Did you call and check on your dad?"

Immediate pang of guilt. "No . . . I, uh, thought you were going to." It was lame to pass the blame, but she didn't want to admit she'd gotten caught up helping Habiba punch up her fliers when she should have been worrying about her own father.

"I'm sure he's fine," Mrs. Waddle responded with a smile. "I'll call after I plate the salads."

Jeez. Her mother had been positively *cheerful* since her dad's accident. It was almost as if she were *enjoying* having her husband laid up in bed, completely helpless. There was probably some kind of psychological term for her attitude, but Harper found it too disturbing to think about. She wished the woman would get frustrated or fed up or scared or generally annoyed once in a while like the rest of the world.

After nearly two hours of serving and clearing plates in the dining room while her mom dished up food in the kitchen, Harper slipped upstairs to check out Beebs's new flier. She imagined Kate thousands of miles away, digging wells and arguing with the mysterious, stubborn, and probably devastatingly dashing Mr. Darby.

"Mr. Finelli asked me how you were doing at school today," Habiba commented as she turned off her iMac. Her bedroom was almost as orderly as Kate's, but she'd covered an entire wall with Foster family photos and a poster of Johnny Depp.

"He did?" Harper tried not to care, but the very mention of Mr. Finelli made her feel tingly with a weird combination of embarrassment and excitement.

"He heard about your dad. Wanted me to tell you he wished him a speedy recovery."

"You're just telling me this now?" Not that it was such an important fact that Harper had needed to know about it *immediately,* but when she was given a message for a person she tried to pass that message on as quickly as possible. It was the polite thing to do.

Habiba shrugged. "Not like you care about Mr. Finelli anymore, right?"

"Right."

She got out of Beebs's room before the girl could start one of her intense grilling sessions. The last thing she felt like doing was analyzing the current state of her feelings for her former teacher. She just wanted to get home and put in some quality time with her laptop. Harper entered the kitchen expecting to find her mom efficiently covering leftovers with Saran wrap, but the sink was still full of dirty dishes, and half-empty glasses of wine were scattered everywhere. Something was wrong with this picture.

She wandered through the Fosters' house in search of her delinquent mother. Mr. Foster sat with a lingering guest in the living room, discussing whether they felt various junior professors should be given tenure. She tiptoed past. Knowing Kate's dad, he'd pull her into a lengthy discussion on the topic, regardless of her absolute lack of knowledge or interest in it. As she neared the cozy library with its built-in mahogany bookshelves and leather armchairs, she heard low, murmuring voices. Her mother and Mrs. Foster were talking about something, but she couldn't make out the words.

I should just go in. But something stopped her. Instead, she hesitated just outside the slightly open door and peered inside. Her mother was standing near the window, and Mrs. Foster had her arms around her.

"I just don't know what we're going to do. I don't have much money coming in . . . and with Harper hopefully going to college next year . . ."

"It'll work out, Cindy. It always does."

Her mother nodded, but tears were dripping down her face. "I don't want the girls to see how worried I am. They don't need to deal with this."

"I know, I know . . . just let it out." Mrs. Foster handed her a tissue and gently patted her on the back.

Harper's insides twisted painfully. Her mother wasn't goddamn cheerful — she was *anguished.* Only she'd kept it hidden, day after day, for the sake of their family. She'd seen her mother cry a few times, like when their dog, Alfred, died, and during some movies, even once when she'd burned herself on the oven. But this . . . it was different. It was horrible.

She couldn't take it.

Harper stepped away from the door and darted back toward the kitchen. She'd deal with the dishes and the Saran wrap and whatever else needed dealing with. And she'd do more, a lot more. From now on, Harper's Dream of writing the Next Great American Novel would have to be second priority, and there was no way she was going to NYU, no matter what the letter said when it came in

April. She'd been self-centered and selfish and totally absorbed in her own life. But those deluded days were over. Her job now was to help her family. And that's exactly what she would do.

Because she never, everfuckingever, wanted to see her mom cry like that again.

△ **AOL** mail

From: waddlewords@aol.com
To: katherinef@ubc.edu, rebeccawinsberg@middlebury.edu, herdivaness@aol.com
Subject: Fringe Benefits

Hi all—

Given the fact that privacy is merely an illusion when it comes to communicating via e-mail, I am not going to share the Judd update over the Internet. The last thing I need are the sordid details published on Page Six of the *New York Post* someday when I'm an award-winning author.

Suffice it to say there has been a development, about which I will fill in each of you when you call me (so call!). Knowing all of you intimately as I do, I anticipate you will inevitably ask certain questions upon receiving said update. Let me answer those questions now, so that we don't have to converse too long on this topic when we could be discussing more important things, such as what I should wear when I race from my triumph at the National Book Awards to the Pulitzer Prize ceremony. Without further ado—

Question: Am I weeping into my hot chocolate?
Answer: No.

Question: Am I totally and unequivocally relieved?
Answer: Yes.

Question: Do I give a shit whatsoever?
Answer: No.

All will be made clear in time.

Thank you and Godspeed,
Harper E. Waddle

ELEVEN

"*Obi* is not a word." Sam pointed at the three light wooden tiles Sophie had laid on the Scrabble board.

"Duh. It's the sash thingie that keeps a kimono closed." During her dark weeks on the bus, she'd taken up the *LA Times* crossword puzzle. *Obi* was the answer to a clue at least once a week.

Sophie had planned to spend her night off doing home beauty treatments. She hadn't had time lately for her usual maintenance routine of facials, salt-scrub pedicures, manicures, and exfoliating, and it was starting to show. At work yesterday Celeste had pointed to her gold strappy sandals and implied customers might lose their appetite if they caught sight of the oh-so-scaly feet peeking out of them. But just as she'd settled on the couch with a bottle of Big Apple red polish and a pair of Revlon clippers, Sam had dropped the Scrabble game in front of her, issuing a silent challenge. She knew he never would have deigned to hang with her if Diaphragm Ellie hadn't had some kind of *Heartland* cast dinner, but she wasn't going to run away from a challenge. Within five minutes, her Sally Hansen pedicure and peach facial scrub were forgotten.

"Fine. Obi." Sam wrote down her points on the gray Mojito scratch pad she'd provided at the start of their game. He looked absolutely ridiculous in the black-and-white ice-cream-cone-patterned cotton pajama bottoms his grandma had sent from New Jersey, which was seriously boosting her confidence. "But it's a stupid word."

"You realize I'm kicking your ass." She grinned. No doubt he'd thought Sophie Bushell would be a lightweight. But thanks to Harper's and Kate's insistence on monthly Scrabble tournaments last year, she knew her way around the board, whether she wanted to or not.

"I realize no such —" Sam broke off as every light in the apartment suddenly lost power at once. "What the hell?"

They were sitting in total darkness. No whirring of the air conditioner, no ticking of the clock that was plugged in over the stove, no sound of the television that apartment 3E blared twenty-four hours a day. Aside from horns honking on the street outside, it was completely quiet.

Sam was already at the living room bay window. "Total blackout," he announced, almost happily. "No lights as far as I can see. Could be hours before we have power."

Of course this would happen on her night off. "You sound *glad*," she accused. Now what were they going to do?

"I happen to find blackouts very relaxing," he informed her as he started digging in the front closet. "It's the city's way of reminding us all to take a break and enjoy the simpler things." He tossed her a half-burned candle. "Pretend we're camping."

"I hate camping." Which wasn't entirely true. She liked the s'mores and the bonding, but she hated the random animal noises, the cold, and the hard ground. She'd only agree to camp up in the mountains with Becca, Harper, and Kate if they let her bring an Aerobed, earplugs, and a down pillow.

Half an hour later, Sophie decided LA-style camping wasn't so bad. Sam had pulled out some cheese and crackers and a bottle of red wine leftover from Ellie's party. In the dim candlelight, she couldn't see that the carpet was stained or that the furniture was frayed. The apartment looked sort of . . . beautiful. So did Sam (pajama bottoms aside), although it was only the glass-and-a-half of wine that made her notice — right?

"I just realized I've been tensing my back muscles for the last two months." She lay back on the couch and snuggled into the cushions.

"The headache I've had for three weeks just went away," he responded, rolling his neck contentedly. "We need to de-stress more often."

"More often? How 'bout *ever?*"

Sam sliced himself a thick piece of Gouda and plopped it on a water cracker. "I'm thinking of leaving."

"To go where? The streetlights aren't even working." She only felt *slightly* hurt that he wanted to abandon their urban camping session.

He chewed for a few moments, brushing a few crumbs off of his black Bruce Springsteen "Nebraska" t-shirt. "Not this second. I'm thinking of *leaving,* leaving. For good."

She choked on her wine. "As in, leave *Los Angeles?*" What the hell was Sam talking about?

"Maybe."

"In other words, you're giving up." It's what he would have said to her, had she made the same declaration.

There were both quiet for a few seconds. She knew what she said must have sounded bitchy, but it was true. Outside, there was a long, loud squeal, and two cars honked. Finally, Sam grinned. "Gotcha."

"You were kidding?"

"Of course." His face was in shadow, but from what she could see, he didn't look like he'd been joking.

Sophie suddenly felt cold and alone. Sam couldn't leave California. He was . . . well, not *all* she had. There was her job. And

Celeste. And Matthew Feldman. She had her car. And some cool clothes. But Sam was . . . What was he? Her sometimes nemesis, her sometimes shelter from the storm. He was what Harper had said. He was *real*.

"Why are you even *thinking* about this?" she demanded, taking a big gulp from her Pottery Barn wine goblet.

"I just said, I'm *not*. It was a joke, okay?" He was scratching the stubble of his pale, patchy beard, which she'd learned from numerous poker games meant he was lying.

"It's because you didn't get that ad, isn't it?" Sam had been up for a Carl's Jr. commercial a few weeks ago, but he'd lost the part to scruffier, brunette version of himself. The ad had been part of a larger national campaign for an LA-based fast-food franchise, and the job would have paid his rent for a year and a half.

He shook his head slowly. "I look at Ellie and the rest of the *Heartland* cast. . . . They're always talking about sunglasses and shoes and what's the hottest nightclub. It makes me wonder . . . even if by some miracle I made it . . . whatever that means . . . is that what this is all about?"

"It's about your *art,*" she reminded him, leaning in close to make her point, which she truly believed. "And there's no law against liking sunglasses and shoes."

"I want to do something meaningful with my life. Stuffing a hamburger in my face for thirty seconds in front of a camera doesn't count."

In the dim light, Sophie couldn't see the gold flecks in Sam's hazel eyes, but she knew they were there. Just like she knew that even if she couldn't see it, his desire to be an actor was somewhere inside of him.

"When I first got to LA, you told me if I lived here long enough, I'd learn not to invest in people. So many come and go, what's the point?"

"Yeah. So what?"

"Don't be one of those people who come and go, Sam."

He looked at her for a long moment, then reached out and mussed her hair. "It was a fleeting, stupid thought. Blackouts make me crazy."

She grabbed his wrist. "Well, if you have another fleeting, stupid thought, make sure you talk to me. Got it?"

"Got it." He kissed the tip of her nose. "Thanks, Bushell. I needed that."

It felt so good to have Sam admit she was right about something that she returned the kiss, planting one on his left cheek. At least, it was supposed to be his cheek. He turned his head at the last second, and her lips landed somewhere dangerously close to his mouth.

Just like that, it was back. The electricity. Only now it wasn't the buzz of a teenage crush. She felt like a woman who wanted a man.

His face was still close to hers. "Do you ever wonder —"

Sam's cell phone chimed. For a second, he looked surprised. Then he stood up and answered it, moving across the living room, away from her, to talk. Sophie took a few deep breaths. Diaphragm Ellie, right on cue. She tuned out their conversation. It was good the girlfriend had called. The girlfriend had saved her. From what . . . she wasn't exactly sure.

Sam hung up and turned back to her. "That was Ellie," he said, stating the obvious. "She's at Cobras & Matadors . . . kinda freaked out from the blackout and everything."

"You should probably go over there. Make sure she's okay."

He nodded and grabbed his car keys. "I know you helped Ellie with her monologue the other night. Thanks."

"I wasn't just going to let her cry. I'm not a *complete* bitch." *Plus, I couldn't sleep with all the bawling,* she couldn't help adding silently.

"You, uh, wanna come with?" He was lingering at the door, staring at her.

253

"Nah. How often does a girl get the chance to paint her toenails by candlelight?"

"We'll finish this," he said, his hand on the doorknob. "Someday, we'll finish this."

As she watched him leave, Sophie wasn't sure whether he was referring to their Scrabble game, their conversation, or their near kiss. But she'd find out. Someday, she'd find out.

"I asked for *iced* coffee." Tie Guy (so named because he wore a navy suit and black tie every day, including weekends) thrust the burning hot medium cup of Columbian-brewed back at Harper, splashing her in the process.

"It's, like, five degrees outside." The boiling liquid had definitely scalded her skin. She ignored the pain in favor of maintaining some semblance of professionalism, despite the fact that she'd gotten only three hours of sleep before her six AM shift at the café. And despite the fact that at that moment she thought Tie Guy was the definition of pure, inappropriately dressed evil.

"I don't need a weather report. I need my iced coffee." His beady brown eyes flicked back and forth, as if he were looking for a large object to throw in her direction.

Harper silently damned Judd for being late to work as she dumped the steaming coffee over a cup of ice and slapped a lid on it. He knew she despised Tie Guy. If he'd been here, Judd would have handled the order himself. As it was, she was exhausted, cranky, and had a line ten deep of people who couldn't start their day without their morning fix of crack caffeine. It was going to be a nonexistent tip day. Generally, serving coffee-without-a-smile didn't motivate customers to empty their pockets for their local barista.

By nine o'clock, she was out of low-fat cranberry muffins, chocolate croissants, and patience. She was also just the tiniest bit worried.

Unlike her, Judd was never late. He had one of those mothers who'd taught him that being on time meant arriving at any destination ten minutes early. And ever since her dad's accident, Harper had felt slightly on edge when she didn't know exactly where every person in her orbit was at any given time. It was like she had a constantly evolving spreadsheet of names, times, and locations in her already overcrowded head.

"Where the fuck are you?" she demanded when Judd picked up his cell on the third ring, feeling vaguely aware that she didn't need to be quite so harsh. Then again, he wasn't the one who'd spent the last half hour wondering if he'd been in a car wreck while simultaneously talking low-fat cranberry muffin–jonesing customers off the angry ledge.

"Good morning, Harper. Your ponytail is crooked."

She looked up from the vanilla cappuccino she was foaming with her free hand to discover Judd sauntering toward her. The shit-eating smile on his face made him look like a curly-haired demonic clown. "Why are you so happy?" she asked, flipping her cell phone shut.

Maybe someone had slipped a tablet of ecstasy into his morning oatmeal. Or he'd found out that Phish was playing a secret reunion gig in Boulder this week. Or maybe he'd just had a decent night's sleep, something she hadn't experienced since she'd decided to help her mom (salary-free) with the constant slew of parties she was catering to up the family income. With all the work, something had to go. Harper had opted to give up sleep rather than stall on her novel, which she'd taken to writing at the time of night when only obsessive Internet porn viewers were the other ones awake.

"One soy latte coming up," Judd beamed at New Mom, slipping effortlessly into his routine. As he started the drink, he turned to Harper. "It happened."

"What happened?"

"My dream."

255

She finished foaming and reached for a lid. "The one where cave-men are chasing you around a cauldron so they can tickle you to death before cooking you for dinner?" She had no idea what it meant, but Judd had told her he'd had the same recurring dream since he lost his first tooth when he was six.

"No. The *Dream*." He wiggled his eyebrows in a jiggly, annoying way. "Y'know, Amelia?"

Amelia Dorf. Virginity. The dream. She was now wide awake. "You guys didn't . . ." For some reason she couldn't bring herself to finish the sentence.

"We did. It just sort of . . . happened. Crazy, huh?" He bounced off to give New Mom her soy latte.

Harper gulped the vanilla cappuccino she was holding for lack of a better response to this news. Judd had *done* it? With Amelia? They barely knew each other. What kind of people went from barely know-ing each other to climbing naked into a twin bed together? Shouldn't there be intermediary phases? The first kiss phase. The groping-under-the-shirt phase. The unzipped-but-still-firmly-placed-around-the-hips-pants phase. The sex phase came last, after much angst-ridden negotiation and testing for STDs. It didn't just sort of *happen*. And if it did, why tell *her*?

"Miss, you're drinking my vanilla cappuccino." The admonition came from the lab coat–wearing med student with crazy hair who stopped by the café every Monday, Wednesday, and Friday.

"Oh. Sorry." Harper turned back to the machines, trying to re-member how to make any sort of cappuccino. Five minutes ago it had been second nature. Now she was a blank.

"It wasn't Amelia's first time," Judd confided as he returned to make a double espresso. "She had a pretty serious boyfriend in high school. But I think I did okay. I mean, she had, y'know . . . an orgasm."

Now he was telling her about Amelia Dorf's *orgasms*? This couldn't be occurring. She was hallucinating due to lack of REM

256

sleep. Or she was *still* asleep. This whole morning had been one long nightmare. Yes. That was it. She was sleeping.

"I owe you big time. If it weren't for our whole friends-with-benefits thing, I wouldn't have had the confidence to go for it." Judd gave her a friendly punch on the arm. "So thanks."

Okay, she wasn't dreaming. "Um . . . sure. Glad to be of service." Making coffee. Wiping tables. Placating disgruntled low-fat cranberry muffin buyers. Getting her best guy friend laid. It was all in a day's work for a writer-barista.

Non-virgin, demonic-grinning Judd set down the double espresso and looked at her. "You're okay with me sharing this, right? I figured, y'know, since you were asking so many questions about Amelia on our stakeout . . . it seemed like you wanted all the details."

"Yeah . . . fine . . . whatever." That's what she said. What she *felt* was a huge surge of anger. Unfortunately, the surge of anger caused her to squeeze the medium-sized paper cup holding the fresh cappuccino, which splattered all over her favorite red hoodie and several square feet of the rubber-matted floor beneath her feet.

"Harper? Are you all right?" Judd's demonic grin was gone. Now he just looked like . . . Judd. Which didn't stop the anger. In fact, it was feeling more like a rolling wave than a surge.

"I'm just surprised." She was trying to tell herself she didn't care. "Last I checked, you two were at the cocoa phase." It wasn't like Judd was a guy she'd actually be *interested* in. Not like Mr. Finelli. *He* was her true love. *He* was the one she wanted to be making out with in cars. Not coffee-grounds-under-the-fingernails Judd.

"We've been hanging out a lot the last couple weeks. And last night . . ." He sighed, fingers pawing at the countertop. "God. It was amazing."

The last couple weeks. Harper did a mental run-down of the fourteen days prior to this one. She hadn't seen Judd much outside of the café, but she'd assumed that was because of her overloaded save-the-family work schedule. And they hadn't fooled around at all. Again, she'd assumed that was because of her. She'd been too engrossed in her own life to notice what was happening with anyone around her. What was happening with one person in particular.

"So obviously . . . I mean, Amelia and I are pretty much together now. . . ."

"No more friends-with-benefits," Harper quickly finished for him. "I get it."

Somehow she managed to get the words out without sounding like a complete shrew. It wasn't that she didn't plan to unleash her fury at some point. She did. But first she had to figure out why it was justified and how to make Judd feel as badly as possible.

"You're sure you're okay?"

"Hey. No harm, no foul." The demonic grin reappeared. Harper wanted to shoot him.

"You and I will still hang out all the time."

She nodded casually. In her head, she was already rearranging her shifts at the café. She could say "no harm, no foul" a million times, but it wouldn't change two things. First, she wanted to be around Non-Virgin Judd as little as possible. Second, she now officially hated Amelia Dorf.

"You're never going to trust me, are you?"

Sitting on the edge of her bed, Stuart looked at Becca as if he'd never seen her before. Then he shook his head slowly, rubbing the knee of his faded Levi's. His white t-shirt was in a heap on her dorm room floor, and Becca imagined that she could almost see his heart beating beneath the bare, muscled skin of his chest — slowly, steadily, painfully.

The air left her body.

How had this happened?

Yes, she had been jabbing at him for days, unwilling to believe that his dance with the blond, wispy girl had only been a dance. Yes, she had shown him — against her will, against her own desire to restrain it — her worst possible side. More than once.

The first time was when he'd shown up at her door ten minutes after she'd run from the Winter Carnival party, worried because she hadn't returned from the bathroom. She'd been covered in tears and snot, and as soon as she saw him she'd slammed the door in his face. He'd tried to get her to open the door again, the concern clear in his voice, until Becca had yelled at him.

"Go back to your blonde!" she'd screamed, knowing even as she did it that she was acting crazy, that she should just open the door and talk to him, that there must be some reasonable explanation for what she'd seen. They *had* just been dancing, after all. And taking someone's hand . . . that didn't mean anything. Maybe. Either way, he deserved the chance to explain.

"Bec," he'd murmured. "Let me in. Whatever you saw, it wasn't what you think."

"Go away!" she'd yelled back at him.

In her defense, she hadn't been herself. But she hadn't been herself ever since Mia's announcement about her parents, and, in its wake, she didn't think she was ever going to be herself again. At least not the naïve, hopeful self she had allowed herself to become over the last several months.

Now she was smarter. Her parents had reminded her that believing in people, trusting people, wasn't safe. Especially the people she loved, who were supposed to love her back. If she gave any one of them a chance, they'd pick up that hammer and drive that nail right through her chest, just like her mom and the bat,. She was done giving them — giving anyone — the chance. Because no matter how many layers of armor she put up, someone always had a bigger hammer and a stronger spike.

Stuart had given her until the next morning, then he'd shown up at her door again, determined to talk. Isabelle, still in her pink flannel pajamas, had grabbed her toiletries case and headed for the bathroom down the hall, flip-flops flip-flopping down the linoleum as the door closed behind her. Stuart had climbed into Becca's bed, grabbed her hand, and pulled her close to him.

"Tell me what's going on," he whispered.

"Nothing." Becca pulled her hand away.

"'The blonde' is Emma Jenkins. She's a junior. She pulled me out on the dance floor while you were in the bathroom. That's it."

"Okay," Becca said, but it clearly wasn't.

"Becca. I know this stuff with your parents is . . . I know it's hard. But I'm not your dad. I'm not cheating. I would never do that."

Stuart looked hurt. And so sincere. Becca almost trusted him. "You were holding her hand," she pointed out quietly.

Stuart frowned, clearly trying to remember. "I . . . It was loud. I think I took her hand to say I was going to go meet you. I wanted to get her attention. It wasn't like a 'hand holding' kind of thing."

Becca could feel herself softening.

"Why would I want to be with her when I can be with you?" He'd looked into her eyes then and her heart had reacted as it always did.

He'd kissed her, and Becca had let it go. Even though she knew the situation wasn't over. Not for her. She wanted it to be — she'd tried, over the next several days, to forget about it. She knew Stuart was telling the truth. He wasn't a liar for one thing. And he loved her. He really did. He showed it in a thousand different ways and he said it at least twice a day. But what did that mean? Loving someone didn't mean you didn't hurt them, and being loved wasn't ever without pain.

And maybe that was why she brought up Emma Jenkins the second time. They'd been walking across the quad, holding hands, under a canopy of new-blooming birch trees. "Aren't you glad I'm not

260

Emma Jenkins?" she'd said, pretending to be lighthearted. But Stuart knew her well enough to know there was more behind it.

"I *am* glad you're not Emma Jenkins." He kissed her forehead as they walked. "Where do you want to go for lunch? Cafeteria or the café?"

"Where would Emma Jenkins want to go?"

Stuart let go of her hand. "I have no idea." He looked as close as he ever got to annoyed. "Cafeteria's probably faster."

"So you don't want to spend time with me." Becca crossed her arms and stopped walking. What the hell was wrong with her? She didn't mean anything she was saying. She didn't *care* about Emma Jenkins either. Why couldn't she just *stop*? When had she turned into one of those psychotic girls that she, Harper, Sophie, and Kate always used to make fun of?

"I always want to spend time with you," Stuart soothed. "You pick."

"The cafeteria's fine." She shrugged.

So they'd gone to the cafeteria. But the entire meal had been spent in an awkward silence. Becca was too scared to open her mouth, not knowing what insane, accusatory thing might come out, and Stuart seemed to sense that the less he said the better.

Then there was today. They'd been studying in their usual position — facing each other, cross-legged on Becca's bed, books open on the mattress between them. Things seemed almost normal. Better than normal — good. The chaos in Becca's brain had faded away as they pored through psych diagnoses and definitions, memorizing the names of the seminal psychologists of the twentieth century.

"What do women want?" Stuart asked, dark eyes smiling.

"I don't know, Dr. Freud," Becca teased back. "Why don't you tell me?"

He leaned forward and kissed her, his hand cupping her cheek. She felt the heat rising within her as his thumb brushed the skin below her eye, and then his hand wrapped around the back of her neck

261

gently. Within moments their clunky psych books were shoved to the floor. God, it felt good to be close to him. He had seemed so far away for so long, and she needed him. Needed to feel how much he loved her. How he would never leave her.

Becca's hands ran up his chest, and he'd raised his arms, letting her take his t-shirt off in one smooth motion. His hands wrapped around her back, holding her on top of him.

"Where's Isabelle?" he'd whispered.

"Class 'til four," she'd answered, pulling his mouth to hers.

And then he said it. "Emma." Becca pulled away. She jumped off the bed, staring at him, horrified.

"What? What happened?" Stuart leaned up on one elbow.

"You said her name!"

"Whose name?" He sat up and swung his knees over the side of the bed.

"Emma! You said 'Emma'!"

Stuart sat perfectly still. "I said 'Becca.'"

"No, you didn't." But Becca wasn't so sure. He'd been kissing her, after all, so the exact syllables could have been garbled.

God, she really was one of those insane chicks.

"I'm sorry," she began. "I . . . I misheard you, and . . ."

Stuart nodded slowly and gave her that look — the one that said he was just now coming to understand something that had hereto-fore been just outside his grasp. For several long seconds, he just stared at her, rubbing the knee of his jeans.

"You're never going to trust me, are you?"

Becca wanted to protest. Of *course* she was going to trust him. She *did* trust him — at least as much as it was possible to trust someone. Which, maybe, for her, wasn't all that much. But it was the best she could do at the moment and that would have to be enough.

Only it wasn't.

Suddenly Becca saw a way out. A way to save herself, yes — but mostly a way to save Stuart. He didn't deserve this. He deserved to have a relationship with someone who would just love him. Who would give him everything without reservation, and trust him — make him feel like the amazing person he was. He shouldn't have to defend himself against a host of imagined wrongs. It wasn't right. Yet she knew she couldn't help herself. Maybe someday, but . . . maybe not. Becca was going to spare him that. Starting right now.

"I can't do this," she managed to squeak out.

"Do what?"

"Be . . . a couple with you." The words were almost impossible for her to grind out, but she forced them from her throat.

"Becca —"

"I am never going to trust you," she pronounced, keeping her voice even. "I just *can't*. Okay? You should go."

Stuart didn't move. He took a deep breath and looked around her room like he was looking for a way to talk sense to her.

"I mean it," she continued. "I thought I could do this. I thought this was what I wanted. But it isn't. It's not you, it's me."

"Don't say that to me." His voice was tense now. "I *know* it's you. I also know you love me."

"That doesn't matter." Becca looked down at the floor. If she didn't, he would see the tears about to overflow onto her cheeks. "We're done. Just go. Please?"

She continued to stare at the floor as Stuart methodically picked up his shirt, put it on, gathered his books, and walked to the door.

"Becca —"

"Get out." She didn't look at him. She didn't look at anything until the door closed behind him. Then her knees gave out and she sank into her desk chair, her tired eyes on the pathway outside the window until Stuart appeared, walking slowly, shoulders hunched.

263

Once he was gone from sight, she climbed into her bed and curled into the wall. It was better this way. Better to get out of it now and save them both from the inevitable pain that would come in the future.

In time, Stuart would be fine. He would find someone new to love. He would recover. And be happy. Someday.

If only she could say the same about herself.

The smell of the market in Kellem would never leave her. Certainly it would never leave her memory. Nor would it ever leave her clothes. No matter how many times Kate scrubbed them and hung them to dry in the cool, dry Mekebe breeze, the pungent conjoined odor of donkey, grain, goat, dirt, dung, and hot human flesh was soaked into the fibers of her khakis and faded Banana Republic black t-shirt forevermore.

Fortunately, the market itself offered ample balance to its own aroma in the form of overflowing stalls full of beautifully crafted natalas; bronze crosses; religious art; honeycombs cut from distant trees and transported in large white plastic buckets dripping with sweet, rich honey; every kind of grain from teff to maize; as well as chickens, goats, sheep, Michelin tire–soled shoes, and an assortment of kitchen supplies made inevitably in China.

She and Dorothé had come to Kellem for the day with the rest of the team to lend a hand — or four — to Darby, Jessica, and Jean-Pierre, who were falling behind in clearing the land for the drainage field. Kate would have bet a month's rent (which, at $22, wasn't much) that Jessica was at least partially responsible for the delay, and it annoyed her to be saving the older girl's butt yet again — although she was happy for the opportunity to see another town.

Kellem was slightly larger than Mekebe, evidenced by the wider streets — many of which were paved — the densely packed compounds, and the much larger market. It was also known for the quality of its weaving. A co-operative of weavers operated in the town, mostly men, all known for their expertise at the craft — making Kellem the perfect place to buy a particularly special natala for Habiba. So when the sun rose to its lunchtime position in the sky and the workers started heading home for their meal, Kate told Dorothé where she was going, pulled a sandwich (injera wrapped around leftover goat meat) from her backpack and started walking toward the market.

More than one stall had an impressive array of natalas, and Kate wanted to be sure to find the perfect one. Habiba would like something colorful, she was sure, and would recognize the quality of the craftsmanship, especially in the intricate weaving along each natala's border. Given the favor that Habiba was doing for her and how helpful her little sister was being about finding Angatu's sister, Kate wanted to find a natala that was unique. Special.

"Can I see that one?" she asked a slim, mocha-colored woman at one small stall, hoping the Amharic dialect in Kellem was the same as that in Mekebe. Apparently it was because the woman passed the natala to Kate with a smile. She had a rudimentary sun tattooed in the center of her forehead, and a little boy, barely a toddler, sat on her lap. He also had a sun on his forehead.

"Is it real?" Kate asked about the little boy's tattoo.

The woman laughed. "No, no," she declared in Amharic. "He's too young. It's blue pen."

Kate smiled and studied the natala. It was beautiful. The cotton, dyed a bright pink shade, was soft and evenly spun. The border, which was black and a bright, lively green, was woven in a complex geometrical pattern. Habiba would love it.

"How much for this one?"

"One hundred forty birr," the woman answered.

Kate knew that the asking price had been increased — maybe even doubled — because she was a *faranji,* but it seemed only fair. As little money as she had, fifteen dollars was still a bargain to her Western sensibilities.

"I'll take it." She nodded, reaching for her purse. She knew she could have haggled the price down at least a little, but if paying an extra twenty or thirty birr meant the little boy with the blue pen tattoo would have a healthier dinner or his mother would be able to buy an extra Chinese-made kitchen utensil . . . well, it was worth it. Kate handed the woman a one hundred birr note and four tens.

Before she could put her wallet back in her backpack, she was surrounded.

"*Faranji, faranji!!!*" There were at least six of them, all children between eight and fourteen, yelling the Amharic word for "foreigner." All boys. Kate had heard that this happened often in Ethiopia — but the team from Water Partners were well known in Mekebe, and they had never really been out on the streets in Addis Ababa. Even in Bahar Dar, they usually drove to where they wanted to go, so most young beggars were seen only through the window of a car or in passing on the street. Kate gave them whatever she could, which wasn't much, whenever she saw them. But she had never seen so many all at once or had them surround her as they did now.

"*Faranji, faranji!!!*" the boys yelled, arms outstretched, reaching for her.

A familiar panic wound its way up from the center of Kate's chest. *This is not like what happened in Greece. They don't want to mug me. They don't want to hurt me. They're just children.*

Kate reached into her wallet, searching for single birr notes. But passing them out only increased the furor around her. Suddenly there were more boys, some older now — maybe fifteen or sixteen. More bodies pressed in against her, more voices rose, demanding money, candy, pens for school. What did she have? What could she give them?

She passed her last birr note to a five-year-old boy in a ratty Coca Cola t-shirt, and dug through her backpack, searching frantically for a ballpoint pen or a piece of gum. She reached the bottom, bare-handed. She had nothing. Her panic increased.

"That's all." Her voice quavered in Amharic. "I don't have anymore."

Still, the boys continued their assault. Kate knew they didn't mean it that way. They weren't hurting her — nor would they. But there were at least ten of them now, all reaching and yelling. The excitement and energy of the crowd fed on itself, but now her back was against a corrugated metal fence at the end of the stall row, and real or imaginary, she sensed a hostility from some of the older boys.

Usually, she would have smiled and tried to engage them. She would have explained to them — she did speak the language, after all — that she had to leave now and could they please clear a path? One of the older boys reached for her, and the second his strong hand wrapped around her upper arm, she cracked.

"Please, go away. Leave me alone." She couldn't take it — all the hands, the noise, the smell, the desperation and neediness. "Please —"

"Kate!"

She searched above the faces of the boys. Where was he?

"Let's go." Darby pushed through the crowd and grabbed her arm. With some quick words from him in Amharic, the boys dispersed, melting into the market populace as quickly as they had appeared. Darby didn't let go of her arm until they had cleared the perimeter of the market and merged back onto the street.

"What the hell's wrong with you?" he yelled, spinning her around to face him.

"I — I wanted to buy a natala for my sister —" Kate began.

"Why were you cowering in a corner? They're *kids*."

"I know —"

"They just wanted a few birr!"

"I gave them —"

"If Africans freak you out so much, why are you in Africa?"

So that was it. Kate stared at him. "Thank you," she said.

"What?" A muscle in his jaw line jerked spasmodically.

"I had almost forgotten what an asshole you are. Thanks for reminding me." She started walking away from him, back toward the well site.

"I'm an asshole for coming to your rescue?" Darby caught up with her in two steps, keeping stride.

"Oh, it was a rescue now? I thought they were just kids!"

"They were. You were the one who got weird about it —"

"I got 'weird'" — Kate stopped and stood in front of him, one hand on her hip, the other gripping Habiba's natala — "because those boys reminded me of something. Okay? Something that's none of your business. I wasn't freaked out by *them*. Just so we're clear."

"That couldn't be *less* clear," Darby shot back, completely unmollified.

She glared at him.

"I got *mugged,* you jackass. In Greece. Three guys, an alley, me in the hospital for two days —" The tears surprised Kate as they materialized, seemingly from nowhere, against her eyelashes. She'd thought she was over all that. Over the fear, certainly over the crying. "And *you* are the last person in the universe I want to talk about it with." She took a deep breath, brushing the tears away with the back of her hand. "Because I'm fine, and it's none of your business, and what the hell do you care, anyway? Excuse me."

Kate was pretty sure Darby was about ten steps behind her all the way back to the well site, but he didn't try to talk to her again. When she saw him next he was elbow-deep in volcanic rock, in the middle of what would be the drainage field.

Rescued me! Freaked out by Africans!

Yet again, who the hell did Darby think he was? More importantly, who the hell did he think *she* was?

And why the hell did she care?

EXAMINATION BLUE BOOK

NAME: _Becca Winsberg_

CLASS: _Psy 240 Mid-Term_

GRADE: _C−_

COME SEE ME.

TWELVE

I'm fine."

"You are *not* fine."

"I am."

"Are not."

Harper considered banging her head against the wall. But the possibility of damaging her black plastic eyeglass frames (which she really couldn't afford to replace at this particular juncture) stopped her from actually doing it. Instead she handed Becca a jumbo bag of Skittles, bought specially for the occasion of their spring break reunion, and popped open a Diet Coke.

They'd been going back and forth on the topic of Becca's state of being or not being fine for the past, oh, hour and a half. So far they'd gotten nowhere. But the night was young, and Harper was determined to get Becca to open up and talk to her — really talk, not bullshit chitchat — before the night was over.

"What's worse? Breaking up with Stuart or your parents getting back together?" It was a simple question. Becca could give her *that* much.

"What's going on with you? What's happening with NYU?" It was a blatant attempt to shift the focus of conversation.

"I find out if I got accepted in fewer than fifteen days, as if you didn't know." The thought made Harper's stomach hurt. "Now spill it."

Becca sighed. "Can't we just watch *Dirty Dancing*?"

Harper was tempted to relent. There was nothing she hated more than someone she was close to grilling her for information she had no interest in divulging. All right, there was *one* thing she hated more. That same person *not* grilling her for information she had no interest in divulging.

"No can do. Sorry."

When Becca had shown up in her basement, Harper had expected her to be irritated about her parents' apparent reconciliation. She also expected her to be aglow with love, calling Stuart every five minutes to tell him in her baby voice how much she missed him. Suffice it to say, Becca was not aglow. She was the *opposite* of aglow, from her vacant stare to her pale cheeks to the stonewashed high-waisted jeans she'd apparently kept since eighth grade.

In a dull monotone, Becca had informed her that she and Stuart had broken up. No, she did not want to talk about it. And, yes, her mother had confirmed that the proverbial flame had been rekindled between herself and Becca's dad. Even worse, she had said they owed Becca for the renewed romance. Her angry diatribe at Parents' Weekend had forced them to open the lines of communication, at which point they had discovered that they were even more fiercely attracted to one another than they'd been when they first met. As far as Harper could discern, it was the "fiercely attracted" part of this equation that had sent Becca over the edge.

"Is it really so bad that your parents are back together? Think about it. No more stepsiblings." Harper had decided to lead with the family situation.

Becca flopped back on the mattress. To pay tribute to her friend's return, Harper had put on the Harry Potter sheets Becca had given her during a frenzy of pre-college purging. "It won't work out. Nothing works out."

So they were back to Stuart. "Bec, he loves you. He'll forgive you. Just tell him you're sorry. Y'know, with a lot groveling."

Becca gave her a forlorn look. "I did the whole apology routine once. It's amazing he forgave me that time." She was referring to the dramatic speech she delivered on Stuart's doorstep after he found out she'd lost her virginity in the most wasted way to Kate's ex-boyfriend. "How many times can I fuck up and expect to be forgiven?"

Her voice was tense and high-pitched now, but Harper didn't try to stop her. Letting it out was the only way to make it better. Besides, her father was probably bored upstairs in his room. Maybe listening to Becca yell would be an entertaining diversion.

"You won't know how many times you can fuck up until you try to make it better," Harper pointed out optimistically. "Isn't Stuart worth it?"

"You don't get it, Harper. *It's over.*" Becca grabbed a pillow and covered her face with Harry and Hedwig, his trustworthy white owl.

"Doesn't sound over to me." Harper paused, picking at an imaginary spot on the bedcover. There was some psychological territory to enter here, but it might turn Becca violent. Oh well, what were a few bruises between best friends? "Is it possible that you think you're not ready for a relationship and you're using the dancing blond as an excuse to push Stuart away?"

Becca sat up, her green eyes flashing. "I really don't think you're in a position to talk about relationships. First, you're infatuated with your *English teacher.* Then you start this weird thing with Judd. A weird thing you claim means nothing to you, although it so *obviously* does."

"No harm, no foul," Harper recited automatically. If she uttered those inane words one more time she might have to commit herself to a mental institution.

"You're *upset* about this Amelia chick. Admit it already."

Harper clenched her fists. *She's not herself. She's heartbroken. She's saying whatever she can to deflect.* All of that was true. It didn't explain why Harper felt like she'd been punched in the gut.

"I'm not upset. I'm ecstatic. I was figuring out a way to end it with him anyway. As it happens, I think Mr. Finelli . . . Adam . . . and I are going to make a go of it."

Why did she revert to lying whenever she felt pathetic? It was more pathetic than being pathetic in the first place.

"Whatever." Becca rolled her eyes. "I accomplished my Dream. I fell in love. No one said anything about staying in love." She stood up. "So why don't you worry about *your* Dream and finish that goddamn novel you're always talking about?"

She was heading for the basement window, ready to make her escape. Harper felt like yelling back, telling her what a shitty friend she'd been since meeting Stuart. Telling Becca that the world didn't revolve around her college sweetheart or her screwed-up parents. There were other things in life. Like having a dad who'd turned from strong and invincible to weak and vulnerable. Like, lots of things.

But Harper didn't say any of that. Because she loved Becca. Maybe there was an evil part of her that had felt almost relieved when she'd found out things at Middlebury weren't as fairy tale as they seemed. Maybe she'd even felt a little superior. There were plenty of crises in her own life, although *she* wasn't falling apart. But the bigger part of her, the part that mattered, didn't want to see one of her best friends in so much pain.

"Stay. We'll call Sophie. We'll e-mail Kate. We'll watch *Dirty Dancing* and gorge ourselves like fat pigs." Harper stopped to take a breath. "We'll *figure this out.*"

Becca turned back. There weren't any tears in her eyes, as if she was past that. "I don't deserve him. Not with my baggage. And the truth is, I don't know if I ever will."

She opened the window and began to climb outside. If Harper thought she could have made her feel better, she would have grabbed her legs and pulled Becca back inside. Instead she let her go.

Forward Motion was Sophie's favorite new TV show. Of course, she'd never seen it and she wasn't even exactly sure what it was about, but she'd just auditioned for a recurring role as Mave, the perky, smarter-than-her-years secretary who confounds her boss every other episode. And frankly, she'd kicked major ass. She'd kicked the kind of ass that already had her wondering when she'd go in for her wardrobe fittings. The *Heartland* debacle was now a distant memory. Who wanted to play angst-ridden Paige Dalloway when she could instead play hilarious Mave whatever-her-last-name-was? Her hand shook as she dialed her cell phone.

"Sophie Bushell for Matthew Feldman, please." She had perfected the cool, professional tone she used whenever she called her agent.

"I'll see if I can get him." Sophie didn't recognize the assistant's voice, which wasn't surprising. In her short time as Matthew Feldman's client, she'd learned that the burnout rate for assistants was so high that few lasted more than a couple weeks. Who knew what kind of political mayhem went on in those corporate offices every day? She was glad she *didn't* know: she had her own daily hostessing/auditioning mayhem to contend with.

As she waited for Matthew Feldman to pick up, she continued to stroll through the Fox lot. She stared up at the huge murals of characters from *Star Wars* and *The Simpsons,* imagining her own face — as Mave — adorning the side of a building.

"Talk to me." As always, Matthew Feldman sounded like he was doing four things at once — and he probably was.

"I think I got the part!" Sophie exclaimed. "I know I totally whined and complained after *Heartland* but that was just so —"

"You didn't get it," Matthew Feldman cut her off. "They decided to go Asian."

"But I just auditioned, like, two minutes ago —"

"Sorry, kid. That's the biz."

"They said they loved me. All the producers were laughing at my delivery . . ." She suddenly hated *Forward Motion* and everyone involved in it. She hoped it was the worst ratings disaster in history. She hoped —

"Yeah, they thought you were hilarious. Turns out the lead gets real twitchy if anyone in the cast comes off as funnier than he is. Producers don't want to deal with the headache." She heard him bite into something. The crunching sound made her want to vomit. "What can I say? You were too good."

The line went dead. Great. Matthew Feldman didn't even say goodbye. Then again, he never said goodbye. But still. Sophie kicked one of the picturesque wooden benches that dotted the lot, wishing it were the head of whoever made the decision not to cast her. How was it possible that a person could be *too* good? What did "going Asian" even mean?

Her cell vibrated in her hand. He was probably calling back to give her a pep talk. Or . . . maybe he'd already booked her another audition. *In thirty seconds?* Hey, anything was possible. "Hello?"

"It's me." Not Matthew Feldman. Sam, sounding panicky.

"What's wrong?" she asked, half-disappointed and half-relieved it wasn't a business call as she headed back to the parking lot. She had three full hours until she had to be at Mojito, and she planned to spend it drowning her sorrows in her favorite vintage clothes shop on Melrose.

"Ellie just called me from her trailer. She's having a meltdown."

Wasn't it bad enough that she'd just lost a gig she was ideal for? Now she had to discuss the Diaphragm Diva's emotional instability? "What now?"

"She's got a tough scene to shoot this afternoon and she's feeling really insecure." *Because she sucks,* Sophie silently informed him.

"Why call me?" It was the obvious question.

"You had an audition on the Fox lot, right? Are you still there?"

Sophie eyed the parking lot fifty yards away. "Barely. Why?" She was getting suspicious. Very suspicious. She happened to know that *Heartland* was shot on the lot, a fact she'd just been studiously trying to ignore.

"Please talk to her. Please. She thinks you've got some kind of magic." If what Sam was asking her to do wasn't so repugnant, she'd be enjoying this.

"No way."

"For me, Sophie. I'm asking for me."

She sighed. Being a softie when it came to Sam was definitely a psychological hazard. But she couldn't say no. "Tell her I'll be there in ten minutes."

When Sophie knocked on Ellie's trailer door on the other side of studio lot, she was already formulating her plan of attack. Get in, hand her a tissue, tell her she's an acting genius, get out. If it went well, the whole process shouldn't take more than seven minutes. She'd still have plenty of time before her shift to hit Melrose to look at all the funky, fabulous clothes she couldn't afford to buy. The door cracked open and Ellie revealed her mascara-streaked face.

"Don't let anyone see you!" she hissed, yanking Sophie inside.

"Why?" Sophie glanced around the trailer, known as a half-banger. There was a small bathroom, along with pea-green carpet, industrial-strength white curtains, and a tiny kitchenette. Not bad for a basically talentless twenty-year-old.

"I told the first A.D. I have a migraine. If anyone sees us, they'll think I'm one of those high-maintenance actresses who holds up production to hang out with her friends."

You are! Sophie couldn't help thinking. Except she and Ellie weren't friends. They were . . . well, whatever it was, it was wholly dysfunctional. "Just tell me what's going on."

"I have this scene with my best guy friend on the show who I'm secretly in love with and I have *no* idea how to play it." Aside from the smeared makeup, Ellie looked every inch the future TV star. She was wearing tight Seven jeans, a powder-pink D&G top, and the snakeskin Jimmy Choo heels Sophie had admired in the Fred Segal windows two weeks ago. Someone had clearly spent the better part of the morning turning Ellie's long butter-blond mane into a casually tousled masterpiece. Next to her, Sophie felt downright dowdy in her J-Crew magenta tank dress and self-styled hair.

"You'll be fine. Just remember all the stuff we talked about the other night. Find a way into the scene, put yourself in Paige's shoes, etcetera." She edged toward the door, hoping the two-sentence pep talk would suffice. But Ellie grabbed her arm again, pulling her down onto the trailer's tiny white sofa.

"No, I need you. If you don't help me rehearse I'm not going to be able to do it." Her voice was desperate and her baby-blue eyes were wild.

Sophie hesitated. Holding the hand of the actress who had stolen *her* part wasn't how she wanted to spend the afternoon, even for Sam. It wasn't like she *owed* him anything.

"I'll give you whatever you want," Ellie pressed, her over-aerobicized butt perched on the edge of the couch. "A hundred dollars? Two hundred? A thousand? *Please.*"

"I won't take your money." Sophie shook her head. "But there is something . . ."

"What?" Ellie grabbed a tissue and dabbed at her baby blues. Clearly, there was an actress *somewhere* in there.

"I want a guest spot on *Heartland.*" The request popped out before it was even a fully formed thought. She leaned back, bumping her head against the wall.

Ellie brightened. "Done."

"Really?" Sophie asked warily.

"I'm totally tight with the casting director. It's *so* not a problem." She jumped up gleefully and grabbed two scripts, handing one to Sophie. "Let's get started."

Sophie smiled as she flipped open the script. After seven months in Hollywood, she'd finally figured out how to work the system. There was hope.

"I still don't get it. You broke up with him to *save* him?"

Sitting across from Harper at the Rainy Day Books Café, Becca nodded bravely. After several days in Boulder, she was finally ready to talk. The café was quiet, apart from a few solitary grad-student types staring at their laptops, and an old guy who looked like he'd nodded off over his newspaper, so Harper insisted it was no problem taking a break. "Everything's just too crazy right now. *I'm* too crazy," Becca tried to explain, although the words sounded lame even to her. "He shouldn't have to deal with —"

"You?" Harper interrupted.

Becca shrugged and stared down into her latte, still too hot to drink. "Yeah."

It would have been easy to go to New York with Isabelle for spring break and hide out for two whole weeks in the back bedroom of the Sutters' glorious Park Avenue apartment. Easy, that is, if Isabelle hadn't been bound and determined to convince her to tell Stuart her body had been occupied by alien beings when she'd suddenly broken up with him, and that she hadn't meant a word of it. Becca knew she couldn't handle two weeks of incessant badgering, and Boulder was really the only other option. If she ruled out gobbling down handfuls of Xanax, which — after some deliberation — she had.

Unfortunately, being in Boulder also meant staying with her parents — *both* of them — who were living in sin in her dad's apartment.

Melissa had moved out, but Becca felt her presence everywhere — the living room was decorated in the ultramodern, clean lines her stepmother preferred, and though most of her art was gone, Becca knew she had chosen the various shades of white that covered the walls, as well as the shiny black granite kitchen counter tops, slate floor tile, Thermador refrigerator, and brushed stainless steel doorknobs.

Her mom's over-squashy Pottery Barn style didn't exactly work in concert with Melissa's sleek sense of design, leaving the apartment a mishmash of shabby chic and actual chic. In the glass-walled living room, the red flower-print sofa she grew up lounging on sat across from an ecru suede armless couch that Melissa had picked out. In her parents' bedroom, the black bamboo platform bed was glaringly out of synch with the antique Shaker bureau her mother had bought right after Becca was born.

The disharmony in which her parents lived unsurprisingly manifested itself in more than just their mismatched furniture. This had been apparent to Becca from the moment she stepped off the plane. Her mom and dad had been standing together, holding hands, at the Denver airport baggage claim, their focus entirely on each other — which had given Becca a chance to study them before they saw her. She had to admit, they did look happy. Without Melissa's influence, her dad was more casually dressed than usual, in faded jeans and an untucked white button-down. Her mom was leaning against him, whispering something into his ear. She looked thinner — and she had always been thin — in her dark jeans and low-cut red sweater.

What disturbed Becca was her father's response to her mom's whisper. He listened, and smiled, just like he was supposed to, but Becca got the feeling that it was a mechanical response — that he would have smiled in just the same way, no matter what her mother had said. That he wasn't really listening at all.

As soon as they saw her, they had dropped each other's hands like teenagers caught making out in the back of a jalopy by the cops. Fear of her reaction was clear on their faces. But Becca just smiled. What was she going to do, make a scene in the middle of freaking Denver airport? She'd known they were coming together to pick her up and had time to prepare on the plane. Not that one could ever really be prepared to see two people who had spent a solid decade detesting each other suddenly holding hands.

Ever since she'd finally talked to them together a week ago, she'd been trying to wrap her head around it all. But they hadn't said anything beyond the most obvious, necessary explanation.

"We reconnected," her mom had explained from the kitchen phone. "We're very happy."

"We didn't want to hurt anyone." Her dad had joined in on the upstairs extension. "If you feel like you want to see Melissa, I know she'd love it. She doesn't want to cut you from her life."

Melissa, the woman who had never once called Becca on her birthday, didn't want to cut her from her life? Gee, what a goddamn comfort.

"Martin's dealing with some anger," her mom had continued, "but I'm sure he'd like to talk to you. And I know how much you adore Mia and Carter, so you should still think of them as your brother and sister."

"Uh . . . okay." As far as Becca was concerned, ditching *them* was the only ray of sunshine in this whole mess.

"So . . . you're coming home for spring break, right?" Her mom's voice had sounded shrill through the phone. "We'll talk about all of this then. You'll see how happy we are!"

At least she had Harper. Becca had spent a good part of the last week in the Waddles' basement and at the Rainy Day Books Café. Her best friend had sat with her when she called Melissa — a call that had been mostly silent on Becca's end. Her stepmother, on the other hand, had quite a lot to say — about *both* of Becca's parents. Her father, apparently, had cheated on Melissa more than once in the past several years. And her mother had regularly made late night hang-ups to their house for the duration of their marriage. Both of these were tidbits Becca would have been perfectly content not knowing. Her stepmother, however, seemed to take great pleasure in sharing them with her. When the phone call was finally winding down, Melissa had asked Becca if she wanted to get together for lunch. Harper, who could hear the whole thing from her nearby perch, shook her head and mouthed an emphatic "nnooooo!"

"I'm pretty busy, and I'm about to go back to school, but next time I'm in town, definitely."

Becca didn't mean it. Hanging up the phone, she knew she wouldn't see or talk to Melissa again, unless her parents split up and Melissa and her dad got back together. So really, as usual, she knew nothing.

The best thing Harper had done was come with her to Martin's house. She'd called in advance and he'd agreed to let her come over to pack up her room. He'd seemed fine on the phone, so when they showed up — the back of Judd's borrowed Saturn loaded with empty boxes — and he answered the door totally plastered, Becca hadn't quite known what to do. She'd tried to step around him, but he'd stood in front of her, blocking the door with his unsteady body. Harper had immediately taken charge.

"Martin," she'd announced loudly, "Harper Waddle. Becca's good friend. We've met. We just want to come in, pack up a few things. . . ."

Martin had looked at Harper, then back at Becca. "She left me," he drawled, sounding as if her mother's defection still confused him, as if he thought, perhaps, Becca might be able to shed light on it all.

"I know." Becca shifted from one foot to the other. "I'm really sorry, Martin. Are you okay?"

"I should have come to Vermont." He shook his head slowly, leaning precariously against the doorjamb. "That's when it happened the first time, with her and that son-of-a-bitch father of yours. But I stayed here. Because of my kids. Don't —" He pointed at

Becca, jabbing his finger like he thought he was close enough to touch her. "Don't ever have kids."

"That's excellent advice, sir." Harper stepped forward. "Why don't you tell me all about it while Becca goes upstairs?"

For a moment, Martin looked like he was about to accede. Then he seemed to remember something. "Hang on," he instructed, closing the door as he disappeared into the house.

"Thanks for trying," Becca whispered. She hadn't expected her stepfather to be such a mess. Even his clothes — which had never been pristine — seemed wrinkled and tattered.

"Somebody's been hitting the bottle," Harper observed in a low voice.

Martin opened the door with a large cardboard box in his arms.

"Almost forgot," he said, an ugly glimmer in his dark eyes, "I packed you up."

"Oh." Becca took the box: it was suspiciously light. There was no way he'd packed everything in her room in that one box, and she knew her mom hadn't packed anything but her clothes. Possessions aside, she just wanted to spend a few minutes in her room. It wasn't the greatest room in the world, but she'd lived in it for seven years, and . . . didn't it help to say goodbye to a place? To make it official and final, just like she had with Stuart?

"Maybe I should just walk through really quick," Becca tried politely, "to make sure you didn't miss anything."

"I didn't," Martin declared definitively. "Anyway, you don't live here anymore, so you don't really need to come in, do you?"

Becca felt like she'd been punched in the stomach. It was one thing for her to blame herself for her parents' resumed relationship; it was quite another for Martin to do so.

Harper had grabbed her arm and steered her rapidly down the front steps back to the car. "Thanks, Martin," she'd said brightly over her shoulder. Her grip on Becca's arm felt both like a vice and a life vest.

By the time they were in the car, Becca was crying. Harper went straight to the Rainy Day Books Café, where her shift was about to start, and after four Green-Eyed Monsters, Becca had decided that the meager possessions in the box — which she'd piled on the crumb-covered corner table — were really the only ones that mattered. Martin was mean, but he wasn't *that* mean. He'd returned all of her yearbooks, as well as her photograph albums and school papers.

As soon as Harper had gotten a break, she'd slid into the wooden chair across from Becca and tried to change the subject by starting in on Stuart again. Becca didn't know how many more ways she could explain it. Stuart was great, she loved him, she couldn't handle being with him, he was better off without her. There. Nutshell.

"Well," Harper shook her head matter-of-factly. "Can't argue with the you-being-crazy part."

"I gotta go," Becca sighed. "Dinner with good ol' Mom and Dad."

"Leave the box here. I'll keep it in Waddle storage for as long as you need."

"Thank you." Becca gave Harper a hug. "It'll be safer with you anyway."

Becca thought about safety on the walk back to her dad's. The times she'd actually felt safe were few and far between — and the foundation of her safe feeling had been built, each and every time, on a lie. Which didn't mean anything: it was just something good to remember. Something to stash in her back pocket for the next time she started to feel like everything was all good.

Her father was sitting on Melissa's ecru suede couch when she got home, remote in hand, tie loose, flipping through the What's Playing list on TiVo.

"Hey, sweetie," he said, glancing up at her. "Good day?"

"Yeah." Becca plopped down on her mom's flowered couch. She just had to ask. "So . . . what's going on with you two? Are you getting married, or . . . what?"

284

Her dad's mouth opened, as if he were attempting to form words, but nothing came out. "Uh . . ." He kept his eyes on the T.V. "It's just . . . we're just seeing what happens. You know."

"Okay. Because Mom thinks you're getting married. As soon as the divorces are final, obviously. Maybe you two should talk about that."

The TiVo *doing*'ed as her dad pressed "play" on some emergency room show. "Yeah, I guess we should."

Becca leaned her back into the cherry-red flowery cushions and watched as a surgeon sliced through some woman's fatty outer layer and stuck his hands in her bloody innards. Without flinching, without thinking about everything that could go wrong. He went straight for the guts.

That's what we humans do. Even if we don't mean to. We go for the guts. Well, from now on, Becca was going to keep her guts under lock and key, and keep her bloody hands to herself.

Angatu giggled.

"What is it?" Something seemed to be wrong with the fliers, but Kate — who had learned to *speak* Amharic, but couldn't *read* it worth a damn — had no idea what. Had Habiba's command of her native tongue grown weak? Had she made some unintentional joke that would undercut the purpose of what Kate was trying to do?

Angatu, in the dim light of her tiny room in back of Abebech's restaurant, held up a flier for Kate and Dorothé. A whole cardboard box of them, marked AIR MAIL, rested on the gray blanket that covered the younger girl's sleeping pallet on the floor.

"It says 'Mulugeta the Fraud,'" she exclaimed, eyes dancing. "It tells the whole story of what his uncle did, and how Mulugeta knows it's a lie."

"Go, Habiba." Dorothé was impressed. Habiba had copied the fliers on brightly colored paper — some were pink, others neon

285

green and yellow. Certainly they were going to be hard for anyone in Teje to miss.

"What's this?" Kate asked in Amharic, pointing to what looked like a list of numbers on the bottom of the page.

"That's the good part," Angatu grinned. "That tells people how many babies die every year in villages without a well, versus how many die in villages *with* a well. Then it shows the same for education, marriage age, hours of work per week."

"I didn't tell her any of that," Kate said, confused.

"She did her research." Dorothé nodded proudly. "Cool sister you've got."

Yes, Habiba was definitely a cool sister. Not only had she gone above and beyond on the fliers, she'd sent along a care package (with packets of real Tide laundry detergent and six Hershey bars with almonds), *and* she had sent a Hello Kitty t-shirt for Angatu. Kate didn't think she'd ever seen Angatu as happy as when she'd opened the paisley wrapping paper and seen a pale pink t-shirt that was just for her.

"It's new?" she'd asked in awe. "No one else had it before?"

"It's brand-new," Kate had explained. "It's only ever been yours."

Angatu had put the t-shirt at the very bottom of her black plastic crate of clothes. She wanted to keep it just like it was, she said — perfect, and clean — until she had a special occasion to wear it.

Tonight was definitely not that special occasion. Tonight they would all be wearing black and sneaking into Teje in the dead of night to tape fliers on every available surface. As soon as the fliers had come in the mail (a week later than even Kate's worst-case scenario, thanks to the Ethiopian mail system), she and Dorothé had set about making plans. First they would borrow a car from their neighbor Isaac, and then, once it was dark, they would drive to Teje and hang the fliers. Habiba, thinking of everything, had even included duct tape in her package. Angatu wanted to come along and Abebech had agreed to let her, although Abebech herself was too nervous about being implicated to participate in person. She had, however, given Angatu a large red cooler full of food and drinks to take in Isaac's car.

"Let's go," Kate urged, feeling a sudden nervousness. She was really going to do this, and once she did, she couldn't go back — whatever the consequences. Mulugeta might not react like she and Dorothé thought he would. He might maneuver politically to get them kicked out of Mekebe or Kellem. Although it was highly unlikely, he might retaliate violently. Mulugeta had a lot at stake. Once the fliers were up and people had read them, it was going to require a considerable amount of diplomacy to help him save face and get him to agree to let them build a well. She hoped, however, that that diplomacy would take place on the village level. If all went well, the Water Partners team wouldn't see Mulugeta again until he had already been shamed and convinced it was in his best interest to allow a well on his land.

Kate had to admit it would have been nice to have Darby on her side for whatever was coming. He wasn't smarter than she was, but he was a more experienced negotiator. But if she couldn't use him, she couldn't use him; she'd figure it out as she went along.

The drive to Teje was more chorus rehearsal than espionage. Angatu taught Kate and Dorothé her favorite folk song, and Kate taught Angatu and Dorothé the title song from "Free to Be You and Me." By the time they neared Teje, they were singing in rounds and laughing so hard Kate almost missed the turn-off.

But as soon as they were on the narrow dirt road, the car grew silent. Angatu, who was up far later than she was used to, started yawning. Teje was silent at night. Even the animals, locked inside the compounds, seemed to be sleeping. Of all the huts on the main road, only a few had lantern light coming through the windows.

"This is it." Kate looked at Dorothé and exhaled, trying to release her nerves.

Dorothé reached over and placed a hand over Kate's on the steering wheel. "We're doing the right thing." She nodded with a certainty that gave Kate the push she needed to get out of the car.

Yes — she was doing the right thing. Too much was at stake for her to give up now, just because she was nervous. Scared, even. What was her own fear compared to the life of a child? And those were the terms of this particular situation. "Life and death" was not an exaggeration.

As she taped the first flier up on a corrugated metal fence on the main road, she still couldn't help thinking of Darby, and not about the practical reasons it would have been nice to have him on her side. No, what she thought, as she ripped of a piece of duct tape with her teeth and pressed it against the cold metal, was *He would be proud of me if he knew. I think he would be proud.*

She looked back at Angatu, who smiled at her from the safety of the backseat, and reminded herself that this year wasn't about making anyone else proud. Not her parents. Not Magnus. Certainly not Darby. Not even her sister. This year was about making *herself* proud. And putting up these fliers — no matter what happened — was something she could be proud of. Getting a well built in Teje was the most important thing she could accomplish in her time in Ethiopia. That, and finding Angatu's sister.

If she accomplished those two things, she could go home in June knowing that jumping on Harper's Dream Train had been the right thing to do. Even if she never went to Harvard. Or if she never saw Magnus again. Even if Darby hated her.

If she didn't accomplish them . . .

Kate couldn't complete the thought in any conscious way, but she couldn't stop the vaguely formed impression, in the back of her mind, that if she failed — either to get a well built or to reunite Angatu and Masarat — she wouldn't be able to go home at all.

At least not with any pride, and not with any peace of mind.

From: mags@stockholmsuniv.se

To: katherinef@ucb.edu

Subject: Kate?

Kate—

Where are you? I haven't heard from you, which makes me think perhaps we've moved on. Am I wrong? Let me know. Because if we haven't, I should feel really guilty about hanging out with the girl down the hall. Her name's Hannah and we've been out for coffee a couple of times. She's no Kate, but no one will ever compare to you.

Say the word, and I'll give up caffeine. Hope taking the water is everything you hoped.

Love always, Magnus

THIRTEEN

Kate never got scared in scary movies. No matter how many blind corners the pretty, scantily clad heroine rounded, no matter how loud or jarring the music got, or how many fake-outs there were before the knife/sledgehammer/chain saw finally hit its mark . . . the suspense never got to her.

But *waiting* was another story. Waiting for her college admittance letters had been *terrifying*. Waiting for a reaction from Mulugeta was even worse. Every night she and Dorothé went to dinner at Abebech's restaurant and planted themselves at the iron-rod table in the center of the patio expressly for the purpose of catching snippets of conversation. In the last week, they'd heard a plethora of rumors, none substantiated and each one wilder than the last. That Mulugeta had committed suicide (false), that he had packed up in the middle of the night and moved to the Sudan (false), that he had found and killed the person who put up the fliers (definitely false).

Only one rumor had potential as truth. The source of the rumor was a village man who'd been in Teje for several days, visiting his sick brother, when the fliers appeared in all their neon glory. The content of the rumor seemed just unsensational enough to be real. Of course, for that reason, no one but Kate and Dorothé put much stock in it.

"How many elders went to see him?" Kate asked Dorothé in a low voice. It seemed the whole village of Mekebe had turned up at the restaurant to hear the latest twists on the Teje drama, and Kate didn't want to be overheard.

"I didn't hear specifics, but it sounded like at least five. Maybe more."

Don't get excited, Kate told herself. They'd been hearing things for days, and none of them had been true. "So then what? How long were they there?"

"At least two hours." Dorothé grew quiet, then leaned in to Kate and whispered. "Somebody else is talking about it. Hold on."

She leaned back in her chair and casually stretched her neck. The two men at the table behind her continued their conversation, heedless of the eavesdropping Frenchwoman. In the several moments it took Dorothé to get the jist of their conversation, Kate crossed and uncrossed her legs, wondering how much weight she'd lost in Ethiopia. The food was great, and she ate tons of it, but the physical labor had turned her thighs to lean muscle under her jeans and her arms had never been more toned.

"They heard the same thing." Dorothé leaned forward, excited. "A group of village elders went to Mulugeta's compound, met with him for several hours, and left."

"When was this?"

"Last night."

"So things are happening." Kate's heart was pounding.

"Looks like it." They exchanged meaningful looks.

"What if he knows who did it?"

"How's he going to know?"

"The paper, for one thing," Kate surmised. "There's no Office Depot around the corner with a wide variety of paper colors. He'll know it didn't come from Ethiopia —"

"Relax." Dorothé smiled. "That just makes it more confusing. The Amharic was perfect. And as good as we all are at speaking

Amharic, we're not that good, and none of us can write worth a damn, so he'll think it couldn't have been any of us."

"Saved by Habiba." Kate took a sip of her pungent St George beer, hoping Dorothé was right.

A sickly combination of hope and fear kept her up for most of the night, tossing beneath her mosquito net as though she had a fever. She tossed as the chickens grew quiet, and turned as Jessica snored "adorably," then tossed some more as the first hint of dawn awoke the rooster. Finally, she got up, pulled on jeans and a long-sleeved purple tee, and started a fire in the cookstove.

Cooking with dung really wasn't so bad, Kate reasoned, tossing a patty into the stove opening. She hardly even smelled it anymore. And it heated up yesterday's coffee pretty damn fast. The Ethiopians in the village would have been horrified to know that Americans re-heated their coffee, but Kate had gotten used to it when water was still scarce in the days before the well, and now she didn't mind the slightly turned taste.

Just as steam started to rise from the mouth of the black, clay coffee pot, a cacophony of voices entered the compound gate. Who would be visiting at this time of morning? Kate leaned over Jessica's cot to unlatch the window and peered into the yard.

Mulugeta stood ten feet in front of her, wrapped in a mud-red natala, his dula held stiffly over his shoulders. At the sound of the window opening, he turned, and his eyes met Kate's, unreadable. She was sure, in that moment, that her eyes gave away everything — but she was too shocked to be able to cover much. *What did this mean? Why was he here?*

A member of Mulugeta's party — which numbered about twelve — walked to the door of Darby and Jean-Pierre's hut and raised his dula to knock. Darby opened the door before wood met wood. Clearly he hadn't gotten much sleep either, Kate thought. He was already dressed for the day, in khaki shorts and a white t-shirt, but he looked weary. She knew he'd been hearing rumors, too. Everyone had. Kate had caught him looking at her at the site in Kellem yesterday. Did he suspect? If so, why hadn't he said anything?

She watched, barely breathing, as the men disappeared into Darby and Jean-Pierre's hut. The second they disappeared from sight, Kate ran to Dorothé's cot.

"Get up!" She reached under the mosquito net and shook Dorothé's arm.

"Quoi?" Dorothé moaned in French. "What's the problem?"

"Mulugeta's here! He just went in Darby's hut with a bunch of elders."

Dorothé shot up like she'd been bitten. "How long have they been here? What did they say?" She fought her way out of the mosquito net and ran for the coffee pot. "Did they look angry?" She poured herself a cup with shaking hands.

"Nobody looked angry. They all seemed very calm. Mulugeta just looked at me — like, *through* me. No reaction at all."

Dorothé was pacing the dirt floor. "Okay, that's good. That's good."

"Why is it good?"

"I don't know, it just sounds good."

Jessica propped herself up on one elbow. "Why are we up?"

"We're not." Kate shook her head. "Go back to sleep."

"Stop shouting." Jessica pulled her flimsy blanket over her head and huddled back into her cot.

Kate rolled her eyes at Dorothé, then whispered, "Should we go outside? Wait for them to come out?"

"It could be hours." Dorothé bit her lower lip. How she managed to look chic in a flimsy kelly-green tank, boxer shorts, and flip-flops Kate would never understand.

"We could feed the chickens?" Kate suggested.

"Perfect." Dorothé nodded, grabbing for one of the white cotton bras hanging from the line over the cookstove.

"That's mine," Kate observed, heading for the chicken enclosure. Dorothé grabbed another one.

Feeding chickens, as it happened, was anything but time-consuming. It involved getting the chickens outside, getting grain from the shed, and dispersing said grain on the ground, hardly an activity designed to run out the clock. Yet somehow they made it last. When the door to Darby's hut opened an hour later, they were standing innocently in the yard, scattering grain to an ever-plumper group of hens.

The men walked silently to the compound gate and disappeared into the street. Mulugeta was the last to leave and caught Kate's eye as he passed. He nodded, lifting a hand in greeting. Then he was gone.

He knows. Kate looked at Dorothé, whose face echoed her panic. Was he going to let them build a well?

"Congratulations." Darby's voice broke the silence from the door of his hut.

Dorothé spoke first. "Why were they here?"

"Oh." Darby looked at Kate, who put on an innocent face. "They came to say Mulugeta will allow us to build on his land."

"Without payment?" Kate managed to ask, joy flooding her chest.

"He sees it as the least he can do to repay his village for the riches the land has granted him."

That was how they were allowing him to save face. He allowed the village to build a well on his land, they allow him to maintain his so-called history. It was exactly what Kate had hoped would happen. She wanted to laugh, cry, scream her joy. But Darby was still looking at her. She cleared her throat.

"Well, good. It's the right thing to do."

"Yes," Darby agreed. "Of course, we didn't plan ahead for this —"

"But we can fit it in. Right?" Kate wasn't going to lose this just because he couldn't plan ahead.

"I may have ordered some extra equipment a few weeks ago." She thought she caught the glimmer of a smile behind Darby's eyes. "Should be in next week. We'll start in Teje as soon as we're done in Kellem."

He'd ordered equipment *weeks* ago! He'd had faith in her!

"Good." A smile blossomed across her face as well. Suddenly she wanted to kiss him. And not a grateful, thanks-for-not-being-an-asshole kiss. She wanted to *kiss* him — full-mouth, tongue to tongue, wet, passionate kiss him. Her stomach somersaulted. "Uh, okay." Kate turned away — fast — barely missing a brown-spotted hen. The hen squawked in her wake as she ran-walked back to her hut.

She wanted to kiss Darby. A lot. For a long time. Which didn't mean she liked him. It just meant that she was attracted to him. It was possible to be attracted to someone and not like them: she just never had felt that way before. So this was new. But unimportant. There was Magnus to consider for one thing. Although that did seem to have dimmed to mere friendship. But the disliking thing was huge. She didn't make out with people she didn't like.

Kate took a deep breath. She had more than enough on her plate — the well in Teje, finding Angatu's sister. Darby would never be anything more than a distraction anyway, and probably not even a pleasant one.

Whatever this attraction was, the best thing to do was just ignore it.

Forget she'd ever noticed.

No problem.

"Cheesie?" Harper walked into her parents' bedroom and offered her father a striped IKEA tray on which she'd placed four mini grilled cheese sandwiches, a bowl of tomato soup, ten celery sticks, and a Dr Pepper.

He looked up from his sudoku puzzle and smiled. Books and DVDs were piled everywhere, along with an iPod Harper had programmed with his favorite Frank Sinatra and Dean Martin hits and several Spanish learning tapes. Her father had decided that his accident was God's way of telling him to learn a second language. "Yesterday your mom made me mini meat loaf, accompanied by mini mashed potatoes and mini sorbet. I think she's finally lost her mind."

"The woman has a passion." She placed the tray on his lap and sat down gingerly beside him on the queen-sized bed. Even though he was healing more every day, she was always afraid of hurting him. "How do you feel?"

Her father still had a cast on his right arm and leg, but he was able to move a little on crutches. He'd even taken a hobbling stroll around the block two days ago. It had taken an hour and a half, and he'd slept for six hours afterward, but the tiny triumph had eased the constant knot in Harper's stomach.

"Itchy." He set the sudoku game book on the blond oak nightstand and picked up a Cheesie. "How do *you* feel?"

I haven't written in three days. Judd and his new girlfriend make me sick. I still haven't gotten up the decency or nerve to thank Mr. Finelli for writing my new college recommendation. Speaking of which, I'm supposed to hear from NYU in a few days and I'm terrified. On top of all that, despite not having eaten chocolate for five days, twelve hours, and thirty-two minutes, I'm still packing twelve of my non-freshman fifteen. . . .

"Harp? Did you hear me?" He was waving his cast in front of her face.

"Me? I'm fine. Great. Eat some soup."

Her father gave her a look but obediently picked up his spoon. He was getting better at using his left hand, although whenever she took a look at his half-filled-in crossword puzzles, she became exceedingly confused by the scrawled letters in the tiny white boxes.

Harper leaned back against the pillows that were piled three deep against the headboard. It felt so good to sit on a real bed instead of her flat, dingy mattress in the basement. Maybe she'd hang out with her father for a while, keep the old guy company. She had at least an hour before she had to change out of her Nike sweats and into the dreaded black-and-white catering ensemble.

"You look more exhausted than I was after my trek around the block," he commented. "Why don't you shut your eyes for a minute?"

"Maybe for a minute," she murmured. Her eyelids felt so heavy, and she was so comfortable. . . .

The room was dark except for the small reading light next to her dad's side of the bed when she jerked awake who-knew-how-long later. A small puddle of drool dampened the pillow beside her. Harper sat up straight, panic setting in. The party started at seven o'clock. She and her mom were supposed to get there at five o'clock — when there was still some semblance of light in the sky. *Shit!*

"Jesus!" she shouted. "What time is it?"

Her father glanced at the clock next to the bed. "Seven-thirty," he answered calmly. The tray with the Cheesies, the soup, and the celery sticks was gone.

"I have to go!" She started to get up, but Mr. Waddle reached out with his good hand and held onto her.

"Relax. Amy's helping your mom tonight. They left over two hours ago." Amy? As in her sister, Amy? The one who never lifted a well-manicured finger for anyone?

"I've been asleep —"

"Forever," he finished. "You were snoring. I couldn't even concentrate on sudoku."

Harper settled back into the pillows. She was the worst daughter in the world. She'd *promised* her mom she would help tonight. It didn't matter that she was working full time at the café and writing her novel in addition to being Caterer Extraordinaire. She had *responsibilities*. Responsibilities that did not include three-hour naps.

"Did I ever tell you I wanted to be an architect?" her father asked suddenly, propping the cushion behind his back. Maybe she'd been talking in her sleep, and this was the continuation of the conversation they'd been having.

"Uh . . . no." She tried to imagine him sitting behind a drafting table, chewing pencils for ten hours a day like Sophie's dad, instead of tramping around construction sites talking to his subcontractors. It was impossible.

"I went to New York one time just to look at the buildings. For three days I walked the streets, staring up, memorizing every detail of the Empire State Building, the Chrysler. . . ." He shrugged. "In the end, I didn't think I had the math skills. Maybe if I'd gone for it, I would have realized I did."

"And half your bones wouldn't be broken right now." She made the joke because she didn't want to say what she was really thinking. That it sucked her father didn't follow his dream. What was up with her parents? Her mother had wanted to be a famous chef, her father a famous architect. Why did they just . . . give up . . . so easily?

He shifted to look at her — not an entirely easy task given the amount of plaster on his body. "This isn't me wallowing in self-pity. I just want you to keep going on that book of yours. Don't let anything stand in the way."

"I'm not!" At least, she wasn't letting anything stand in the way by *choice*. It wasn't a *choice* to spend every free minute helping her mother cater parties to keep the family afloat. It was a necessity. And she wasn't going to bitch about it. Not even to her father. Especially not her father.

"You've officially got the night off," he announced. "Go down into your dungeon, lock yourself in the bathroom, and *write*."

"You know about the bathroom?"

"Mom tells me everything."

"Oh." She pictured her parents huddling together, discussing their daughter's strange habits. It was unnerving.

But when she finally hauled herself off the bed, she found bits of dialogue running through her brain. Her characters wanted to talk, and it was her duty (one of many) to turn on her computer and *let* them. She needed to see this through.

"Dad?"

"Yeah?"

"When the letter from NYU comes, hide it from me. Hide all of the college letters."

He peered at her over his drugstore-bought reading glasses. "You're joking."

"I don't want to know. Not until the book is done." She shook her head, trying to find the right words. "Besides, I'm not sure I should go even if I *do* get in. Y'know, with everything that's happened . . ."

"You're right. We're very lucky you didn't get into NYU last year."

"I know." She couldn't imagine the disaster their finances would have been if they'd been paying for a private college education on top of everything.

"We're lucky because it gave us the opportunity to see what our daughter was made of. To see we raised her to turn something bad into something good . . . to see her stand up and help out when her family needed her most." Her father sounded suspiciously close to crying, which made Harper want to bawl like a baby. "But know this. Whatever college is lucky enough to get *you,* we'll find a way to pay for it. Period."

Harper swallowed hard. "Thanks, Dad."

As she headed back to her dungeon to lock herself in the bathroom as commanded, she realized that for the first time since her dad's accident she felt . . . light. And it had nothing to do with her three-hour nap or his promise to pay for college. Her father was proud of her. No daughter could ask for more than that.

"*There* you are!"

Isabelle's shrill voice startled Becca out of her reverie. She closed her collection of Grace Paley short stories and smiled wearily up at her friend, who stood at the end of a massive bookcase, one hand on her jean-covered hip.

"I've been hiding," Becca admitted. She'd chosen to study for her upcoming English midterm in the most tucked away carol in the library — partly because she wanted to avoid Stuart, and partly because she genuinely couldn't afford any distractions. Her grades hadn't exactly been stellar lately, and she needed to ace this exam. It would have been a tall order in the best of circumstances. The teacher was a notoriously hard grader and the readings were challenging, but for the last several weeks, it had been verging on impossible for Becca to stay on top of her schoolwork.

Part of the problem was her general state of melancholy. There was no doubt about that. But it was extra-hard to study without Stuart. They'd developed a rhythm, a process that worked for them, and she missed having him there to challenge her.

She missed everything about him.

But it was better this way. He was better off without her. And in a way, she was better off without him. Without Stuart in her life, she didn't have to worry about pretending to be happy all the time when she wasn't. She didn't have to spend all of her time with him either, which meant she was seeing a lot more of Isabelle. All in all, breaking up was definitely the best thing. She'd even stopped wanting to cry when she saw him in class five times a week and he'd stopped staring at her from across the room. At first it had been unbearable, knowing he was watching her. But eventually, when she had refused to look at him, he'd stopped looking.

Leaving class was the tricky part. Fortunately, they seemed to have decided by some sort of unspoken signal that Stuart would leave first while Becca dallied over her books.

"Time for a dinner break," Isabelle announced. "Can you say, fusilli with meatballs?"

"Mmmm," Becca responded, packing her books. She pulled on her black fleece and threw her backpack over her shoulder. "We're not going to . . ."

"No," Isabelle replied, tucking her hands in the pockets of her skinny jeans. "We're not going to Stuart's dining hall. I wouldn't do that to you."

"Just checking."

Isabelle opened her mouth, then closed it.

"What?" Becca looked at her friend, suspicious.

"It's just . . . I talked to Stuart."

Becca kept looking at her.

"Well," Isabelle continued defensively, "he's a friend. And he's hurting."

Becca's insides caved in on themselves. Isabelle gave her a look back. "I know you don't want to hear it, but he's in pain. Just as much as you. And you know I think this whole break-up thing is stupid."

"I can't —"

"I know. You can't. Whatever." Isabelle shook her head. "You and Stuart are not your parents."

"I'm just going to hurt him —"

"You *already* hurt him." Isabelle was silent for a moment. "He misses you."

"He said that?"

"He didn't have to say it. He misses you. I could tell."

Stuart missed her. What did she expect? She would have been upset if he *didn't* miss her. But it didn't change anything. Smokers missed cigarettes when they quit. Alcoholics missed alcohol. Drug addicts missed drugs. That didn't mean they should relapse, just to get rid of the craving — because, ultimately, cigarettes, alcohol, and drugs were bad for them. And she was bad for Stuart. They were naturally going to crave each other — at least for a while. But over time, those cravings would diminish and finally fade away. She was sure of it. Almost.

Tabasco. Anything tasted better with a little Tabasco. Standing at the kitchen counter in Sam's apartment, clad in the burgundy terry robe she'd borrowed from J.D.'s closet, Sophie shook the bottle several times over the watery Ramen noodles she'd boiled for dinner. She dug in, confident that the hot sauce would add zing to the dreaded Ramen. The first bite indicated she'd made a terrible mistake.

"Aaack!" Thank goodness the nearly overflowing trash can was nearby. She leaned over it and unceremoniously spit out the noodles as they landed on top of that morning's coffee grounds. So much for dinner.

"Are you okay?" Dressed in his best pair of just-right faded jeans and a crisp white button-down, Sam was heading from his bedroom to the kitchen. Judging from the way his usually unruly blond hair had been brushed out of his face, he seemed to have spent some time in front of a mirror.

"Ramen noodles." She didn't need to say more. He hated them as much as she did. "Where are *you* going?"

"CTI's having a huge bash in Malibu."

"CTI? As in Creative Talent International? As in *my* agency?" She dumped the rest of the noodles into the garbage and shut the lid.

Each of the big three agencies in town were known to have star-studded parties at least once a year. They always invited their clients, along with whatever other big or small stars they could draw with the promise of flowing champagne, great sushi, and expensive favors.

"They invited the whole cast of *Heartland.* I'm Ellie's date." He went to the hall closet and pulled out the leather jacket he reserved for special occasions. Sophie considered pouting. *She* was a client of CTI. *She* should have been invited. "Maybe Matthew Feldman's assistant forgot to e-mail you the invite," Sam reasoned.

Of course. The guy had a new person on his desk every other day. Whoever the latest grunt was probably got overwhelmed amid all the party planning. It happened. "Give me five minutes. I'm coming with you."

Sam hesitated. "Maybe you should try Matthew Feldman's cell. Y'know, just to make sure."

She adopted her signature cold, formal tone. "I happen to be one of his most valued clients. To not show up to this affair would be nothing short of rude. And I don't intend to be rude."

"Fine. But make it quick. Ellie gets pissed when I'm late to pick her up."

She had no problem keeping Her Lady of the Diaphragm waiting. She'd kept Sophie waiting long enough. Every few days she promised she was going to talk to the casting director about Sophie's guest spot, but so far nothing had materialized. Nonetheless Sophie wanted to get to Malibu while everyone was still sober enough to remember meeting her. She raced toward J.D.'s room. Her vintage Halston halter dress was balled up in one of her duffel bags. With any luck, it wasn't wrinkled beyond hope.

Sophie hadn't been to Malibu since she ditched a play audition Sam had gotten her, and instead went to the beach with Trey Benson. She pushed the memory out of her mind as Sam stopped his gray Honda in front of one of the six black-jacketed valets waiting outside the ultramodern white beachfront mansion. That error in judgment had been months ago, back when she was naïve and stupid. Having sworn off boys of all ages and levels of fame, she knew she'd never again risk her career for a date.

The valet made a face as he slid into Sam's beat-up car. "Don't worry, baby," Ellie cooed, peering into her MAC compact mirror for a final makeup check and almost tripping over the first step. "Someday you'll be driving a seven series."

Sam snorted. "Ugh. I'll pass. But thanks for the vote of confidence."

"You don't want a BMW?" Ellie sounded incredulous. "Huh."

Sophie smiled to herself as she followed the couple to the two headset-wearing girls who were posted outside the front of the mansion, carefully checking off each guest's name before allowing them to enter. It was a relief to see Sam and Ellie have *any* disagreement. Up until now, he'd been so blinded by her perfectly perky breasts that he hadn't seemed to notice she lacked a brain.

After Ellie gave her name "plus one" and got waved forward, Sophie stepped up. "Sophie Bushell," she enunciated clearly. The girl in the headset flipped through several pages, then shook her head.

"Sorry. You're not on the list."

Sam looked back as Ellie pulled him by his hand toward the front entrance of the glass palace before them. "Just a little glitch," Sophie called. "Go ahead. I'll be right in."

Sophie turned back to the Keeper of the List. "I'm a CTI client," she announced in her most authoritative voice. "You can check with Matthew Feldman's office if you need to."

"Not on the list, you can't come in." The sleek brunette was already looking over her shoulder at the next group of arrivals. The other girl, dressed in a rainbow-striped figure-hugging number, readjusted her headset and studiously avoided Sophie's gaze.

"But I came with my friends," Sophie insisted. "I'm a *client*. What am I supposed to do? Sit on the curb?"

Before the dark-haired girl could slap her with yet another snarky remark about The List, Sophie felt a warm hand grip her shoulder. "She's with me."

She knew it the second she felt his skin touch hers. Even though she hated him, she had to admit he looked hot in a casual pale gray t-shirt, worn khakis, and brown leather flip-flops. Like always, Trey Benson's olive skin was so flawless it looked air-brushed. As he headed past Sophie, his entourage in tow, Brunette beamed at him. "Of course, Trey! Great! Welcome!" She waved Sophie through, but didn't make eye contact.

Sophie didn't want to accept even the smallest favor from Trey. But she also didn't want to loiter on the Pacific Coast Highway for the next three hours. She swallowed her pride and followed him into the party.

Inside, music pounded as waiters circulated with drinks. Every beverage had been dyed lime green, the agency's signature color. Sophie grabbed a lime green champagne as she looked around for Sam and Ellie, who'd already disappeared into the massive throng. The back wall of the mansion, which was made entirely of glass, had been opened for the party. A wide expanse of the Pacific Ocean glistened in the moonlight outside. Whoever owned the place had done it exactly like the CTI offices — all the furniture was made of glass, steel, and chrome, and colorful modern art hung everywhere. This space was cold, intimidating, and awe-inspiringly impressive, also like CTI. Sophie headed outside to search for Matthew Feldman and get a glimpse of what promised to be the coolest infinity pool she'd ever seen.

Thirty minutes later, she came to the conclusion that agency parties sucked. Matthew Feldman was nowhere to be found, Sam and Ellie were heavily ensconced with the entire cast of *Heartland*, and every person she tried to talk to snubbed her once they realized she wasn't famous. She'd finished off her green champagne out of boredom and frustration, and followed it with two appletinis. It wasn't until the infinity pool began to sort of roll back and forth that she realized she might have hit her alcohol limit. *I'll lounge on one of the chaises until Sam and Diaphragm Dora are ready,* she decided sleepily, stumbling a bit as she walked around the vast pool.

"Hey! I don't even get a thanks?" Trey was walking toward her in all his tanned glory, gesturing with his green Cosmopolitan. "You'd have stood out there all night if it wasn't for me."

"Thanks. Now if you'll excuse me." She started again toward the white canvas-covered chaise, but Trey reached for her arm.

"Come on, babe. That's no way to treat an old friend." He pronounced the words gently, his saucer-shaped brown eyes smiling at her.

"But I guess lying to an old friend to get her to go to Aspen with you for Christmas is okay?" Sophie stared hard at him.

He held up his hands. "I would've apologized if you'd ever returned my calls. That's *your* bad."

"I didn't see you issuing any *mea culpas* when I saw you at Mojito," she responded tartly. Her voice was a little louder than she wanted it to be — a typical side effect when she drank too much.

He walked a little closer, and she could smell his musk-scented soap. God, how she used to love to smell his soap. "The girl I was with was a jealous type. I didn't want a scene. Never know when a camera might be there to catch the moment, right?"

Sophie knew he was referring to the photo of him and his costar Pasha DiMoni kissing. The photo that had sent her running back to her friends in Boulder, swearing she'd never set foot in LA again. Rage, fueled by lime-green appletinis, boiled up inside of her. "You are such an ASSHOLE!" she couldn't help yelling. "You USED me!"

He rolled his famous eyes. "*I* used *you?*"

307

"Duh." Nothing more eloquent came to mind. A few black-clad partygoers were watching now, but she was beyond caring. This was her chance to tell off Trey and she was taking it.

"Every time you looked at me, you saw your shot," Trey told her, his voice calm and even. "You wanted my agent, my contacts, my ability to get you in the door of an audition. I didn't mind. I get it. When you're starting out, you have to make every opportunity. They don't come to you, that's for damn sure."

"You're wrong. I liked you —"

"Maybe. Or maybe you liked the idea of me. Now you can get off your soapbox, because if I'd been Miguel Estoban the bus boy you wouldn't have given me the time of day. We both know that."

Sophie was stunned. Trey *was* an asshole. But he was also . . . right. She *had* seen him as her way into the Business. She couldn't help it. Still, she'd never *lied* to him, never humiliated him. He was the one to blame for what had happened in Aspen. Not her. She wanted — needed — to lash out.

"I'm just glad I never had sex with you!" she seethed, her voice still louder than intended. "I've got no doubt it would have been as shallow and unsatisfying as every one of your movies."

"Sophie!" Sam was walking toward her, a concerned expression on his face. She saw Diaphragm Ellie hovering in the background, staring at her as if she was insane. Maybe she was. "Let's get out of here."

"Hold on!" Sophie felt free now. The martinis and her big mouth had freed her. She felt like going swimming.

Trey wasn't done either. "Right now, you're a semi-attractive, semi-talented hick who doesn't have a clue how to make it in Holly-wood. Either get on the bus and go home or smarten up. Pissing me off isn't going to get you anywhere."

He turned and walked back into the crowd of admirers who'd now gathered. She heard someone telling him what a bitch she was

308

and how he'd handled her crazy rant like a gentleman. She wanted to barf. The night couldn't get any worse.

"It's *over.*" Sam swiped at her arm, but she pulled away. "We're leaving."

"*After* I go in the infinity pool," she insisted.

"You'll go now," a man's voice said. Sophie looked over to find none other than Mr. Peter Alterman, class-A pervert and CTI partner, staring sternly at her.

"I'm a client at this agency. You can't tell me to go anywhere." She knew she sounded like an idiot, but she couldn't stop. Especially for this grandpa.

His eyes narrowed. "Who's your agent?"

"Matthew Feldman. He's the *best.*"

"That little twit was fired this afternoon." He smiled smugly. "You're no longer represented by CTI. I'd like you out of my house. Now."

As Sophie finally let Sam take hold of her elbow and lead her out of the penis-flasher's house, his words echoed in her brain. *That little twit was fired this afternoon. You're no longer represented by CTI.* So much for the night not getting any worse.

JOE WADDLE'S POTENTIAL HIDING PLACES
(A.K.A. OH WHERE, OH WHERE, MIGHT MY NYU LETTER BE?)

1. IN THE BOWELS OF THEIR MATTRESS

2. UNDERNEATH THE GUEST ROOM MATTRESS,
   OBSCURED BY DUST BUNNIES

3. BEHIND THE LIVING ROOM TV,
   STRANGLED BY ALL THE WIRES/POWER CORDS

4. IN MOM'S PURSE
   (CLEVER WOMAN KEEPS IT WITH HER ALWAYS)

5. INSIDE HIS CAST GETTING SWEATY

6. IN THAT OLD TRUNK IN THE ATTIC

7. AMONG THE TANGLE OF X-MAS TREE LIGHTS
   IN THE GARAGE

8. IN MY OLD POWER PUFF GIRLS' E-Z BAKE OVEN

9. BETWEEN THE PAGES OF A BOOK
   (ONLY A FEW THOUSAND OR SO OF THOSE AROUND)

10. IN MOM'S BRA

11. IN THAT REALLY OLD TUB OF BUTTER

12. TAPED TO THE BOTTOM OF SOME RANDOM
    PIECE OF FURNITURE

13. HE ATE IT BECAUSE I DIDN'T GET IN

FOURTEEN

I t's probably in their bedroom somewhere," Harper theorized as she placed a poppy seed bagel into the aluminum slicer. "Or in the garage. I never go in the garage."

Habiba continued to froth her mocha latte in silence. She'd been making all her own drinks at the café since Harper determined her amateur barista skills were better than Harper's own professional ones.

"Do you think it's in the garage?" Harper pressed, wiping the poppy seeds on the sides of her favorite pair of old jeans.

Habiba took her freshly whipped mocha latte and headed back around the other side of the counter. "You told your dad to hide those acceptance letters for a reason. Stay strong. Finish your novel. Worry about college when it's done."

"They might not *be* acceptance letters. They might be *rejection* letters."

"I'm being optimistic." In her well-worn Gap jeans and black knit J. Crew sweater, it was hard to believe Beebs had ever been anything but an all-American teen. She also understood the massive importance of anything related to college admission. With the Fosters as parents, it would have been impossible not to.

"If by some miracle I *do* get into NYU, I've got to tell them by a certain date," Harper pointed out. "It would be irresponsible to miss the deadline."

"Then I suggest you write faster. And if you start feeling the urge to snoop, come to me. I'll talk you out of it."

Harper didn't tell Beebs that she'd already done some snooping, looking under her parents' mattress during one of her father's epic trips around the block. She'd found a note in his heavy, angular handwriting. *You will not find it. Give up.*

"You look good," Habiba noted, studying her. "I like your hair." She took her mocha latte and the PSAT study book she'd taken to toting everywhere and settled into the small brown corner table.

Lately, Harper had exchanged her sloppy hoodies for form-fitting sweaters. She'd even been wearing her hair loose around her face instead of in its usual ponytail. Not for any special reason. It was her *right* to improve her appearance — every fashion magazine said so. She perched on the stool behind the cash register and surveyed the café. Judd was taking a break, hanging, she guessed, with some CU friends she didn't know. Poppy and George hadn't been in lately, and Harper missed getting snippets of Poppy's snarky take on life between her beverage-making duties.

They're probably too busy enjoying their "benefits," she decided, wishing she and Poppy had never had that conversation in the bathroom. Maybe they had mastered "no harm, no foul," but Harper and Judd decidedly had not. They'd been ultra-polite to each other since Amelia entered the scene with a literal "bang," but their old rapport just seemed to have disappeared.

Every minute or so, Judd glanced toward the front door of the café. Harper was about to attribute this gesture to a newly developed nervous tic, when the door opened and Amelia walked in. Judd popped out of his seat and kissed her. Eventually, Amelia caught sight of Harper and waved.

I'm glad for them, Harper told herself calmly, waving back. *They're cute.* Well, Judd was cute. Upon closer viewing, Amelia's eyes were abnormally close together and her skin was pale to the point of appearing Albino. Though judging from the way Judd was now pulling her onto a sofa next to one of the overflowing bookshelves for a full-on makeout session, he didn't seem to mind these obvious flaws. Which was sweet. Really. Harper was so busy surreptitiously observing Judd and Amelia's tonsil-hockey session that she didn't notice a couple of customers had approached the counter.

"I'd like a soy latte, please."

Harper turned to find a pretty twenty-something with long chestnut brown curls, green eyes, and a heart-shaped face staring at her expectantly. Usually, she didn't make a mental catalog of her customer's physical traits. But this particular customer happened to be standing next to Mr. Finelli. Holding hands with Mr. Finelli. Her stomach, which was already feeling funky, constricted. Period cramps felt like they were migrating to her large intestine.

"Hi, Harper. Just coffee for me." Mr. Finelli looked at the woman whose hand he was holding and gestured toward Harper. "Meet one of my best-ever students. Her essays were always searing and incisive."

The woman smiled warmly. "High praise, coming from Adam. I'm Tara." Adam. She called him Adam. Of course, she did. They were clearly "together."

"Hi." There was being polite, and then there was subjecting oneself to random chitchat with the enemy. Harper had already decided this woman was the enemy, so she went off to get their drinks without another word.

Grabbing a carton of soy milk from the fridge behind the counter, Harper forced herself to take a deep breath. Was there some reason that every guy she'd ever kissed felt the need to parade in front of her with his new girlfriend? Maybe Albert Greenbaum, who'd pecked her on the lips during their family vacation to Estes Park, would drop by next to introduce her to whoever the hell *he* was dating these days.

By the time she returned with their drinks, she was fully engaged in a mental rant, but nonetheless managed to smile as she handed over the soy latte. "Nice to meet you," Tara trilled, walking away to get a packet of Splenda.

That left Mr. Finelli and Harper alone at the cash register. "Thanks for the message about my dad." She nodded. "He's doing a lot better now."

"That's great to hear." He handed over a five-dollar bill. "Keep the change." As he turned to go, she thought she heard him say something else under his breath. It sounded a lot like "I miss you."

She shook her head. Along with public humiliation, she was now suffering from public insanity. More sleep was imperative. *Not to mention a different job.* Preferably one in Alaska, where she'd run no risk of bumping into anyone she'd ever met in her entire life.

Hours later, Judd contemplated the rain that had just started to fall outside. "I say we close early."

"Why? Hot date?"

Harper was doing her best to forget about the entire afternoon by rereading *Gone with the Wind* for the fortieth time. So far, it wasn't working.

"Might hail. Roads could get icy. And it's not like anyone's going to die if they can't get their café au lait."

"Please. You just wanna make cocoa and snuggle with what's-her-name." She wasn't being a bitch, just a bantering friend. There was a difference.

Judd set down the yellow sponge he was using to wipe the glass case that housed Mr. Finelli's favorite raspberry scones and the rest of the pastries. "Are you okay?"

He sounded concerned rather than pissed. She hated it when

people were concerned. Even more than she hated it when they were pissed. "I'm great."

"You don't seem great."

"I just think engaging in PDA next to the bagel slicer isn't the most professional behavior." She looked down at her tan V-neck sweater, searching for some lint — or a poppy seed — to busy herself with.

"Amelia and I were nowhere *near* the bagel slicer."

"Sofa. Bagel slicer. Same difference."

"I think we need to talk." Judd was tugging at his dark curly hair, a sure sign something was on his mind.

Harper mustered a bright grin. "Like you said, icy roads. And I have chapter twelve waiting for me at home. Close up, would you?" She grabbed her black puffy jacket and her red backpack and race-walked toward the door.

Talking was overrated.

Breathe in. Breathe out. Breathe in. Breathe out. In . . . Out . . .

Cross-legged on her dorm room floor, Becca leaned against her bed and breathed. *So far, so good.* If this was all there was to therapeutic visualization, it was a piece of cake. Resting her hands lightly on her black sweatpant-clad knees, she consciously relaxed her shoulders.

Okay, here goes. Her new therapist — Isabelle had recently insisted she take advantage of Middlebury's therapy services — had talked her through this several times, but this was Becca's first time going solo down the visualization road.

Imagine Mom and Dad, she told herself. *Picture them tied to me by thick ropes. Hundreds of thick ropes. The ropes dig into my waist and legs and arms. I want to get them off. Off!*

When Dr. Bleiweiss had guided the visualization, her parents had been expressionless, almost like mannequins. But now they gnashed sharp, pointed teeth and struggled against the ropes, raging at her with wild, savage glares.

Becca breathed evenly. *Mannequins. Be mannequins. I am not scared of you.* After several rounds of breathing, her parents slowly grew placid. *Okay, now imagine a big pair of scissors. Big enough to cut through the ropes.* A pair of shears materialized in Becca's hand. *Use the scissors to cut the ropes. Free yourself. Cut yourself free. . . .*

Her fingers twitched against her knees as she imagined herself slicing at the ropes that bound her to her parents. Dr. Bleiweiss had said this was a common quitting-smoking visualization, and when Becca had used an addiction analogy in their second session he'd thought it might help.

If only she'd started dealing with her feelings in a mature, adult way *before* she went crazy and broke up with the only guy she'd ever loved.

Snip, snap, snip. The ropes connecting her to her parents were endless. As many as she cut, there were that many more to go. *Breathe,* she reminded herself. No matter how fruitfully the ropes multiplied, she would keep cutting. For years, if that's what it took. It had taken years for all the ropes to develop, so it made sense that it wouldn't be easy to break free.

"Sorry!"

Becca opened her eyes to find Isabelle backing out of the just-opened door.

"No, come in," she beckoned, getting up. "I'm done. I mean, I'm not *done*. But it's an ongoing thing, as Dr. Bleiweiss says. Anyway, I wanted to talk to you."

"Uh-oh." Isabelle dropped her gray messenger bag on the floor by her bed. She was dressed for the ever-improving weather in white Banana Republic pants and a red short-sleeved polo shirt. Becca felt like a shlub in her dark sweats and white ribbed tank. She pulled her knees up under her chin and looked down at the floor.

"I owe you an apology."

"Tell me you didn't fry my Nano —"

"No," Becca laughed, and glanced up. Isabelle looked scared. "Your Nano's fine. I mean, for being so . . . difficult the last month. And before that for . . ."

"Dropping off the face of the planet?"

"Yeah, that." Becca smiled apologetically. "I didn't mean to disappear. I was just . . . when I was with Stuart, I was . . ."

"Happy." Her roommate sat on the floor across from her, and put a hand on Becca's knee.

"Yeah." She tried to hold back the tears. She *had* been happy. And because of that she had abandoned her friends, treating them as if they weren't important. She was lucky they still even spoke to her. Especially since she had no one to blame but herself — both for how badly she'd acted toward them when she was with Stuart and how badly she'd treated Stuart when she'd found out about her parents.

"I know I wasn't a good friend to you for a while." Becca squeezed Isabelle's hand. "And I'm just really grateful you didn't hold it against me."

Isabelle winked at her. "I did, actually. And then I let it go. You just did what we all do."

Becca made a disparaging face. "I know. Why do we do that?"

Isabelle shrugged. "We're idiots when it comes to the boys." She raised her shapely eyebrows. "And speaking of boys, when are you going to talk to Stuart?"

Becca shook her head. It was too awful and embarrassing. He must hate her, the way she had behaved. He *should* hate her.

"Okay." Isabelle raised an I'm-backing-off hand. "Just so you know, I'm gonna keep asking."

Becca smiled wistfully. Maybe . . . just maybe . . . if she managed to cut through enough ropes, she would feel free enough to talk to Stuart again. To tell him the truth about why she'd freaked out and broken up with him.

If that time ever came, Becca knew she would still love him. She always would.

She just prayed he would still love her.

"I bet he murdered his girlfriend. Or his gay lover."

"Probably got drunk and ran a red. That's what it usually is."

Sophie moved her cell to her other ear and leaned forward on the couch. On Sam's nineteen-inch Sony hi-def TV, a dark blue pickup truck was traveling northbound at sixty miles an hour on the 110 freeway. Its occupant appeared to be a white male, midforties, wearing a white wifebeater. She was experiencing one of LA's greatest institutions, the televised car chase. And she wasn't experiencing it alone.

"Holy shit! He almost hit that Mercedes," Matthew Feldman laughed into the phone.

"What?"

"I was just fantasizing that the driver of the Mercedes was one of my asshole bosses. I'd like to see any one of those guys go up in flames."

"Goes without saying." Sophie grabbed the bag of Cool Ranch Doritos she'd opened when the chase started at least an hour ago and dumped the last of the crumbs into her open mouth.

Since the CTI party last week, she'd gone into what she was calling "self-reflective hibernation." Her mom probably would've called it "depression." She'd been living in her oldest Juicy sweats, eating junk food, and watching way too much daytime TV. Her days of rushing to auditions in the morning and to work at Mojito at night seemed like a hundred years ago. The morning after the party she'd called Celeste at home and told her she was sick and wouldn't be at work. Indefinitely.

Since then, her manager had called her at least once a day, but Sophie never answered. Every time she imagined going to Mojito, she pictured herself at the CTI party, screaming at Trey Benson, preparing to make a drunken dive into the pool and getting ordered to leave. Aside from periodic trips to the 7-11 up the street for supplies, she never wanted to go outside again.

"Unemployment is awesome," Matthew Feldman was saying. "If I was slaving for my clients right now, I would have missed this."

Matthew Feldman hadn't taken getting fired well. The first time she'd talked to him, he was so devastated he was threatening to burn his closet of suits in front of CTI as a form of protest. As the days passed, he'd relaxed to the point that he was swearing he was going to move to Hawaii's Big Island to be a bartender at the Four Seasons. In fact, he was probably wearing a Hawaiian shirt at that very minute. He was just waiting for the general manager he knew there to return his call. They'd developed a habit of watching TV together over the phone. In between providing running commentary on old game shows, soap operas, or whatever talking head was on CNN, they commiserated.

"Is he running out of gas?" Sophie asked as the pickup slowed almost to stop. It had to happen eventually. Then came the good part, when all the CPH officers jumped out of their vehicles, guns drawn, and made the poor bastard surrender.

"False alarm," Matthew Feldman announced. The pickup had sped up and was now racing toward the freeway exit.

"I give up," Sophie repeated for the millionth time. "I just can't do the actress thing anymore." Matthew Feldman had been her great hope. They were supposed to make it together. Now that their mutually beneficial business arrangement was over, she'd lost her will.

"No shit. I'd rather be a tollbooth collector than get back in the tank with the piranhas that pass as agents in this city." She could hear him chewing — probably either a Fig Newton or a Mars bar. She'd learned they were his favorites during an intense *Project Runway* marathon on Bravo.

The apartment door opened. Sam walked in and flipped on the overhead light. Sophie squinted in the unaccustomed glare. Turning on the light had seemed like too much effort earlier, so she'd just let the apartment grow dark around her. Sam looked at Sophie sitting on the sofa, then at the TV.

"You're pathetic."

"Let me call you back," she told Matthew Feldman.

"Cool. I have to call and order a pizza, anyway." He clicked off.

"I'm *resting,*" Sophie informed Sam, as she did every day when he came home from work.

He walked over to her and grabbed the remote control from her lap. "Hey! I'm watching!"

"I can tell you how it ends. Unemployed screw-up ruins his life because he tried to run instead of facing the music. Sound familiar?" Sam switched off the TV and threw a padded manila envelope in her lap.

"What's this?" The package had a Boulder postmark.

"The key to getting your ass off the couch," he declared. "Courtesy of your friend Harper Waddle." Sam headed into the kitchen and clanged the tea kettle, filling it with water.

"If it's from Harper — why's it addressed to you?"

"Because I called her and told her one of her best friends was wasting away in a huge abyss of self-pity."

"You had no right —" Sophie felt a hot flash of shame, imagining Sam and Harper talking about her behind her back. *Poor pathetic Sophie. She's lost it.*

"I had every right. I was worried. So is she." He pointed at the envelope. "And as a result of our mutual worry, she sent *that.* To me. For you."

"Why don't you go have sex with your idiot of a girlfriend and leave me alone?"

The vein pounding in Sam's forehead suggested that maybe she'd gone just a teensy bit too far. But ever since her self-imposed, self-reflective hibernation period had started, Sophie's rage toward Ellie Volkhauser had been building. It was becoming painfully evident that the girl had no intention or desire to get Sophie a guest spot on *Heartland.* She'd been had.

"I'm going to pretend you didn't say that because of your current psychosis," he informed her calmly, setting the teakettle down on the stove. "But if you ever talk about Ellie like that again, I *will* kick you out of here. Now open the fucking package."

Sophie's curiosity got the better of her. She ripped open the package and pulled out an unmarked DVD.

"I give up. What is it?"

Sam turned on the gas stove. "Put it in and find out. Believe me, by the time our chamomile tea is ready, you'll feel like a new person."

Sophie did what Sam told her. She was still pissed about him turning off the TV, but paying her share of the rent was going to be hard this month and she needed an understanding and tolerant Sam, not the pissed, sick-of-Sophie's-abuse version. But there was no way that whatever was on this DVD was going to make her feel like a new person. She was going to wait out the rest of the Year of Dreams sitting on Sam's sofa, and then she was going to go home and attend CU. Given all that had happened — and *not* happened — it was obvious she should have done that in the first place.

Dorothé put a calming hand on Kate's arm. "Take it easy," she whispered in French.

"*Je lui detest,*" Kate murmured through clenched teeth, her eyes on Darby and Mulugeta.

"Darby ou Mulugeta?" Dorothé had the gall to look amused.

"Les memes." Kate almost grinned. As frustrated as she was, there was something slightly humorous about her — a confirmed pacifist — wanting desperately to smack Darby upside the head. But from the moment their team had arrived in Teje that morning, he'd been alternating between praising Mulugeta for "his generous contribution" of the land for the well, and taking all the credit for negotiating the agreement with Mulugeta and the elders. He hadn't even glanced in Kate's direction when he made a speech to the villagers who'd gathered at the well site to celebrate.

"We're honored to be building a well here in Teje," he'd declared, going on and on about how Mulugeta had offered the land out of the goodness of his heart, and how Darby was more than happy to bring his team to such a deserving village. As if *he* were responsible! He'd even referred to his many conversations with Mulugeta — *his* many conversations! — as they had worked together to come to the terms of the deal to donate the land.

Not that Kate expected him to mention the fliers. According to Abebech, who had heard from family in Teje, the fliers had been torn down almost immediately by Mulugeta's wives. But their brief wall-time didn't mean they weren't essential in persuading the greedy elder to come around. If it hadn't been for the fliers, the other village elders would never have pressured Mulugeta, and he wouldn't have been forced to donate the land in order to save face.

The fliers were *the* reason they were building a well. They were *why* Mulugeta had agreed to let them use his land. The least Darby could do, as he blew smoke about how great Mulugeta was and aggrandized himself, would be to *look* at Kate and acknowledge in some way that she had succeeded. That *she* was saving lives, dammit!

Really, would it kill him to just *look* at her?

But he didn't. Not once.

The fact that Darby had been almost sort of nice to her lately made it even more frustrating. He'd ordered the parts for the Teje well before she'd even posted the fliers, which showed he had faith in her, even if he wouldn't have approved of her methods. So would it kill him to give her a little credit?

"You ready?" Dorothé's soft voice jerked Kate out of her irritated reverie.

"For what?" Kate looked at her blankly. Then she saw Darby walking toward them.

Dorothé groaned. "Time to split up into teams. How much you want to bet I get the drainage field?"

Darby had the dreaded clipboard clenched under one tanned arm. Kate couldn't help noticing that he looked unreasonably good in tan cargo shorts and her favorite orange t-shirt.

"Dorothé," he called, all business, "you're drainage crew leader." Then he turned to Kate, holding out the clipboard. "Kate —"

"You can't be serious."

Darby looked at her, his eyes growing cool. "What can't I be serious about?"

Dorothé threw a breezy "Have fun, you two" over her shoulder as she walked off toward the drainage site.

Kate crossed her arms. "I will not be Clipboard Girl."

"Clipboard Girl?" Darby's eyebrows rose.

"The chick who can't do anything else so you send her around to make check marks on a little form. I don't think so."

Darby nodded slowly. "So you think you're 'the chick who can't do anything else.' Interesting."

The irritation Kate had been fighting all day morphed into full-blown anger. How could he be so *calm*? So totally *unaffected* by everything she said and did?

"You know what's *interesting*?" Kate shoved her hands into the pocket of her grubby jeans. Her white t-shirt suddenly felt too tight, almost stifling. The very *air* felt too tight. "First you ignore me all day as if I'm not *completely* responsible for us being here in the first place, and then you want to shove me off on some bullshit task that doesn't mean anything —"

"Oh," Darby drawled, tapping the clipboard, "*you're* completely responsible? Someone has a high opinion of herself."

Kate stood her ground. "Yeah, you. You're pissed off because you said there was no way to get this done, and I got it done anyway."

"*That's* why I'm pissed off?"

"Damn straight. Which is why you're going around taking all the credit!"

Darby nodded slowly. "See, I thought I was taking all the credit so Mulugeta wouldn't figure out you were responsible for his smear campaign. *I* thought I was maybe *protecting* you. But I guess you *want* to be the sworn enemy of the most powerful man in a hundred square miles. I don't know, maybe that turns you on —"

Kate didn't even sense the motion before it happened, but suddenly she was in his arms. One powerful hand grasped the base of her neck, tangling in her hair, as the other spun her into the darkness of a storage hut. His mouth was on hers, hard and angry. Like they were in some kind of battle that he was determined to win — but Kate wasn't going to let him. She kissed him back, all of her pent-up fury and frustration finding release in the grip of her hands against his chest, the pressure of her lips against his.

Slowly a reluctant gentleness crept into the kiss. Darby pulled away.

Kate stared at him, dazed, her heart thundering.

"I shouldn't have done that," Darby muttered, looking down at his feet.

Kate frowned. *He shouldn't have done that?* What did that mean? More important, had the world stopped spinning? Because she was feeling a decided lack of gravity.

Darby clenched his jaw and pressed the clipboard into her hand.

"Enjoy being 'Clipboard Girl,'" he said flatly, and ducked out of the hut without a backward glance.

Kate leaned into the thatched wall, breathless.

Darby's kiss made one thing explicitly clear. He definitely didn't hate her. Yes, he found her frustrating, challenging, stubborn, even annoying. But he liked her — even if he didn't want to. The thought made Kate's cheeks twitch with an irrepressible smile.

Darby liked her.

And the boy could *kiss*.

FIFTEEN

Thank God for Genevieve Meyer's cast-off Chanel suit. She'd given Sophie the ensemble (light lavender tweed, from the winter 2005 collection) in a fit of generosity last December. Since then Sophie had kept the suit, carefully encased in its plastic bag, for a time when she really needed it. That time was now. She was going into battle, and the suit, along with a pair of four-inch gray Prada pumps she'd found at a Beverly Hills garage sale, was her armor.

She pulled the Oldsmobile up to the guard gate at the Fox lot. "Name?"

"Sophie Bushell. Here to see Michael Rinkin." In fact, she had no intention of seeing Michael Rinkin. But she couldn't get onto the lot without a "drive on." And she couldn't get a "drive on" without an appointment. Enter J.D., who'd used his connections to get her a fake appointment with a friend of his in reality TV development.

The guard handed her a pass. "You know where to park?"

"Sure do." *As close to the* Heartland *trailers as possible,* she thought.

"Have a nice day!" Sophie waved at the guard, and he buzzed open the gate. She was in.

Thanks, Harper, she thought, driving slowly through the lot. If she hadn't sent the DVD of Sophie's performance as Blanche DuBois in

A Streetcar Named Desire from last spring, Sophie would still be sitting on Sam's couch, stuffing herself with chips and phone-wallowing with Matthew Feldman. The first viewing had done nothing to bring her out of her depression. But Sam had forced her to watch the DVD again. And again. The layers of frustration had melted away and she'd been transported back to the stage. As Blanche, she'd been in total control, using her gift as an actress to pull the captivated audience into the charged world of Blanche, Stanley, and Stella. They'd done six performances, and Sophie had been drenched in sweat and emotionally drained after every single one. She'd also been exhilarated. Maybe Sophie wasn't a straight-A student like Kate, or an awesome writer like Harper, or an amazing athlete like Becca. But she had something else, something her own — and she wanted to share it with the world.

After watching the DVD four times, Sophie got up from the couch. She'd spent an hour in the shower, washing off the cynicism and hopelessness of everything Hollywood, and emerged stronger, surer, and cleaner than she'd been in months. In the following days, she'd returned to work at Mojito, silently chanting mantras and making plans in every free minute. Trey, dick that he was, had given her good advice. He'd said she had to make it happen. She planned to.

Sophie slid her enormous yellow vintage convertible into a spot reserved for visitors and glanced at her makeup in the rearview mirror. By the time she left this place, she intended to have a guest-starring role in *Heartland* in her back pocket. She was going to confront Ellie about her promised guest spot, and plant herself in the girl's makeup chair until she called the casting director or executive producer or whoever the hell needed to be consulted. Sophie had given up several hours of her life to keep Ellie from humiliating herself playing *her* role, and she was going to get what she deserved for her effort. The girl could try to play for time or make excuses, but Sophie wasn't going to let her get away with it, not this time.

When she reached Diaphragm Ellie's trailer, she considered knocking, but thought better of it. What better way to let the blond bombshell know she meant business than to barge in unannounced with her one-item list of demands? If nothing else, Ellie should appreciate the dramatic nature of the move.

I've tried to play nice. Now it's time to play to win. Sophie felt as if she were channeling Trey: this was probably the kind of thing he did when he was just a struggling Mexican kid from Whittier.

She grabbed the handle of the flimsy trailer door and pushed it open hard. "Ellie, I'm not leaving until you call the casting director and get me —"

Sophie stopped. And stared. Even the protective layer of her lavender Chanel suit didn't protect her from the shock. Ellie was practically naked, which wasn't especially noteworthy — the girl seemed allergic to clothes. The shocking part was what Ellie was doing *while* practically naked. She was having sex on the floor of the trailer, legs open, blond hair spread out over the pea-green carpet.

But not with Sam. Cody Howard, the hottest young star of *Heartland* was on top of her, his jeans and boxer shorts around his ankles.

"Ellie?" Somehow, despite the moaning and grunting, Ellie managed to hear her.

"Sophie! Shit! This isn't —" She was already pushing Cody away and reaching for a tiny blue tank top.

"What it looks like? Right." Sophie knew she'd come here for a reason, but it was currently escaping her. *Need to get to car,* her flustered brain commanded. Sophie turned without another word and raced out of the half-banger.

By the time she was halfway back to her car, she remembered that she'd come for her guest spot. But that no longer seemed to matter — not when she pictured Sam's face when she told him. *If* she told him. Oh God . . . *should* she tell him?

"Sophie. Stop." Ellie was running up behind her, dressed in the tiny tank and a pair of plaid boxer shorts. Probably Cody's, Sophie thought. "Tell me what you want. I'll give it to you."

"What I want?" *I want you and your overactive diaphragm never to have come into my life. I want to have gotten the part of Paige. I want to be home in my Juicy sweats, eating chips and watching car chases.* "From you? Nothing."

"I'll get you the guest spot!" Ellie blurted, her face red, scrubbing at her eyes with the back of her hand. "But you can't tell Sam about this. He wouldn't understand." Her voice sounded completely different. The bubbly, sweet-but-stupid girl was gone. In her place was a cold, calculating businesswoman. Sophie guessed she'd been there all along.

"There's nothing to understand." Even as she spoke, Sophie considered taking the deal. She was sure people had done a lot worse than use emotional blackmail to get a role. Would it be so wrong?

"I love Sam. I need him to keep me grounded. This thing with Cody . . . it was one time only. We just got too into character. . . . You get it, right? As a fellow actress?"

Sophie shook her head, all thoughts of making a deal with Ellie gone. The scene she'd just witnessed made her sick. She did not get it. She did not *want* to get it. This incident was the icing on her Hollywood cliché cake. Sophie had no doubt that if she wanted that guest spot — if she was willing to do whatever it took to make it happen — she could have it in the palm of her hand.

But she didn't want it. Not like this.

"Good luck, Ellie. I hope you get what you want." Sophie climbed into her convertible, leaving the stunned pseudo-actress in her wake, and realized she hadn't needed her Chanel suit after all. A few good old-fashioned morals were all the armor she needed.

On the way back to Sam's apartment, Matthew Feldman called her cell phone. She hadn't heard from him in several days and assumed he was somewhere on the Big Island mixing up piña coladas for sunburnt tourists.

"Sophie Bushell. Talk to me."

"If there's a car chase on, I don't care. I'm done with those." The light turned red, and she took the opportunity to kick off her Prada pumps and flex her sore toes.

"Never mind that shit. How's my favorite client?" He was using the patented Matthew Feldman staccato sentence-styling. She hadn't heard it since he got the ax.

"Your favorite *ex-client*," Sophie corrected.

He cackled. "Not anymore. You're talking to ICA's latest and greatest agent. Even got my own office. With a window."

"No." International Creative Agency was another of the Big Three. Which meant that in the world of agents, Matthew Feldman was no longer shit.

"Made me an offer I couldn't refuse." He sounded very pleased with himself. "I got auditions for you coming out of my ass. TV, movies, you name it."

Sophie smiled as an image of herself as Blanche DuBois flitted through her mind.

"Forget TV," she told him. "Forget movies. I want to do a play."

The light turned green. Sophie pressed the gas, and her car surged forward. For once, traffic on Wilshire was light. She was flying.

"Best TV shows of all time. If anyone says *CSI*, we're no longer friends."

"The Sopranos."

"Overrated."

"So *not* overrated!"

"The Shield."

"Did anyone watch that show? Like, apart from the Hollywood Foreign Press."

"Yeah, about six people in the Midwest."

"My mom got the DVDs of *Northern Exposure.* Totally amazing. Genius."

Becca leaned back on her elbows and closed her eyes against the sun. *Now this,* she thought, *is college.* She, Isabelle, Taymar, and Luke were stretched out on a blanket in the large quad near the center of campus doing absolutely nothing. Above them, the sun shone hot in a sky so clear and blue it almost glowed, and green mountains loomed behind them. Students crisscrossed the quad on their way to and from classes, looking enviously at those — like Becca and her friends — who were lucky enough to have Thursday afternoons free. From the number of blankets scattered across the crowded quad, Becca guessed that more than a few students were skipping — and after the long Vermont winter, and a pretty dreary spring so far, she couldn't blame them.

Only Isabelle knew it wasn't just the weather that had brought Becca to this particular spot on the quad — a spot that just happened to be only steps from Stuart's dorm room. After much thinking, a month of therapy sessions with Dr. Bleiweiss, several rounds of phone calls with Harper and Sophie, e-mails with Kate, and a few all-night marathon conversations with Isabelle, she'd decided to talk to Stuart. She *had* to talk to him. First, to apologize. Second, to tell him she still loved him. And third, to see if there was any way he might be interested in giving her another chance — a chance to show she *could* trust him. Not just that she could — that she *did.* That, really, she always had. The thought of Stuart existing in the world believing that she didn't have faith in him was like a growth in her heart that had started small and easy to ignore, but every day it grew — more painful, more present, until she felt it with every breath.

She just wanted him to know. What happened after that . . . well, she had her hopes. Big hopes. But her friends had all warned her that she might have burned that bridge already. Of course, Becca thought, burning one bridge didn't mean a new bridge couldn't be built in the same place — maybe a better bridge. She just hoped she got the chance.

Isabelle had defined her choice in stark terms. Becca could stay scared and keep running like "a punk-ass bitch," or she could be scared and love Stuart anyway. And eventually, Isabelle promised, the fear would go away.

"Hey." Isabelle tapped Becca sharply on the arm.

She opened her eyes. There he was, coming out the door of his dorm — a door she'd walked through with him a hundred times at least — wearing a t-shirt she'd bought for him at a ski meet at Wesleyan. That had to mean something, right?

"Get ready," she murmured to Isabelle as Taymar and Luke argued about the relative merits of *The Honeymooners* versus *The Three Stooges*. Isabelle was a key component of her plan, which went a little something like this: Stuart would see them all hanging out on the blanket (he couldn't *not* see them where they were planted); he would smile; he would feel uncomfortable about coming over, so Isabelle would give him no choice by yelling his name and waving her arms in a crazy, beckoning windmill. Then, after Stuart had hung out with them for a few minutes, Isabelle would take her leave — making sure Taymar and Luke followed suit.

What could go wrong? It was a foolproof plan.

Only Becca hadn't counted on Emma Jenkins.

Just as Stuart saw them and Isabelle yelled "Stuart!" Emma Jenkins emerged through the door. Looking utterly carefree and perfect in a floral miniskirt and layered white and pink tanks, she wrapped her arm around Stuart's elbow, then slid her hand down to grasp his in a smooth, confident motion. Like they held hands all the time. Like she had the right.

Like she was his girlfriend.

Becca's chest felt like a water bottle left too long in the freezer — ice cold, constricted and exploding at the same time.

He was *with someone.* Already. How could that be? And why hadn't she dressed up more? She'd wanted to look like she wasn't "trying," but now she just felt frumpy in her khaki shorts and blue cotton top.

Becca saw Stuart spot her. She couldn't help noticing his awareness of Emma, how much he *didn't* want to come over to their blanket. Isabelle had stopped waving as soon as Emma had come out the door, but the damage was done. He and Emma were walking over.

"Hey," Stuart said awkwardly, addressing the whole group.

"What's up?" Isabelle asked brightly.

Stuart said something about heading to the library and Becca stared intently at her knees, trying not to feel sick. *They study together. We used to study together.* She wanted to leap over her friends and tackle Emma Jenkins. Rip her hand out of Stuart's, tear out that perfect little pale throat with her teeth.

Instead, her eyes drifted to Stuart's scuffed tennis shoes. They were the same Nike trainers he was wearing the first time she saw him on the football field. And now he was wearing them and holding Emma Jenkins's hand. They looked enormous beside Emma's white strappy sandals.

The Nike trainers took a couple steps back, and Becca looked up.

"See you later," Stuart was saying to everyone at large.

"Bye." Emma smiled. She never once looked at Becca. Like Becca didn't exist — like she had never existed.

Stuart's eyes landed on Becca for just a moment as he turned around, but she couldn't read them. Was it pain she saw there? Or relief?

Isabelle, Taymar, and Luke were all looking at her.

"What?" She tried to smile — and ignore the fact that Stuart was walking away from her with another girl, clutching her hand in his. "I'm fine."

"Right," Taymar snorted. "That explains why the blood has literally drained from your face."

"Hey!" Luke mock-punched Becca's shoulder. "It doesn't mean anything, whatever's going on with Emma. He's just falling back into old patterns."

Becca frowned. Old patterns? What did that mean? "I don't understand."

"He didn't tell you?" Luke looked guilty.

"Tell me what?"

"About Emma?"

Whatever blood had drained from Becca's face was now pumping viciously through her chest. "What about her?"

"They dated last year — and part of the year before. He met her when he visited — you know, back when he was a senior in high school, and she was a freshman."

"So . . . he came to Middlebury to be with her."

"Well, not exactly . . . ," Luke muttered, unconvincingly.

"Remember, they broke up," Isabelle told her.

"And now they're back together." Becca was too stunned to move. She'd thought her jealousy was just a reaction to her parents' screwed-up relationship, all in her head. If she could just deal with her own issues, Stuart would love her again and she would be smart enough to not screw it up. Emma was supposed to be nothing more than a bump on Becca and Stuart's path to happiness. Except all along he'd really wanted to be with Emma Jenkins.

The path to happiness wasn't Stuart and Becca's at all. It was Stuart and *Emma's*.

Which made Becca the bump.

Sometimes, Kate thought, the universe just smiled.

The well in Teje had been done in record time. Yes, the path to getting there had been shadowed by one huge universal frown — but once Mulugeta had been handled, every element of the preparation and construction couldn't have gone more smoothly. The parts had come in on time and unbroken, the water table was high, the crews were hardworking and organized, the weather was ideal. The schedule had been met and exceeded.

Today — one whole week early — had been the grand well-opening celebration. A long, happy day of dancing, speeches, feasting. And she'd missed it all — for a search on which the universe had apparently decided *not* to smile.

She finally had a lead on Angatu's sister — Abebech had found a woman in the village who claimed to know the man who'd driven Masarat to Addis Ababa after she ran away from the farmer who wanted to marry her. It wasn't the most solid lead: Masarat had fled from the farmer over six years ago. But at least this man might remember where he had dropped her off, and if she had mentioned having any plans or acquaintances in the city. Visiting him couldn't wait because according to Abebech's friend, he was sick — waiting even a day or two could be too long.

So instead of participating in the ceremony for the Teje well, Kate had walked — with a big stick for protection — nearly three miles on dusty roads to the nearby village where the man, Eschetu, was staying. The village was even smaller and scrappier than Mekebe, and it hadn't taken long to track him down.

Kate had found him in bed at his parents' hut, shriveled with AIDS. He was probably only about thirty, she guessed, but his taut face was lined with pain and a vein-deep exhaustion.

He remembered almost nothing about the twelve-year-old Masarat. He'd picked her up hitchhiking on the road outside his village, and didn't remember if she'd wanted to go to Addis Ababa specifically, or if she'd just gone there because it was where he happened to be driving. Either way, he thought he'd dropped her off by Meskal Square, but he couldn't be sure — it was so long ago. He didn't think she'd mentioned knowing anyone in the city, but wasn't certain of that either. And the last he'd seen her, she'd been walking down the crowded sidewalk, her meager belongings wrapped in a dirty white natala slung over her shoulder.

It was discouraging, to say the least, and frustrating. And on some deep level, enraging. What had happened to Masarat when she was forced to run from the only home she knew? How had she survived? *If* she had survived . . .

Kate forced herself *not* to think about that possibility for the entire walk home to Mekebe. What she'd thought about instead was her family. How lucky she was to have them — even when she'd disappointed her parents by not going to Harvard, even when she hadn't been the best sister to Habiba. No matter what, they loved her.

And now, more than ever, she needed them. Angatu needed them.

The second she'd gotten back to the village, Kate rushed to Abebech's restaurant, paying the older woman well above market price to use the phone. It was the only phone in the village and Abebech guarded it judiciously. For two one-hundred birr notes, and Kate's insistence that the call was about Angatu, the old woman slid the old black phone out from under the plastic-covered back counter.

Kate's fingers had trembled as she dialed the international codes, and then finally her own familiar number.

"Hello?" Her father's tenor came clearly across the line.

Kate's eyes welled up. "Hey, what's for dinner?"

"Katie?" Her father, whose even temper was legendary, actually sounded excited. "Is that you?"

"It's me," Kate laughed.

"Let me get your mother and sister."

Ten seconds later, her mother, father, and Beebs were all on various phones in their house, talking over one another, jockeying for verbal position.

"When are you coming home?" That was her mother.

"How's the well coming?" That was Beebs.

"We haven't heard back from Harvard yet." That was her father.

"I need a favor," Kate told them.

"Anything, sweetie," her mother said at once.

"Now let's not get crazy," quipped her father.

"It's a big one. It might mean you have to come here."

There was silence at the other end of the line. Then Habiba said, "We're in."

Her parents started laughing — a sound Kate hadn't heard in a long time — and it made her long for home. In all the months that she'd been gone, she'd never once felt homesick. Now it hit with such force she had to take a breath. She missed her family and her friends, not to mention sleeping on an actual bed.

Soon enough she would be home. Her team's work in Ethiopia was almost completed, and before she knew it she would be on a plane back to Colorado with some real decisions to make. Was she going to go to Harvard? Had she figured out what she wanted to do with her life? And then there was the Dream issue. That had been the point of this whole year, after all — to figure out who she *really* was, separate from her parents' dreams and expectations. But had she succeeded? Had she found her Dream?

Kate shook the question from her head. The only thing she needed to find right now wasn't a thing at all, but a person — Masarat. She filled her parents in on everything done so far to find the missing girl, and shared what little information she had on a possible location and contacts.

"I can do some research from here," her father suggested. "Then we'll see."

"Okay." It was the best Kate was going to get — her father didn't make quick decisions. He was a thinker, a planner. He was what she had been ten months ago, Kate realized on the walk back to the compound from Abebech's restaurant. Deliberate and a little obsessive. A one-step-at-a-time kind of person.

She opened the front gate, stepping into the yard. The moon had just risen over the street, and the lack of candlelight in the huts said that everyone else had gone to bed. Kate was still her father's daughter, but she was also a whole new person. Less afraid, for one thing, and more spontaneous. Certainly more daring. Instead of trusting others to make decisions for her, she trusted herself. That change alone had made the year of dreams worthwhile.

Smiling, Kate pushed open the door to the women's hut. From their cots, Dorothé and Jessica breathed the steady, rhythmic breath of sleep. Dorothé had thrown a log on the fire, which bathed the hut in a warm orange glow. On the off-white goatskin beneath her mosquito net, a small glass jar glistened in the dim light. Pulling the gauzy net aside, Kate picked up the jar and unfolded the note placed beneath it.

"This is the first water out of the Teje well. I thought you should have it. Congratulations."

Kate held up the jar. The water looked silty and gray. The screw-on lid was rusty and dented. A label had been unsuccessfully peeled from the glass, leaving a thick, gummy residue black with dirt.

Kate smiled. This dirty jar, with its silty water, was . . . well, it was by far the best present she'd ever received.

English 234 – Modern African-American Literature
Professor Anita Smith
Class Hours: M,W,F 11am-12:15pm
Office Hours: Th 3-5 / Humanities Bldg. Room 204A

Grade: 1/4 class participation
1/4 final exam
1/2 papers

PLEASE NOTE: Papers purchased off the Internet will receive an "F." Papers with sections cribbed from Cliff's Notes or, even worse, from someone else's scholarly work will receive an "F." Offending student will be referred for disciplinary action. I, personally, will do my best to see that anyone who knowingly rips off anyone else's work is expelled. Got me? Good.

Enjoy your reading.

SYLLABUS:

Week 1: *Their Eyes Were Watching God* (Zora Neale Hurston)

Week 2: *Invisible Man* (Ralph Ellison)

Week 3: Paper #1 (Topic TBD)

Week 4: *The Color Purple* (Alice Walker)

Week 5: *Native Son* (Richard Wright)

SIXTEEN

Harper had a strategy. She would drink two beers, and then she would go home. One beer wasn't enough. One beer said, *I'm here against my will, and I'm going to leave as quickly as possible.* Two beers said, *I'm having so much fun that I made a return trip to the keg, but unfortunately circumstances dictate that I get home before eleven o'clock.* Maybe even ten-thirty, if she drank fast.

Judd only told her about the party he was co-hosting in his dorm at approximately six o'clock this morning, as they'd been opening up the Rainy Day Books Café together. Because he'd caught her before her first three cups of coffee, Harper's brain cells had not been firing at a rate sufficient to devise an excuse to get her out of it. She'd considered bailing at the last minute, but she knew what a no-show would lead to. Judd would threaten her with another "talk." This was something to be avoided, for reasons she wasn't quite sure of. So here she was, standing in the shabby, crowded common lounge of Elmer Hall, surrounded by overloud drunken freshmen, sipping her first of two Coors Lights.

"I'm so glad you came." Amelia smiled and pushed her cat-eye glasses higher on her nose. Despite the fact that her eyes were too close together, the girl looked amazing in a short red wool dress, black tights, and knee-high leather boots. Harper wished she were wearing something besides her requisite jeans. She felt positively *masculine.*

"Thanks." Harper wasn't sure what to say next. This morning, Judd had led her to believe he wanted to bond with her tonight. Hang out together "like the old days." But now she realized that had been a ruse. What he really wanted was for Harper to bond with *Amelia* while he manned the two kegs illegally obtained for the party.

"He talks about you *all* the time."

"He does?" Harper tried to imagine what he would say. *Harper gained another pound today. Harper spilled a one-pound bag of coffee grounds all over the cash register today. Oh, did I mention Harper and I used to make out all the time? That was before you and I shared cocoa and fell in love. . . .*

On the other side of the party, Poppy (wearing skintight black leggings that only she could pull off and a cinched-in royal blue tank dress) was playing darts with a guy in a giant moose head. *George.* Harper wondered if it would be impolite to ask one of them to throw a dart at her head.

"I think it's awesome that you guys are best friends." Amelia set her empty cup down among about twenty others littering a beer-stained Ping-Pong table.

Best friends? He'd said they were *best friends?* The idea made Harper's heart ache a little. Not because she and Judd hadn't been anything *approaching* best friends lately. It just seemed sad that Harper filled that role in his life. She had Sophie, Becca, and Kate, even if they'd barely talked much the last few months. Judd had . . . no one — apart from Amelia.

"I mean, the idea that men and women can't have totally platonic relationships is so twentieth century."

Harper nodded, tapping her beer against her chin. Obviously, Judd had left out the "benefits" part of their awesome best friendship. She wondered how Amelia would react if she knew the truth.

Not that Harper would tell her. That would be a bitch move, and Harper wasn't a bitch — grouchy, maybe, but not a bitch. Anyway, she had no *reason* to disabuse Amelia. It wasn't like she wanted to drive a wedge between her and Judd. If she did, why would she be here, drinking her first kind-of-tasteless beer, acting all pleasant and likeable?

"I was actually kind of jealous of you at first," Amelia confessed, leaning one slender hip against the flimsy table. "I thought Judd was in love with you."

Harper took a large gulp of her Coors Light. "That's crazy."

"I know that *now*. We sort of had a fight about it one night." She lowered her voice. "But he told me about the English teacher."

"Mr. Finelli?" How nice that Judd was selling out her most private and humiliating secrets to the girl who devirginized him.

Amelia caught Judd's eye across the room and waved at him. "Judd told me you're still in love with him. I'm sorry that he broke your heart, but you're so lucky you had Judd to help you through it. He's the most understanding guy I've ever met."

Harper never said Mr. Finelli *broke her heart!* Okay, maybe she'd implied it. But a gentleman would have kept that information to himself. Besides, *he* really hadn't done the breaking. She'd managed that all by herself, by behaving like an utter ass. And did Judd *really* think she was still in love with Mr. Finelli, or had he just said that to throw Amelia off their "friends with benefits" scent? She downed the rest of her beer and tossed the cup onto the table.

"I need another drink," she announced, spinning on her heels. One more trip to the keg and she was out of this nightmare.

"Tell Judd I'll be right back," Amelia called. "I've had to pee for an hour."

As Harper headed for the keg, she decided her second beer was going to have to go down a lot faster than the first. She wasn't sure how much more girl talk she could handle.

"Having fun?" Judd filled her cup to the very brim with lukewarm Coors Light.

"Mmm . . . yeah." She managed to spill at least an inch when she raised the flimsy cup to her mouth.

He beamed. "Isn't Amelia great? I knew you guys would hit it off if you had a chance to talk."

"Yeah . . . yeah . . . great. Just great." Harper clapped him on the back in a way-to-go-buddy sort of manner. "She's peeing, by the way. Amelia. She wanted you to know."

Judd gave her an intent look. "You really like her, right? You're not just saying that?"

"*Love* her." Across the room, Poppy was laughing: one of her darts had lodged itself in the head of George's giant moose costume. Harper felt a wave of guilt. Why was she the only person on earth who seemed to have a problem with the friendship/benefits idea? "I'm gonna say hi to Poppy."

She threaded her way through the shouting, jostling partiers, sipping doggedly at beer number two.

"Hey, guys." Harper toasted them with her already half-empty cup. Poppy grinned. Her black hair was wound into a tight bun, and she was wearing dramatically dark red lipstick. She looked like she should be dancing at a night club in Manhattan rather than throwing darts with a guy in an animal costume.

"Harper! I wanted to come say hi but I was too busy winning meal points from Liam."

"Who's Liam?"

The guy in the moose head stuck out his hand for Harper to shake. "Pleasure to meet you." He had a sexy, if muffled, Irish accent.

"You're not George?" Duh. This was fairly obvious, but Harper was still confused. If Poppy had been playing darts with Liam all night, where *was* George? She thought the two of them never spent an evening apart.

Poppy lifted a giant CU travel mug from a low cigarette-burned table and poured something that smelled like cleaning fluid into her mouth. "We haven't spoken in two weeks."

"What? Why?" Harper was so surprised she forgot to swig her beer.

"Hey, Liam — how 'bout another?" Poppy thrust the travel mug in his direction and Mr. Moosehead obediently ambled off toward the huge bowl of "punch" near the kegs. Then she turned back to Harper and leaned in, lowering her voice. "Turns out the whole friends-with-benefits thing doesn't work so well. Thank *God* you and Judd never tried it."

"What about no harm, no foul?"

Poppy snorted. "Please. That's such a crock of shit. I met Liam at a poetry slam and went a little gaga over the accent. We kissed once, and when I told George he freaked. He hasn't talked to me since." She rolled her eyes. "Apparently, he was secretly in love with me the whole time. When I suggested that maybe we should explore our relationship further, take it to the next level, he said the fact that I kissed another guy ruined everything. Asshole."

"Wow." Harper took a huge gulp of beer. She'd reached the bottom of the cup without even trying.

"Like I said, thank *God* you and Judd never went for it. Someone *always* gets hurt." Poppy sighed, patting her perfect bun. "Truth is, if George and I had just started dating like normal people, we'd be snuggling up watching skateboard videos right now. Instead, I'm stuck playing a never-ending game of darts with a guy wearing a giant moose head."

"Wow." Oddly, Harper felt better. Poppy and George weren't even *speaking*. At least *she'd* managed to have a coherent conversation with Judd's new girlfriend.

Ten minutes later, her two-beer tally accomplished, and her goodbyes-to-all mumbled, Harper was riding her bike home through the Boulder streets. She inhaled the cool night air, trying to block out the noise of the party. But as she pedaled faster and faster, the conversation with Poppy played over and over in her mind. Their situations were completely different. Harper didn't long to snuggle with Judd watching skateboard videos. Not at all. Like Judd told Amelia, she was in love with someone else.

Instead of making a left at Pearl Street, Harper veered her bicycle to the right and rode up Rose Drive. She hadn't planned it. Or maybe she had. Either way, she found herself braking in front of Mr. Finelli's duplex, gazing at the light on in the kitchen. She imagined him drinking coffee from his percolator, grading papers or reading the *New Yorker* at the table. Up until tonight, she'd tried not to think about him, the same way she tried not to think about her novel unless she was actually locked in the bathroom writing it.

But now . . . Harper realized Judd had been a distraction from what she really wanted. Mr. Finelli. Adam. And she was ready to go for it. She would apologize for turning serial-killer crazy when he'd criticized the fifty pages of drivel she'd given him. She would articulately express her deepest feelings and win him back. He'd cast aside Tara, take her in his arms, and make mad, passionate love to her. Then they would snuggle and watch skateboard videos together. It would be sheer bliss.

"Harper?"

Oh God. Adam wasn't in his kitchen drinking coffee and grading papers or reading the *New Yorker*. He was standing next to her, dressed in faded jeans and a gray sweater, a bemused expression on his handsome face. He was also holding a leash, at the end of which was a small Jack Russell terrier, who was looking at her with equally curious eyes. Tara's dog, no doubt.

"I thought my bike had a flat," she blurted, nudging herself onto the seat. She *had* to get out of here. "But I was wrong. Have a good night."

"Don't run away," he called after her, his voice plaintive. "You're always running away!"

As Harper pedaled away as fast as her nontoned legs could take her, she decided it wasn't a lack of courage that had made her flee. It was commitment. Last fall, she'd told Mr. Finelli she wasn't going to kiss him until she finished the first fifty pages of her novel. Well, now she had a whole lot more than fifty pages of a whole new novel and it was a hell of a lot better than the last one. She needed to finish it. *Then* she'd apologize for acting serial-killer crazy.

And if Adam took her back ... who knew? Maybe she and Judd had a double date in their future.

There was always that moment just before Sophie walked onto stage, when the world seemed to pause, as though it were waiting for her. She'd experienced it over and over again, since her first performance as a giant tooth in the first grade play about dental hygiene. In that moment, nothing else mattered. Not a fight she'd had with her mom that morning, or an F on a history test, or a broken fingernail. Whatever forces she felt gathering in the universe to conspire against her fell away. In that moment, she wasn't even Sophie Bushell. She was living, breathing art, about to be unveiled before whomever lay just beyond the curtain.

Right now, she wasn't experiencing anything even close to that moment. Instead, she was sitting in one of the velvet-covered seats in the echoing Mark Taper Theater, wearing an old pair of Levi's and a yellow Gap t-shirt, her curly black hair tied back in a loose ponytail. And she was in heaven. Because for the first time since she moved to LA and started The Year of Dreams, she knew that moment would come again.

She'd gotten the part.

Sophie was playing seventeen-year-old Debbie in Tom Stoppard's *The Real Thing,* a role that had launched Cynthia Nixon's career when she performed it as a teenager on Broadway. Whenever she thought about it for more than twenty seconds, it was almost hard to breathe.

"We're not just going to *rehearse* this play. We're going to *be* this play." On the stage, Sebastian Kramer, a Tony award–winning director, paced back and forth, pulling at his graying hair and occasionally making the boards creak by jumping up and down for no apparent reason. He'd been talking for over an hour, but Sophie couldn't get enough.

She'd auditioned for the part six days ago. When she'd first told Matthew Feldman she wanted to forego film and television to concentrate on theater, he'd accused her of being on an overhigh dosage of Xanax. Then she'd pointed out that doing theater would give her the kind of credibility that TV and even movies never could. If the stage was good enough for Julia Roberts, it was good enough for her. Eventually he'd succumbed — with a caveat.

"You're not trying out for some jerk-off part in some jerk-off production of some jerk-off piece," he'd ranted. "I don't want you running around stage draped in a sheet screaming about the wind. This has to be legit."

Sophie laughed. "No screaming about the jerk-off wind. Understood."

"As long as we're clear." He'd hung up on her.

For two days, she'd heard nothing. She went back to work at Mojito, jogged, gave herself a long-awaited pedicure. And she waited. Every time the phone rang, her heart raced. She believed in Matthew Feldman, because he believed in her. Well, because he believed in her *and* because he had that new office with the window.

He called on the third day. She'd been standing around at work reading her horoscope in the *LA Times* with Celeste while they waited for the dinner rush to start. *Leo's star is on the rise.*

"Be at the Taper tomorrow morning at nine," he ordered. "This is it. Your chance to rise above the shit. We got one shot, so make it count."

Sophie had stayed up all night studying *The Real Thing,* a play about love, marriage, and betrayal. But when she arrived at the theater, she never felt more awake in her life. She sat in the lobby for two hours, watching other hopefuls enter and exit from the stage area. There were one or two semi-famous faces and some recognizable character actors, but mostly other nobodys like herself.

For once, she hadn't allowed herself to make comparisons. No "she's prettier," "I'm taller," "he looks more nervous than I am." She'd sat in her zone, trying to block out everything around her.

When Sophie finally got her chance to audition, Sebastian Kramer had watched her from the back of the theater, slouched in a chair. If she hadn't been so completely consumed by the monologue she'd prepared, she might have been insulted that he appeared to be asleep. But when she finished, he stood up and called out to her.

"Someone will call with my decision tomorrow. Meantime, clear your schedule for the next three months." His voice was hoarse from too many years of smoking cigarettes and yelling at actors.

She hadn't gotten the lead. She hadn't expected to. But the role of Debbie was juicy, deep, and delicious, despite having just one scene. Sophie planned to wring every drop out of it.

"I want you all to wear your costumes to the grocery store, to your boyfriend's soccer game, in the shower. You're no longer yourselves. You *are* your characters." Sebastian finally stopped pacing. "Now let's do some acting."

"Yes, sir!" Sophie hadn't meant to say anything. The enthusiasm just sort of seeped out.

The dark guy next to her leaned in close. "This isn't boot camp," he muttered, smiling. "You can relax." She recognized him from Steve Buschemi's first movie. Brown hair, soulful hound dog eyes. If she hadn't sworn off men, Sophie would've flirted back.

Sebastian grinned down from the stage. "Leave her alone. A little respect never killed a performance. Let's go, people."

Sebastian's idea of rehearsal was quite different from her high-school drama coach's. Instead of performing the actual scenes in the actual play, he had the small cast improvise as their characters for hours. After six hours, Sophie's throat hurt from screaming at her fictional parents about their fictional wrongdoings. Everything she'd ever wanted to say to a real mom and dad had come pouring out on stage.

"I want everyone to get their eight hours tonight," Sebastian bellowed at last. "Tomorrow we start working on your English accents."

Sophie grabbed her black Gap tote from the first-row seat where she'd left it during rehearsal. Tomorrow they would do this all over again. Tonight she felt so drained she wanted to take a nap in the parking lot before driving to Sam's.

As she started toward the exit, a hand came down, hard, on her shoulder. Sebastian. "Guy back there was watching you for the last hour. I think he liked what he saw."

Sophie glanced toward the back of the long theater. In the shadows she saw a middle-aged man, a Dodgers cap pulled down low over his face, sitting doing a crossword puzzle. "Who is he?"

Sebastian shrugged. "Got me. I guess security isn't shit around this place." He squeezed her shoulder. "'Night, Debbie."

Great. She'd attracted the attention of yet another over-the-hill pervert. Sophie briefly considered complaining to the theater manager to at least make an attempt to keep out the riffraff. Then she decided Sophie Bushell might care who was watching. But Debbie didn't.

Nonetheless, she didn't want to be prey for The Lurker. A nap in the parking lot was definitely out.

Kate reached into her backpack — not because she actually wanted lip balm, but because it was the only way she could think of to steal a sideways glance at Darby. He'd been sitting silently beside her for five full minutes, ankles crossed casually in front of him, arms outstretched on the backs of the neighboring chairs. He seemed oddly comfortable, here in the Addis Ababa airport, waiting for her parents.

But she hadn't quite figured out why he was here.

When she'd told everyone that her family was coming to Ethiopia and she was going to meet them in Addis Ababa, Darby insisted on flying down with her. Apparently, he had some meeting with Water Partners administrators scheduled — which explained why he was in Addis Ababa, but not why he was determined to stay with her at the airport to wait for her family's plane.

It wasn't as if they had bonded on the flight down from Bahar Dar. Kate, in fact, had been uncharacteristically nervous. The kiss — that one, intensely amazing kiss — kept replaying in her head. Nothing that surrounded it seemed to matter — not that he had walked away, not that he had been angry. That was all just background rumbling, lost in the roaring thunder that was *the kiss*.

Kate had thought about it a million times in Mekebe — whenever she saw him, or heard his voice, every time someone mentioned him, every time she saw the particular shade of his orange t-shirt — which, as it happened, was quite often. Orange was not as uncommon a color as she'd once thought. It was *everywhere*. It *stalked* her.

Even the backs of the seats on the airplane had been orange. Not that it made a difference in terms of how much she thought about him — he was sitting right next to her, his elbow resting against hers on the arm rest. Kate couldn't have gotten him out of her mind if she'd tried. And she *did* try — first by pretending to sleep, then by reading the same page of *Mama Day* forty-three times. Thank God it was a short flight.

And now he was casually stretched out next to her, as if waiting for her mom, dad, and sister was the most natural thing in the world for him to be doing. She'd told him not to wait, to go on to the hotel. So . . . why was he here? Was he *trying* to drive her crazy???

Kate spread the Burt's Bees balm slowly across her lower lip. Why wouldn't he say anything? She pursed her lips together self-consciously.

"Can I use some of that?" Darby held out his tanned hand.

"Uh . . . sure." Kate passed him the little yellow tin. Oh God, something that was on her lips was also going to be on his lips. It gave her little butterfly thrills in her tummy. Damn, she was ridiculous. She didn't even *like* him.

Okay, yes she did.

But so what? They were wrong for each other.

Except that maybe they weren't.

Darby held out his hand. "Thanks." He smiled as he handed back her lip balm, his hazel eyes twinkling. "So . . . are you not talking to me for a reason?"

Kate opened her mouth. She wasn't not talking to him!

"I'm not . . . I'm . . ." She didn't know what to say.

"You haven't spoken a word to me in, like, two hours."

"Neither have you!"

"Yeah, but I'm trying to back off because I kissed you and I think it freaked you out."

Kate swallowed. "I wasn't freaked out."

Wow. This was really happening. They were going to talk about it, have a real, actual conversation. She wasn't sure she was ready.

"You've barely spoken to me since," he said, twisting toward her.

"I didn't . . . know what it meant." It was a struggle to meet his gaze without lunging at him with her lips. "You got all pissed and stormed out. And I've been a little busy. With the well, and finding Angatu's sister."

"I haven't been a priority, is what you're saying." He gave a rueful smile.

358

Kate smiled back, then looked down at the white tile floor. "I didn't know you would want to be." There was a lip lunge coming very soon in her future. She could feel it.

"Maybe I —" But whatever Darby was going to say was chopped short by the very noisy arrival of her parents. Habiba's high-pitched screech didn't help either.

"Katie! It's Katie!" Her mother was almost shrieking.

"There's my girl!" Her dad's voice echoed through the cavernous airport.

"We're here!" Beebs yelled, skipping with excitement.

Kate felt a completely unexpected moment of joy. After almost a year, seeing her whole family rushing toward her in their practical travel clothes was overwhelming. She laughed and stood up, rushing toward them with open arms.

As her father pulled her into a hug, Kate thought about the morning she'd told them she wasn't going to Harvard. The look on his face would be pressed in the pages of her memory for the rest of her life. He'd been so still, so furious, so stunned. And her mother had been devastated. They accused her of setting a bad example for Habiba, a blow that Kate still considered unfair. For several months after she left for Europe she hadn't spoken to them at all.

And now, here they were — her fair-haired mom and dad both holding her in their arms, having flown halfway around the world to support and help her. She knew that their willingness to do so was a direct response to all she'd accomplished. If she *had* just spent what would have been her freshman year of college backpacking around Europe, they never would have come so far for her. They wouldn't even have welcomed her home with the joy and pride they were expressing now. But she hadn't just backpacked — she had set out on a mission to discover herself, to grow, to explore and learn. And she'd focused her energy on more than just herself, something she knew her parents valued highly — not that she had done it for them. They weren't even part of the equation when she decided to come to Africa.

But Habiba was. Kate pulled away from her parents and flung her arms around her sister, whose dark eyes were glistening with tears.

"I love you, kid," she whispered into Habiba's ear.

"Me, too," Habiba murmured back. Over her sister's shoulder, Kate saw tears in their mother's eyes.

"So is it weird being back?" Kate asked Habiba, releasing her from the hug, but keeping one arm firmly around her shoulder.

"I don't know." Habiba grinned. "I just got here."

Habiba looked toward the sliding glass airport doors at the misty afternoon. Even this far out of the city, the air was thick with the smell of smoke. "Wow." She breathed. Then she caught her breath and turned to Kate, eyes wide. "Who's the hottie? Is that *Darby*?"

Kate almost choked.

"That's me," Darby said, coming forward with his hand out. He shook her father's hand first, then her mother's, then Habiba's.

Her father smiled. "What happened to Magnus?"

Kate wanted to crawl into a hole. Were they *determined* to embarrass her?

"Oh, that's over," Habiba said. "Darby thinks he was a . . . I'm not allowed to say the word."

Kate glanced over at Darby, and he held her gaze, his eyes sparkling. Then he turned to her parents. "Kate's been amazing," he said. "She got more done in four months than any volunteer I've ever worked with. We wouldn't have gotten a well in Teje without her —"

"And me," Habiba piped in, smiling.

"Yeah," Darby laughed. "I'm beginning to see how Kate managed to get those fliers done so perfectly. Nice job with that."

Habiba glowed. "Thank you."

"You should be really proud of her," Darby continued, looking sincerely at her parents.

Kate's throat tightened when her father reached out to grasp Darby's shoulder. "We are." He nodded. "And thank you for taking such good care of her."

"He didn't take care of me —" Kate protested.

"Well, there was the night with the hyenas," Darby teased.

"We don't have to talk about that." Kate gave him a warning look.

"Oh, yes we do," her mother said, eyebrows shooting up. She nervously patted the pockets of her TravelSmith safari vest. "We most certainly do!"

"It was nothing." Darby shook his head. "Actually, I was just looking for an excuse to talk to her."

Kate blinked at him. What was going on? Who was this person, and what had he done with Darby? Habiba wrapped her hand in Kate's and gave her a pointed look. "I like him," she mouthed.

Kate was desperate to change the subject. "So . . . ," she began, "Angatu's sister. Did you have any luck tracking down someone who might know where to find her?"

"We did." Her mother ran a hand through her airplane-mussed, shoulder-length blond hair. "But there'll be time for that at the hotel. Right now, I just want to wrap my arms around my girls and never let you go."

Kate couldn't stop the tears when her mother pulled her and Habiba into a tight embrace. Behind their mother's back, Habiba wove her fingers through Kate's. For a moment, she forgot all about Darby. And all about Angatu, Masarat, Magnus, the wells, her friends, everything that had happened in the last year.

In that moment, there was only one thought. One word. A word that she had wanted so badly to understand, and now did — suddenly, with all of its complexity and emotion.

Sister.

Duran Duran. Hall and Oates. Pat Benatar. Blondie.

What other seventies and eighties bands had her mom been obsessed with? Tears for Fears. And that other one . . . with the weird name . . . what was it? Kajagoogoo!

Becca continued listing bands (the Police, a-ha, the Thompson Twins) as she walked past the last building on campus and headed into the surrounding woods. So far on this walk, she had listed carpet manufacturers (Karastan and Dalton were the only ones she could remember), vacuum brands (Hoover, Dyson, Dirt Devil), and every teacher she'd had since Miss Anne in Montessori School — who had changed her name many years later to Sunshine, which meant she counted twice.

The second she stopped *listing,* Becca knew she would start *thinking.* And there would be more than enough time for that once she got to where she was going. Until then . . . lists, lists, lists.

She'd covered the presidents of the United States (or, at least, the ones she could remember), current Supreme Court justices, and writers of the Beat Generation, and she was just starting on potato chip flavors when she turned a corner of the pine-needle-strewn path and stopped. This was it: the middle of nowhere.

Becca filled her lungs with warm spring air. The campus buildings looked like miniatures in the beautiful valley below her, and the mountains pointed upward in front of her, green and alive. Carved through the trees, the ski trails where she had felt so alive, so happy, during the winter were crooked scars, already dry and brown.

Like the scars on her heart.

She pulled off her Pumas and let her toes nestle into the crisp pine needles. These woods were part of why she'd come to Middlebury. Harper and Sophie were the city girls and Kate was comfortable anywhere. But Becca needed trees and mountains and air — the thinner the better. Open spaces always made her feel stronger, freer, released from pressures she wasn't even aware of until they were left behind.

Today, however, she'd carried her burdens with her. After blocking them out for an hour, the instant her feet were still, they invaded like a marauding army. Stuart. Her parents. Emma Jenkins.

Becca wanted to scream.

If only she could make *sense* of it all. Line it all up in a row and see where everything started. Maybe it began with Harper's announcement, and her friends making her promise to fall in love. Or maybe it had started when her parents got divorced or when her dad first started his affair with Melissa. The beginning almost didn't matter. What she really wanted to know was if there was an end. Because what if there wasn't? What if this was it? What if she was always going to be this miserable, this . . . alone?

The cruelest part was that she had just started to feel — really feel — like she was past it all. Now that she had moved away, her parents' fights were going to be just an unhappy memory. Wasn't that what college was supposed to be about? Starting your own life? Leaving your childhood behind — with all its fears and fucked upness? Wasn't that the *point*?

Noooo. Not for *her* parents. They had psychically stalked her all the way to Vermont. They had reached their arms out to smack her from halfway across the continent and made her lose the only guy she'd ever loved.

No. She couldn't blame them for that. At least, not entirely. For that, she was to blame. She was the one who'd pushed Stuart away. Even if he *had* always had feelings for Emma Jenkins, for a while — at least — he'd wanted to be with Becca. He couldn't have faked the way he looked at her, the way he held her. He cared about her. Maybe not as much as he cared about Emma, but . . .

Becca swiped a tear from her cheek.

Damn it, she thought. She was going to be miserable and messed up for the rest of her life. Why fight it? Why try to be healthy? Why work so goddamn hard, when this was all she got out of it — this horrible, sick feeling in her heart and head and soul. She should just quit college and move into Harper's basement. Harper would probably be going to NYU next year. The Waddles' basement would be empty. And it was semi-decorated — barely worse than a dorm room. Yeah, she would take over Harper's job at the Rainy Day Café and be friends with Judd Wright —

Behind her, pine needles crackled under the weight of approaching feet.

"Afternoon."

Becca turned to find Coach Maddix pulling to a stop from a full-on run. He assessed her with blue eyes that were no less icy in the summer sun. His hands were on the hips of his red running shorts, and his US Olympic Team t-shirt was drenched in sweat.

Becca suddenly felt as if she'd done something wrong. Like she'd gone off campus without permission, or invaded his private sanctum.

"Nice spot." Maddix walked up to her.

Becca nodded, trying to keep her face averted. The last thing she needed was Coach Maddix to see she'd been crying.

"Good spot to get away." Maddix seemed to be waiting for Becca to respond. Why? Why did he want to *converse* all of a sudden? It wasn't like they were *friends*.

But suddenly the words were bubbling over. She couldn't stop them. "I just broke up with someone I loved a lot, and now he's with someone else, which is probably for the best. I mean, I'm just not ready — my parents are doing this weird thing, and it's totally my fault. It's not, really, but . . ."

Becca closed her mouth, feeling like an idiot. Maddix put a hand on her arm.

"I know about Stuart," he said. Becca's eyebrows rose in surprise.

"I'll tell you something," Maddix began, and immediately Becca was riveted. "I've been inside your head coming down that mountain. I know what you're thinking every second."

Maddix's eyes were on the rolling Berkshires. "Not a goddamn thing. At least, when it's working. When you're at your best — which is not all the time, and we both know it — the only goddamn thing in your head is the getting to the bottom of the hill, and what you need to get there. That's it."

Becca nodded. Maddix was right. Coming down a mountain, all the bullshit fell away.

"Life is no different," Maddix said quietly, glancing down at her. "Focus on what you need to get down the hill. You let all that other crap in, it's gonna be a bumpy ride."

Becca nodded, her throat too tight to speak. Maddix, as always, was right. She was letting too many things get to her, destroy her focus. The only things she needed to be worried about right now were her classes and her friends — they were her mountain. If she was lucky, maybe Stuart would come around. But she couldn't waste her whole life dreaming about him or anyone. She just had to get down the hill.

"Yes, sir," she said, chancing a smile.

Maddix nodded briskly. Then he smacked a hand against her back in a gesture that felt like a two-by-four to the spine. "I thought you had your shit together, Winsberg," he called, kicking back into his run. "I hate being wrong."

His last words drifted back to her from the other side of a grove of trees, and then he was gone. Becca stared after him.

Wrong? Well, he wasn't going to be wrong anymore. Because Becca was going to forget everything that didn't help her get down the mountain — her parents were first and foremost on that list.

But Stuart was on the list, too.

It was time to let him go.

Dear Harper—
You were right. I'm definitely
glad I came. I owe you a
Green-Eyed Monster! Being here is
great and scary and emotional...but
my parents and Kate have been
really cool. I decided not to go
to the place where I used to live.
Saving that one for the next trip.
Kate says hi—she has SO much to
tell you. I'm really proud of her.
Is that weird? Only a few more
days til you get to open your NYU
letter—I'm holding my breath!

XO, Habiba

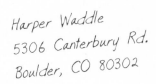

Harper Waddle
5306 Canterbury Rd.
Boulder, CO 80302

SEVENTEEN

I still can't believe you turned down that Brett Ratner audition." Sam chewed thoughtfully on a French fry, regarding her. He'd let his patchy, gold-flecked beard grow in the last few weeks, which gave him a slightly dangerous look.

Sophie rolled her eyes. They were sitting at a small vinyl-seated booth at the In-N-Out on Sunset Boulevard, LA's ultimate in fast food. They'd both ordered the house special, Double-Double burgers with everything, strawberry shakes, and delicious fries.

"How many times do I have to tell you?" She took a long slurp of her cool, just-sweet-enough milkshake. "I'm a serious actress."

Since catching Diaphragm Ellie getting jiggy with her co-star on the set of *Heartland,* Sophie had tried to avoid Sam whenever possible. To tell or not to tell: that was still the question. But when she'd gotten home from play practice for *The Real Thing* tonight and he'd suggested they grab dinner, she couldn't say no. For one thing, she'd eaten nothing except a Zone bar since eleven AM. For another, she missed him.

Across the booth, Sam shook his shaggy blond head in disbelief. "The little gal from Boulder I picked up from the airport back in

September never would have passed an opportunity to strut in front of a camera."

"People change," she sniffed. "*I* changed. This play *means* something. What was I gonna do? Spend the rest of my life telling the world I have a love-hate relationship with my hair?"

She was referring to the national shampoo ad she'd shot last fall. At the time, it seemed like the biggest thing that had ever happened to her. Millions of people seeing *her* on TV. But for every commercial and every three-line part in a movie like *Stud,* Sophie had to go on hundreds of auditions — auditions where the casting directors cared more about what she looked like than what she had to offer as an actress.

"Whatever." Sam stuffed another fry into his mouth. "I'm just glad you finally got off the damn couch. You were starting to smell a little funky."

"I was not!" Sophie felt herself blushing with indignation: she'd made sure to use extra deodorant on the couple of days — OK, *many* days — she hadn't bothered to shower. "And that time on the couch was important for my mental health. I was in self-reflective hibernation."

"You were a slug." He was right, but she didn't appreciate the critique.

"What about you?" Sophie challenged, wiping her greasy fingers on a paper napkin. "When was the last time you auditioned for anything besides Pool Boy #2?"

Sam averted his gold-green eyes. "We're not talking about me. We're talking about your claim that you've suddenly lost the desire to be a movie star. *Viva La Stage.*"

"Hey, if Steven Spielberg decides he wants to offer me a part in his next film . . . I'm there."

Duh. Of course Sophie wanted to be a movie star. But how could she explain to Sam that she'd needed a break from the . . . *Hollywood-*

ness . . . of it all? Something had pushed her over an intangible ledge — probably the combination of watching her purer, less LA-savvy self in the DVD of the high-school *Streetcar* production and stumbling into Ellie's impromptu sex scene in the trailer. Though it wasn't just seeing Sam's so-called girlfriend turn not-so-slowly into a Hollywood cliché. It was how Sophie herself had reacted, that awful moment when she'd considered using the situation to get ahead — at Sam's expense. Betraying a friend to further her own career: when Sophie came to her senses, she shuddered at the thought. This wasn't the kind of actress — or the person — she wanted to become.

Unfortunately, Sophie could only explain her tortured thought process if she told Sam what she'd witnessed in Ellie's trailer. Part of her knew she should, but another part of her didn't want to be the messenger. Messengers always got shot.

And another thing — she wasn't entirely sure of her own motives. Was it really *just* for his own good that she wanted Sam to know his girlfriend was a lying, cheating, manipulative bitch? Or did she want to tell him because she hoped he would dump Ellie and then he and Sophie could pick up where they'd left off the night the lights went out?

"What?" Sam, his lips shiny with grease, was staring at her as if he knew she was hiding something. "Tell me."

"Nothing." She nervously jiggled the zipper of her pink Juicy hoodie. "Shouldn't you be at a *Heartland* cast party or something?"

He swallowed the last messy bite of his Double-Double. "Yeah. Not so much."

"What's that mean?" Sophie took a sip of her strawberry shake, trying not to fixate on the way Sam's messy blond hair fell adorably into his green eyes.

"We broke up."

"Aacckk —" Choking on the shake, she started to cough. Oh God. Did he know? Was that why he brought her here? To bust her

371

for keeping Diaphragm Ellie's cheating ways to herself? "Why?" she managed to get out once she recovered her ability to breathe properly.

He twirled a French fry in a small blood-red puddle of ketchup on a napkin, avoiding her eyes. "We grew apart, blah, blah, blah."

Sophie raised an eyebrow. "Blah, blah, blah? That's it?" It was so male to leave out every relevant detail of a major happening. But she relaxed a little. He didn't know about Ellie and Cody. Or if he did, he didn't know *she knew.*

"Don't act surprised. You never liked her anyway."

"Yes, I did," she lied, reaching for a fry. "Y'know, aside from the fact that she's a shallow airhead whose only talent is her dedication to Pilates."

Sam bristled. "I'm not the only person in this booth who's fallen for the wrong person." He pointed the droopy French fry at her. "And unlike a certain guy with the initials T.B., Ellie never cheated on me."

Sophie pursed her lips. Leave it to Sam to bring up her least favorite subject. The guy was a sadist. "I'll have you know —"

"What?" His gold-flecked hazel eyes were boring into hers now. That's when she noticed that there was something different in them from usual. Sadness. Sam might have been acting like he didn't give a shit that his relationship with the Diaphragm Ditz was over, but he was lying. Telling him what she saw that day in the trailer would be unnecessarily cruel.

"I'll . . . I'll have you know that Ellie's lips are fake," Sophie improvised. "One hundred percent collagen. She admitted it during one of our acting sessions."

Sam smiled grimly. "Haven't you learned anything, Bushell? In Hollywood, everything's fake."

Not us, Sophie thought, staring down at the white Formica of the table. *What's between us is as real as anything I've ever experienced.* But as quickly as the thought entered her mind, she brushed it aside.

She'd sworn off guys for a reason. And she wasn't going to let Sam suck her back in. No matter how cute he was with his scruffy beard and sad, heartbroken eyes.

"Is he here?" Isabelle held a red plastic beer cup up to her lips — a makeshift shield as she scanned the crowded party.

"Are you sure he was coming?" Becca rubbed her neck and did a casual twist-and-glance around the room. Left to her own devices, she would have been hiding in a corner — or better yet, back in her dorm room — but she owed it to Isabelle not only to act as her wing-woman tonight, but to pretend she was enjoying it. Tonight was her chance to even up the friendship scales — even if it meant hauling her ass out of her self-inflicted seclusion and reentering the land of the alive and kicking.

"I heard him talking to Andi at the end of Poli Sci," Isabelle shouted over the party din. Apparently, the guy throwing the party had the same musical taste as Becca's mom — Pat Benatar was blaring from the iPod speakers at the other end of the rec room. Becca assumed it was supposed to be retro-cool, but she just found it annoying. "He and Matt are like, old friends," Isabelle continued, lasering the room with her eyes, the red cup an exact color match for her halter top. "He's here. He's totally here. We just have to find him."

The Matt in question was a junior whom Becca had never even met. Every year he threw a legendary pre-finals birthday bash — students drove in from at least three other New England schools, and several people were guaranteed to make asses of themselves in some egregious way. Last year, the party had ended with a naked wrestling match on the lawn of the college President's house, after which several students from Harvard were permanently banned from the campus, and three Middlebury students were suspended.

Why am I here? Becca thought, forcing a ready-to-party smile, and smoothing the skimpy floral swing dress that Isabelle had persuaded her to wear. That's right: she was here for Isabelle. Her friend needed her, and Becca was going to — what? March up to Josh, Isabelle's new crush, and demand he make out with her friend immediately? No, she reminded herself. It was all about support.

Isabelle had certainly been supportive after Becca saw Stuart and Emma Jenkins together. She'd been there while Becca talked, cried, and finally came to terms with the incredibly painful thought of moving on. She'd ordered in pizza when Becca couldn't face the cafeteria, and she'd kicked her in the ass when Becca couldn't face studying. If it hadn't been for Isabelle, there was no way Becca could have hauled her grades back up to acceptable levels.

Though it was hard to tell in the undulating clot of bodies packing Matt's suite, Stuart did seem to be one of the few Middlebury students *not* in attendance. He and Emma Jenkins. Not that it would have been a problem if he were there. Becca was fine. She was over it.

"Holy shit! Bec!" A pair of hands wrapped around Becca's waist from behind. She felt herself pulled backward, tanned masculine hands splayed across her stomach.

"What the hell —" Becca's voice broke off as the hands at her waist spun her around and she stared up into the drunken blue-gray eyes of Jared Burke. Kate's ex-boyfriend. The guy she'd lost her virginity to last Thanksgiving. What was *he* doing here?

"I totally forgot you went to Middlebury," Jared slurred, his face too close to hers. His breath stank of beer.

"Yeah." Becca tried to move away, but Jared's hands were tight around her waist. The last time she'd seen him was in the reflection of a twentieth-story window as he pulled on his pants. She hadn't been able to turn around, hadn't been able to face him. Until she had torpedoed her relationship with Stuart, it had been the biggest mistake of her life. Having his hands on her now made her skin crawl.

"You look hot." His blond hair was damp with sweat and his gray polo shirt reeked of smoke. "I am so stoked to see you. Is your room around here?"

Becca felt her face contort with disgust. "Jared, let go of me." She looked around for Isabelle, trying to wriggle free from Jared's persistent hands, but Isabelle had found Josh and was standing with him several feet away, completely preoccupied.

"Okay, that's enough." Becca winced, dodging Jared's lips and wrenching herself out of his clutches. She managed a fake smile. "I was actually leaving. So I'll see you."

But Jared grabbed her hand. "I just want to spend some time with an old friend." He gave his hips a lascivious swivel, and pulled her toward him. Becca jerked her hand away.

What had she and Kate ever seen in this guy? Becca didn't remember him ever being a complete drunken ass in high school. But maybe he was one of those guys who lost it when they went to college — who started drinking too much and bailing on classes, and ended up working in the mail room of their dad's companies.

Jared pulled her toward him. "Come on, you know we're good — oh . . ." She felt a warm hand wrap around her shoulder, firmly drawing her out of Jared's clammy grip. Suddenly she was nestled warmly in the crook of another guy's arm.

Stuart's arm.

"Are you hitting on my girlfriend?" Stuart's voice was calm, but Becca could feel tension radiating from his body.

Jared blinked as Stuart's words — and, in all likelihood, his size — registered. "Fuck, man. I didn't know." He held up his hands in a lame gesture of surrender.

"Now you do," Stuart said coldly. Becca closed her eyes for a moment, the party a distant blur of noise. She wanted to sink into him, wrap her arms around him and never let go. Was this really possible? Was Stuart really coming to her rescue? He'd called her his *girlfriend*. Maybe it was just a way to get rid of Jared, but there was more to it than that. He'd clearly been watching her, and when she couldn't get Jared to back off, he'd cared enough to step in.

When Becca opened her eyes and looked up at Stuart, she caught a flash of something in his hazel eyes. He missed her . . . and something else. *Holy shit, he still loved her.* It was written all over his face, as hard as he was trying to hide it. But it seemed clear — Stuart wanted her in his arms as much as she wanted to be there.

Jared grinned, backing off. "Good to see you, Bec," he slurred, stumbling toward the bottles of cheap booze lined up on a table by the wall.

Becca opened her mouth to say thank you, but as quickly as Stuart had appeared he was gone, melting back into the crowded party without another word.

Still, Becca's heart ballooned with hope. *He loves me.* Yes, maybe Stuart was with Emma Jenkins right now. But if Becca had learned anything from her parents, it was that true love didn't just go away. This fight wasn't over after all. She was going to find him right now and convince him that they were meant to be together.

And once she had him back in her life, she would do things differently. Becca was more in control of her fears now, and she'd learned a lot about trusting herself — and trusting other people the way she had always trusted Harper, Sophie, and Kate. She would tell Stuart how different she was going to be and he would forget he'd ever met Emma Jenkins. Everything would be just like it was, only better.

Only better. The words repeated in Becca's head as she circled the party, but Stuart had disappeared. *He loves me.* The thought carried her out into the mild, breezy night and across the dark campus to Stuart's dorm room. He didn't answer when she knocked — which was almost a relief. If he'd been in his room with Emma Jenkins, Becca was sure all of her newly discovered resolve would have evaporated into a thin mist of cowardice.

She could go back to her room and talk to Stuart tomorrow. But if she did that, the moment would be lost. When she woke up in the morning, Becca would start second-guessing what she'd glimpsed in his eyes tonight and this resolve would falter. So she was going to stay. And wait. For as long as it took. Sooner or later, he would be back. Maybe he'd be with Emma, but Becca couldn't let herself think about that.

She also couldn't stand in the hallway all night. So she slipped into the messy student lounge next to Stuart's room and propped herself on the gray velour couch facing the open door. When he came home, he would see her and they would talk. Somehow, everything would be fine.

But after an hour of sitting and waiting, all the late nights of catch-up studying caught up with her. The next thing Becca knew, a guy's voice broke through her sleep. "Becca? Dude, what are you doing here?"

"Wha —" She opened her heavy-lidded eyes, and for several seconds couldn't quite figure out where she was. Or why Mason's tall form was looming over her, or why he was staring down at her chin. Then — *oh.* There was drool covering the lower half of her face. As she took a swipe at her chin with the palm of her hand, Becca's encounter with Jared and Stuart came back to her. And in the clear light of day — and day it seemed to be, from the sunlight streaming through the dusty vertical blinds — she knew she'd made yet another humiliating mistake. Camping out in Stuart's dorm was . . . ridiculous. Totally misguided. Verging on psycho.

And now Mason was going to tell his football-buddy Stuart that Becca was stalking him —

Fuck. She had fallen asleep waiting for Stuart, and he had never come home. That meant — *he had spent the night with Emma.* Tears stung Becca's eyes. She clambered up off the sofa, beelining for the door.

Sorry," she mumbled. Mason awkwardly reached out a hand, as though he wanted to help but didn't know how or if he should. Becca stopped at the door, long enough to make a last plea. "Could you *please* not tell him I was here?"

"Yeah, sure." Mason sounded like he felt sorry for her.

Could she *be* more pathetic? *No,* she thought, heading out into the sunlight for her walk of shame. Of all the embarrassing things she'd ever done, being woken up by one of Stuart's friends having spent an entire night waiting for him like a lost puppy dog was by far the pathetic-est. God, she had to get a grip on herself. She didn't want Maddix to be wrong about her. Becca wanted to be together and confident, totally capable of dealing with a stupid break-up. Break-ups happened all the time. What, did she think Stuart Pendergrass was the love of her life or something?

But that was the problem. The answer was: she did.

A year ago, when Kate had opened her acceptance letter to Harvard, it felt . . . well, sort of like her whole life was a perfectly browned Thanksgiving turkey. She'd made the stuffing, done all the roasting and basting, and what came out of the oven was better than a magazine picture — it smelled perfect, looked perfect, and would undoubtedly taste perfect, too. Nothing could have been better. Her parents were prouder than they had ever been. Her teachers were unsurprised but still impressed. Her friends were happy for her. And she'd felt . . . not much, actually. Kind of like after the turkey's eaten and the tryptophan sets in. Yum. Yippee. Yawn.

That feeling — or lack of it — was part of what persuaded her to hop on Harper's Dream Train. And now her life felt less like a turkey, and more like . . . like a life. Her life. She'd spent almost an entire year living it, wholly and completely, and with purpose.

And she had still managed to make her parents proud.

She couldn't imagine them being any prouder than they were now, sitting in the back of the dust-covered Range Rover on the bumpy road back to Mekebe, listening to Kate and Habiba explain to Masarat — for the tenth time — how they had managed to track her down, working in the hot, claustrophobic kitchen of a small hotel on the outskirts of Addis Ababa. It was a miracle, really, that they had. Between all of their contacts — gathered from her father's friends, Habiba's orphanage director, Abebech's relatives, and even a few people Darby suggested — they'd spread the word throughout Addis Ababa that they were looking for an eighteen-year-old named Masarat from Mekebe. People had contacted other people, who had contacted others, one of whom had spread the word through the massive Merkato marketplace. On her parents' third night in Addis Ababa, Kate received a phone call from a woman who sold grain to the hotel where Masarat worked.

The next day, the entire Foster family took a yellow Mercedes taxi to the hotel. The look on Masarat's thin, exhausted face when she heard her sister's name — part pain, part joy, part terror that she was about to get bad news — would stay with Kate forever. The Fosters had reassured her that Angatu was fine — but that Abebech was quite old, and would not be able to take care of her much longer. Masarat had immediately decided to bring Angatu to Addis Ababa — she had a shanty in the city, she told them, and she had missed her little sister desperately.

Kate knew what kind of life Angatu would have if she moved in with her sister in one of Addis Ababa's shanty neighborhoods. Her parents knew it, too. Which was why they had made arrangements even before they came to Ethiopia, communicated with the help of Kate and Habiba. Mr. Foster knew a professor at Addis Ababa University, they told Masarat. The professor and his wife had grown children who'd moved away, and now they had a spare room — for Masarat and Angatu. The Fosters would be happy to pay for Angatu's and Masarat's education. They had arranged for Angatu to attend a private grade school, and Masarat would have a private tutor to prepare her for the university. If she wanted to, she could start in the fall.

For several tense moments, Kate wondered if Masarat was stricken with paralysis. Her mouth was frozen open, her brown eyes wide and stunned. And then she was sobbing, rushing from Foster to Foster, embracing one then the other, over and over. Kate had never seen such unrestrained crying. It was as if years of sadness, pain, and fear had found a jagged crack in Masarat's strong exterior and wrenched it open with gale force. Kate watched, teary herself, as Habiba held Masarat's hand and reassured her that everything the Fosters said was true.

Finally, Masarat calmed down and stood quietly, shaking her head slowly. *"Amese genando,"* she said. *Thank you.*

Masarat had said thank you more times than Kate could count as they packed up her meager belongings from the half-collapsed tiny shanty, boarded a plane to Bahar Dar, flew north, and piled into the rented Land Rover for the final leg of their journey. But the closer they got to Mekebe, the quieter Masarat grew. Her slender hands alternately picked at the loose threads of her white natala and smoothed her brown hair, which was pulled back into a stubby ponytail. And when they arrived at Abebech's restaurant, Kate had to take Masarat's trembling hand and lead her from the car.

"She will not know me," Masarat whispered, fear in her eyes. "She will be angry at me for leaving."

"She knows you had to leave," Kate told her, squeezing her hand. "She's just missed you."

"She's your sister," Habiba agreed, one hand on Masarat's arm. She looked over at Kate. "Sisters forgive everything."

Kate thought she caught her mother giving her father a satisfied smile when she took his hand and led their party of five into the restaurant.

"Are you ready?" Kate asked, and Masarat bowed her head.

Angatu was coming out of the kitchen as they entered, and she smiled widely at Kate. Then she noticed the girl walking in with Kate, and her brow knit together in confusion. Kate suddenly wondered if she'd made the right decision in not telling Angatu she was looking for her sister. She hadn't wanted to get her hopes up and then disappoint her — but what if Masarat was right? What if Angatu *didn't* want to see her?

But Angatu's eyes lit up like Christmas morning. "Masarat?" she whispered, as though she couldn't believe the mirage in front of her.

Masarat nodded and held out her arms. Angatu ran into them.

And that was that. In that moment, every question Kate had a year ago was answered. Every doubt that had plagued her in the last ten months was gone. Every inconvenience and every danger she'd suffered was worth it. Without taking her eyes off of Masarat and Angatu, Kate reached out and clutched Habiba's hand. Habiba leaned into her shoulder, and Kate rested her head against her sister's. She knew who she was and what she wanted with a clarity that had eluded her for eighteen years. And being in possession of that knowledge meant one thing.

She could go home.

Home. The word stuck in her chest and spread a warmth that dimmed just briefly when she saw Darby standing in the doorway, watching. He smiled at her — the first *real* smile he had ever given her — open, happy, generous. And the warmth in her heart became something else entirely.

She was going home. But that would mean leaving Darby.

Three hundred and sixty-six. Three hundred and sixty-seven. Three hundred and sixty-eight. Harper let out a breath as her wheezing laser printer spat out the last page of her still-untitled novel.

381

Three days ago, she'd called the coffeehouse and told them not to expect her for the rest of the week. Then she'd gathered her mother, father, and sister together in the kitchen. "I'm going to finish my novel," she'd announced. "I'll be unavailable for catering duty until further notice."

Amy had whined for a minute about getting stuck with extra work, but a look from their father had silenced her. "Do what you have to do, Harper," he'd said. "We'll send down supplies."

Then Harper had descended into the basement and locked herself in the bathroom. For the last seventy-two hours, she'd been alternating between writing and sleeping. She'd turn on her computer and write until the power died, at which point she'd plug it in to recharge while she took a long nap. After scarfing down a hasty bowl of cereal, a plate of her mother's mini grilled-cheese sandwiches or a GOLEAN bar, she'd start the whole process over again.

And finally . . . she was done. Harper pulled the three hundred and sixty-eight pages from the printer and slipped the fat bundle into a manila envelope.

Since January, her novel had been hers and hers alone. Now she was tempted to stick it in a drawer and forget about it. Maybe it was enough that she'd done what she set out to do. Maybe she didn't need to bare her most personal thoughts to the world. . . .

No! The voice in her head was loud and not to be argued with. She was a *real* writer. Real writers shared their work with an audience. That was the whole *point.*

Her heart hammered as she looked at the name and address she'd written on a Rainy Day Books Café scratch pad.

Caroline Sutter
965 Park Avenue
Suite 311
New York, NY 10112

Caroline Sutter was the mother of Becca's Middlebury roommate, Isabelle. She was also a literary agent. The kind of literary agent who represented authors who won National Book Awards and had novels on the *New York Times* bestseller list every Sunday. Becca had acted so casual when she'd given Harper the address a few weeks ago. *Send the book to her when you're done. She's nice, I promise. There's nothing to be nervous about.*

Nothing to be nervous about? That was easy for Becca to say. She hadn't poured her entire life into those three hundred and sixty-eight pages. She wasn't the one whose heart would be crushed beyond recognition if Caroline Sutter thought she was a total talentless hack.

Harper headed toward the shower — her first since the Final Descent into the basement three days ago. She *was* going to send the book to Isabelle's mother. She *had* to. But first she needed to know if it sucked. Unfortunately, there was only one person who would give her an honest opinion. And when she heard that opinion, she at least needed to be clean.

"Is Tara here?"

"You came to my apartment to see Tara?" Leaning against the frame of his front door, arms folded, dressed in an American Apparel t-shirt and worn khakis, Mr. Finelli looked closer to eighteen than twenty-four.

"No!" This wasn't going the way Harper had planned. He sounded kind of pissed.

"Good thing, because she moved to Boise three weeks ago. And for the record, what we had was fun but not worthy of a long-distance relationship."

Harper took a deep breath. She wanted to process that information. She really, really did. But she had something to say, and she was going to say it.

"You were right. I was wrong." Harper hugged her manuscript tight against her new black tank top. "I've wanted to tell you that for a long time."

"Are you going to run away now?" Mr. Finelli asked, one eyebrow raised. "Or, to be more accurate, pedal away?" He glanced over at the bike she'd left lying in the grass in front of his duplex.

She shook her head and held out her manila envelope. "I'm going to ask for a huge, huge favor."

Mr. Finelli glanced at the envelope and grinned. "Is that what I think it is?"

"Three hundred and sixty-eight pages of blood, guts, and soul. I started over."

"And here I thought you came by to talk about us." He slipped off his glasses and rubbed the lenses against his t-shirt. "Then again, there never really was an 'us,' was there?"

A familiar sensation of imminent barfing washed over her. "I thought there was," she croaked out, ignoring the bile simmering in her throat. "I just totally screwed it up."

"Yeah, you did."

This was the part where Harper was supposed to give her big speech. The one where she confessed her undying love and begged him to give her another chance. But the envelope in her hand felt like a bomb about to explode. If she didn't get rid of it immediately, all that would be left of her was a pinkie finger and her black plastic eyeglass frames.

"Will you read it?" She thrust the novel toward him with more force than intended, almost whacking his stomach.

"I don't know. . . ." He hesitated, still rubbing his glasses. "I can't promise I'm going to like it."

"But I can promise I won't freak out if you don't," Harper insisted. "I'm sorry about how I acted last time. It won't happen again."

She could have given the book to her mother or father or Habiba. They wouldn't have said it sucked. They would have heralded her for being brilliant and insightful and amazing. And she would have savored their words, basked in the glory of her accomplishment. But she'd come too far to be safe. Harper needed to know the truth.

"Please."

He nodded and took the envelope from her outstretched hand. "I'll read it tonight."

Harper sat down on his front steps. "Great. I'll wait here."

He gave her a bemused look. "You're going to sit on my stoop while I read three-hundred-and-whatever pages?"

"Uh . . . yeah." She gave him a weak smile. The steps were cold and hard. "If that's okay?" She couldn't get up if she wanted to. Her legs seemed to have forgotten how to work.

"First you won't talk to me, now I can't get rid of you." But Mr. Finelli smiled, shaking his head, before he went inside.

For the first half hour, she sat rigidly on the front steps, counting the seconds and then the minutes. *He's probably read the first line by now. The first paragraph. The first page. Okay, he's maybe done with Chapter One. Unless he took a break to make coffee . . .*

Finally she forced herself to stop. This kind of obsessive thinking couldn't be healthy. It wasn't even sane. She forced her mind to travel to the one topic that could provide distraction.

Kissing Adam Finelli.

Harper thought back to the night when he'd surprised her by pulling her close and touching his soft lips to hers. Closing her eyes, she tried to relive the sensation. She knew there'd been stubble on his cheeks, and he'd rested his hand against the small of her back, shooting tingles up and down her spine. When he'd caressed her face, she'd thought she was going to faint. Those were the facts. Unfortunately, she couldn't *feel* any of it. Not anymore. *Why not?*

385

Behind her, the door opened. Harper jerked out of her daydream. Could it be possible that she'd been so lost in her thoughts about kissing that enough time had passed for Mr. Finelli to finish? Was she *that* depraved? She turned to find him staring at her.

"You hated it." She could tell by the look on his face.

Her first thought was that she was going to die. Her second thought was that first she would burn this novel, the way she burned the first fifty pages of the last one, and *then* she would die. No need to leave a legacy of non-literary crap for everyone to snicker about at the funeral. She deserved a bit of postmortem dignity.

"I love it." He smiled, scratching his messed-up dark hair. "Correction. I love the first five chapters. I couldn't keep reading until I put you out of your misery."

Harper hopped to her feet, ignoring the fact that both of her legs had fallen asleep. "You . . . what?"

"I love it, Harper. It's . . . *you*."

She was terrified that he was lying to avoid a scene. Only . . . people didn't *beam* when they lied. They didn't look right in another person's face and *beam*. That just didn't happen. Which could only mean one thing. Mr. Finelli loved her book. Or the first five chapters, anyway. And it only got better from there.

Harper didn't intend to leap into his arms. She didn't intend to leap it all — it just sort of happened. He stumbled back, surprised, but then she felt his arms encircle her waist, holding her steady.

"Sorry, I —"

He held her tighter. "It's okay. Really."

Mr. Finelli's boyish face was close to hers. He smelled minty and fresh, like he was part of a toothpaste ad. They were both wearing short sleeves, and she felt their skin touching. "I have a big speech," she whispered, suddenly shy.

"I hate big speeches." He pulled her even closer. "Remember what I taught you in class. Show, don't tell."

Harper felt like laughing, crying, screaming, or some combination of the three. She also felt like *showing* him exactly how glad she was to be back in his arms where she belonged. She was kissing him before the thought was even complete in her mind.

And he was kissing her back, hard and urgent. She leaned into him and they clung together, their lips moving in unison. It was everything she dreamed of. Mr. Finelli — Adam — loved her book. Maybe he even loved her.

There was, however, a problem. All the time they were kissing, she could only think about one thing. Actually, one *person*.

Judd.

Dewar's

TWELVE **12** YEARS OLD

Special Reserve

BLENDED
SCOTCH
WHISKEY

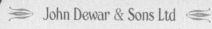

John Dewar & Sons Ltd

TWELVE YEARS OLD

BLENDED SCOTCH WHISKEY

EIGHTEEN

Becca and Isabelle took the stairs to their dorm room two at a time. "I wish I still drank," Becca laughed, feeling almost giddy. "This is definitely a moment for celebration." She, Becca Winsberg, had just finished her last final exam of her freshman year of college. It had been a bitch, and she definitely didn't ever want to take another psych class again, but she felt she'd done well — better than she would have expected, given that Stuart was sitting in the back of the room. She'd been able to block him out for most of the two-hour exam time, but it had been a relief when he'd finished before her and headed for the door. And she'd been grateful that Isabelle — who'd also just finished her last exam — was waiting outside for her when Becca finally emerged, exhausted but euphoric.

"I've got a bottle of scotch in the back of my closet." Isabelle paused at the top of the stairs. "Feel like a snort?"

"A *snort?*"

Isabelle shrugged. "I dunno. That's what my grandma says."

"I'm up for a snort," Becca nodded. "But a very *little* one."

"Oh." Isabelle suddenly looked awkward, fingering the platinum chain around her neck. Becca followed her eyes down to the end of the door-lined corridor where . . . oh.

Stuart was sitting outside their door, staring at the floor.

Isabelle pivoted and hurried back down the stairs. "See you later. Good luck."

Becca felt her knees turn to jelly as she walked the twenty remaining feet, watching Stuart clamber to his feet.

"Hey." He shoved his hands in his jeans pockets, still looking at the floor. Wearing a pale-blue button-down open over a white t-shirt, he looked like an Abercrombie model. Only cleaner. And significantly more stressed.

"Can we talk?" Stuart was having a hard time meeting her eyes.

Becca realized she'd just been staring at him. "Uh, yeah." She reached in her pale yellow North Face backpack for her keys, and fumbled the door open. She felt oddly calm. Or numb. That was what happened when people went into shock, right? And she couldn't imagine a bigger shock than seeing Stuart in front of her door.

She dropped her backpack on the floor and stood awkwardly waiting for him to close the door behind them. For a long moment, they just stood there, facing each other, eyes nervously locked. Becca's heart thudded, her mouth too dry to say a word. Finally Stuart cleared his throat.

"Did you . . . Mason says you slept in the lounge at my dorm last week," he began, shifting from foot to foot.

Shit. Mason had sold her out. Stuart probably thought she was some kind of stalker now. That's probably why he was here — to tell her to keep five feet away from him at all times.

Becca took a deep breath. She was going to be adult about this. "I'm sorry," she said slowly, then finished with a petulant, "But Mason promised he wouldn't tell you!" So much for being adult. She might as well stomp her feet.

"He thought I should know." Stuart stared down at the floor again. "Since I'm in love with you and everything."

He glanced up at her, and Becca instantly felt transported into an alternate universe. The one where things worked out the way they were supposed to work out. The one where love was amazing and real, and where it lasted.

But this was *her* universe, where things like this didn't happen. She might not have heard him right.

"You . . . what?"

"I thought, maybe — you know, after the lounge thing — that maybe you still had feelings for me, so . . ." Stuart's voice trailed off, uncertain. His eyebrows were knit together, a muscle pulsing in his jaw.

Becca didn't know what to say. *Of course* she still had feelings for him. She would always have feelings for him. Strong feelings. *Love* feelings.

Stuart misread her silence. "I'm sorry, I'll go." He turned for the door.

"Wait!" Becca grabbed his arm, and then she was grabbing *him,* wrapping her arms around him, burying her head in his chest. "I love you," she said, her cheek pressed against the cotton of his t-shirt.

Stuart gripped her shoulders and pulled her far enough away to see her face. "Seriously?"

"Seriously." Stuart's grin would have lit up the Arctic circle in the no-sun months. Becca beamed back at him, until she remembered. "What about Emma?"

Stuart shook his head, looking slightly embarrassed. "Emma's an old friend. An old girlfriend, but . . . I was never in love with her. We just dated for a while, and . . ." He took Becca's hand and pulled her down beside him on the edge of the bed. "I was really . . . I was kind of a mess when we broke up, and she was there for me. And I thought . . . I don't know, I guess I thought maybe I could get over you if there was someone else."

The numbness was starting to wear off, and Becca wasn't sure her heart could take what was happening. Stuart was here. In her room.

He loved her. The night he'd saved her from Jared, she was right. She *had* seen love in his eyes.

"But you didn't come home that night . . ."

"Emma and I were . . . breaking up, I guess. She figured out I wasn't as over you as I wanted to be."

"You wanted to be?"

Stuart nodded. "And then I realized . . ." He grinned, his eyes sparkling. "You are not the most . . . *balanced* human being I've ever known."

Becca laughed out loud. That was an understatement. "I'm trying," she said. "I'm going to therapy —"

"I'm just trying to say, I'm sorry. I should have known what you were going through. I should have seen it, and I shouldn't have let you push me away."

Becca blinked, stunned. Was Stuart taking responsibility for her craziness? "But . . . I was horrible —" she stammered.

"You were freaked out and scared. I should have given you more time. I got all hurt because you didn't trust me, but *of course* you didn't trust me —"

"I do trust you." Becca twisted toward him and took his hand. She held it to her heart.

She loved him. She trusted him.

And he loved her.

I got in.

No, I didn't.

Yes, I did.

Harper stared at the letter from NYU, wondering when she'd be ready to actually open it. She carried it with her everywhere she went — the basement, the bathroom, the Rainy Day Café — figuring that eventually the right moment would present itself. So far it hadn't. She kept taking the letter out of her pocket, looking at it, then folding it up and putting it back again. She was in the looking-at-it phase right now.

"Holy shit." Judd was standing behind her, his eyes glued to the New York University address printed on the creased top left side of the envelope. She tried to ignore the nauseous feeling she got every time she was near him, ever since the Mr. Finelli kissing incident. "When did you get that?"

"A few days ago." Harper re-folded the envelope and rammed it into the pocket of her dark Levi's. "Tie-Dye Guy is waiting for his ice coffee." She nodded toward one of their regulars.

"We're opening that baby tonight," Judd informed her, tapping out coffee grounds. "I mean it."

Her dad had given her the letter two nights ago, when she got back from Mr. Finelli's. He told her he was proud of her no matter what the contents, then hobbled up the stairs to go to bed. Harper didn't know what she'd expected to feel when she finally had the answer to her future in her hands. Fear. Excitement. Anxiety. The hope of redemption.

But holding the thin white envelope, she'd felt an overwhelming sense of gratitude. Gratitude that the last time she'd gotten a letter from NYU, they'd rejected her. Despite living in a basement and missing her friends and having to be a barista and various other personal catastrophes, this had been the most satisfying year of her life. And she wasn't ready for her Year of Dreams to end. Not yet. Which was why, days later, she still didn't know her fate.

Now Judd reached past her to hand Tie-Dye Guy his iced coffee. As his arm brushed hers, she felt her face sizzle. The whole blushing thing was an extremely annoying development. It had started, along with the nausea, the day after KMF — i.e., Kissing Mr. Finelli.

"We're closing early," Judd called out to the three customers who were still lingering in the café. "Personal business."

Judd put an encouraging hand on her shoulder and squeezed. Harper almost jumped out of her skin. "We are *not* closing early!" she yelled. "Everyone, please enjoy your beverages."

"Good luck with NYU," Tie-Dye Guy told her, tipping his iced coffee in her direction. "They should be stoked to have you." Jeez, even the café's resident pothead knew about her letter.

God. Harper was nervous. Like, *really* nervous. She wasn't sure if the sweat forming under her arms was about opening the letter from NYU or being alone with Judd. Either way, she wished she had a stick of deodorant in the red backpack she kept behind the counter. Or possibly a cold shower.

"Are you okay?" Judd asked. "Your face is red."

"I'll be in the storage room — storing stuff." Harper grabbed an unopened bag of coffee beans and headed to the cluttered, shelf-lined room at the back of the café.

She dropped the coffee on top of a giant box of toilet paper and pulled the door shut behind her. Except for a small sliver of light seeping through the crack under the door, the room was dark. She perched on the small stepladder and forced herself to breathe slowly. *Everything is okay,* she told herself. *It's no big deal.*

Either she got into NYU or she didn't. If she didn't, there were seven more letters just like the one in her pocket waiting for her at home. She had to get accepted *somewhere.* This wasn't like last April, when her whole life seemed to depend on getting a Manhattan address. It didn't matter anymore what a nameless, faceless group of admission directors thought of her. What mattered was what she thought of herself. Okay: what Isabelle's mom thought of her manuscript mattered a little, too. But that simply wasn't something she could obsess about right now.

Harper pulled out the much-folded envelope. The Year of Dreams was coming to a close, and she was ready — finally — to see what would happen next. In the near darkness, she felt along the flap of the envelope, slowly ripping it open. She squeezed her eyes shut as she removed the single sheet of paper and unfolded it. This was it. The moment of truth. She opened her eyes.

And saw nothing. It was too dark. *So much for a dramatic moment.* Just as she was about to heave herself off the stepladder and turn on the switch, the door opened.

"Everyone's gone," Judd announced, light flooding the room. He stopped and stared at her. "Were you sitting here in the dark?"

Harper didn't respond right away. She was transfixed by the letter. One word in particular.

Congratulations.

She'd gotten in to NYU. Should she scream? Dance? Execute some kind of ancient tribal war cry? What?

"Harp?" Judd was standing right in front of her. "What does it say? You can tell me."

"I'm sorry I hate Amelia." It wasn't what she'd expected to come out of her mouth at that moment, but it was true.

He grabbed the letter out of her hands and scanned it. "YES!" His shout reverberated off the metal shelves. "YES!" He dangled the letter in front of her face. "You did it! YES!"

She smiled. "Cool, huh?"

He grinned. "Very." Then he frowned. "You hate Amelia? You said you love Amelia."

"I lied. I'm sorry. I'm sure she's a very nice person, but I hate her guts." Harper took the letter from him and ducked out of the storage room. She couldn't stand that close to Judd without her face registering a third-degree burn. "We should mop tonight. It's pretty nasty behind the counter."

She'd almost made it to the cash register when she felt his hand on her arm, spinning her around. "You're acting very strange."

"I got in. Yay! Now let's mop." Harper *was* happy. But suddenly going to NYU didn't seem like the biggest deal in the world. It almost seemed a little . . . sad. She liked her life just the way it was, aside from all the horrible stuff. Even mopping wasn't that bad, really.

Judd looked annoyed. "This isn't fair, Harper. We're *friends*. I should get to hug you or something."

"Okay, hug me."

He put his arms around her and pulled her close. After a few seconds, she relaxed enough to hug him back. "I'm sorry I'm such a bitch," she whispered. "Don't take it personally."

"Why aren't you smiling?" he asked, jerking his tousled head back to look at her. "I'm very troubled that you're not smiling."

Because I'm going to miss you. Because until I kissed Mr. Finelli again I didn't realize that the most awesome guy on the planet was just one espresso maker to the left. Because I want to throw myself at you, but I can't.

"I just feel sort of weird," she finally answered. "You know me. Harper Waddle. Weird, weird, weird."

Judd laughed, letting her go. "I'm the one who should be apologizing. I never should have suggested that whole friends-with-benefits thing. I was a total asshole."

"We both agreed," she reminded him, willing herself not to blush. "It's not like you forced me. No harm, no foul, right?"

"Except there was harm." He leaned against the counter. "Our friendship isn't the same, and you know it."

She shrugged. "Things change. It's natural."

Judd crossed his arms in front of his chest. His thick black hair was even messier than usual, and he'd spilled coffee on his t-shirt. "Since this night is already incredibly bizarre, can I make it even more bizarre by telling you something?"

"I'm a shitty kisser?" It was one of her worst fears. That and having BARISTA-UNPUBLISHED AUTHOR engraved on her tombstone.

"I never wanted to be friends-with-benefits," he said quietly, moving around some spilled coffee grains with the toe of his shoe. "I had a thing for you since sophomore year, and I figured . . . I don't know. It was a way in."

Harper stared at him, incredulous. "You obviously have me confused with someone who needs a bullshit ego boost."

"It's true."

"Hello? You're the guy whose Dream was to lose your virginity to Amelia Dorf, remember?"

Judd shook his head. "I wanted it to be you, Harper. That's why I wrangled you into working here. That's why I went with you on your stupid stakeouts and took you to buy a Christmas tree and showed up at your house the night you finished the fifth chapter of your book. I wanted *you.*"

Now she was *really* confused. Addled, even. None of this made sense. Judd had *had* her. They'd been making out very nicely when Amelia showed up for her cup of cocoa *a deux.* He could have kicked her out and gone back to touching Harper's breasts. But he hadn't. He'd disappeared off to Amelia Land and never come back.

"You're lying," she insisted. "As soon as Amelia came on the scene, you were gone."

He tugged at his hair. "Only because you kept asking me about her. It was like you *wanted* us to get together. Eventually I got the hint that you were *never* going to like me the way I liked you. So, yeah, I forced myself to move on. Turns out, Amelia's pretty awesome." He sighed. "Look, it's no big deal. I just wanted you to know."

For a moment Harper thought about leaving the conversation there. She'd come out of it looking desirable and unobtainable, which wasn't a bad way to be perceived. But Judd had been her best friend during the Year of Dreams. And she didn't want to tell another lie, even if it was a lie of omission.

"I like you, too," she said softly, gazing into his dark eyes. "I didn't realize it at first. But I saw Mr. Finelli the other night, and I realized . . . maybe I'd known it for a long time. I'm not sure yet. I'm still sort of figuring it out."

"So Mr. Finelli blows you off, and you decide you like me? Nice."

"He didn't blow me off. He kissed me. For a very long time, I'll have you know. But all I could think about was you."

"Really?" Judd's face softened.

"When he stopped kissing me, I told him I felt a case of the flu coming on and ran like hell." Harper shrugged. "Probably wasn't the best way to handle the situation, but I think he got the hint."

"Wow."

"Yeah. Wow." They were staring at each other. Harper itched to be in his arms — not as a friend-with-benefits, but as something else. Something more.

But Judd didn't sweep her into a movie kiss. "Shit. I have a girl-friend. A really nice girlfriend who loves me." He paused. "And I kinda like her a lot, too."

That's when Harper started to get the feeling that this night wasn't going to end with her and Judd riding off into the sunset in his battered old Saturn. She forced back the crushing wave of disappointment. Harper was a good talker — if she'd convinced her friends to abandon the college plans they'd worked toward for years, she could probably convince Judd to abandon a girlfriend he'd had for a few months. But what then? In three months, she'd be gone. Judd and Amelia would still be here. If he could be happy with her . . . Harper was going to make his decision easy. After everything he'd done for her, it was the least she could do for him.

"Hey, don't worry about it," she told him. "We're probably better off as friends, anyway. We'd screw up anything more."

He didn't say anything at first. He just stared at her as if he was trying to read her mind. Then he smiled in a fake over-cheerful way, just the way she was smiling at him. "You're right. Friends."

Harper grabbed the mop. This was the second time she'd lied after reading an NYU admissions letter. The first time she'd spiraled into a pit of self-loathing and ended up turning her friends' lives upside down. This time was different. She knew she'd done the right thing.

Still, if she'd had the choice, she would have written a different ending. In her story, Harper would have finished her novel, gotten accepted to NYU, *and* ended up with the boy. She shook her head. *Oh, well. Two out of three ain't bad.*

"So what's next for you?"

Kate felt Darby's presence at the door of her hut a full second before he spoke. For the last several days — ever since she'd noticed him watching her with her family when Angatu and Masarat were reunited — she had known intuitively where he was almost at all times. She sensed when he was in the yard in the mornings, where in the village he was working during the day, and when he returned to the compound at night. As it grew dark, she could almost count down to the exact moment when the glow from long rays of his lantern, beaming through the window over Jessica's cot, would flicker off. If she tried, Kate was sure she would feel the exact moment when he fell asleep.

She herself wasn't doing much sleeping. She was alone in the hut now. After a tearful goodbye with Abebech, the Fosters and Habiba had taken Angatu and Masarat to Addis Ababa to get them set up in their new home. Dorothé had gone with them, hoping to catch the earliest plane back to France. She was meeting up with Mira, the other woman Kate had met in Paris on the long-ago day when she'd first heard the words "take the water." Dorothé and Mira were planning a fund-raiser for Water Partners in Paris, and Chantal, Kate's much-loved professor friend, had agreed to host the event in her book-lined apartment. Even Jessica had abandoned her cot and taken up residence in the Hotel Tana in Bahar Dar. She'd woken up one morning, a few days ago, and announced that she'd had enough of "shithouses" and was going to spend her remaining days in Africa at a place with indoor plumbing. Kate suspected that Jessica had finally realized Darby was never going to fall madly in love with her — she couldn't be bothered to continue pretending she gave a damn about anyone or anything but herself.

So for the last two nights, Kate had been on her own. Each night she had dinner with Darby and Jean-Pierre, then played soccer with the children — though every laughing girl reminded her of Angatu, a bittersweet memory. Part of her was happy about bringing Angatu and Masarat together again — but a selfish part of her missed the little girl she'd grown to adore.

For the past few nights, after the children returned home, she and Darby ended up sitting on tree stumps in the yard and talking. A lot. She'd learned more about him over the last three days than in the previous four months. His parents were in Boston, setting up an AIDS education N.G.O. They would be returning to Africa — the Sudan, specifically — in several months, which worried Darby. The older he got, he confided, the more he was aware of the dangerous situations his parents put themselves in. And although he understood that they had to do what they believed in, he worried about them all the same.

"It's important, what they do," Kate told him. "They save lives. Probably more lives than most doctors in their entire careers."

"I know," Darby had nodded, his face glowing in the light of their campfire. "And I'm proud of them. It's just . . . you know, I want them to be safe."

They talked about Kate's parents, Habiba, the Year of Dreams . . . even Magnus.

"Do you still love him?" Darby asked her, his face unreadable in the twilight.

"Definitely. But not romantically, anymore. I don't know, he gave me exactly what I needed at that time in my life. I'll always love him for that. But not . . . you know."

"No more making out," Darby grinned.

"Exactly." She smiled back at him.

She had laughed more in those hours with him than she had ever laughed with her old boyfriend Jared, or even with Magnus. But it didn't really matter, did it? He hadn't made an actual move since the day of the fierce kiss. Yes, he'd been great with her parents. Yes, he liked her. But it wasn't as if there was a future for them. This was the end — her last night. Tomorrow she would be in Addis Ababa and two days after that she would be back in Boulder. This was goodbye.

As Kate shoved a final t-shirt into her backpack, Darby walked into the hut. "Home is next for me," she told him.

"And then what?" Darby stepped toward her.

"I don't know. Mac and cheese, for one thing."

Darby was closing in now. Kate felt her heart jerk to life. "What then?" he said, his face intent.

"Harvard, in September," Kate answered, fighting the urge to step back.

"And then?" Darby was so close they were almost touching. Kate felt a pull — it was all she could do not to lean toward him, press her hands to his chest.

"I don't know," she whispered. "Why do you ask?"

Darby lifted one hand and cupped Kate's neck, sliding his fingers into her hair. She concentrated on not letting her knees buckle. "I thought," Darby said quietly, "maybe you'd like to come to Boston. My parents want to meet you."

"Your parents . . . know about me?"

Darby nodded, his eyes locked on Kate's. She couldn't resist the pull any longer. Why wouldn't he just kiss her, dammit?

403

And then he did. This was a different kind of kiss — not angry at all. This kiss was gentle, and warm, and urgent.

Kate had spent her whole life trying to be perfect. But what she learned from Darby — over the next several hours that night — was that perfect doesn't require trying.

Perfect just is.

"You wanna grab a beer, drink away rehearsal fatigue?" Jackson Achebe was tall, dark, and handsome. They'd been onstage together for the last twelve hours, during which they'd participated in Sebastian's numerous intense acting exercises, practiced their English accents, and exhausted themselves with calisthenics.

Sophie glanced up from her cell phone. She'd been scrolling through her missed calls. Harper had left a message and so had Becca. In a few days, the two of them would be reunited with Kate in Boulder. The fact that Sophie wouldn't be able to go home for the big reunion still hadn't sunk in. But as soon as she got the part in *The Real Thing* she knew that the Year of Dreams wasn't going to end, not for her. She'd called her parents and told them that she was going to stay in Los Angeles and be an actress. It was who she was. It was what she wanted. To keep them from freaking out over her decision not to enroll in college full-time, she'd promised that in the fall she'd take a few classes at UCLA. Just because she was an actress didn't mean she had to be uneducated.

"I can't tonight," Sophie told Jackson. "Roommate thing."

"Excuses, excuses." Jackson asked her out every day, and every day she came up with another reason why she couldn't hang out with him after hours. But this time it wasn't just an excuse.

Her heart skittered thinking about her meeting with Sam tonight. He said he had something important to tell her. In between trying to talk like Bridget Jones and doing jumping jacks, she'd wondered what "something important" meant. Maybe tonight was the night. Maybe they were finally going to finish the conversation they'd started the night the power went out. Just in case, Sophie planned to spend a good twenty minutes in the bathroom redoing her hair and makeup. It didn't hurt to be prepared.

By the time she got to the parking lot a half hour later, Sophie was convinced that Sam had called the meeting to inform her he was raising her rent. Or worse, J.D. was finally reclaiming his room, effectively kicking her out onto the street. *Homeless twice in nine months,* she thought. *Stellar.* She'd had to quit her job at Mojito to do the *The Real Thing,* and the pay for playing the role of Debbie was hardly enough to rent a cozy one-bedroom anywhere closer than Tarzana. *I've always got Bessie,* she thought as she approached her enormous yellow vintage convertible. She'd rather live in her car than commute an hour and a half each day.

As she threw her black tote into the backseat, the little hairs on the back of her neck suddenly stood up. The pervert in the baseball cap was back, and he was walking toward her in the now-empty parking lot. Sophie hadn't noticed him in the theater earlier. Had he been lying in wait, hoping to catch her alone and vulnerable?

"I have Mace!" Sophie shouted as he neared, reaching for her bag. She didn't, but maybe the threat would be enough to scare him away.

"Sophie Bushell, right?" He'd ignored the Mace comment. Great. He was a perverted stalker with no sense of self-preservation. "I'm Steven."

He was only a few feet away. Close enough for her to see that under the Dodgers cap he had salt-and-pepper hair and expensive-looking eyeglasses. He didn't look scary. In fact, he looked like —

"St — Steven?" It couldn't be. It absolutely could not be.

"Sebastian and I have been friends since before *Jaws.* He always invites me down to the theater to take a look at the new talent he's discovered."

405

"I — I . . ." The pervert wasn't a pervert. He was one of the biggest names in Hollywood. He was a living legend. He was the director of all directors. . . . Sophie was gonna pass out.

He smiled, undisturbed by the useless mass of jelly she'd become. Apparently, he was accustomed to people becoming stuttering masses of jelly in his presence. As Sophie listened in shock, *Steven* informed her that he was taking a break from the blockbuster movies he'd been directing for the past few decades. In a few months, he was shooting a small film, an independent with no A-list stars attached. He wanted to prove to himself that he didn't need a hundred million dollars to wow audiences.

"There's a part I haven't cast yet," he told her. "I think you'd be perfect."

"Me . . . ?" Sophie had yet to form a complete sentence in front of the man.

"You."

This wasn't happening. It was impossible. Wasn't it?

Sophie looked around for a hidden camera. She didn't see one, although she did notice a new black Mercedes parked on the other side of the lot. But . . . this had to be some kind of sick joke.

"What about the play?" *Who cares about the play? Why aren't you jumping in this guy's arms and thanking him for making your dreams come true?*

"You'd have to drop out. Our shooting schedule conflicts." He shrugged. "Sebastian will hate me, but what else is new? He hates everybody."

Yes! Tell him yes! All the auditions, all the humiliation, all the disappointment. . . . It had all led to this.

She'd been discovered.

Because of the play. Without insane Sebastian Kramer taking a chance on her, she wouldn't be standing here, getting discovered. She'd be at Mojito, answering the phone and showing TV starlets to a table.

It killed Sophie, but she had to say it. "I can't." She gave a deep sigh. "I can't leave the play. I'm sorry."

He sighed. "Sebastian told me you'd say that. Said you were the genuine article. He was right." He pulled a card from his wallet. "Call me when the play finishes its run."

"Okay." That wasn't what she was expecting to hear. Sophie took the card, staring at the name neatly printed across the top. Any moment, she'd wake up.

Steven tugged at his baseball cap. He turned to go, then stopped. "Y'know what, Sophie? I think you're going to be a star."

The first thing Sophie noticed when she sailed into Sam's apartment were the boxes. There were several of them, stacked one on top of the other next to the front door. She immediately flashed back to walking into the guesthouse to find Genevieve and Marco redecorating *her* place. This wasn't good.

"What the hell?" she yelled to Sam as he walked out of his bedroom carrying a stack of CDs. He was wearing his favorite green cargo shorts and a Mojito t-shirt she'd snagged from the restaurant. "I don't even get two weeks notice?"

"Hello to you, too."

Then she saw that all the boxes were marked with a Newark, New Jersey address. Newark was Sam's hometown. "What's going on?"

He set down the pile of CDs. "I'm leaving."

"What?" But she already knew. He'd tried to tell her before, only she hadn't been willing to listen.

"I don't want this life."

Sophie wanted to scream at him. She wanted to remind him that he'd promised to talk to her the next time he had some crazy notion about giving up. She wanted to cry.

"Sam, you can't —"

"It's not a bad thing, Bushell. It's a good thing."

"How can you say that?" The high she'd been on since her magical getting-discovered parking lot encounter was suddenly gone. Why did everything awesome have to be counteracted with something awful? She hated the whole balance-of-life thing.

Sam took her arm and pulled her onto the sofa. Sophie flopped down, overcome with impending loneliness. What would she do without him? Who would she fight with? Who would she depend on?

Sam pushed his straggly blond hair back. His gold-flecked hazel eyes were serious, but not sad. "I've lost it, Bushell. I don't have the drive anymore. I look at you . . . and even at Ellie . . . it's like, you want this so much. The idea of going to an audition makes me feel bored and tired. Not because I'm discouraged . . . I'm just not interested."

"But you did so well in *The Cherry Orchard*. If you stick it out, I know you'll make it —"

"Being in that play was amazing," he agreed, slumping against a cushion. "But when our run was over . . . I felt done. I tried to ignore that feeling for a long time, but I can't anymore."

"I don't get it."

He smiled. "How could you? This is who you are. It's what you're meant to be. I want to find out what *I'm* meant to be."

"You want your Year of Dreams," Sophie whispered.

"I guess I do."

She didn't want Sam to leave. But she didn't want to hold him back, either. She knew what it was like to be living in the wrong place, doing the wrong thing. It was stifling and frustrating and generally horrible all around. She'd be okay on her own. Hell, she'd be better than okay. She'd be great.

"Can I have your room?"

He laughed. "Only if I get to stay here when I visit. I have to see you open in *The Real Thing,* you know."

"Deal."

Sophie remembered the first day she met Sam. He'd been a total dick, convinced she was some rich airhead killing time in Beverly Hills until her trust fund kicked in. When she'd called him on his rudeness, he'd shrugged. *Stay in this city long enough, you see a lot of people come and go. No point investing time and energy into just anyone.* Now she knew what he'd meant by that. It was a rite of passage she could have done without.

"I *am* sorry about one thing," he admitted.

"What? You're going to miss torturing me?"

He shook his head. "I wanted to be around when you decided to stop swearing off men. I was kinda hoping I had a shot."

She looked into his eyes and smiled. "I might consider a one-night moratorium. For the right guy."

Sophie never got around to telling Sam about being "discovered" by Steven. Because in less than thirty seconds, they were all over each other. They ended up among the boxes in her soon-to-be new bedroom, where they spent the next eight hours experiencing what might have been. And in the morning they were both in perfect agreement, for once: it would have been phenomenal.

Harper Waddle
5306 Canterbury Rd.
Boulder, CO 80302

Mrs. Caroline Sutter
965 Park Avenue
Suite 311
New York, NY 10112

Dear Mrs. Sutter:

My name is Harper Waddle. (Yes, Waddle. Feel free to take a moment to giggle. Everyone does. I'm used to it. Totally not offended. Really.)

Anyway, I'm a writer. At least, I'm trying to be. A year ago (nine months but let's round up), right before I was supposed to leave for NYU, I made a decision. If I wanted to be a writer, I should BE a writer. Why defer my dream?

Instead, I deferred college. Just for a year, long enough to write the next Great American Novel...the novel that would Define My Generation. It seemed a reasonable enough plan at the time.

I gave a rather moving speech to my three best friends—Kate, Sophie, and Becca—about creative vision and seizing the day, and I must have some talent with words, because they decided to join me. We'd all take a year to pursue our dreams.

So I stayed at home to become the brilliant, Pulitzer Prize–winning author I was always meant to be....

Sophie moved to Los Angeles to become the next Halle Berry....

Kate bought a one-way ticket to Paris and set off to discover the world and herself along the way....

And Becca...well, Becca went to college. Partly because skiing for a college team was her dream, and partly because...

Well, it's complicated. Dreams always are. They almost never turn out like you imagine-they almost always change. Sometimes, they change you.

I say this from personal experience. Here's the thing: I tried to write the next Great American Novel. I really, really tried. I started it, like, fifty ba-zillion times, and then I realized...

I don't know anything about Greatness—yet. Although after everything we've been through this year, I think I'm learning. And I don't know that much about America yet. Not in the Big Picture, anyway—I'm eighteen.

What I do know about is my friends. And though we may have spent the last year apart, in some ways we're closer than ever. Because when you don't get to talk to someone every day—when it's just a phone call here or an e-mail there—you don't have time for the b.s. You have to get to the heart of the matter, the guts. The stuff that counts.

We gave ourselves one year, and we followed our dreams. We followed them, and found them, and lived them. And that is what this book is about. It may not be the Defining Book of Our Generation.

But it is the Defining Book of Us.

I hope you enjoy it.

Sincerely,

Harper Waddle

Harper Waddle

P.S. One more thing. The speech about deferring college and pursuing my dream was kind of a lie—at least the part about deferring. The truth is... I didn't actually get into NYU. Which was a truth too horribly humiliating to admit.

P.P.S. In case you're wondering, I confessed all this to Becca, Kate, and Sophie on Christmas. I'm forgiven. I knew I would be. It was, after all, the best year of our lives.

P.P.P.S So far.

EPILOGUE

Home. Kate stood in the doorway, her tattered black backpack slung loosely over one shoulder, and took in her room. *Her room.* The big, comfortable brass bed was in the same corner, her antique desk was still piled high with course catalogues from Harvard and high-school English books. Everything was exactly as it had been when she left Boulder almost a year ago. The young woman returning to it was exactly the same, too. The same, and completely different. She was tanner, for one thing. Her hair was impossibly lighter, and her muscles leaner under her wrinkled khakis and long-sleeved purple tee. She still loved her family — only more now, and deeper. And, Kate thought, dropping her backpack and drifting toward the dark window, she was a hell of a lot smarter. She'd always been book smart, but now she actually knew a little something about the world — enough to know that there was still a lot to learn.

Kate gazed out her window at the roof deck where the Year of Dreams had begun. If Harper had imagined what she was getting them into all those months ago, she would never had lied to them about being rejected from NYU. She would have come clean, no matter the humiliation — which would have been a terrible mistake. Kate wouldn't have traded this year for anything — it had been the most amazing and important year of her life.

And she would tell Harper exactly that when she saw her tomorrow morning. Right now, though, she was just going to step out on the roof, and revel in being *home*.

But as Kate slid open the window, she saw three forms . . . lumps that seemed to be . . . were they *moving*?

"Welcome home!!!!" Harper, Becca, and Sophie shouted in unison, leaping to their feet. Before Kate could even process that her three best friends were there — really there! — they were grabbing her and hauling her the rest of the way through the white-framed window. And then all four of them were jumping and laughing and shouting and talking all at once —

"Your plane was late!"

"We missed you!"

"Habiba gave Harper a key so we could surprise you!"

"How can you be *skinnier*?"

"Becca and Stuart are back together —"

"Stop!" Kate laughed, pulling back to look at her friends. They looked so . . . like *themselves*. Even though they'd never really been out of touch, she'd missed them.

Sophie's perfectly shaped eyebrows shot up as she looked at Becca, then Harper. "Is she crying?"

Which, of course, made Becca cry. "Katie! You learned how to cry!"

Harper rolled her eyes, flopping down onto the vinyl roof. "Great, now we have two criers."

Sophie grabbed Kate's hand and propped herself against the crumbling rim that surrounded the gabled roof. "Okay, we want to hear all about Magnus."

As Kate sat down and crossed her legs, a bottle of chilled pinot grigio materialized in Harper's hands. Becca pulled four plastic cups from her purse.

"Keep up, Sophe," Becca said as Harper poured the wine. "Magnus is history. It's Darby, now."

"Details!" Sophie grinned, reaching for a cup of wine.

"He's good." Kate blushed. "I think I'm going to go see him in Boston this summer."

"Not for a few weeks," Becca said, glancing at Harper and Sophie.

"Why? Do we have a plan?" God, it was good to be home. Weird, but good.

"We thought we might take a little cross-country trip." Harper gave her a sly grin. "Sophie's transplanting permanently, so she's gonna need her stuff."

"Wait, what are you doing here?" Kate asked, remembering Sophie's last e-mail. "Aren't you in a play?"

Sophie gave her inimitable shrug/head turn. "Director got a perforated ulcer, which is apparently the only thing that trumps that whole 'show must go on' thing. So I've got a few weeks before my dream goes back into action."

Harper held up a hand. "Speaking of dreams . . ." She looked at Kate. "Time to report in."

Kate smiled. "Well," she began, "thanks to all of you —"

"And to yourself," Becca interrupted.

"And to myself," Kate nodded, "I do indeed know what my dream is." She let the tension build for a moment, as she scanned the gorgeous faces of her three best friends, who looked at her, rapt. "First, I *will* be going to Harvard in September, where I will be studying economics and international public policy with a focus on Africa. And I plan to spend every available minute raising money for Water Partners."

"Are you going back to Ethiopia?" Becca wanted to know.

Kate nodded. "You want to come?"

Becca laughed. "As long as I don't have to sleep by the chickens."

Kate smiled. "Done."

Harper looked disappointed. "So . . . you're just going to do what you were going to do a year ago?"

"No!" Kate grabbed Harper's hand. "A year ago, I would have gone to school, and probably taken a bunch of English classes because I didn't know what I really wanted to do. I wouldn't have known what a gift it was to be in a place where I can really learn what I need to know to change things in a fundamental way —"

She could have gone on for fifteen minutes, but Harper held up a hand, laughing. "Okay, I got it. You're gonna save the world. Good dream." Then she looked down, and Kate wondered if Harper, too, were going to cry. "If anyone can do it, you can. I'm kind of proud of you," Harper said softly.

Sophie cleared her throat and raised her plastic cup of wine. "To Kate," she said, dramatically projecting in her actressy way, "and to the Year of Dreams."

Kate smiled, raising her cup. "To all of us."

"To all of us," her three best friends echoed. "And to the Year of Dreams."

What a year it had been, Becca thought. She had found Stuart, then lost him, then found him again. Then lost him. And, finally, found him for good. As Harper and Sophie filled Kate in on their planned road trip to California, Becca fingered the latest charm on the bracelet Stuart had given her for Christmas. The night before they left Middlebury, he'd given her a new charm — a tiny, platinum ring. It wasn't an engagement ring, or a pre-engagement ring, or even a promise ring — at least not in the traditional sense.

"This is to remind you," he'd said when she opened the box, "that no matter what, I love you. Even when you get scared and think I don't."

It was going to be hard, she knew, adding Stuart to the very short list of people whom she trusted. Harper, Kate, and Sophie were on that list. Isabelle was close. Everyone else in the world . . . well, she was trying, even with her parents. She had finally realized that whatever was going on with them was just about them — she didn't have anything to do with it, either in a good way or a bad way. She neither blamed herself nor invested too much in their future — if they had one. She kind of thought they didn't, if her father's late nights and her mother's bitchiness were any indication.

"You're thinking about your parents again," Sophie said, nestling her head in Becca's lap and looking toward Kate. "She's got two looks — her Stuart look, and her parents look."

"It freaks *me* out that they're back together," Kate sighed. "I can't imagine how you feel about it."

"I'm actually okay," Becca said, playing with Sophie's beautiful hair. "It kind of sucks, but whatever they do — it's not about me."

She laughed as Harper, Kate, and Sophie all clapped and cat-called. "Yay, Bec! Woo hooo! It's not about you!!!"

"Damn" — Harper grinned — "we've grown up. We're *mature*. I can't stand it, pass the wine."

"Enough about me." Becca turned to Harper, who was adjusting her rectangular black glasses and spilling her wine in the process. "*You,* lady, have some information for us, I believe."

Becca and Sophie had been bugging Harper about NYU for the last three days, but Harper had annoyingly refused to say a word until Kate was back. Something about it not meaning anything if all four of them weren't together. Which was a nice sentiment, but Becca hadn't been able to think of much else (besides Stuart, of course) for the last seventy-two hours.

Harper gave a coy smile. "Perhaps."

Becca shot her a warning look. "I woke up at three AM thinking about this," she said, "and I get grumpy without my sleep. Spill it."

Kate was gripping her wine so tightly a tiny crack slivered down the side of the plastic cup. "Eeek!" She took a long drink, emptying the glass. "Let's hear it."

Harper, her face completely straight, reached behind her and stuck the cup-free hand into her jeans pocket, pulling out an envelope. Becca, Sophie, and Kate all shared a glance. More than anything, Becca knew, they all wanted Harper to have this. Whether she had written the Next Great American Novel or not, Harper had always wanted to go to NYU. She deserved it. She'd worked hard for it.

"It's a thin envelope," Kate said, worried.

Harper's face cracked into a wide, radiant smile. "That's because it's the form about *housing*! Because I'm going to *live there*!"

Becca clapped her hands and Kate threw her arms around Harper. Sophie reached over to wrap her arms around Harper's knees. "My girl here understands drama," Sophie said, relief in her voice.

"Drama and dreams," Becca smiled.

For Becca, this year had delivered both — more than she wanted, maybe, at times. But the reward . . . well, the reward was right in front of her. And, of course, there was Stuart.

The look on Harper's face when she talked about NYU reminded Becca of what Coach Maddix had said about getting down the mountain. To get down her mountain, Harper needed to write, and now she needed to go to NYU. But Becca . . . she just needed her friends. With them, and with Stuart, no matter what the mountain threw at her, she would get to the bottom just fine. More than fine. Safe. Balanced. Warm.

And, best of all, loved.

"Call me when you stop for the night. And don't speed. Stay in the slow lane. If you're tired, *stop* for God's sake. Do you know how many teenagers die in car accidents?"

Sophie set down the box of shoes she was carrying and made a face at her mom, who'd been shouting out orders at fifteen-second intervals. "Angela, I've lived on my own for nine months. I think I can figure out how to haul my stuff from here to LA without an instruction manual."

Her mom put one hand on her hip and tossed back her long braided hair. "Mothers worry. Even cool, progressive mothers such as myself."

Sophie glanced toward Kate, Becca, and Harper, all of whom were grinning at her from beside the U-Haul she'd rented this morning. The four of them were going to take the scenic route to Los Angeles. They figured a two-week road trip was a fitting way to end the Year of Dreams. Besides, Harper had some decorating ideas for Sophie's apartment. It was a scary thought, but she'd been so enthusiastic that no one had the heart to tell her that the nubby orange couch she'd purchased for almost nothing from the Salvation Army indicated a terminal case of bad taste.

Kate stepped forward, pulling her still-perfect blond hair into a ponytail. "Actually, Ms. Bushell, I've mapped out our route and itinerary. We'll be hitting every significant landmark, and I've made sure we don't have to drive more than seven hours each day. That way we won't be a danger behind the wheel."

Harper rolled her eyes. "And Miss Anal-Retentive claims she changed this year."

"I resent that!" Kate exclaimed, hands on hips.

"We may make a detour to Kansas City," Becca informed Sophie's mom. "Y'know. For the barbecue."

"We are *not* going to Kansas City," Kate told her as she hopped into the driver's seat of the ugly white Nissan they'd rented to pull the U-Haul. "It's completely the wrong direction."

"You can live without Stuart for two weeks," Harper added, flicking Becca's charm bracelet.

"It was merely a *suggestion,*" Becca answered, her nose in the air. "No need to jump down my throat because you still wish you'd told Judd to break up with Amelia."

Sophie laughed. Sure, they'd all changed this year. Each of them had grown deeper and more complex and more *herself.* But it didn't matter how many thousands of miles they traveled — together or apart — they'd always be the same four friends who'd bonded in the girls' bathroom one day in seventh-grade. They'd always be *them.*

As her friends continued their familiar back-and-forth, Sophie loaded the last overstuffed box into the back of the U-Haul and pulled the heavy door shut. She'd managed not to cry when she said goodbye to her father this morning, but when she hugged Angela, a few tears escaped down her cheek. She knew she'd be back for Thanksgiving, but this time it felt like she was leaving forever. In a way, she was. Boulder wasn't her town anymore. This house wasn't her home.

"It's all starting," her mother whispered as she held her close. "Remember everything, because it goes by fast."

"Any other advice?" Sophie asked, sniffing a little.

Her mother looked at her and smiled. "Just be Sophie. That'll never steer you wrong."

Be Sophie. She could do that. She'd been doing it for almost eighteen years. And so far, it was pretty good. She got into the backseat of the white Nissan next to Becca and slammed the door. "California, here we come."

"Who's got snacks?" Becca asked once they were driving up Sophie's street, the U-Haul bouncing along behind them.

"Harper was in charge," Kate answered from the front seat. "I requested Twizzlers."

Harper pulled a plastic bag out from under her feet and handed Becca an orange. "I've got fruit and sunflower seeds," she informed her friends. She'd lost thirteen of her non-freshman fifteen, and she intended to keep it that way.

Sophie groaned. "Harper Waddle, health nut? What have we come to?"

Harper reached back under the seat and grabbed a bag of Lays potato chips she'd gotten for emergencies. "They're *baked,*" she told everyone. "So it doesn't really count." She popped open the bag and stuck a chip in her mouth. Pure baked heaven.

"Where do you guys want to go first?" Kate asked, adjusting her sunglasses with one hand.

"Don't ask us," Becca responded, grabbing a handful of the Lays. "You're the one with our itinerary."

"Are you kidding? I have no idea where we're going or how to get there."

"But you said —" Becca started.

Kate grinned. "Gotcha."

"I've got an idea," Sophie announced, slipping off her green Pumas to settle in for the ride. "Let's just head west, see where the day takes us."

"We'll know where we want to be when we get there," Becca agreed.

Kate flipped on her blinker to turn toward the highway. "Sounds good to me."

"I just have one request," Harper told everyone. "When we get to LA, I want to go see Sophie's photographer."

Sophie raised an eyebrow. "Armando? The guy who did my headshots? Why?"

"Isabelle's mom called me this morning. She loved my book so much she already sent it to an editor. It seems I'm going to need an author photo." She paused. "They're publishing it."

The screams were deafening. Kate actually took her hands off the wheel to hug her, while Sophie and Becca pumped their fists in the air in triumph. Since that night on the roof, when Harper had accidentally convinced her friends to jump on the Dream Train, she'd learned that pursuing *any* dream was as much about the journey as it was the destination. She didn't need to see her name in print to know she was a real author. But hey, who was she to deny her adoring public?

"You know what's weird?" Kate asked, once their screams had semi-quieted down. "If it weren't for Harper's book, none of us would be where we are right now. I'd be spending the summer interning at some dreary law firm to beef up my transcript."

"I definitely wouldn't be in love with Stuart," Becca mused. "I would've spent my whole freshman year holed up in my room IMing you guys."

"Without that book, I'd probably be on trial for killing Maggie Hendricks, the boring roommate from hell." Sophie added. "And I *definitely* wouldn't have Steven's card in my purse."

"Steven!" Harper pinched Sophie's arm.

"Not that it wasn't awful a lot of the time," Kate clarified, merging onto the highway, heading west.

"*God* awful," Sophie agreed. "I may never be able to eat Ramen noodles again."

"And there's a reason they call it *falling* in love," Becca said. "I landed on my ass a thousand times — literally *and* metaphorically."

Harper sighed, nostalgic. "I'm going to miss the Year of Dreams."

Kate and Sophie nodded. A feeling of melancholy settled over the stale-smelling rental car, each of them lost in their own thoughts. Finally, Becca spoke.

"I guess I learned something in college that all the real-world experience you guys got didn't teach you."

Harper turned around to look at her. "What's that?"

"Following our Dreams isn't about a year. It's about a lifetime."

Harper grinned. "In that case . . . there should be plenty of material for my sequel."

They all laughed. Then Kate pressed the gas and moved the car out of the slow lane. They were heading nowhere and everywhere at sixty-five miles an hour. Harper rolled down her window. She wanted to let the world in. She wanted to let it all in.

THE END

ACKNOWLEDGMENTS

EC & SF: What can we say about Cindy Eagan? She's our editor. She rocks. Thanks, Cindy, for everything. Thanks, also, to the rest of the team at Little, Brown — especially Alison Impey and Christine Cuccio. To our agents, Richard Abate and Matt Solo, and our lawyer, Eric Brooks — thank you for the unfailingly smart, incisive advice and guidance. A special thanks to Paula Morris, who came through big time.

EC: Thanks and apologies to my friends and family. There were a lot of unreturned phone calls during the writing of this book. Special thanks to my brand-new husband, Adam Fierro. Yay! And an extra big shout-out to Karen Schwartz and Mike Feldman. Love, love, love to you guys.

SF: My deepest thanks and respect to everyone at the Abebech Gobena Children's Care and Development Organization (Yehetsanat Kebekebena Limat Dirijit) in Addis Ababa. Especially to Ato Anchelew, Ato Echetu, Ato Tesfaye, Azeb, "Mirror," Isaac, and most of all Weizero Abebech, who has selflessly devoted her life to women and children in need. Thank you to Simenen and Tashome, our generous guides in Addis Ababa. Thank you to Maserat, and all of the teachers at the Fregenet Foundation kindergarten, and thank you to Tafesse Woubshet for founding such an amazing organization and allowing me to visit. Thank you to Heather Arney at WaterPartners for helping me seem not totally clueless about the well-digging process, and for being so kind in sharing her experiences. I fictionalized, of course, but the core truths remain. Thanks, as always, to all of my parents, but a special thanks to my mother, Judy Strong, for taking the journey with me and for sending me duplicates of her pictures. But most of all, for me, this book is for Angatu.

For more information on any of the organizations above, please visit their Web sites:

Abebech Gobena Children's Care and Development Organization: www.telecom.net.et./~agos/Pages/aboutus.html

The Fregenet Foundation: www.fregenetfoundation.org

WaterPartners: www.water.org